WHAT NOW?

SHARI LOW

Boldwood

This updated edition first published in Great Britain in 2021 by Boldwood Books Ltd.

Copyright © Shari Low, 2021

Cover Design by Alice Moore Design

Cover Photography: Shutterstock

A CIP catalogue record for this book is available from the British Library.

Paperback ISBN 978-1-83889-142-8

Large Print ISBN 978-1-83889-784-0

Hardback ISBN 978-1-80162-569-2

Ebook ISBN 978-1-83889-144-2

Kindle ISBN 978-1-83889-143-5

Audio CD ISBN 978-1-83889-237-1

MP3 CD ISBN 978-1-83889-781-9

Digital audio download ISBN 978-1-83889-141-1

Boldwood Books Ltd
23 Bowerdean Street
London SW6 3TN
www.boldwoodbooks.com

To every reader who has picked up my books and allowed me to share my stories for 20 years... Thank you.

With love,
Shari x

BEFORE YOU TURN THE PAGE…

A NOTE FROM SHARI

Lovely readers,

Twenty years ago, in January 2001, my first novel, What If? was released. It was the story of Carly Cooper and her merry band of friends, Kate, Sarah, Carol and Jess, all of them navigating their way through life and love.

In that book, Carly was having a pre-Millennium crisis. Single and restless, she quit her job, her home and her life and set off to track down the six men she'd almost married, determined to see if she'd accidentally said goodbye to her soulmate.

It hit the shelves for the second time, when my publisher, Boldwood Books, rereleased a special anniversary edition in 2020.

If you haven't read What If?, don't worry. All that matters is that you know that in the end, Carly found her happy ever after and as the new century dawned, she celebrated with her rekindled flame, Mark Barwick, her best friends, and cocktails. Lots of cocktails.

So what happened next?

It's a question that many readers have asked over the years, and to be honest, I was pretty curious too.

Did Carly and Mark stroll hand and hand into the sunset? Did Sarah find happiness after escaping an abusive marriage? Did Jess ever recover from her scandalous affair? Did Carol's marriage to Carly's brother, Callum, go the distance? And did Kate get a sainthood for being the cool, loving voice of reason in every situation?

All the answers are right here, in the pages of What Now?

Thank you for coming back to catch up on Carly. And thank you, thank you, thank you, to all of you have read my books over the years. You've changed my life and I'm so grateful to have spent two decades telling stories.

As for the future? Well, I'm already wondering what Carly will be up to twenty years from now...

Much love,

Shari xxx

PROLOGUE – AUGUST 2019
INDEPENDENT WOMEN – DESTINY'S CHILD

There are so many clichés in the story about how this whole thing started that I'm embarrassed to revisit them. Or 'pure morto', as one of my teenagers would say, right before he calls me a 'beamer' and asks why I can't be the kind of mother who has a mature dignity, cooks edible meals, does Pilates and keeps their disasters private. Thankfully, I suffer from chronic oversharing, so my mortification threshold is low enough for me to just blurt it all out and then pretend I said nothing. I'm a big fan of self-denial. Except when it comes to anything involving chocolate, cocktails or Robert Downey Jr.

Cliché number one: there was alcohol involved. Number two: it seemed like a good idea at the time. Number three: we should have known better. And number four: we shouldn't be allowed to gather without the presence of a responsible adult. The fact that four of the people who were present are approaching middle age with the speed of a bullet train rushing towards Menopause Central, and the fifth one has already passed that station, tells you everything you need to know about the maturity levels of my friends. There isn't an ounce of responsibility between us.

And yet, should I really be surprised? After all, I have form for being irresponsible and spontaneous in the face of adversity.

I'm Carly Cooper. Mother of teenagers, Mac and Benny. Soon to be ex-wife of Mark Barwick. Turns out that keeping my own name when we married twenty years ago saved me a whole lot of paperwork then and now.

Not that keeping my name was some statement of independence or pessimism. It was just one of those things I never got round to, too caught up in a whirlwind of fast love, great sex, and transforming just about every other thing about my life.

When I married Mark, I gave up a varied career that included everything from managing nightclubs in Hong Kong, Shanghai and Scotland, to selling the toilet rolls that took care of corporate bottoms all over the UK.

Now, I make my living as a writer, thanks to two confessional novels I penned many moons ago: *Nipple Alert* (please don't judge me for the awful title – it was the nineties and my publisher wanted something that would stand out, no pun intended) and *Sleeping Under A Star*.

I wrote *Nipple Alert* in the months after our wedding. It was based on the true story of how I chucked my job, my flat and my life, and went off to track down six blokes I'd almost married in my twenties. Disastrous doesn't even begin to cover it. If you haven't read it, all I'll say here is that the story, and my life, had a most unexpected ending, when I found myself in the arms of Mark Barwick, high-school sweetheart and all-round male-type superhero... Or so I thought. But I'll come back to that.

My second book, *Sleeping Under A Star*, told the story of a regular girl who contemplated leaving her husband for an ex-boyfriend who'd become an A-list movie star. You know, just your average, everyday, common-as-chips-type tale. And Sam Morton, my real-life movie star ex-boyfriend (I swear I'm not making him up) says he believes me when I say it's not based on him. My face flushed a little when I wrote that last sentence because it's a blatant lie. Sorry. Full disclosure – a few years after I married Mark, I went to live with Sam in LA for a couple of months to try to land a movie deal for the first book. While I was there, some feelings began to bubble under the platonic surface, and I briefly wondered if I'd picked the wrong man. However, Mark swooped back in and I realised our marriage was worth saving, so I said goodbye to Sam for the second time. Thankfully, he forgave me and he's been one of my closest friends ever since.

For a while it looked like that trip to LA to flog my novels would lead to a starry screenwriting career and I'd be best friends with Kate Winslet, but that never happened. Both books did okay, but Danielle Steel wasn't exactly budging up to give me a space on the bestselling author bench.

Like so many other nineties writers whose funny, romantic books were labelled at 'chick lit', my pink-covered flames burned brightly at the turn of the millennium, only for my publisher to chuck me as soon as sales dipped and the next literary trend took over. If my memory serves me right, 'misery lit' became the next big thing. I could have written about the tragic demise of my career as a novelist, but luckily, my two works of (almost) fiction led to a couple of side gigs that have put money in the bank for the last two decades. First, I landed the dubious honour of penning an unbearably smug, achingly obnoxious weekly parenting column for the lifestyle magazine of a broadsheet newspaper. I hate every word and have to shower after I've written it, but I got over the complete vacuum of integrity by reminding myself that it pays the bills. In real life, I supress the shallow cow who writes the column by trapping her under the wheels of a fictional £3000 designer buggy and only bringing her out when she needs to get in 1000 words of chai-drinking, nanny-hiring, personal-trainer shagging, pretentious yummy mummy nonsense. I'm not proud.

More recently, I've made a living ghost-writing fiction and non-fiction for people who are cashing in on their fifteen minutes of fame. I've done two novels by former contestants on *Love Island*, one for a dancer on *Strictly Come Dancing* (and he's still proclaiming in interviews that he wrote it himself) and a couple of autobiographies for reality TV stars. I'm naturally nosy and happy to exist in the background, so it suits me fine.

Lately, however, my own life has been as turbulent as the ones I write about. You see, it's fairly safe to say that I've hit an all-time, and quite unexpected, low.

A flashback to a day almost two decades ago ricochets into my head.

It was one year into the new millennium. I was with my girl-friends, Sarah, Kate (Smith, not Winslet), Jess and Carol – the four women who have been my pals since primary school and, remarkably, we'd all reached a happy plateau in life. I was twenty-nine, at the end of my epic adventure, and I'd found the man of my dreams, the house of my dreams and I was pretty sure I was in for the life of my dreams.

Actually, let me rewind a second, and take you back to my thoughts in that very moment, twenty years ago. Here's the scene exactly as it played out:

We're now coming to the end of the year 2000, and I've been Mrs Barwick for six months. Mark always jokes about two things: one is that he's spent his life saving my ass and the other is that he always had money in the bank until he met me. His wedding present to me was to pay off the credit-card bills I'd run up trekking the world to find my ex-boyfriends, much to the relief of the financial institutions involved. My present to him was to throw away three packets of contraceptive pills, two diaphragms and a family-size box of condoms (you can never be too careful) and start trying for his much-wanted brood. We decided to settle in London and he transferred to his company's office here, so he's now the hardest-working lawyer in London. I don't want to be nauseatingly sentimental, but God, I love him. He's everything. We fit perfectly and I still can't believe that the right guy for me was there all along, and I didn't see it.

Our future kids will have two gorgeous cousins to play with as Carol and my brother, Callum, are expecting twins next month. Carol is delighted about it now, but it took her six months to get over the shock of losing her supermodel figure and her life on the catwalk. She's covered up every mirror in the house. They can't decide on names for the babies. We suggested 'American' and 'Express'; at least then she'll bond with them immediately.

Sarah and Nick also got married this year. Sarah is still studying and hopes to be a qualified teacher by next summer. Nick treats her like a princess. They were made for each other.

Our MENSA-member, Jess, is still working as a researcher in the House of Commons, however, she is now awash with passion for the very journalist who exposed her affair with a married MP to the nation. It brings a whole new meaning to having press contacts.

And Kate? Well, Kate's been fired from her job in a desperately trendy salon for threatening a diva client with a hot-brush. It's probably for the best. Since Bruce won the award of 'UK Architect of the Year', she's been frantically busy moving house, hiring nannies and cleaners, shopping and socialising. Now she's the one having her hair done every week. We live next door to each other now so we see each other every day. Bruce and Mark joke that we should get a bridge built between the two houses to save us from getting wet when it rains. We took their idea literally – the builders are coming to give us a quote tomorrow.

I sometimes wonder if I made a mistake by chasing my rainbow, but I know I didn't. I've found everything I ever wanted. From now on, there'll be no more 'what ifs...?' No more uncertainty. We've all got life sussed out.

'Sometimes I can't believe we all managed to settle down and sort out our lives,' Kate says one Sunday morning as we sit around her kitchen table eating brunch. 'Especially you, Cooper,' she adds, to the amusement of the others.

'I know. It's miraculous,' I tell her, breaking off a chunk of cinnamon bagel from the pile on the plate in front of me. 'We're like fully formed grown-ups.'

'You know what I was thinking about the other day though?' Carol asks, then waits for an answer, as if we could genuinely read her thoughts. Eventually she realises that no one is going to take a guess and she carries on. 'What will we all be like when we're fifty? Because you know what they say, with age comes maturity... And bunions, but we can get them lasered off.'

There were amused groans all round.

'I reckon we'll be drama-free and enjoying quiet, peaceful lives,' Jess offers.

'Really?' asks Sarah, one eyebrow raised in cynicism, and I catch her glancing at me.

'I agree with Jess,' I say indignantly. 'Look, I've already had enough dramas and disasters to last a lifetime. There's no way I'm messing up my life again.'

The others nod in agreement and I sit back, satisfied, happy and positive that from now on I'm in for a smooth ride.

But what if... what if I couldn't be more wrong?

Dear reader, wrong I certainly was.

Twenty years later, I have two gorgeous teenage sons and although our friendship group has faced tragedy and heartache, the bonds are unbroken and the love has got us through some dark days. And that's a good thing, because I'm fairly sure that I've just plummeted down a well of despair. You see, at this very moment I seem to have found myself unemployed, skint, single, I've been publicly shamed, faced national humiliation, my mother has denied knowing me, my kids may never forgive me and...

'Your lawyer is here.'

Did I mention I'm in a holding cell in a police station and in a whole heap of trouble?

Well, hello, rock bottom. Let me take you back a few months and tell you how I got here.

HOW IT ALL STARTED...

1

LONDON, SUNDAY 31ST MARCH, 2019
ONE – U2 AND MARY J BLIGE

Mother's Day. My soon-to-be ex-husband really knew how to pick his moments. Almost eight months after our separation, it was the first time I'd woken on the annual celebration of motherhood without Mark lying next to me – a thought that was blasted out of my head by the sound of my teenagers banging open my bedroom door. There had been a split second of anxiety until I'd ascertained that it wasn't a SWAT team breaking into the wrong house, and that it was in fact my sons, bearing a mug of tea and a bacon roll. I pushed myself up, ran my fingers through my short blonde hair, transforming it from 'loo brush' to the more subtle 'Charlize Theron Fast & Furious 9' bowl cut. Sadly, this is the only thing I have in common with the wealthy, slim, drop-dead gorgeous mega star.

'Happy Mother's Day, Ma,' Mac cheered, as he dive-bombed the end of my bed, sending a card flying my way like a frisbee, while Benny put the breakfast treat on my bedside table, making sure the mug was positioned on a coaster. He's thoughtful that way. In fact, that whole moment summed up their personalities. At sixteen, Mac is an adrenalin junkie, wild, driven and prone to choose whatever is more fun in any given moment, regardless of whether it's a good decision or not. I know – that apple fell right under my tree. My sweet, smart Benny, on the other hand, is almost fifteen on the outside, but about forty-two on the inside. He's comfortable in his own skin, couldn't care less what anyone thinks of him, and fills his low-key life just partaking of the things he loves: reading, movies, sport.

When the boys were babies, my Auntie Val, gin drinker, Glasgow-dweller and wise oracle of all knowledge, gave me the best nugget of mothering advice I've ever received – keep them fed and exhausted. Taking that on board, I encouraged (some may say 'pushed', but I'm admitting nothing) them both to take up a sport and thankfully they each found their own thing. Mac's life is basketball and Benny is our swimming champ. Traipsing to their daily and nightly training sessions takes up half my waking hours, but the payoff is that they don't have time to loiter outside the local off-licence on a Saturday night, asking passing adults to buy them a bottle of Mad Dog and six cans of Dragon Soup. The endless sport and working out (definitely theirs, not mine) means I need a HAZMAT suit and a barge pole to tackle the laundry basket, but it's a price worth paying.

'That's the worst T-shirt I've ever seen,' Mac pointed out with a teasing groan and a woeful shake of his head.

I glanced down at my sparkly grey pyjama top, that announced, 'ALL'S GOOD IN THE MOTHERHOOD.' He might have had a point, but it was Mother's Day so I wasn't rising to it. Instead, I took the mug of tea and wedged it between my knees and then gingerly balanced the bacon roll on my lap, while Benny flopped down on the available bed space not already consumed by Mac's six foot three inch frame.

'How did I get this lucky?' I was having one of those 'I love my kids more than life' moments – the ones that balance out the pants on the floor and the discovery of a week's worth of manky plates under their bed. My life may have turned out nothing like I'd expected it to, but these boys more than made up for it. 'Thank you, my lovelies. You two are my very favourite people...' They looked chuffed until I added, 'That I've ever pushed out of my birth canal.'

Benny closed his eyes and shook his head, clearly unwilling to absorb any form of mental image.

'I can't believe you remembered it's Mother's Day,' I gushed, only for Mac to swipe his phone screen and hold up the text I'd sent them both yesterday.

Tomorrow is Mother's Day. Just sayin'. Love yoos!

'Never seen that before in my life,' I said innocently. The heat from the mug was radiating through the summer duvet, giving me third-degree burns as I opened the card. My eyes went to the heading.

To A Special Mum On A Special Day...

Aw, shucks.

My tired, green peepers moved downwards.

If you could cook and play football, you'd be perfect.

My laughter sent the tea sploshing on the white bed linen, but I didn't care.

'Right, you have choices,' Mac declared, and while he ramped up the tension with a dramatic pause, I was struck with the recurring thought that I've no idea how I managed to make these two. Mac's black hair and almond-shaped blue eyes are his dad's, and Benny's ash blonde hair and green eyes are mine, but that's where similarities end. Both of them spend half their lives in the gym, on court or in the pool, so they've both got the kind of athletic frames that I could only acquire if I had them tattooed on my size fourteen body.

But back to the moment. Choices? Had they both cleared their day to spend it with me? Was I being relieved of all taxi duties for a full twenty-four hours? Did they have some wonderful surprises up the short sleeves of their muscle-fit T-shirts?

Mac enlightened me. 'We can stop and pick you up either a Subway or a McDonald's on the way back from the gym.'

Those were my choices. Subway. McDonald's. Oh, and they came with the standard side helping of guilt I felt every time they had the motivation to work out, only to be reminded that I haven't sweated since I gave birth to Benny.

'Or...' I said, trying not to let my disappointment show. Okay, so they hadn't actually planned to spend time with me today, but that didn't mean the whole day was a lost cause. 'Kate is having a Mother's Day barbecue next door at 1 o'clock and it's an open invitation. All the usual suspects will be there. Maybe after you come back from the gym we could go?'

'Are Charlie and Toni going to be there?' Mac asked, and I immediately realised I had played a winner. Charlotte and Antonia are my eighteen-year-old twin nieces, the darling, gorgeous offspring of my brother Callum and my lifelong pal, Carol.

Carly. Callum. Carol. There are way too many names that begin with Ca in this little trifecta. It would have been much less confusing if Callum had married Kate, Jess or Sarah. Anyway, Charlie and Toni are my sons' much-loved cousins. They've been pretty much brought up together so they're more like brothers and sisters, but closer because they don't live in the same house and fight about who's taking longest in the bathroom in the mornings.

'I think so,' I replied, resigned to the fact that the girls would be the deal sealer, not the fact that my sons wanted to spend the afternoon with the woman who still has their stretch marks.

'We'll come with you, Mum,' Benny said, one of his arms going around my shoulders and giving me a hug.

I couldn't resist teasing them. 'Because you feel like you don't spend enough time with your really cool and trendy mother?'

'That's exactly it,' Benny confirmed, in his most certain and definite tone.

'And you're absolutely lying about that?' I said, with a grin.

Benny's eyes crinkle when he laughs. 'Completely and utterly.'

Honestly, they could wreck their rooms, stay out all night and eat the last Kit Kat and I'd still adore them because they make me laugh.

'Look, I'm your mother. It's my job to be needy and clingy. You can prise me off when you're forty and I'm ready to let you go.'

Was it my imagination or did a look pass between them that didn't quite fit with the light-hearted moment? For a split second I thought about ignoring it, but years of motherhood ninja training kicked in and I knew further investigation was required.

'What is it?' I asked, eyes narrowing as they went from Benny to Mac and back again. 'What don't I know about?'

'Nothing,' Mac countered with the same innocent shrug he perfected when he was about five and going through a phase where he only wanted to be the bad guys from action movies. He made us call him Dr Doom and every time our backs were turned, he tried to thump his brother with my best table lamp.

They both shifted, climbing off the bed, then took it in turns to give me a kiss.

Mac didn't meet my eyes as he said, 'Right, Mum, we need to go. We'll be back in time for the barbecue.'

Benny was next, no eye contact there either. 'Happy Mother's Day,' he said again. 'We love you.'

They were almost at the door.

'Freeze!' I ordered. I removed the mug from between my scorched knees as I watched their shoulders slump like armed robbers who'd just been apprehended with a bag full of balaclavas. 'What's going on?' My voice dipped a few octaves. It was an interrogation technique I'd picked up from *Criminal Minds*.

They looked at each other again, and Mac broke first.

'Nothing, Mum, but... eh... Dad called us earlier and he wants you to phone him back.'

'Why?' I had only spoken to Mark a few days before. We kept everything painfully calm, mature and polite for the boys' sake. He was great at that. Those were three of his main personality traits throughout our whole marriage. Unfortunately, I'm easily excitable, like a giggle, and blurt out everything I think and feel. The writing was on the wall, really.

Benny was too slow to get out the door and had to answer. 'Em, just ask Dad, Mum. Love you,' he repeated.

And they were gone. This couldn't be good. Two 'love you's, and the avoidance of full disclosure when it came to a call with their father. My mama senses were tingling. They're the same as spider senses, but they can also detect dirty plates under their beds and underlying guilt.

I considered delving straight to the root of the issue by calling Mark, but stopped myself. It was Mother's Day. I wasn't going to let anything spoil it. I would finish my tea and bacon roll, perhaps while watching a rerun of a highbrow programme on international criminal justice (in other words, *Hawaii Five-0*), then I'd read a few chapters of the latest Dorothy Koomson, then get up and give myself plenty of time to throw on a pair of jeans and a T-shirt for Kate's barbecue, and then...

The ringing of my mobile phone interrupted my thoughts. I didn't even look at the screen before picking up because I knew that it would be Kate's daily morning call.

'Hello, you've reached Carly Cooper's Sex Chat Line. Press one for some heavy breathing, press two for some filthy language, and press three if it's been so long since you had sex, you can't remember how to do it.'

That last one would make her laugh, because she'd know it was me projecting my reality. Since my marriage ended, my dating game had been non-existent.

My amusement was kneecapped by a very male voice saying, 'How about I press four, for a bloke who probably shouldn't be discussing his sex life with his ex-wife?'

I choked on my tea. Bollocks.

'Sorry, Mark, I thought you were Kate,' I spluttered. And it didn't escape me that he'd called me his ex-wife, even though the divorce wasn't technically official yet. We'd started the paperwork, but neither of us were in a rush. It wasn't as if we were running into the arms of someone else.

'I guessed that. Sorry to disappoint you,' he said, and I detected a tiny hint of tension beneath his usual calm, mature, politeness. Mark Barwick. Father to my two sons. My husband for approximately nineteen years and the man that I'd legally separated from approximately 226 days ago and counting. My brain had gone rogue and somehow insisted on keeping a running tally, despite my heart's express orders to stop it.

'I'm not disappointed.' I hoped I'd hidden the sigh from my voice. We'd been some variation of best friends, lovers or partners since I was fourteen years old and now it was like we were in that awkward stage that came after a one-night stand with someone you barely knew. Not that I can remember the last time I was in that situation. I used the bottom of my pyjama top to dry the tea off my blanket as I ploughed on. 'I was going to call you. The boys said you were looking for me and they were acting like *Crimewatch* suspects. Is everything okay?'

'Eh, yeah.'

Oh, sweet Jesus, there was something hesitant in his voice now too. My stomach began to churn. What the hell was going on? Were the boys in trouble? Had one of them done something and was too scared to tell me? Mac was sixteen – oh God, had he knocked someone up? How many packets of condoms had I put in his drawer?

'I'm too young to be a granny,' I blurted.

'What?'

'Sorry, my imagination is running away with me. Please tell me Mac hasn't got anyone pregnant.'

His laugh was both a heart-warming relief and a condescending dig. 'Not like you to be dramatic. No. At least, not as far as I know. I didn't even know he had a girlfriend.'

'He doesn't, I'm just...' I stopped myself before I came out with something that suggested I was neurotic, anxious, or prone to catastrophising. He knew all that already. 'It doesn't matter. Anyway, why were you calling me?'

'I just wanted to talk to you about summer. We haven't got around to finalising when we'd have the boys and I just wondered if you had any plans?'

I hadn't known this man for over half my life without picking up a few things. Other than the fact that he was a workaholic, there was a reason he was a very successful lawyer – he never entered a negotiation without a battle strategy. However, my bacon sandwich was getting cold, so I had no time for playing games.

'No, no plans yet. I was thinking I might take them over to see Sam at some point, but I hadn't got any further than that.'

Sam. Benny's godfather. Who just also happened to be my aforementioned ex-boyfriend and a drop-dead gorgeous human being who went on to be a bona fide Hollywood star and *GQ* magazine's Sexiest Man of the Year, 2009. It's a long story and I promise I'll come back to it later.

There was a pause and I imagined that I could hear Mark's teeth grinding. He knew without a shadow of a doubt that Sam and I had no romantic interest in each other – that ship sailed long ago – but I think the boys' general hero-worship of their uber-cool godfather hit him smack bang in the ego.

'Okay, it's just that I was thinking I might take them away too.'

'That would be great,' I agreed, surprised but enthusiastic. Mark worked such long hours that Mac and Benny only spent alternate weekends and the occasional midweek night with him, so a boys' week at the beach or city-hopping around Europe would be great for them. A real bonding experience and one that they hadn't had before now.

'Yeah, I agree. It'll be the first summer since... you know...' He didn't seem to be able to say 'since we split up', but I let it go as he went on, '... So I thought we could do something special.'

Ooooh, maybe catch some big sports event? Perhaps an F1 race somewhere? I didn't get the chance to question him as he cleared his throat and continued.

'And I spoke to the boys about it and we thought we'd hire an RV and spend a month touring the east coast of the States.'

I had to rewind it at least twice to make sure I'd heard correctly, and even then, I had to check I wasn't mistaken.

'A month? You want to take the boys away for a month?'

Was this an April Fool's joke? No, that was tomorrow. Mark was way too grown up and sensible to pull a prank on the wrong day. Or any day, for that matter.

'Yes. Is that a problem?' There was a hint of challenge in there and I had to clench my jaw to stop myself rising to it with full-force sarcasm along the lines of 'No, of course not. Why should it be a problem? It's not as if I begged you for years to take more than a week off work. And when you did grudgingly agree to a short break, it's not as if you'd then spend every day on the phone and trying to get Wi-Fi so you could answer your emails. It's not as if one of the very real reasons that I called time on our marriage was because I couldn't bear to carry on living a life in which I always felt the kids and I were below work on your priority list. It's not as if you promised me a hundred times that you'd show more interest in us, and then immediately reverted back to showing zero interest. And it's definitely not as if I eventually gave up trying to make it work, we finally separated and you've suddenly decided you've got positively oodles of free time and you're father of the bloody year.'

Nope, I didn't say any of that because I understood now why the boys were being shifty – they knew this would blindside me and they didn't know how I'd react. Despite Mark's initial objections to the separation, we'd both agreed to be amicable, to go with the line that we'd just outgrown each other and parted as friends. However, this morning I could sense that they felt stuck in the middle, and that was somewhere I didn't want them to be.

I forced myself to reply in a non-fricking-furious tone. 'No, it's not a problem. I just wish you'd discussed it with me before talking to the boys.'

A sigh at his end. 'God, I can't win. Look, I know I haven't been around as much as I should have, but I'm changing that now. And it just came up in conversation with them...'

'And I take it they want to go?' I swear my ovaries clenched. *Say no. Please say they don't want to leave me for a whole month, that they were positively inconsolable at the very thought of it.*

'They do.' *Dammit.*

'Then it's fine with me,' I blurted.

'Are you sure?' I could make out surprise, relief and a tinge of disbelief.

'Absolutely,' I assured him, trying so hard to sound sunny and enthusiastic that I was now using the same voice as the actors in washing powder commercials. 'I think it's a smashing idea and I'm all for it.'

2

FIFTEEN MINUTES LATER – KATE'S HOUSE NEXT DOOR

NOT READY TO MAKE NICE – THE CHICKS

'And *are* you all for it?' Kate asked, her jaw almost hitting the hot tray of stuffed peppers she was clutching between her oven gloves. Apart from the distraught and needy pal, this was Kate's idea of a perfect Mother's Day – cooking and baking up a feast for everyone she loves. The best thing about living next door to your best friend was that you could slip through the gate connecting your gardens and be in their kitchen in seconds. Right now, I'm not sure Kate felt the same. She went through far less biscuits when we lived at opposite ends of the country.

The defection of most of our high-school girl-gang from Glasgow to London had begun back in the late eighties. At eighteen, Carol had been the first to go in search of fame, fortune, or at least enough modelling gigs to keep a roof over her beautiful head and maintain an endless supply of black coffee and Marlboro lights. Jess had followed at twenty-one, when she left uni with a degree in politics and came south to fulfil her dream of working in the epicentre of government. Back then, when we were all catching lusty feelings for Brad Pitt and we were yet to discover that Clooney bloke in *ER*, Jess could come over all sexually giddy at the sight of a well-written manifesto. Kate had joined the other two, when she landed a junior position in a swanky London salon. The only one whose path didn't bring her down the M6 was Sarah, who'd lived in Scotland until she moved to the USA in her thirties.

I'd been the last to make the move, finally settling here when I decided my world travels were over and it was time to grow up and put some roots down. My brother, Callum, was already living just off the King's Road, my brother, Michael, visited often, and my parents stayed back in Scotland, which suited us fine because they had pretty much zero interest in what their offspring were doing anyway. Years later, Mark had no objection to making it our home after we married. His parents had moved abroad, so he had no family ties to Glasgow. We'd bought the house next door to Kate and strictly speaking, that's where I'd lived ever since, but I spent so much time in Kate's kitchen that she could probably justify charging me rent.

I lifted my head off the battered but beautiful oak table that had been the centre of the room for two decades, and realised she was still waiting for an answer. 'Of course not! Nineteen years, Kate! Nineteen years and he has not arranged or organised a single thing in our lives...'

Kate interrupted me. 'Are you about to go full-scale martyr and rhyme off everything he's ever done to upset you, because I'm not sure how long I can hold this tray for.'

'I am,' I confirmed.

'Okay, give me a sec to get organised so that I can give your rant my undivided attention.'

In the time it took her to put the tray on the drainer, grab a mug, pour a coffee from the pot and join me, I fired off a text to Sarah's daughter, Hannah.

Hey, luvly, just thinking about you. All good? Sending hugs and big love.

I didn't expect a reply. It was about six in the morning in New York.

Ping.

All good, Aunt Carly. Miss you all. Xx

Since Sarah left us, I'd texted Hannah and her brother, Ryan, at least once a week, and called Hannah once a month or so. We all did. It was a thin line. We didn't want to bombard them with calls that would inevitably remind them of what they'd lost, but at the same time, we wanted them to know we cared and that they had four non-biological aunts who loved them. It was the least Sarah would expect and the least I could do. I owed her.

Kate plonked down across from me. 'Okay, I'm all yours until I need to take the chocolate sponge out of the oven. You've got...' she consulted the big brass clock on the kitchen wall. 'Twelve minutes. Go.'

I didn't waste a second of my allotted time.

'All those years I begged him to take time off. He never planned a holiday or a trip or even a day out. I'm not saying he wasn't a good dad, because I know how much he loves the boys, but you know he's never been the proactive type, so yes, I'm struggling with the notion that he's suddenly turned into Thomas bloody Cook.'

'And maybe struggling with the thought of not being involved in this too?' she probed gently. There is a reason you should never discuss your problems with the person who's been your friend since you were five. They know you far too well and can cut through any narrative and get to the root of your feelings before you even understand them yourself. Also, when they're sitting there looking like a petite, chestnut-haired, Nigella-esque goddess in a pretty sundress, having cooked for and rustled up a party for twenty without even breaking sweat, they can make you feel wholly inadequate, but that's beside the point right now.

'Well...' I began weakly. 'It's just that... Aw, bugger you're right.' I took a sip of coffee from the bright blue mug with my initial on it. Kate had bought one for each of us – Sarah, Jess and Carol too – about ten years ago on a girls' weekend to Dublin. My throat constricted at the thought of Sarah's mug, sitting there for so long, unused.

I swallowed. Now wasn't the time to go there. Domestic disagreements with my soon to be ex were easier to bear. I forced myself to focus on the present. My mug had definitely faded over the last year with excessive use. Illness, divorce, loss and way too much emotional trauma had pretty much made me a permanent resident at Kate's kitchen table over the last twelve months.

'A month touring the States is the kind of thing I used to beg him to do, and he'd always say it was impossible to take that much time off. How come he can do it now?'

'And you feel it shows how unimportant you were to him? That he couldn't do that for you, yet now you've split, he's becoming the person you wanted him to be?'

She was doing that whole spooky insight thing again. In a minute, she'd tell me I was thinking about putting my wedding dress on eBay and that I'd bought an abdominal crunching machine thingy I would never use off a late-night infomercial last night. Both of which were sadly true.

I nodded. 'Am I pathetic?'

'Yes,' she reached over and took my hand. 'But it's also totally understandable that it stings. Thing is, maybe it's taken every-thing that's happened to make Mark realise what's important and to make the changes in his life that he should have made long ago.'

I let that one hang for a minute. This wasn't the moment to rehash all the reasons that Mark and I are no longer together, but Kate's analysis of one of our issues was painfully accurate.

Her eyes flicked to the clock again, and I knew that she was mentally counting down the chocolate sponge deadline, but she didn't rush me. Instead, she put her hands on mine. 'So what are you going to do about it?'

I thought about it. 'Slash his tyres and put fish under his car seat?'

'That could work,' Kate shrugged. 'I've got a couple of cans of tuna in the cupboard. I was going to have them with a baked potato, but I'll make the sacrifice.'

'That's devotion,' I said, laughing for the first time since I'd burst in the back door. It was what I needed to put it into perspective. At least for now. 'Or I could get behind it, encourage them to have a great time and wave them off with a smile on my face.'

'Smiling gives you wrinkles – I'd avoid it at all costs,' deadpanned a new addition to the room. And she should know.

My sister-in-law, Carol, all five foot ten, size eight, willowy Cindy Crawford lookalike wafted in. Years on catwalks meant that while us mere mortals trudged or shuffled, she glided, head held high, everywhere she went. It would be easy to hate her, but she was one of my original lifelong gang, and we were friends for decades before she fell in love with my brother and married him. Did I mention that at the time he was also travelling the world, making bucketloads on the catwalks too? It was a modern-day fairy tale: gorgeous woman meets gorgeous man, they marry and have gorgeous kids and now earn a living as social media influencers, getting paid thousands to post pictures of their fave brand of washing powder (a tad misleading, since they have a lovely woman called Bella who comes three times a week to do their cleaning and laundry). I should deeply resent her for being so perfect, but on the inside, she has just as many hang-ups, worries and flaws as the rest of us, so I love her madly.

She put a couple of bags on Kate's gleaming white granite countertops, slung her white leather biker's jacket on top, then took her mug out of the cupboard. Thoust Shall Treat Each Others' Homes As Our Own, was definitely one of the ten commandments of our friendship – it sat between Thoust Must Always Listen To Each Other's Worries Even If They're Irrational and Thoust Must Not Covet Thy Neighbour's Shoes (but if thoust does, then thoust must return them asap).

Kate gestured to the section of her kitchen designated for the coffee station. One of the benefits of being married to an architect was that her kitchen – with the exception of the beloved old centre table that she wouldn't part with – was constantly updated to accommodate all the latest trends. There was a juice bar there for a while, but we told her we were disowning her if she didn't swap it back for coffee, tea and a large tin of chocolate Hob Nobs. 'There's fresh coffee in the pot.'

Carol was way ahead of her. 'Nope, I'm in need of something a little stronger,' she said, reaching into one of the bags and pulling out a bottle of champagne, which she popped like a pro and poured straight into her mug. 'Help yourselves.'

I might just do that. Day drinking at 11 a.m. was something I could totally get on board with today.

Mary Berry got up to attend to the chocolate cake, while Carol took a sip of her plonk, then slid into the chair next to me. I realised we were both wearing the same outfit: white jumpers, ripped faded jeans. However, with my size fourteen figure and her size eight, we looked like a before and after poster advertising weight-loss shakes.

'Wow, who's rained on your pavlova?' she asked, meeting my gaze for the first time. Carol's brain is like a war zone where metaphors, common sayings and phrases battle for supremacy and then stagger out wounded and confused, but her meaning was generally clear enough.

'Mark. He wants to take the boys away for a month in the summer and go touring around America.'

Carol went straight to my side of the marital woe, making her the instant winner of the Sister-In-Law of the Year Award. 'You're joking? I thought he was too busy...'

I put my hand up to stop her. 'Don't proceed unless you want to see me cry. Anyway, why are you on the booze at this time in the morning? If you could make it something awful that'll take my mind off my problems, I'd appreciate it.'

'Mother's Day,' she replied, as if that explained it. 'I had to get up at 6 a.m. to get the kitchen looking perfect, then drag everyone out of bed at eight, spend an hour making us all look like we rolled out of bed gorgeous, in colour co-ordinated pyjamas, all so we could get some Insta pics of the girls pretending to give me some inedible bloody chocolates that taste like feet. It was a good earner, but Callum was pissed off, Charlotte says she's moving out and I've no idea what Toni thinks because she hasn't spoken to me for a week. As soon as I'd posted the pic, they all went back to bed and left me sitting there like a saddo, not even a "Happy Mother's Day" between the lot of them. Parenting teenagers is hardcore. Tell me again how much of a nightmare we were when we were nineteen?'

'Complete nightmare,' I said, trying to reassure her. Actually, I wasn't lying. 'You'd run off to London and were shacked up with someone double your age, and I was in Amsterdam working in a club in the red-light district. And we did it all with no mobile phones, no internet, no common sense and no way for our parents to know what we were up to.'

Carol took another sip as she pondered that, nostalgia making the corners of her perfect pout turn up. 'Ah, we were happy, though. God, I miss the nineties.'

'I think you'll find that was the end of the eighties,' Kate pointed out, shaking a perfect chocolate sponge onto a cooling tray.

Carol shook her head. 'Sorry, you've clearly got your dates mixed up. I'm in my late thirties. God bless Botox.'

Since her twenties, Carol had been getting every age-defying treatment – freezers, fillers, peelers, lifters – often before they even came on the market, and there was no doubt they were working for her. Never too much though – just enough that they did the job but still looked natural. They'd wiped at least ten years off her, fifteen in a dim light. Meanwhile, I'd neglected myself to the point where my roots were like zebra stripes and my cleanse, tone, moisturise routine had long been replaced with a quick slap with a baby wipe.

Carol deflected back on to me. 'What are you going to do about Mark and the boys then?'

'I'm going to be extremely mature...'

'That'll be a stretch...' She interjected.

I ignored her.

'And I'm going to smile and wave them off. Then I'll either cry or comfort-eat my way out of my jeans. I haven't decided yet.'

Carol sighed, and turned to Kate. 'Are you going to say it, or am I?'

Over at the kitchen island, Kate flushed, shoved a wooden spoon in a bowl and started furiously stirring. 'I'm making icing. Can't do two things at once. I'll leave it to you.'

My gaze went from one to the other. 'Say what? What are you talking about?'

Carol put her mug down. 'I'm saying this because I love you and I want you to be happy.' In my mind, I got ready to retract the Sister-In-Law of The Year award. To the outside world, Carol would have my back until the death, but in our little circle of trust she was bold, blunt and, as she would say, the type of person to just rip that bandage right off. I mentally donned my bullet proof bra for the assault.

She didn't miss. 'You need to give yourself a shake and find the old Carly Cooper and drag her back into your life.'

'What do you mean, the *old* Carly Cooper? I'm still the same person I always was.' I could feel my face flush with the lie, even as I said it.

'Am I still flying solo here?' Carol asked Kate, who murmured, 'You're married to her brother – it'll be harder for her to take a hit out on you,' then went back to focusing 100 per cent on her bowl.

You know that thing where the hairs on the back of your neck stand up because you realise that people have been discussing you and you knew nothing about it? Well, that. My friends clearly had an issue with me, and I'd been blissfully unaware.

Before I could swallow my outrage and delve deeper, the back door opened again and Jess came in, sporting hair like a matted red setter and huge sunglasses.

Kate stopped stirring. 'Wow – rough night last night? I was about to send out a search party when you hadn't texted that you were home safe by 3 a.m. You're lucky you answered my call or we'd have broken down your door.'

'Sorry. I was otherwise engaged and lost track of time,' Jess admitted, taking a free seat at the table and immediately putting her head in her hands. 'I'm deleting Tinder. I swear it this time. Here, take my phone. Delete it. Or hit it with a hammer.'

This time, the comeback was mine. 'I deleted it last time you said that. You must have downloaded it again.' It wasn't surprising. Since her son, Josh, had gone off to university, her empty nest had been fitted with a revolving door to accommodate an endless stream of no-strings hook-ups.

Jess groaned. 'I did. I have no willpower. Hit *me* with a hammer. On the thumb, so I can't swipe. I swear I won't press charges. Happy Mother's Day, by the way. Did you all have a nice morning and do you all feel loved and appreciated?'

Kate put a coffee in front of Jess, then said, 'Yes,' at exactly the same time that Carol and I chorused, 'No.'

'Don't think you're getting away with not telling us about last night,' I warned her, 'because we'll come back to that. But did you know that these two think I've changed and need to find my "old self again". Whatever that means?'

Jess raised her sunglasses and looked at the other two. 'Seriously? You had to do this today? When I've got a hangover, a bad back and I'm still trying to remember the name of the guy I swore undying lust to last night?'

My eyes widened in shock. 'You know about this too? Is this some kind of conspiracy? I. HAVE. NOT. CHANGED,' I blustered, more than a little bit miffed. This was like one of those interventions you see on American reality shows featuring a soap star from 1984 who is trying to reclaim his moment in the spotlight despite having a grand-a-day crack habit. Not that we didn't have our own addictions, I thought, reaching for my third chocolate Hobnob of the day.

Kate obviously decided she'd be the best one to take this further, given that the other two had all the subtlety of a smack in the face. 'Honey, you were the funniest, wildest, craziest chick when you were younger. You fell in love every six months, you were fearless and you loved life. You lived for adventure and excitement and you laughed more than anyone I've ever known. These days... well, you've pretty much lost your mojo.'

'It isn't lost!' I argued, before climbing right back down. 'It's just a bit misplaced. I still love life.' That was true. Especially if there was a Gerry Butler movie on the telly.

'Do you?' Kate asked.

'Yes!' I protested, a little too sharply.

Jess winced at the pain of my shriek and let her sunglasses fall back down over her eyes. 'And are you actually doing any of the things that you said you were going to do after you and Mark split up?'

Ouch. That one stung. I'd had such big plans. I was going to figure out what I needed to do to reclaim life on my own terms and then I was going to go for it, to have adventures, to change my path, to stop just existing and start living. Trouble was, after the strength it took to actually make the break, I'd got stuck in the figuring out stage, and given up like a marathon runner who collapses on a pile of foil blankets and Mars Bars at the end of a race.

'No, but I'm going to. I am. I just need to get to the right place and...' I stopped. Even to me it sounded weak.

'I know it feels like we're ganging up on you here,' Jess said, before pausing to pour coffee down her throat, 'but we'd be crap pals if we weren't honest with you. You're the one who said that you want to live your best life. So maybe it's time to get moving on that. Now that the boys are older, more independent, you've got time to focus on your own life again.'

I gave up objecting. The only thing worse than brutally honest pals is brutally honest pals who are right.

The last few years had been tough for so many reasons and it would have been easy to keep plodding along with Mark, but I'd decided that I wanted more than a mediocre marriage with someone who'd lost all the funny, sexy ways that I'd fallen in love with. Mark and I were coasting. Just existing. And I didn't want to do it any more. But what had I done to change my life since he'd moved out? Nothing. Not a thing. No dates. No interest in anything or anyone new.

'I just wanted to give the boys a chance to get used to the new normal,' I said in my defence. It was true, but I knew what was coming next even as I said it.

'Carly, the boys are fine,' Jess said. 'By some miracle, you've managed to breed two balanced, grounded guys and they've totally adjusted to you and Mark's split.' I knew she was right, but I wasn't going to admit it in case the lump that had formed in my throat at the thought of my boys sent a sprinkler system to my eyes. Breaking up their family had been the hardest decision I'd ever made, and I put it off for a long time because the guilt was paralysing me. If I was being completely honest, what I didn't expect was that the same guilt would hang around after I'd made the break.

And then there was the other guilt, the one that had nothing to do with my impending divorce and everything to do with the person who was no longer in our lives. None of us had mentioned her, but we didn't have to. I felt the weight of losing Sarah every day. I felt the grief, but worse, I felt the responsibility. And that blocked all motivation to forge a new, exciting path for myself.

If I dropped the fleecy jumper of denial I'd been hiding behind for the last year, it was obvious. I'd kept myself so busy with the boys that, despite all my talk and big plans, I'd avoided making any fundamental changes to my life.

'You're the person that used to grab life by the whiskers...' I don't need to say that little confused nugget of observation came from Carol.

Jess took over. 'And now – don't get pissed off – but the truth is that these days you're all talk and no action. You need an adventure!'

'I'm not getting Tinder,' I railed, feeling my toes actually curl at the thought of having to re-enter the dating scene. I couldn't remember how to flirt. I had zero dating game. And there was no way I was letting a stranger see my wobbly bits without a dim light and a non-disclosure agreement.

Jess laughed. 'Okay, a Tinder-free adventure. Have you thought about Plenty of Fish?'

I threw a caramel wafer in her direction.

I knew they were right, though. My days were just passing me by, while I stood still in a swamp of habit. I'd work during the day, then spend every evening chauffeuring the boys to and from their sports activities, then when the weekends came, I'd chill out with a takeaway and a good movie, in the company of whatever pal was free. Maybe it was time to stop procrastinating and get started on a future that included the core things that used to be my motivations for life: excitement, love, laughs and new experiences.

I just wasn't sure I remembered how.

3

LATER THAT AFTERNOON
WE ARE FAMILY – SISTER SLEDGE

By early afternoon, the barbecue was fired up and the drinks were flowing. Over at the grill, Kate's husband, Bruce, her son, Cameron, and her daughters, Zoe and Tallulah, all wrapped up in chunky jumpers, jeans and boots, were bickering good-naturedly about something or other. Where had the years gone? Those kids were in their twenties, yet I still expected them to break out the lightsabres and challenge me to a death-defying battle to save the universe.

Kate's garden was understated chic. As opposed to mine, which was an overgrown wilderness, thanks to my gardening skills, which extended to nothing more than a once-monthly run around it with a Flymo and the addition of a deckchair that collapsed if you sat down too quickly. In Kate's oasis, there was an outdoor cooking area, a circle of comfy chairs around a firepit in the centre, two sumptuous cream sunloungers and a cedar wood dining table under a rich, ebony pergola. As long as it wasn't raining, she had us out here winter, spring, summer and autumn, determined to make the most of the space and the fresh air. Thankfully, today was mild, and we were all wearing enough layers to keep the chills away. The outdoor Christmas dinner of 2012 had left us with two chest infections, one case of chilblains, and a cremated scarf caused by dancing too close to the firepit.

Kate was still in the kitchen, having shooed us out because we were getting under her feet, so Carol and I were sitting at the outdoor table and chairs, next to the patio heater that was making our cheeks glow, while Jess was lying on one of the loungers, despite the fact that even if sun managed to break through the March afternoon cloud, no rays whatsoever could permeate her black sweater, tweed trousers and the towel that was over her face. The hangover wasn't subsiding then.

I was still ruminating over the headlines from my chums' intervention, when the side gate opened and the rest of the Cooper squad arrived. At the front was Callum, who was both my brother and Carol's husband, and if I wasn't mistaken, he was looking a bit pleased with himself. I wasn't sure why. Behind him, came Charlotte, who was deep in conversation and laughing uproariously with my boys, then came Antonia, her head down and hands shoved in the pockets of her hoodie.

Charlie was an absolute clone of her mum, all glossy mane and perfect bone structure, enhanced by a grooming schedule that rivalled Carol's intense regime. Toni shared her family's Amazonian height, but she was the quieter twin, low maintenance and natural, a little awkward and uneasy in her skin. She reminded me of my youngest brother, Michael, who'd always been in Callum's shadow but had found his own niche later in life when he turned his love of computer games into a career that now earned him bucketloads of cash in Silicon Valley. I had no doubt our sweet, lovely Toni would find her groove too.

Over her head, I could see someone else was behind her, so I leaned back in the chair, squinted and the surprise almost landed me flat on my back. Thankfully, a deft stunt manoeuvre rectified the situation and I made it to my feet and threw my arms open wide.

'Val! Oh my God, I don't believe it. What are you doing here?'

'Och, I went out for a paper this morning, took a wrong turn and just kept going,' she joked.

Beside me, Carol was giggling. 'I may have forgotten to tell you we had a surprise visitor. Callum just collected her from Heathrow.'

My Aunt Val. One of my favourite women in the world. An indomitable force of nature that I only usually got to see when I travelled up to Scotland for weddings and funerals.

She was already powering across the lawn, making surprising speed for a woman of her sixtyish vintage teetering in four-inch-high pink suede boots.

Her hair reached me at least five seconds before she did. When I was a child, I was endlessly fascinated by her huge, platinum blonde, Ivana Trump updo, but a few years ago she'd updated her style to a chin-length bob that was almost the width of her shoulders and sprayed to the consistency of steel. If she ever partook in an activity that required her to wear head protection, she was safe in the knowledge that she came fully prepared.

I wrapped my arms around her and squeezed, inhaling the giddy scent of her Estée Lauder Dew Youth perfume. 'It's been so long. Oh, I've missed you.' As I said it, I realised I truly, wholeheartedly meant it.

Over her shoulder, I could see Carol's eyes narrow as they followed her girls across the garden. Something was definitely bothering her, and I made a mental note to ask her about it later. But first, I had an aunt to catch up with.

Val pulled out a chair and plumped herself down next to us, just as Callum reached us, kissed his wife on the cheek and then stretched over to hug me.

'All right, sis?' he asked, still looking chuffed with himself. In our family, I was the one who loved planning surprises, organising get-togethers and bringing everyone together. Admittedly, when it came to blood relatives, that wasn't too easy because my mother was a law unto herself, Michael and his family were in the land of technology and we had no other DNA sharers to speak of, other than Val and her family, who lived 400 miles away. We all decided long ago that our true family consisted of the friends we chose to spend our lives with – Kate, Carol, Jess, Sarah and me, and all our partners and extended broods. One big, dysfunctional, chaotic, eventful 'framily'.

I stretched up and ruffled Callum's perfectly messy hair. I'd never massage his ego by admitting it, but he was wearing his upper forties well. He kept himself in great shape with daily workouts, the grey that peppered his hair only made him look more handsome and the sultry eyes and lazily attractive smile were still getting him work in catalogues and on the catwalk. And yes, it icked me out even to think about women lusting after my brother, but, to his credit, he only had eyes for Carol. Especially as she'd assured him that she'd take her straightening irons to his pubic hair while he slept if he dared to consider infidelity. Again, not a mental image I wished to hold on to.

'All right, Mum?' Benny asked, hand up ready for a fist bump. It wasn't as great as the cuddles he doled our unreservedly when he was a kid, but I'd take it. My knuckles bounced off his. Mac was just behind him, blocking out the sun with his shoulders.

'I'm good, son. How was your workout?'

'Great,' Mac responded first. 'Although the wee man still can't keep up with me,' he teased his brother.

Benny sighed and made everyone laugh with a dry, 'Disown him and kick him out, Mum. I'll give you everything I've got.'

I patted his arm. 'I would, but he'd only come back for food.'

Benny moved on from his disappointment with, 'Eh, did you get a hold of Dad?' He tried for nonchalance, but I could see a little twitch of concern across his eyes. He was definitely the more empathetic of my sons. Mac, bless him, wouldn't spot a potential emotional minefield if it wore a high vis vest and shot up a flare.

'I did, and I think you going away with him is a great idea. You'll have a fab time.' My jaws were hurting with the effort of forcing my facial muscles to feign enthusiasm.

Mac's excitement was obvious. 'Really? Yassssss!' He high-fived Benny, then nudged him out of the way to hug me. 'That's amazing, Mum. Thanks.'

I was grateful when Charlie, my gorgeous sporty niece, interrupted the moment by shouting over from the other side of the garden. 'Hey, are you two up for volleyball or what?'

Mac kissed me on the cheek, then off they went, and I was finally able to let the fake smile muscles stand down.

'Back in a sec. I'm just going to have a quick chat with the girls,' Carol said, following them. 'I'll come in case you need a referee,' Cal joked, his hand slipping into the back pocket of Carol's J Brand jeans as they wandered off. That's what Mark and I should have been like after twenty years – still tactile and crazy in love. Instead, he'd have spent half of Sunday at the office, and then dashed in at the last minute, stressed and preoccupied by whatever case he was working on.

Val squeezed my hand, making me throw off the melancholy. 'It's so good to see you, lass.' Her gorgeous Scottish accent always made me a little homesick for Glasgow, even though I hadn't lived there for almost thirty years. 'How are you doing? And don't be fobbing me off with pleasantries, because at my age I could pop my pink boots before I get to the bottom of things.'

That made me chuckle. 'Rubbish, you're indestructible, Val. And I'm okay. *Mostly*,' I added, with a tinge of uncertainty. There was no point fudging it. She could home in on half-truths like a heat-seeking missile, and woe betide anyone who got in her way.

I still remember the first time I met her. I was about eight or nine when my Uncle Don, my dad's brother, brought home his new girlfriend. They were in their early twenties and I thought they were the coolest couple ever. Uncle Don wore baggy jumpers and drainpipe jeans, but he looked a bit like Christopher Reeve (without the superman suit) and Val was the spitting image of Debbie Harry and had a fondness for patent leather skirts and eyeliner that went out to her ears. They've added on a few decades and Don's lost the drainpipes, but they've been together ever since and they're still the coolest couple ever.

When I was growing up, Val was the aunt that always knew when you needed a hug, who could spot a problem at a hundred yards and who had an open door in her house and an endless supply of love and biscuits. Although, she always insisted that we drop the 'aunt' and just called her Val, because she said it made her feel old.

'Better now that you're here, Val,' I said, with genuine affection. 'Every time I see you, I think it's been way too long since the last time. When was it?' I asked, confused for a moment as I tried to put the pieces together.

She got there before I did. 'Two years ago, when I came down on that theatre break to see *42nd Street*. Och, it was fabulous. Before that... Oh, darlin', I think it was when you came home for your dad's funeral. Six years ago. What a heartbreak that was – in so many ways.'

We both knew what she meant. The biggest heartbreak was that it could have been avoided. My dad had always been a heavy drinker. He was the one who started every party and who finished them by keeling over somewhere. He wasn't a bad person, but alcohol came first and last, and his family was somewhere in between, walking on eggshells because we never knew what state he was going to be in.

After thirty years of marriage, my mother reached her limit of disgust and left him. They had a couple of half-hearted attempts to work things out, but it didn't happen. The irony was that in the last five years of his life, he met someone – the landlady of the local pub, of course – and with her support, he finally got sober and cleaned up his life. He had no idea that it was too late. The damage was done and he died of liver failure on the fourth anniversary of his second wedding.

'Your Uncle Don still misses him,' Val said, with a sad sigh.

Val's husband had been called so many times to drag Dad out of pubs, or to sit with him in A&E after a fall or a fight, but he never gave up on him.

'Uncle Don was so good to him. You're a lucky woman, you know,' I said, with a wink, trying to lift the conversation back up to a happier place. Today wasn't the day for sinking into the challenges delivered by my parents. It was a miracle that Callum, Michael and I had survived them without serious hang-ups and a lifetime of therapy, but that thought was for another time and Val felt it too.

'Aye, and I tell him that every day,' she chirped, with a cackle. 'Handsome big devil that he is.'

Her raucous laughter made the blue baubles around her neck quiver. Here was a perfect example of Aunt Val's very specific style. Somewhere in her sixties now (I was too many vinos in to work it out), she still had her very own sense of style and fashion: rarely trousers, usually a pencil skirt, with a polo-neck jumper in the winter, swing-style shirt or kaftan blouse in the summer, always accessorised with many items of the same or contrasting colour. Today, the big blue baubles of her necklace were matched by the two blue gobstoppers on her ears, and blue eyeshadow the same shade as her calf-length skirt. Meanwhile, her pink polo-neck, knitted poncho was on the same colour palette as her lipstick, bag and boots. If she was a gender-reveal party, she'd be announcing the arrival of male and female twins.

Callum strolled back over with a bottle of beer in his hand and a glass of Prosecco for Val. She beamed at his presence as he sat beside her and took her hand.

'Is everything really okay, Val?' he asked. 'We're thrilled you're here, but when you called to say you were coming, it was a bit of a surprise. You're not delivering bad news?' He articulated my thoughts so much better than I could have done.

Val shook her head. At least, I think she did. Her platinum helmet barely moved. 'I promise, son. It's just that... well, Mother's Day isn't my favourite. You know, with Dee and Josie... And our Michael has gone off to Australia with his family, and Don was at a golf weekend and I just thought this one here...' she squeezed my hand, 'has had a rough time of it, so we could cheer each other up. If you fancy a lodger for the night, that is.'

'That's the best offer I've had all year,' I replied, giving in to an urge to hug her again, for my sake as much as hers.

There was so much to unpack in what she'd said. My cousin, Dee, Val's daughter, was killed by a drugged-up driver almost a decade ago, and I knew that Val still felt it every day, but especially on special days like today. She'd also lost her lifelong, closest friend, Josie, a couple of years ago. And with her only other child, Michael, off to visit his Australian wife's family, it made total sense that she didn't want to be alone today. I was just so touched that she thought of me in the midst of all that, especially when our contact over the last few years was limited to texts and the occasional FaceTime calls.

I realised my bottom lids were feeling moist and I shook it off. 'Damn it, Val, you'll have me sobbing into my gin in a minute. A bit of warning when you're going to make me feel loved, warm and bubbly please. I'm a hormonal woman. I need notice of any situation that might make me sweat or cry.' I wasn't kidding. Don't even get me started on my peri-menopausal woes.

'Have you spoken to your mother today?' she asked both of us.

Cal shook his head. 'Haven't heard from her in months. That's nothing unusual though. It's been years since she even bothered to call the girls on their birthday or at Christmas. We can take a hint.' My mother's disregard had long ceased to bother him. Or me.

I shook my head. 'I called her mobile, but she didn't pick up. That's nothing new, though. Last I heard she was in Italy, living in a vineyard and loving life. Feels crap that we don't mark Mother's Day with her, but she's made it clear to us all that she wants to live her own life now.'

My mother and I had never been close. In fact, my mum wasn't particularly fond of any of us. As far as she was concerned, she'd done her bit by sticking by my dad while we were growing up, and now was her time to enjoy her life on her own terms. I didn't begrudge her that and I didn't miss the running commentary that had been going since I was a kid on how much she disapproved of me, my choices, my habits... There had never been any danger of her overloading on that love, warmth and bubbly stuff that Val shared so easily.

'Ach, she's a funny one,' Val said, taking a sip of her Prosecco, then raising her face so she could catch the rays of the sun. 'Always was. She could have married George Clooney and she'd still have found fault. She always had that sour expression – like her knickers were on too tight.'

I was still choking with laughter when Val's analysis was interrupted by raised voices over where Carol was talking to the teenagers. I glanced across just in time to see Toni storming off inside, leaving Carol to throw her hands up in the air.

'Christ, here we go again,' Callum murmured.

'What's happening?' Val asked, squinting in the direction of the commotion.

Callum sighed. 'Toni. We don't know what's going on with her. You know that thing where everything you say and do is wrong...?'

'Happens to me every day when I'm watching *Countdown*,' Val nodded. 'I noticed she was quiet in the car coming here. I'll try to have a wee chat with her later if you want.'

'We'll take all the help we can get,' he said gratefully, getting up. 'Especially from the Mother Yoda,' he added, giving Val a kiss on the top of her blonde helmet, before heading over to the war zone.

'I remember our Dee went through a phase like that. God, she was a wild teenager. The joke is that when she made it to adulthood, I stopped worrying about her so much.' I could hear the sorrow in her voice.

'How about,' I began, nudging her playfully, 'I take our minds off all of this by telling you what an arse my soon-to-be former husband is?'

'Will there be lots of swearing and biased judgements?' she asked warily.

'There will.'

'Excellent,' she laughed, lifting her glass. 'Then please proceed and don't spare the insults.'

So I did. Jess finally prised herself off the sunlounger and joined us, followed by Kate and then Carol, who'd managed to broker a temporary cease fire with Toni. All our woes were parked for the day, pushed aside by great chat and cackles of laughter, the loudest of them coming from Val.

By nightfall, I was merrily tipsy and loving the background music coming from round the firepit. Benny had nipped home for his guitar and the blokes and kids, Toni now back in the fold, were murdering the Oasis back catalogue.

Today had turned out to be absolutely nothing like I'd expected, but I'd loved every minute. At least, every minute since Val had wandered in the gate.

The fairy lights around the perimeter fence were a perfect starry backdrop to Jess and Carol, who were holding up tealights and swaying in time to the music, adding their backing vocals to 'Champagne Supernova'. If the Gallagher brothers heard my friends' unintentionally skewed version of the lyrics there would definitely be tantrums. I don't think Liam or Noel ever woke up the prawns to ask them why. There was a reason we never formed a band in high school and Val hit it right on the head.

'Och, thank God you're good-looking and you're smart,' she gestured, chuckling, to Carol and Jess in turn, 'because you couldn't get a song right or hold a tune in a bucket.'

They both took it in the spirit it was intended: harmless fun with a definite grain of truth.

More wine, more laughs, more chat, until the singing was temporarily suspended when Callum and Bruce broke out a football for a moonlit light kickabout, and Kate appeared with a bowl of marshmallows for the teenagers to roast over at the firepit. At our table, a tray of Irish coffees and a pile of thick, fluffy throws were delivered for those of a more advanced vintage and as we wrapped up against the night chill, we fell into a happy, contented silence.

Val was the first to break it.

'I'm just thinking...' she announced.

'That's never a good thing,' Jess teased. 'It usually ends with one of us in trouble. It's crazy how I'm a forty-something woman and one penetrating gaze from you makes me want to go to my room and listen to my Wham albums.'

'Oh, I adored that George Michael,' Val said, wistfully. 'I'd have had his babies in a heartbeat.' We left that one there as she went on, repeating, 'I was thinking... What are you going to do when Mark takes the boys away? You'll have a whole month to amuse yourself.'

It was the second or third time today someone had asked me that and I still didn't have an answer.

I took a sip of my coffee, trying to buy time. 'I'm not sure. I'll need to think about it.'

'There's your problem,' Val chided. The garden lights were reflecting off her hair now, making it look like she was sporting an iridescent halo. Saint Val of the Blessed Prosecco.

'What is?' Once again, I braced myself for a blunt truth. Sometimes I really wished I was related to people who humoured me and sugar coated everything.

'You've started thinking about things. When did that happen? The Carly Cooper I knew never weighed up pros and cons in her life – she just jumped right in and took a chance on where she'd land. I mean, suffering mother, chucking in your job and your home to travel round the world looking for your ex-boyfriends, with nothing to fall back on? That was the most ridiculously, bloody brilliant thing I'd ever heard, and I admired you for it, pet.'

There was a heat rising in my neck and I tried to tell myself it was the furry blanket, firepit and the whisky in the coffee, but I knew better. It was the pained acceptance that what she was saying was right. Just as, much as I preferred my little oasis of denial, I knew everything Carol, Kate and Jess said earlier was true too.

'I don't know... I guess life taught me a few lessons and somewhere along the line I started playing safe and got sensible.' There was so much more I could say, so many more reasons I could give them, but I didn't want to spoil the party.

Kate grinned. 'I wouldn't go that far.'

'Okay, slightly more thoughtful and careful,' I acknowledged. I could see that they weren't going to let me off the hook, so I went with an explanation that had a grain of truth, without telling the full story. 'I had to grow up a bit after I had the kids. I couldn't be rash and do crazy things that would land me on my arse when I had the boys to look after. I think the time I took them to LA when they were still toddlers to try to sell my book to a movie company taught me a sore lesson. I ended up skint, nothing substantial came from it and I almost wrecked my marriage.'

'Well, there you have it!' Val said.

'Have what?'

'You're still acting like you've got something to lose. You haven't. Carly, growing up you were the boldest child I'd ever known. Then you became the boldest twenty-something. And thirty-something. So how come the forty-something Carly Cooper is too afraid to live her life?' The words were harsh, but her voice oozed tenderness. We both knew that she was right and just doing that tough-love thing that aunts can get away with.

Oh God, snot alert. I blinked back the tears that were forming again. Bloody hormones.

The others, for once, were wide-eyed but silent, waiting for my reply.

'You're right. I know you are. I'm just not sure I'm ready to change it.' I'd never prayed more than I did right then for someone to burst into song and take the heat off me. If they kept going, I'd crack and blurt out everything – my sadness, my sorrow, my guilt for the part I played in what happened to Sarah – and there would be no taking any of it back.

Thankfully, Val rescued me with some words of wisdom.

'There's only one way to get back on that horse, love. When the boys are away, plan something for yourself, something that will enrich your life. If you could go anywhere and do anything, what would it be?'

'Shag Tom Hardy on a beach in Bermuda,' I answered glibly, hoping humour would divert the attention.

'Yup, me too,' Carol piped up, just as Jess quipped, 'Count me in.'

'Dear Lord, you lot are like nuns that all have their monthlies at the same time,' Val chirped, exasperated. 'Let's try that again, but this time something a shade more realistic.'

I was tempted to say 'Shag Matt Damon on Blackpool beach,' but I could see she was trying to help.

'I don't know. I was thinking maybe I'd go to the States this summer too, but I can't do that, because I'll look like a saddo who's stalking my ex and my boys.'

'I think you might manage to go to a country of 330 million people without bumping into them,' Jess pointed out helpfully.

'True,' I conceded. She had a point. Could I really do that though? Did I really want to spend money I didn't have, going somewhere on my lonesome? And was there any chance whatso-ever that I'd fit into any of my summer holiday clothes, since I'd opted for the cinnamon bagel and Frosties separation diet? I'd gained at least a stone since Mark had moved out. Maybe two. I avoided the scales because I didn't want to deal with them either. 'Okay, I'll think about it,' I said for the second time, just to appease them.

'No, you won't,' Val challenged. 'Decide right now. This minute. Because that's what the Carly Cooper I used to know would have done and it's time you clutched back some of her devil-may-careness.' Her eyes flicked to Jess, who had taken a breath as if she were about to speak. Val cut her right off. 'And I know that's not a proper phrase, Miss Smarty Knickers, but we all know what I mean.'

I knew. I absolutely knew. She was right. When I went off to live in Amsterdam and Shanghai and Hong Kong, in my teens and early twenties, I hadn't given any of it a second thought. I'd fallen in love with giddy regularity, swept up in the moment. When I went back to find all my exes years later, it was a ludicrous plan to everyone except me. But the truth was, the chain of events I'd kicked off on that trip created a sliding door that set us on a collision course with heartbreak years later. It was the first domino in a twenty year chain and when the final one fell it caused so much pain and loss to people I loved. Sarah. Her family. Mark. Me. That loss had changed me. Now, somewhere deep inside, I was scared of seizing the day because that's how people got hurt. It was better to play safe, to burrow down and do nothing.

I could feel my throat start to tighten again and I feigned a sneeze to cover up the tears that were filling my eyes.

'Aaargh, hay fever,' I said, ignoring quizzical looks from Kate, who was the only one of the girls with the wherewithal to realise that I'd never had hay fever in my life, and even if I did, it was hardly likely to flare up at midnight in March.

Countless Proseccos in, Val was not for deserting her mission. 'What do you say then, my love? Are you doing it?' she badgered excitedly, while everyone else stared at me expectantly.

It was crazy. Mad. Ridiculous. And my stomach clenched at the very thought of it. I knew they were right, but I wasn't ready.

However, right then and there, I'd have agreed to anything to get them off my case, so I decided to just play along. By tomorrow morning, everyone would have forgotten about it and I could go back to my plan to spend the month at home in my pyjamas, with Ben & Jerry providing daily consolation for the absence of my boys. I had to make it convincing, though, so I downed the last of my Irish coffee, slammed the glass mug on the table, gave silent thanks that it didn't break and slapped on a beaming smile.

'Yep, I'm doing it.' I ignored the parts of my lie-detecting brain that were now holding their palms to their foreheads in horror. 'But you lot might want to start saving the bail money, because if I get into trouble, I'll be expecting you to be the cavalry.'

The irony is that I was joking.

Given how things turned out, the joke was definitely on me.

4

SUNDAY 28TH JULY, 2019
WRECKING BALL – MILEY CYRUS

After a sleepless night, I finally drifted off at dawn, then woke with that sick feeling in my stomach, the sadistic, non-specific kind that forces your mind to run through everything in your life to find the problem. It didn't take long. This was the day I'd been dreading for the last four months, since Mark suggested taking the boys away. My hopes for a national flight ban, a plague of locusts, an alien invasion – anything that would derail Mark's plan had come to nothing and in just a few hours they'd be leaving.

My throat tightened as I reached for my phone, force of habit every morning. Last thing I remember was scrolling through old photos of the boys as kids and weeping pathetically at 5 a.m. The screen was black. Bugger, forgot to charge it.

Sighing, I plugged it in to the pink wire on my bedside table and forced myself to leave the cosiness of the duvet. If I lay there, I'd just drive myself crazy. Much better to get up, get busy and...

I heard the toilet flushing in the bathroom next door. Whoever that was, he knew how to twist the knife. Not only was this the day that they were leaving me FOR ALMOST A WHOLE

MONTH (I could only think of that reality in capital letters – like my brain was screaming the words), but one of my sons had just reached that incredible teenage milestone – he'd managed to get out of bed on a weekend morning with no nagging, shouting or bribery from a parent. That had only ever happened on birthdays, Christmas and Mother's Day.

I padded out into the hall, determined to get eye-witness proof of this momentous occasion. I was just in time to meet Benny, in shorts and a Simpsons T-shirt, hair going in twenty-three different directions, coming out of the bathroom. Wrapping my arms around his waist, I went in for a hug, noticing that my head only reached his shoulders now that he was almost the same height as his brother. I was fairly sure I was either going to have to invest in a box to stand on or spend the rest of my life with a sore neck from gazing upwards. When did that even happen? It seemed like a heartbeat ago he was toddling around my knees, wearing a hard hat and wellies, planning a career as either Buzz Lightyear or Bob The Builder.

'Morning, my love. Congratulations on getting yourself out of bed without intervention from your mother.'

He gave me an affectionate squeeze and I glanced upwards to see a cheeky grin as he replied with, 'Congratulations on managing to sleep past noon.'

It took me a moment. 'Past noon?' For the first time since I woke, I checked the Fitbit on my wrist. I tended to avoid looking at it, as I couldn't handle being step-shamed by an inanimate object. What I saw there forced my brain to ramp up the decibels again as it screamed, 'HOLY CRAP, IT'S ONE O'CLOCK!'

One o'clock. Mark would be there any minute and the boys would be leaving and all I'd be left with was my new trophy for being the worst mother of the fricking year. For over a decade I'd been doing that bloody school run every single morning and I hadn't been late once. Okay, maybe a couple of times, but I'd claimed car trouble and tied it in with a life lesson that sometimes a little fudging of the truth was necessary. I did, however, stress that the only exception to that rule was when it came to confessing misbehaviour to their mother. Those blips of tardiness aside, I was on time for their sports practice, swimming galas and basketball games at the crack of dawn on Saturdays and Sundays. And today, the one day that an actual flight depended on it, I'd decided to audition for Sleeping bloody Beauty.

'Shit, shit, shit – your dad will be here any minute.'

Just at that, the doorbell rang. Damn his need for punctuality. That man needed to lighten up and be late for once in his life.

'Benny, go get your brother up and for the love of all that's holy, try to be downstairs in five minutes looking like you've been awake for hours and you're totally organised.'

The only thing stopping me from escalating to full panic was that I'd told them both to pack last night, before we ventured out to the dizzy heights of Taco Bell for a farewell dinner (sobbing into nachos is never a good look), so I knew they should be pretty much ready to just grab their luggage and go. Presuming I didn't crack at the last minute and barricade the doors so they couldn't leave. I'd watched enough Bruce Willis movies to recreate a fairly decent siege situation.

Passing the hall mirror, I ruffled my hair and tried to make it look like it was deliberately messy as opposed to serious bedhead, wiped yesterday's mascara flakes from under my eyes and then groaned as I saw the reflection of the T-shirt I'd worn in bed last night. It was a Christmas pressie from Kate, and said, 'If it's men or chocolate, pass the Crunchie.' I clearly had to address my slogan T-shirt phase.

'Please be the postman. Please be the postman,' I prayed, as I slowly pulled the door open.

'Hey,' Mark said, and I could see the forced cheeriness in the tightness around his mouth. He'd probably been out there thinking, 'Please let one of the boys answer the door.' 'I thought for a minute you guys had overslept,' he scoffed, as if that was the most ridiculous thing in the world.

'No, of course not. The boys are almost ready.' My fingers were crossed behind my back. 'Do you want to come in for a coffee?' It was a year now since he'd moved out and into his own place and it still felt weird inviting him into the house we'd lived in together for almost twenty years.

The mercury on the uncomfortable scale rose even further when his eyes went to my T-shirt. 'Trying to tell me something?' he asked, those gorgeous blue eyes going into a cynical frown that threatened to expose the chirpy act.

That was one of the toughest things about this situation. The physical attraction to the first guy I ever snogged had never gone, although it irritated the life out of me that, let's be honest, he'd aged way better than me. The flecks of grey around his temples just made his dark hair look more interesting, and he still had that cute grin that had always made me melt.

And the body... Since we were teenagers, his answer to the daily stresses of life had been to run five or six times a week, whereas mine had always been to drink coffee or wine and eat biscuits with my pals. I felt the vein in my neck start to pulse as his finely toned torso and curvy biceps reminded me that for the last few years he didn't have the energy to have a night of passion with his wife more than once a fortnight, but apparently he had no issue at all summoning up the motivation to do a 5K jog or to spend a couple of hours doing sweaty stuff with weights down at the sports centre. The flat he'd moved into was in one of those service apartment blocks near his office in Bishopsgate, in the City, and the boys had reported back that there was a gym in the basement. I hoped Mark and his chest press would be very happy together. Not that I was in any way bitter. I'd always hold a little nugget of sadness that, just like my dad had put his chum, Jack Daniels, first, Mark had prioritised work over family. And sure, it stung that when Sarah died, and I fell down a well of pain and regret, he didn't even try to lift me up. But in the end, I was the one who'd called it quits and I truly wanted him to find a life that worked for him.

'Boys, your dad's here,' I shouted up the stairs. We both pretended we didn't hear the loud thud, followed by a hissed 'Shit on a stick!' from Mac.

My almost-former husband followed me into the kitchen, and I flicked on the coffee machine and pulled our cups out of the cupboard. His DAD mug still sat where it always had, front and centre on the bottom shelf of the cream cabinet above the Dolce Gusto. I slipped his favourite cappuccino pod into the machine, wondering if it was out of date. I was a straight-up, strong Americano drinker, so I hadn't touched that box since the day he'd moved out. He'd been in the house a few times in the last year, but only when he needed to discuss the boys. It was never a social call or a comfy chat over a hot beverage. I'm not sure why. He would have been welcome, but perhaps it had been easier for both of us to take a step back and maybe – as long as out of date coffee didn't give him an ulcer – this meant we were making progress on working towards some kind of new friendship frame for our relationship. I hoped so. I missed him. Not husband-missed him, but definitely friend-missed him. God, I was turning into Val and making up new terminology. I'd have a blonde bob the size of a wheelie bin before the month was out.

The thought made me smile as I flicked the coffee machine off and took out his positively in date (I was going with optimism) coffee. It was all going fine until I reached over to give it to him and jolted with the realisation that I wasn't wearing a bra. Now, when I was twenty, my 34Cs could hold their own. In my thirties, my 38Ds definitely appreciated support. Now? It shouldn't matter, because he'd seen my 42 longs braless countless times in recent years. But somehow, in our kitchen, with me making him coffee, wearing daft pyjamas with my nipples pointing at the floor... well, it bloody mattered today.

My body went into some kind of self-protection spasm that involved snapping my arms across my chest just as he was reaching for his mug, which then jolted upward, splashing frothy cappuccino all over his arm and hand, with a spray reaching the front of his jeans – never a good thing when you're about to get on a flight.

'Carly, what the...?' he spluttered.

'Sorry! Oh bugger, I'm so sorry. I just...' Panic took over, I leapt into action and before I had the sense to stop myself, I was dabbing the front of his genital area with my finest Lidl kitchen roll.

'Carly, it's fine. Honestly, you don't need to...'

I stopped. Mortified. He was right. I didn't need to. I was no longer married to this man, so if he was heading off to Heathrow airport looking like he'd had an episode of incontinence, well, it wasn't my problem.

However, the fact that he was taking my boys definitely was. A pang of devastation crept up from my gut and he must have seen it in my face and recognised it for what it was.

'How are you doing?' he asked, moving back to lean against the counter and taking his groin area out of my reach. I appreciated that he was attempting to steer this catastrophe back on to some kind of neutral territory, but his choice of diversion needed work.

'Oh, you know,' I said dolefully. 'Like I did on their first day of school, when I sent them in with my phone number written on their hands and then parked at the end of the road in case they needed me quickly.'

We both smiled at the memory. In fairness to him, he'd stopped by a couple of times to pass me tea and snacks through the car window.

'I'm trying not to be pathetic,' I added, 'but you may need mechanical assistance to prise my fingers off Benny's ankles.'

As he smiled, his shoulders lowered a couple of inches and his eyes stopped darting to the door, as if he was starting to relax a little. 'So did you make plans to do anything while they're away? Are you going anywhere nice?' he asked, making polite conversation.

I switched the coffee machine back on to make my own drink, looking for a much-needed caffeine boost and a distraction to keep the chat light. 'Oh, you know... Nothing planned. Thought I'd do a bit of decorating and fumigate the boys' rooms. The smell of sports kits is pure evil.'

'I think you can buy Hazmat suits on Amazon,' he suggested. This was the closest thing we'd had to our old easy banter, and I was about to throw back some other surface-level quip when he burst my bubble. 'I wasn't sure if you were still going to see Sam...'

Was I imagining it, or did he stiffen slightly as he said that? I wasn't sure why. The obvious answer would be that despite our separation there might be a shade of jealousy, but it couldn't be that because it was a legendary fact that Mark Barwick was officially devoid of the jealousy gene. It didn't exist in his DNA. We used to joke that I could strut down the high street in a mini skirt and nipple tassels with his entire football team strolling behind me and he'd just ask me to nip into M&S and pick him up some new boxers. It wasn't far from the truth.

'No, I don't think so. If I were to go to LA, I'd feel bad if I didn't stop off in New York, and you know...' My vocal cords wouldn't finish the sentence, but he knew where I was going with that. Sarah had lived in New York. Her amazing children, fully grown adults with their own lives, were still there. I couldn't cross the Atlantic without visiting them, and that came with a price. One that I wasn't ready to pay.

He shrugged, and I could hear the sadness in his voice as he murmured, 'I know.'

I stopped myself from going to him for the comfort of a hug. Old habits die hard.

'I'm sorry, Carly.'

'For what?'

'If this trip with the boys hurts you.'

I tried to bluster, determined not to let my true feelings show. 'Not at all. I think it's great that you're finally taking time off.' Okay, I'm not proud of getting the slight dig in with that one, but he'd have known that I was faking nice if I didn't, and I softened it with a smile to show I was teasing.

He didn't take the light-hearted bait.

'It's just that...' he went on, 'it should have been all of us heading off on this trip. I'm sorry about that. We talked about touring America for so long, and it was my fault that it never happened.'

This was a moment of conciliation, the first time since the split that we'd acknowledged each other's feelings. There was a palpable overtone of regret, of care, of tenderness and it required delicate handling.

So, of course, I blew it by panicking yet again and blurting out a bad joke that could understandably be interpreted as a dig. 'Yeah, by the time we'd actually have got round to it, I'd have needed special permission to get on Space Mountain with my Zimmer.'

His jaw set into a firmer line as the cosy moment instantly evaporated.

Damnation buggersome fuck. Why had I said that? And had he forgotten that inappropriate humour is my fallback in moments of anxiety? It's why I don't get invited to many funerals.

'I'm kidding!' I exclaimed, making it ten times worse.

Once upon a time he would have rolled his eyes and laughed because he found my bad jokes funny. I'm not sure when that stopped, but it was a dim and distant memory.

'Hey, Dad, we're just about ready,' Benny said, arriving just in time to rescue me. My relief was short lived. If he was here and ready, then he'd been leaving soon. I swallowed back another sob.

It suddenly felt like someone was holding a Dyson to my body and sucking out my guts. My boys were leaving. For twenty-two days, ten hours and approximately thirty-five minutes, depending on the traffic back from Heathrow in just over three weeks' time. It's amazing what you can work out when you're lying awake at 5 a.m.

Don't cry. Do not cry. It wasn't even any consolation that the month they'd planned had now been cut short by a few days due to some big case that Mark was working on. In fact, it made it worse because, oh, the screwed up irony of it, now they were going on a date that was significant to us both. I wasn't going to mention it and I was fairly sure that he'd forgotten. Wouldn't be the first time.

'All right, bud,' Mark greeted him, and my anxiety dipped a little. I told myself again that this would be good for all of them. Although they were only eighteen months apart in age, Mac and Benny had completely different personalities and lives that didn't overlap much, so this would allow them to build a friendship.

And the fact that I wasn't there to be a communication link between them all would make Mark stay in the moment and build experiences and memories that would last a lifetime.

Mac came in a few moments after his brother. Benny had managed to pull off an illusion of organisation, but that was a step too far for Mac. He was wearing shorts, a Kobe Bryant T-shirt, a baseball cap and a pair of Prada sunglasses he'd persuaded his Uncle Callum to part with. His Beats dangled around his neck, the volume so loud that we could all hear Drake's dulcet tones, he had a basketball under one arm and he was wearing a pair of trainers so huge it wouldn't surprise me if a customs officer detained him under the suspicion that he was smuggling a consignment of crack in the soles.

To Mark's credit, he didn't make a comment about the fact that Mac was late, or that he had obviously just rolled out of bed and pulled on the first clothes he'd found – both of which would almost definitely be making Mr OCD Fastidious Punctual Lawyer's teeth grind.

'Have you got everything?' I asked him, raising my voice over the sound of Drake.

He shrugged as he gestured to his backpack. 'Think so: iPhone, PlayStation, chargers, ball, extra pair of boots.'

'Hang on – didn't you tell me you'd finished packing last night?'

'Yeah,' he agreed. 'Got this stuff sorted,' he pointed again to his backpack.

Sigh. I should probably have checked. Rookie error. Clearly my separation anxiety had temporarily blocked my mamma skills.

'Excellent. And what about the frivolous stuff like underwear, socks, toiletries, clothes?' I asked casually.

He put his muscly big arm around me. 'Don't worry, Ma, I'm

travelling light. I'll borrow from these two or pick up stuff at the mall.' With his incorrigible grin and laid-back attitude, that boy could get away with anything. All that mattered to him was that he had the stuff he needed to have a good time. As the girl who went off to Amsterdam at sixteen, with just a duffel bag and a big bucket of optimism, I could relate.

Mark put what was left of his coffee in the sink. 'Right, lads, let's get moving then.'

As we trooped out to the front door, I swallowed, desperately hoping that whatever blockage was choking up my throat would shift itself pronto.

'Are you going to cry, Mum?' Mac teased me.

I rolled my eyes as if the notion was ridiculous. 'Nope. I'm just worried that you'll hang about much longer because Snoop Dog, his posse and two hundred ravers are invited round in half an hour for a party. I don't want you to get in the way.'

My boys laughed, and I ignored Mark's glance of pity.

Benny came in for a hug. 'Yeah, right. You'll be on your phone tracking us on Find My Friends before we leave the end of the street.'

'Nope, I won't.' I so would.

His eyes were questioning as he looked at me suspiciously. It was no secret that I was the overprotective mother who checked on them on a regular basis despite the fact that most criminals would have to stand on a ladder to mug them. 'Why not?' he asked.

'Because you know they're with me and they'll be fine,' Mark interjected confidently.

'Nope, because I put a tracker in their food last night. Even if you switch off your phones, I'll find you.'

The boys knew I was joking, but I could see Mark wasn't 100

per cent certain. Obviously his sense of humour was still in the gym doing forty-five reps on the ab cruncher.

'I'll just take these to the car,' Mark said, going down the path with the boys' bags.

Grateful he'd been diplomatic enough to give me a private moment to say goodbye, I hugged them both tightly. 'Okay, I want a daily text of more than just emojis, a FaceTime call every second day, and once a week just humour me and tell me you miss me,' I said, holding it together. 'Have an amazing time. And if you happen to see a huge pot plant moving around everywhere you go, I'm probably behind it. Just saying.'

Laughing, Benny gave me another hug. 'We knew that already. Love you, Mum.'

'I love you too, son. I'm going to miss you both so much. Please take care of each other. And your dad.'

'We will, Mum, don't worry. Love you.' That reassurance, and another hug, came from Mac. 'Don't be crying when we're gone.'

I shook my head. 'I won't. Snoop Dog hates it when I cry.'

As they strolled down the path, I fixed my face into a set smile, determined to hold it together until they were gone. Maybe another minute. I could do this. I could. They climbed into Mark's car, a Volvo estate. It was a long-standing joke that it fitted his personality perfectly. Steady. Sensible. Definitely not prone to racy sexiness or wild rides. His office had a parking contract at Heathrow, so I knew the discounted rate would be far less than taxis each way and it made the logistics of going back and forward from two households much easier.

Smiling. Still smiling. I was waving too, but it was an awkward elbows-in, wrist-movement-only gesture, because my folded arms were holding my boobs up.

Okay, bags were in the boot. Mac was in the front passenger

seat, Benny was in the back. Mark just had to climb in, drive off, and I could close this door and wail.

He shut the boot, took a few steps forward and... stopped.

My heart was thudding like a drumbeat as the agony was prolonged. What was he doing? Had he forgotten something? I watched his brow furrow as if he was thinking hard, then he turned, met my gaze and came back up the path.

'Is everything okay?' I asked as he reached me. Was there a problem? Or had he changed his mind about going. Yes! That one. Please make him have decided it was a crazy idea and now he was going to tell me he was just going to take them to the nearest Burger King for a quick snack instead.

He ran his fingers through his hair, in a gesture that I once found crazy sexy.

'Yeah, it's just that... em...' This couldn't be good. Mark Barwick didn't do hesitation. He was confident, solid, always sure of himself, but in a quiet, understated way. 'Look, maybe when we get back you and I could... em... talk.'

'Of course. Is something wrong? You know you can call me any time,' I replied, a bit concerned.

'No, nothing's wrong, but, em, this isn't a phone conversation. It's just that, I've...'

Oh fuck, he was going to tell me he was getting engaged. Or married. Or he'd got someone pregnant. Yes, I realised I'd just transferred that particular thought from the panic I had about my sons on a regular basis. My range of potential catastrophes clearly needed to be expanded.

I think I stopped breathing as I waited.

Finally Mark continued. 'I want to talk to you about us. I've realised some things. Some mistakes I made. Maybe we could... have dinner?'

My cardiovascular system kicked back in with a major gulp and managed to splutter out, 'Yes, sure. Of course.'

About us? We'd been married for almost two decades. What sudden realisations could he possibly have had? And why did he want to talk now, and not a year ago when I was reaching the end of my tether with our life together?

I wanted details, but this wasn't the time. The boys were waiting, and he had a flight to catch.

He took a step backwards and then stopped again.

'And, you know, if you've got nothing on while we're away you'd be really welcome to come over and join us for a while.'

He was saying now. On my doorstep. As he was leaving for the airport. Clearly that was a total last-minute pity offer because he was feeling bad.

Despite the fact that I was feeling extremely sorry for myself, I wasn't going to give him the satisfaction of thinking I was about to spend the next twenty-two days drowning in loneliness. That was between me and the well-stocked ice cream drawer in the freezer. 'Thanks, but I've got some things planned, so I'll be fine. You enjoy your time with the boys. I think it'll be great for you all.' I'm pretty sure the lie made my eye twitch. I was never great at duplicity.

My stomach flipped when I saw what could have been a flinch of disappointment. Or maybe pity offers made his eye twitch too.

'Yeah, of course,' he said, uncomfortable and backing away now. 'Well, erm, take care. And I'll make sure the boys keep in touch.'

'Thanks. Lov...' I bit down on my tongue. Bloody hell, I almost said 'Love you.' What the hell was I thinking? Force of habit, I told myself. And his surprised eyebrow arch turned to something like puzzlement when I fudged it to, 'Lov... ing your jeans!'

'Eh, thanks,' he said tightly, as he turned away.

I wanted to bang my head off the door frame until I fainted.

He was halfway down the path for the second time, when he stopped again. Dear God, what now?

'And Carly... happy anniversary.'

He'd remembered.

For the first time, I really wished it had slipped his mind.

'Yeah, you too.'

Nothing more to say, he walked away.

I plastered on an inane grin in case the boys were watching us, and did a bit more boob-supported waving.

Only when the car finally pulled away and turned out of the street did I stop, step back, slam the door, then slide down the wall, some weird strangled sound coming from my throat.

Devastation, sadness, and a ridiculous longing to phone my boys and tell them to come back hit me first, and it was only after that had passed that I replayed Mark's words in my head.

What did he want to talk about? What had he realised? What did it mean? And why the hell had he wished me a happy anniversary?

Shit, how had we got to this? We were once the happiest couple I'd ever known.

Still on the floor, I pulled up my legs and rested my head against the wall. As I did, my eyes fell on the photograph on the console table on the opposite wall. Mark and me, on our wedding day, nineteen years ago today. Our love was all-consuming, fun, crazy and I truly thought it would last for ever. That woman in the picture, flushed with happiness and excitement, had absolutely no idea what was to come.

5

NEW YORK, FRIDAY, 28TH JULY, 2000

FALLIN' – ALICIA KEYES

'Okay, how do I look?' I asked my bridesmaids, as I smoothed down the ivory satin on the bodice of my dress. 'Only, I think Kate's pierced at least two of my ribs lacing up this corset, so I want it to be worth it.'

'Definitely worth it,' Jess said, from her prone position on the bed, where she was sipping champagne in a bathrobe and full make-up. 'If an asteroid hits New York today and wipes us all out, at least you'll always know you died pretty.' She took a sip of her drink, then realised that we were all staring at her. 'What?' she yelped, indignantly. 'It could happen.'

'Thanks for that little snippet of optimism,' Kate retorted. 'I think I prefer you when you're boring us to death about manifestos.'

Carol, lying next to Sarah on the other double bed in the room, both of them in the same robes as Jess, interjected, 'I always get confused between manifestos and mandates.'

'Hello?' I yelled, hands on hips. 'Bride over here looking for reassurance!'

Thankfully Sarah had the ability to stay on message. 'You're gorgeous,' she promised, hugging me as tightly as she could manage, given the barrier of my flared skirt. 'I love you, Cooper,' she whispered. 'I can never thank you for all you've given me.'

'Tell me I look like Kate Moss and we'll call it quits,' I joked.

As far as I was concerned, she didn't owe me anything. I was just happy that her life was working out for her. Despite being friends since primary school, we'd all lost touch with Sarah when she'd gone off to Edinburgh University years ago. Thankfully, a chance meeting just a few months ago in the frozen foods aisle at Tesco had brought her back to us. But she wasn't the same carefree, bundle of joy she'd been when we were teenagers. Over the next few heart-breaking hours, my sweet pal had revealed that she'd recently escaped from an abusive marriage and was back at college studying to be a teacher so she could support her two kids. The turnaround in her life had continued when I'd taken her along on stage one of the ex-boyfriend hunt. We'd found Nick, a throwback to a holiday romance when I was seventeen. It soon became clear that there was zero chemistry between us, but, sweet joy, Nick and Sarah had fallen madly in love and she, Nick and the kids, Hannah and Ryan, had been a family ever since. They were perfect for each other and the relationship had transformed her life. I couldn't be happier for her.

'I love you too,' I told her, and when we eventually pulled apart, our eyes were teary with emotion. Or it might have been the mascara they'd used in the dodgy beauty salon we'd all visited that morning. It had been a last-minute decision and the only place we could get bookings for hair and make-up was a salon in SOHO run by three sisters in their sixties who looked like they'd been stuck in a time warp after being in close proximity to an explosion at a Max Factor factory in 1984. It didn't give me much hope for my request for a natural look, but other than having to firmly refuse blue eyeliner, it had been a largely successful outing.

My blonde hair was in the pixie cut I'd been wearing since an unfortunate incident with too much hair dye the year before, and my finished face was definitely preferable to anything I could come up with using a make-up bag that I'd barely updated for a decade. The whole look had a fifties vibe, which perfectly matched the dress I'd picked for my big day. White satin, off the shoulder, tight bodice, with a tulle skirt that flared out, thanks to several underskirts, until it reached mid-calf level. Carol had used her extensive contact base of stylists and fashion insiders to find it for me and it had the whole 'Breakfast At Tiffany's' vibe that I'd always pictured for my big day.

Kate, Jess, Carol and Sarah had also let the salon sisters go to work, and they all had updos that perfectly accented their style. Kate's chestnut hair was in a sleek but understated ballerina bun, Sarah's ebony mane was in a simple but elegant ponytail, Carol's dark waves were intricately woven into a high-fashion, elaborate twist, with a few messy strands escaping around her face, and Jess had gone for a no-nonsense chignon that would serve her well if she ever decided to be a school teacher or Princess Anne.

Over on the chair by the window, where she was recovering from the exertion of getting me into this dress, Kate cleared her throat. She'd been emotional all day. Kate was the softest of us all. Even when we were kids, she was the caring one who looked out for the rest of us and always said the right things to make us feel better. 'You are stunning, honey. Mark's a lucky guy.'

There was a poignant pause, before the other three burst out laughing at the obvious absurdity of that comment. I had to agree with the implication from the majority – I was definitely the lucky one in this relationship. After I first touched tongues with Mark behind the youth club fire exit, we became love's young dream... if the dream was punctuated with several episodes of interrupted sleep. We broke up many times over the next few years, finally going our separate ways when I ran away to live in Amsterdam in my late teens. Over the next decade, I'd somehow managed to almost marry several different men, before bumping into him again six months ago at Carol and Callum's wedding. On the day we met again, I was single, skint, drowning in debt, and I'd made a complete arse of myself by bringing Sam, another ex, to the wedding and pretending he was my boyfriend, only for everyone to find out I was lying.

The pamphlet version of the happy ending is that Mark had scooped me up, declared his love, and I realised the right guy for me had been there all along. If I'd had a crystal ball, I could have saved myself a whole lot of heartache and air miles.

Anyway, if fairy-tale endings came with true love, unimaginable happiness, and a boyfriend who didn't faint when he saw the size of your credit card bill, then this was it.

'I think we all got lucky,' Sarah said. 'I still can't believe I'm here.'

'I still can't believe I'm married,' Jess interjected. Ah, yes, Jess. After an affair with a married MP had gone public in the Sunday tabloids, she'd got together with Mike Chapman, the journalist who'd spilled the story. Not the most conventional start to a relationship. And now she'd had a pretty unconventional start to married life too. On the flight over here, Mike had ambushed her with a vicar and they'd got married in mid-air between Heathrow and New York. They'd have to make it official when they got home, but as far as they were concerned, the deed was done.

Carol's turn. 'Is it just me who thinks this is just like any Saturday night back home when we were teenagers and we were all getting ready in your bedroom to go to the school disco? The only thing that's changed is you lot have some wrinkles and George Michael has ditched Andrew Ridgeley.'

'And there's no way this arse is getting into those gold hot pants I bought in the Miss Selfridge sale in 1986,' I said wistfully.

'Not without a public indecency charge,' Jess agreed.

'Bugger, look at the time,' Kate squealed. 'The car will be here in ten minutes.'

That rustled up a flurry of activity as everyone jumped off their beds, discarded the pre-wedding drinks and swapped their robes for dresses. I hadn't done that thing where all the brides-maids looked so similar they could be in a girl band. Although, if we did, Kate would be Mamma Spice, Carol would be Sexy Spice, Jess would be Smart Spice, Sarah would be Survivor Spice and I'd be Mastercard Spice, the one who – thanks to her recent round-the-world search for all her ex-boyfriends – would be paying off her debts until the end of time. Instead, the girls had all picked their own pastel frocks. Carol was in a powder blue Hervé Léger dress that clung to her curves. Jess had gone for a shift dress in mint. Kate's yellow tea dress had a similar fifties vibe to mine. And Sarah was exquisite in pale pink, bias-cut silk.

On the outside, we actually looked like a group of successful, mature, together women. The world didn't need to know that on the inside we were still those fifteen-years-olds who loved a laugh because we knew that we were only ever one wrong turn away from a drama, a disaster or a regrettable snog at the school disco. Thankfully, we'd grown out of that last option.

We were just about to leave when I stopped at the door, causing a slight pile-up behind me as the others ground to a halt. 'Okay, so I know we don't do mushy stuff, but I just want you all to know I love you. You're the best friends anyone could have.'

'We love you too,' Kate said, squeezing my hand.

It should have been a beautiful moment of reflection and

gratitude, but Jess couldn't bear to be late for anything. 'Okay, that's our sentimental interlude over. Now let's go, and make it snappy, before Mark sees sense and makes a run for it.'

'Oh my God, that reminds me...' Carol exclaimed, while Jess herded us out of the door and into the corridor. 'I was watching a talk show at the gym this morning and a brother and sister ended up ditched when their partners ran off together. So if Mark says he's going to the bathroom and I'm not in the room...' she let that drift off with a mischievous grin.

Maybe beautiful moments of reflection and gratitude just weren't our thing, but I wasn't complaining. I'd take this lot over anyone else on any day of the week. And I'd also take this unconventional wedding day too. The thought of a big, formal celebration filled me with absolute dread. My dad would get blitzed, my mother would criticise everything, and there would be all that stress about photos and cars and whether we had the right shade of napkins. It was an easy decision to go for a short-notice, destination wedding.

We'd decided on New York in a philosophical and analytical way just a month or so ago – we'd put the names of all the places we loved into one of my Converse sneakers and pulled out a winner. Thankfully, everyone we loved could make it, except my Auntie Val and Uncle Don, who were celebrating their twentieth wedding anniversary on a Mediterranean cruise. She'd called from Palma the night before to wish us luck and let us know that she'd stashed away several bottles of sangria for a party when we all got home.

The wedding itself was to be low-key too. There was no booking system at the Marriage Bureau, so it was a case of turning up and hoping for a slot. If it worked out today, then great. If not, we'd come back tomorrow. It would give me a great excuse to wear my dress again. After the ceremony, we planned a quick change at the hotel, and then a jaunt to Coney Island for some serious candy floss, funfair rides and the weekly Friday night fireworks. Perfect. My mother was going to have to lie down for a week to get over the lack of pomp and formality. To be honest, I was surprised my parents had come. It was difficult for people with a loving mum and dad to imagine, but Ma and Pa Cooper were a law unto themselves. My dad would have to be prised off a bar stool to get him to the ceremony, and my mother, well, cosy mother daughter moments had never been her thing. She'd shown absolutely no interest in the wedding, until we'd decided to have it in New York. I was pretty sure she was only here for the shopping. Still, I'd tried. 'Mum, the girls and I are getting ready in my suite then going to the registry office together. Why don't you come over and get ready with us, then we can all travel together?'

I didn't have to wait long for the inevitable rejection. She'd looked at me like I'd just suggested we did a line of crack behind a dumpster, 'Darling, that would be such a hassle. I've already arranged for a hairdresser to come to my room and I'm not getting my dress crushed by squeezing into a cab. I've also booked a car for me and your father and I suppose we'll bring your gran as well.' Gran was dad's mum, but at least, to her credit, my mother accepted her as part of the package. It would be uncharitable to think that the only reason for that was because she'd needed Gran's constant babysitting service when we were kids. Definitely uncharitable. And almost definitely true. Anyway, I brushed her refusal off. I wasn't letting my mother's disdain and general disinterest spoil my day. Not when I was with my girls and they more than compensated for the lack of fuzzy family stuff.

And they knew how to dish out orders too.

'Walk and talk, walk and talk,' Jess commanded, all the way to the lifts. We made it to the front door of the hotel at one o'clock on the dot.

The Manhattan Marriage Bureau was only ten blocks from our Greenwich Village lodgings, but we'd been warned it could take an hour in mid-afternoon traffic, so we'd left ourselves plenty of time. Mark, and his best man, who just happened to be my brother, Callum, were meeting us there at two o'clock with the rest of our guests: my parents, my brother, Michael, Gran, Mark's parents, Kate's husband, Bruce, Jess's husband, Mike, and Sarah's fiancé, Nick. Hopefully we'd get a slot before it closed at 3.45 p.m.

As the car moved steadily along the streets, though, I saw that we'd been overcautious. There were a few minor hold-ups at traffic lights, but there was almost no congestion, so twenty minutes later we were sitting outside the stunning steps of the government building with forty minutes to spare until our meeting time with the rest of the wedding party. Unsurprisingly, there was no sign of the others yet.

'There's no way we're going in just now,' Carol exclaimed. 'It's your job to make an entrance.'

'Want me to ask him to go around the block?' Kate asked.

Biting my lip, I scanned the street. Carol was right. We didn't want to be hanging about some hallway waiting for everyone to get there. It wasn't exactly the romantic option.

'We passed a pub just round that last corner. We could go in there for a pre-wedding drink.'

'From your lips to Jack Daniel's ears,' Kate said, laughing.

We paid, hopped out, and then sprinted back across the road at the first non-jaywalking opportunity.

As soon as we opened the doors of O'Reilly's Tavern, we knew it was our kind of place. Like so many Irish bars we'd loved before, the wood-panelled walls and traditional decor beckoned

us in, and the music was playing, the chatter was loud and it had
a huge free table right next to the bar.

'In half an hour, remind me I'm getting married today, otherwise we'll end up staying here and I'll be starting off a sing-song
by six o'clock.' I was only half joking.

'No problem,' Carol agreed. 'You know what they say…'

She paused and the rest of us waited with bated breath. Carol
hadn't got a popular saying right since, well, ever. If today was the
day, it had to be a good omen for the wedding.

'A drink in time saves nine,' she said breezily.

Forget about that omen thing.

I'm not sure who giggled first, but it was contagious.

'What?' Carol asked, genuinely puzzled. 'What did I say
wrong?'

I hugged her and landed a kiss on her cheek. 'Not a thing,
Carol Cooper, but I fricking love you. I just hope you're not on my
team if we ever go on Catchphrase.'

'Hello there, ladies! Sit yerselves down, and I'll be over for
yer demands in just a minute,' shouted the barman, a portly
gent, somewhere around his late fifties or early sixties. I recognised his accent as being from Dublin, one of my favourite
cities.

That was definitely a good omen.

As promised, our pastel-clad buttocks had barely hit the seats
when he appeared at our side. 'Going somewhere fancy or is this
your usual daywear?' he asked me, with a completely straight
face.

'Usual daywear,' I replied, as if it was the most natural thing in
the world. 'I put on a wedding dress every morning and wander
up and down outside the Marriage Bureau around the corner in
the hope that someone will take me on.'

There was a twinkle in his eye. 'Well now, it's yer lucky day. I get off at five, and I'm willing to give it a go. My wife might object, but she's not so fast on her feet, so I reckon you could take her.'

'I might never leave here,' I announced, desperate to giggle. 'Sorry, what's your name? If we're going to be married, I feel I should know that.'

'It's Daniel,' he said, with a bow. 'But you can call me sugar lips.'

That was it. I crumbled into laughter. 'I'm Carly. Or Mrs Sugar Lips. I'll answer to either.'

Daniel was still hooting with laughter when he headed back to the bar with our order.

One round of drinks turned to two as the bar continued to fill up. I had to raise my voice to be heard over the background music and increasing volume of chatter.

'Can someone call Mark and tell him I'm ditching him for Daniel?'

'I think that's the kind of thing you should tell me to my face,' came a voice from behind me.

My head whipped round and there was my groom, my gorgeous love, looking utterly handsome in his suit. My brother, Callum, was with him, and it was fair to say they were attracting attention. If there was a reality TV show called 'Thirty-Some-things of Abercrombie and Fitch', these two would be in it.

'Babe!'

'Eh, who's Daniel?' Mark asked. His eyebrows were raised, but a smile played on that entirely kissable mouth. Superstitions about not seeing him before the wedding didn't even register. I was marrying this amazing man. That was the kind of good luck nothing could spoil.

I gestured over to Sugar Lips. 'The barman. He says he wants to marry me just as long as his wife, Big Bernie, doesn't kill me first.'

Mark took a moment to absorb this, then shook his head. 'Cooper...' Like my girlfriends, he often called me by my surname. It was an old habit from primary school because there were another two Carlys in my class. 'I've left you alone for one day, and this is what happens?'

'Yup,' I confirmed, sheepishly.

His stern demeanour cracked into laughter as he slid in beside me. 'And that's why I'm marrying you,' he said, while the others cheered. His hand went to my face and he gently tugged me towards him for a long, smoochy kiss. 'You look incredible,' he murmured, before kissing me again.

'Excuse me, can you take yer hands off my future wife,' Daniel roared from behind the bar.

'Only if you bring me beer,' Mark jibed right back.

Daniel bowed. 'Sounds like a fair swap to me.'

Another tray of drinks had just materialised, when the pub door opened again, and in came our parents, my gran and my brother, Michael. It was like we were the mothership and we were calling our people home. Shocked, they stopped dead when they saw us, then came over to greet us with a flurry of hugs and kisses.

'We were ten minutes early, so we just popped in for the ladies to use the loo,' my dad announced. God love him, he was a terrible liar. The man had never knowingly walked past a bar in his life.

'Budge up there, Mark Barwick, or I'll sit on your knee.' That was my gran. A hilarious, irrepressible force of nature.

'But since we're here, might as well have a quick one before we kick this wedding stuff off then,' my dad said, before taking everyone's requests and going off to the bar, a happy man.

When my mother returned from the loo, I could see she was furious, but, for once, she bit her tongue.

Callum and Michael pulled another table across to join ours and the profits of O'Reilly's tavern soared for the next hour, until Jess finally broke the revelry by loudly and repetitively clinking her new wedding ring on her glass.

'Eh, Mr and Mrs,' she said, looking at Mark and me. 'Unless you really are ditching him for Sugar Lips, we've only got half an hour left to get round there and get married.'

Bugger! We'd been enjoying ourselves so much, I'd completely lost track of time.

'Daniel,' I shouted over to my bit on the side. 'Can you keep these tables for half an hour and we'll be back?'

'The amount you lot are spending, I'll keep them for a week,' he answered with a wink. 'The live music starts at five o'clock, so you won't want to be missing that.'

'Will they let me do a wee number for the bride and groom?' my gran asked, beaming. If there was a musical instrument within a hundred yards, she automatically started warming up her vocal cords. She didn't always hit the right notes, but she made up for it with enthusiasm and a set of lungs that ensured everyone within a mile radius could join in.

There was every chance Coney Island would have to wait until another day, but I was all for it. The best parties were always the spontaneous ones.

Daniel didn't even break off from pouring a Guinness. 'Indeed they will.'

I blew him a kiss, and there was a scramble for the door, as one bride, one groom, one best man, four bridesmaids, and assorted family members mobilised.

We made it in the nick of time, handed over the licence we'd bought the day before to a smiling clerk and, thankfully, were ushered straight through to the registrar. It seemed not many other people left their wedding until twenty minutes before the place closed for the day.

Bursting with joy, with excitement, and with the absolute certainty that I'd found my happy ever after, my grin never left my face as I stared into the eyes of the love of my life while we took our vows.

'I now pronounce you man and wife,' the registrar announced. 'You may kiss... Oh.'

We were already way ahead of him, Mark's lips were on mine as the people we loved clapped and cheered.

Mark eventually pulled back, his hands on my cheeks, his face still only inches from mine. 'I will adore you every day of our lives,' he whispered.

It had been the perfect day. The perfect wedding to the perfect man.

I just had no idea that those words would turn out to be the perfect lie.

6

SUNDAY 28TH JULY, 2019

LANDSLIDE – STEVIE NICKS

I was still sitting on the floor in the hall, ten minutes after Mark and the boys had left for the airport. My buttocks were numb and I was desperate for more coffee, yet the churning feeling in my stomach hadn't subsided enough for me to get up or even think about what I was going to do for the rest of the day. Or the rest of the week. Or the rest of the month.

How could I miss them so much already when they would barely be out of Chiswick yet?

Nothing was shifting me from here. Nothing. I was going to sit and drown in self-pity for as long as I damn well wanted. Or at least until I needed to pee. Or…

'Carly? Carly?'

Or until Kate used her key to come in the back door and shout at me.

'I'm in the hall, but you don't want to see this. Run. Save yourself,' I hollered back. Mark might have had a point when he accused me of being dramatic.

She appeared in the doorway, hands on the hips of the white jeans, her flowery top setting off the perfect summer look. I really had to swap her for a messy pal. 'Nice T-shirt,' she said, as if there was absolutely nothing strange about me sitting there in my feminist-statement pyjamas in the middle of the day.

'Thanks. You bought it for me.'

'I know. I've got great taste,' she joked. 'Right, pity party over. I'm making you coffee...'

'I'm staying here,' I argued weakly.

She delivered her smoking gun. 'And I've brought you pie.'

'What kind?'

'Banoffee.'

My favourite and she knew it. Damn that woman. She'd hit me right in the weak spot.

'Okay,' I grudgingly agreed. 'But only if you're prepared for me to be a miserable cow. Don't say I didn't warn you.'

Thighs aching, arse still numb, I pushed myself up and plodded through to the kitchen. I plonked myself down and, as always, Kate sat down directly opposite me. It was one of those comforting things about our friendship group – out of sheer force of habit, we all sat in the same seats every time we visited each other's houses.

Kate slid a coffee, a large banoffee pie and a spoon in my direction.

As I picked up the spoon, I glanced up at her. 'Are you not having any?'

She shook her head. 'I saw Mark leave with the boys. I think this is a full-pie kind of moment for you.'

'That's why I love you, oh wise one,' I said, taking my first bite. 'Can I moan about my sad, solitary life while I'm eating it?'

'Okay, you've got ten seconds to get it all off your chest, and then we're over it,' she said, indulging me.

Spoon in mid-air, I paused. 'I know that I should be happy for them, and I promise I am, but there's just a bit of me that wishes it was different.'

'Do you want Mark back?' she probed gently.

'No... at least... No!' I repeated, more firmly the second time. 'I think I just want my family back.'

'That's understandable, hon,' she said, taking my non-spoon hand. 'They've been your whole life for the last twenty years. But maybe this is a good thing. Remember when you first found out they were going? At my Mother's Day barbecue, you told Val that you were going to find yourself again and plan something fantastic for when the boys were away.'

I swallowed an exquisite chunk of thick gooey caramel. 'I know. I think I was high on the fumes from your firepit. If I'm going to find my old self, she's going to have to pitch up at this kitchen table. I can't think of anything worse than going away on my own. Are my ten seconds up?'

She checked her watch. 'They are.'

'Okay. Wanna go binge-watch some trash telly?'

Before she could answer, a sound took my gaze to a new shadow outside the back door.

'Who's that? And why don't you look surprised?' I asked her, suspicious now.

The door swung open and Carol and Jess trooped in, making straight for their usual seats – Carol next to me, and Jess across from her, next to Kate.

'Bloody hell, you lot are like some kind of Avengers squad that kick in in times of trouble. Middle Age Pals Assemble,' I muttered, secretly delighted and grateful they were there. I took a deep breath. 'Look, I realise that in the grand scheme of things I've got absolutely nothing to moan about, so I'm going to save you all the pep talk. I'm fine. I'll be okay. I just needed a moment for reality to sink in and to consume calories that will stay on my arse for ever. That's now been achieved,' I gestured to the large chunk that was missing from Kate's pie, 'so I'm going to pick myself up and get on with it.'

'Get on with what?' Jess asked. She'd always been a details person. In school, she made up all our timetables, colour-coded and laminated, complete with handy hints and reminders. Later, she'd studied politics at Aberdeen University and at the end of the nineties she'd become a researcher for Basil Asquith, MP. Unfortunately, she was then caught shagging the aforementioned MP and was plastered all over the pages of the Sunday newspapers. Thankfully, twenty years later, that's been largely forgotten by the British public and she's built a hugely successful PR company that specialises in scandal and damage limitation. Handy, because if the world discovers she's meeting blokes from Tinder for sex, she'll know how to deal with it. What's important here, however, is that she's the absolute kickass kind of friend every woman should have. Even if she occasionally scares me.

I saw they were waiting for an answer and I hesitated, squirming a little. 'Ah, I'm... not exactly sure yet.'

Jess continued to probe like this was a House of Commons committee on rogue arms deals and I'd just been caught with a cache of AK47s next to the fold-up table, the Flymo and the bucket of old wellies in my shed. 'So you've no plans?'

'No, I'm—'

'And you've no work for the next month?' Jess went on. I was under so much pressure here that I couldn't even object that Carol had taken my spoon and was now dipping into my banoffee pie.

'Just my usual columns,' I said, referring to the load of pretentious, mummy-chic nonsense that I wrote for *Family Values* magazine. 'I don't start my next ghost-writing gig until the beginning of September. That bloke off morning telly who spent all his money on cocaine and hookers.' I don't know why I felt the need to add that. Maybe I just wanted to make the subliminal point that, in comparison, my life was tickety-boo.

Kate took over. 'We think you should go to LA and visit Sam like you said you would.'

Buying time, I lifted my coffee and held it to my lips. I'd thought about it. I mean, what wasn't there to love about a friend of twenty-five years, who just happened to have made it big in Hollywood and who lived in a Pacific Palisades resort-like home down the road from Ben Affleck? Something had stopped me making the booking though. Maybe I didn't want to irritate Mark. Perhaps I wasn't ready to hold the failure of my marriage up to the sun by discussing it with an ex. Or maybe it was just that, given the current state of my body, my roots and my wardrobe, I was pretty sure I'd be stopped by the Los Angeles Glamour Police and packed off on the next flight home. 'No. It's just not the right time,' I argued.

Jess leaned forward, elbows on table, hands clasped, going full-scale inquisition on me. 'Why not?'

I decided to bluff it. 'Because I think it's important that I read-just to all these changes in my life in a holistic way and the first steps are reconnecting with my inner self and learning to embrace being alone.'

'Is she talking about stuff that requires sex toys?' Carol asked Kate, who nearly choked on her tea.

Jess's steely glare didn't leave me, and she continued as if Carol hadn't spoken. 'You're lying.'

I shrugged. 'Was it the whole "holistic" thing that gave it away? I thought that might be too much.'

Kate and Carol were both laughing now, but Jess still wasn't letting me off the hook. 'Come on, Cooper...'

Time to go on the offensive and see if that threw her off.

'Look, Jess, I'm just knackered. In the last year, I've gained thirty pounds, none of my clothes fit me, insomnia has aged me five years and the last thing I want to do is go to the land of the beautiful people where I'll feel totally self-conscious and spend the whole time trying to cover my wobbly bits.' It was so shallow, so superficial, and so me, that she was bound to believe it.

'I think that's part of it,' she conceded, her tone suddenly softer, 'but we both know it's not the whole story.' Damn it. Not for the first time, I wished she didn't know me so well.

The temperature in the room dropped about ten degrees as silence descended. Meanwhile, someone took a chisel to my heart and widened a crack that had been there for way too long.

She was right. It was so much more complicated than that. If I delved really deeply into my soul, I knew what was going on, I just didn't want to say it out loud. I couldn't. It hurt too much.

Carol's head dropped on to my shoulder, while Kate leaned over and put her hand on mine again.

'Babe,' Kate said, gently, 'Sarah wouldn't have wanted you to live like this.'

No matter how many times I heard her name, the pain still hit me like a cannonball to the chest, taking my breath away and making every cell in my body scream in pain.

I could feel Carol's breath on my cheek as she said, 'What happened to Sarah wasn't your fault, Carly.'

'I know that,' I lied, my words strangled. Of course it was my fault. The one thing I'd learned in the last couple of years was that when I made crazy choices, when I was the old Carly Cooper, the woman who went off searching for her exes, who risked her marriage by galloping off to LA to try to land a movie deal, who sought out fun, excitement, thrills and adventures – when I was that woman, people got hurt. If I hadn't done any of those things,

Sarah would still be here. I wouldn't have married Mark. I wouldn't have then asked my husband of twenty years to leave. I wouldn't have split up my family. Taking wild, spontaneous risks might have seemed like a great idea, but look where it had got me this afternoon: sitting alone on the hall floor, with my family gone, and facing the rest of my life without one of my best friends.

Nope, I was done with risks and rash decisions. It was over. My actions had consequences for me and for the people I loved. I had no right to throw caution to the wind and go off in search of excitement and happiness when I'd already done so much damage to us all.

I didn't verbalise any of that, though. I didn't have to. We all knew each other so well, we'd all lived through the pain of losing Sarah together, so they knew I carried the scars and the guilt, even if they didn't realise the depth of it.

Jess reached around to her handbag, slung over the back of her chair. It took me a moment to notice that she'd pulled out a document, which she unfolded and pushed in front of me. I really hoped it was a voucher for a make over. Or a recipe for cake.

'Cooper, you have to get over this and the only way to do it is to get back out there and live your life, so here's what's happening.'

My eyes followed hers to the paper, and immediately picked out the important bits.

Flight Confirmation:
    Carly Cooper.
    28th July 2019.
    20.05 – Flight BA2934 – Heathrow to Los Angeles LAX.

I tried to process the words, but they weren't computing. 'I don't understand. What is this?'

Carol answered first. 'It's your Christmas and birthday presents for the next year, from all of us. And you need to take it, because it's the only way you're going to find a way to get past this.'

'But... but that's ridiculous. I mean, thank you, but that's mad. It's today's date. And it's... it's...' I checked the kitchen clock. 'Five hours from now! I can't just pick up and take off tonight...'

'Why?' Jess asked, innocently, knowing full well that it was exactly the kind of thing I used to do on a regular basis when we were younger.

'Because... because... I just can't. I don't even have a visa.'

Kate winced. 'You do. The ESTA you got last year when we were thinking about going to New York is still valid. I checked.'

New York. We'd been planning to go over to see Sarah's kids. In the end, we hadn't gone on the trip for a whole load of reasons: Hannah had been too busy with work, I'd been too busy wrecking my family, and Jess couldn't go because Josh broke his leg playing rugby and came home from uni for six weeks to recuperate. The Gods conspired against us, and if I was being honest with myself, I was glad. New York came with too many memories and I couldn't face them. Not then, not now, maybe not ever.

As for this insane plan to hop on a plane to LA tonight... my palms were sweating and my stomach was lurching like a tumble dryer on the highest setting. And I couldn't even vocalise that because my mouth had completely dried and my lips were stuck together.

I couldn't do this. I wouldn't.

An almighty thud interrupted the panic and I realised that someone was battering my front door. My surge of relief was short-lived.

'We thought you might say that,' Kate said. 'And we knew there's only one way to change your mind.'

Jess laughed, and there was hint of triumph in her voice when she said, 'We've called in the big guns. And you're not going to be able to refuse.'

7

STILL SUNDAY 28TH JULY, 2019

I'M EVERY WOMAN – CHAKA KHAN

Carol slipped out of her seat to go and answer the door, while I stared at Kate, then Jess, then back to Kate again, before deciding that she'd be the easiest to crack.

'Kate, what have you done? Who is at the door?'

'Our insurance policy,' she replied. 'And even if you're mad at us now, just remember we're making you do this for your own good, honey. You're not going to solve anything by sitting at this table for the next three weeks.'

'Carly, your visitor is here,' Carol announced, before stepping back, holding the door from the hall open and taking a bow, while the new arrival breezed past her.

'Hello, ma darlin'! Surprise!' bellowed my Aunt Val, arms wide, just stopping short of doing jazz hands. Her platinum bob was the width of the door frame, and she was dressed in a white skirt and floaty top, accessorised with electric blue wedges, belt and handbag. Her cerise lipstick was an identical shade to her nails and toenails. She was like a cross between Joanna Lumley in *Ab Fab* and Kanye West at his Sunday Service.

My chin hit the floor. 'Val! What are you doing here?'

What the hell was going on? I hadn't seen my lovely Val for years and now she'd shocked the life out of me twice in six months.

'I'm going on holiday,' she chirped, hugging me, before pulling out the seat at the end of the table. It was only then I saw that Callum and my niece, Toni, had come in behind her. Callum kissed me on the cheek and then headed straight for the coffee machine, while Toni slouched against the door frame. I guessed they'd been dispatched to collect Val from Heathrow.

'You are?' This was clear as mud. Was she off somewhere that required a layover in London and she'd decided to visit us en route? 'Where are you off to?'

'Los Angeles,' she said, with casual nonchalance. 'I've never been, so I'm proper excited.'

'Oh. My. Lord,' I gasped, as it all fell into place.

'I think the pound just dropped,' Carol observed with acute perception and rubbish articulation.

I could barely get the words out. 'You're in on this too, Val?'

Her face beamed with pride. 'I am. And let me tell you, Carly love, there's no getting out of this, because it's for your own good. All this moping isn't helpful for the cerebral cortex. Or something like that. I read it in the paper. Anyway, the gist of it is, you need to get out there and start living. And so do I. I've been in a hellish rut since my Josie died,' she said, her voice dipping a little as she mentioned her best friend, who'd passed away last year. 'Her and I took a trip together every year, and she'd be spitting feathers at me for wasting the days I've got left, so you're coming with me instead. You and me. We're going to Los Angeles to stay with that bloke from the films...'

'Sam,' Jess interjected.

Oh God. Sam was in on this too? I'd kill him for letting them ambush me like this.

Val was still on a roll. 'Although, my Don made me pack my housecoat, because he said I wasn't to be wandering around in my nightie in case that Sam one found me irresistible.'

The world had actually gone mad.

'And we're going to come over too,' Carol said, beaming. 'Aren't we, Toni?'

I spun to see Toni shrugging, as though this idea wasn't exciting her. Her long toffee brown hair was pulled back in a ponytail and she was swamped by the sweatshirt she was wearing with her denim shorts and white trainers. It struck me that I couldn't remember when I'd last seen Toni laugh and made a note to get her alone and check in on her. My nieces were the closest thing I had to daughters and I adored them.

'Right, that's it,' I said, unable to stop the explosions in my head caused by the utter confusion of what was going on here. 'Tell me exactly what's happening.'

'You might need wine for this. I brought my own in case you didn't have any.' With that, Val produced a bottle of Lambrini from the depths of her tote bag.

Kate immediately jumped up, and retrieved a few wine glasses from my cupboard, before grabbing a bottle of Prosecco from my fridge. Today was blowing my mind, but I had to admit, that bubbly feeling of being in a room with all my pals was beginning to lift my mood from devastation to something a bit more bearable. But I still wasn't going to LA. Definitely not.

Was I?

'Here's the plan,' Carol finally said. 'You, me, Toni and Val are flying to LA tonight and we're going to stay with Sam. He's got some film commitments going on, so I'm not exactly sure if he'll be there, but he said we can stay in his home whether he's there or not.'

'It has a jacuzzi,' Val said knowingly. 'And I've brought my pink swimming cap for the pool.'

I was fairly sure that everyone was biting their tongues so they wouldn't point out that Val's swimming cap would need to be the size of a space hopper to go over that hair.

Kate took up the travel-service baton. 'Carol and Toni are coming home after two weeks, and Jess and I are flying out to replace them. We thought we could maybe do some travelling or tour around a little bit. Oh, and Val wants to go surfing in Malibu. Apparently it's a whole *Baywatch* thing.'

'I do,' Val agreed, lifting her Lambrini. 'I've packed my red cossie and I've been practising running in slow motion for the last month.'

Oh, she was good. They weren't kidding when they said they'd brought in the big guns.

'And that's as far as we've got, but the flights are all arranged and we've all booked the time off, so you've got no choice but to go along with it,' Jess concluded. The world of politics had been crazy to let this one go. There wasn't a task force that she couldn't sort out or a crisis she couldn't solve. And she'd do it in great shoes. I realised this thought was somewhat distracting me from what was important at that moment.

'For my sake, if nothing else,' Val added, piling on the emotional persuasion.

Exhaling, I sat back in my chair and scanned the room, every other set of eyes staring right back at me. I felt pressured. Shocked. Stunned. Most of all, though, I realised I felt absolutely grateful that these people loved me enough to come together to dig me out of the hole I'd slid into. How lucky was I? I may not have parents looking out for me, or a partner I was going to grow old with, but I had a gang of pals who cared enough to see that I was struggling and to come up with a plan to help. They'd paid for this ticket, they were giving up their time and they were doling out some tough love and pushing me out of my comfort zone. Whether I liked it or not.

I just wished Sarah was here with us and part of the plan. She'd love this. She'd already be in my room, throwing my stuff into a suitcase and fantasising about meeting George Clooney in the supermarket.

Blinking back tears, my gaze fell on the travel confirmation on the table in front of me as I contemplated what it actually meant. If I went along with this, then this time tomorrow I'd be in a swanky pad in Los Angeles, easing my cellulite into a kidney-shaped swimming pool in the sunshine, next to a woman whose bright pink bathing cap would make her look like the closest thing to a nuclear warhead that Glasgow had ever produced.

I needed some perspective, someone to balance out all this badgering.

'What do you think of all this then, Toni?'

My niece shrugged again. She matched her mother's five foot ten height, but she had her dad's lighter brown hair, and the green eyes that ran in our side of the family. 'It's like, a hostage situation. Apparently, I don't have a choice,' she said, summing it up perfectly. She'd always been the quietest, most bookish of the kids, but now she just seemed, well, deflated.

On the surface, she had everything going for her: great parents, a lovely home, decent grades and the potential to be anything she set her mind to. She'd just finished her first year at college, studying fashion, but I'd never been convinced it was a great fit for her. It was almost like she'd taken the obvious option and had gone into the family business.

It crossed my mind that one positive of going along with this ambush was that I'd get to spend time with Toni and perhaps even cheer her up a bit.

'Yep, we're terrible parents,' Carol said tightly. 'Imagine forcing your child to go on an all-expenses paid trip to LA.' It was supposed to be a joke, but the tightness in her voice and the exasperated glance she threw Callum combined to make it fall flat.

Toni just rolled her eyes and slunk off into the lounge, the door thudding as she closed it behind her.

'I know,' Carol said, to no one in particular. 'I'm messing this up. She hates me.'

'She's a teenage girl,' Jess said, trying to take the edge off the situation. 'At that age, it's part of the job description to hate your mother.'

My relief at the focus being taken off me was short-lived, as a room of inquisitive, raised eyebrows (with the exception of Carol, whose Botox regime had prohibited her from raising her eyebrows since 2002) swivelled back in my direction.

'What do you think, then?' Kate asked, and I couldn't miss the hope and concern in her tone.

This was ridiculous. I was a grown woman. I controlled my own destiny. Yet... I knew when I was beat.

'I think I'd better go and dig out my swimming cap.'

8

LATER THAT EVENING – 28TH JULY, 2019
LET'S GET THE PARTY STARTED – PINK

'Carol, I swear to God, I'm going to take that phone off you and slip it in the drinks trolley the next time the cabin crew pass,' I warned my pal, as she took the thousandth photograph since we'd left my house just a few hours before.

We'd arrived at the airport for our LA flight just as the boys took off for their flight to Miami. This was so very different from how I'd expected today to play out.

'Welcome to my life,' Toni sighed.

I decided not to point out that while she wasn't quite as prolific as her mother, she had done her fair share of selfie snapping too.

'Urgh, I know it's irritating,' Carol admitted. 'But it's just part of the job. You've got to admit, it has its perks though, so it's swings and seesaws.'

My brain automatically corrected it to 'roundabouts', but I said nothing because Val chirped in first.

'Aye, it does, pet. You snap away and keep those perks coming,' she said, adjusting the eye mask that she'd procured from the complimentary toiletry set we'd been given when we boarded. She was also wearing the complimentary pyjamas, the socks, the slippers, the lip balm, the moisturiser and she'd brushed her teeth at the first available opportunity with the complimentary toothbrush. If the head of British Airways walked past right now, they'd think she was a brand ambassador.

I couldn't argue with my sister-in-law's point though. Travelling with Carol was a very different proposition to my usual experience of transporting myself from one country to another. There was no sprinting through the boarding-gate scrum to board first so there would still be room for my cabin bag in the overhead locker. No getting stuck next to a bloke called Jez who snored while he slept and hogged the armrests. No agonising over whether to choose chicken or beef and then inevitably picking the wrong one. No wondering if Marge from Blackpool on the other side was ever going to stop chatting so I could open my Jilly Cooper retro bonkbuster or make spontaneous purchases I couldn't afford from the duty-free magazine.

Nope, none of the above, because travelling with a well-known former catwalk star and social media influencer with over three million followers on Instagram was like travelling with a minor royal.

It started when we arrived at the check-in desk and bypassed the normal queue to deposit our bags at the Priority Boarding desk, where we were informed that we'd been upgraded to first class and they hoped we'd have an enjoyable flight.

'It was a bit of a risk booking business class, but I contacted their PR people to say we were coming and I knew they'd shift us up to First if the flight was quiet,' she'd whispered, while taking a selfie at the check-in desk and then singing the praises of the airline to her cult on Insta, Twitter, Snapchat and Facebook. I'd never had the slightest interest in social media. I'd set up Facebook and Twitter accounts when they were first launched (mostly out of curiosity to see what had happened to everyone I'd ever known), but it had been so long since I'd used them that I'd forgotten the passwords. I did have an Instagram account and Snapchat, but the only two people I followed were Mac and Benny and that was strictly for supervision purposes and their own protection. Also known as spying. Not that there was much to look at. The boys rarely posted, usually too busy in the gym, pool or on court to bother with them. Or perhaps they were just sick of the lectures I gave them on a weekly basis about not putting their lives out there and not speaking to anyone they didn't know.

'Would you like us to arrange a chauffeur service at LAX to take you to your final destination?' the check-in agent had asked, sending Val into a coughing fit of astonishment.

'No, we're already organised, but thank you,' Carol had said sweetly, acting like this was the kind of thing we did every day. Actually, this was pretty much her life.

I'd only flown in first class once in my life. It was on a flight from Hong Kong to the USA in the nineties, and I only got the seat because I'd slept in for an overbooked flight and when I rushed to check in at the last minute, economy was full. It would have been wonderful, if it wasn't for the sad reality that I had a hangover from hell and spent the whole flight simultaneously sleeping and sweating pure gin.

Today's experience had definitely been more indulgent. After check in, we went to the VIP lounge, where we were treated to free beverages and snacks that were so posh I couldn't pronounce them. More pics and online praises duly followed. The sight and sound of Val's pink toenails dangling off a massage table while she oohed and ahhed with every stroke in the first class spa area is one that will stay with me forever.

Afterwards, back in the bar, with more complimentary cock-

tails (Diet Cokes for Toni), Val had exhaled like a truly contented
and relaxed passenger. 'How much would this cost then, if Miss
Fancy Pants there hadn't flashed her pearlies and got us
upgraded?'

Carol had sipped back the last of her Kir royale. 'About six
thousand each... One way.'

'Pounds?' Val had spluttered.

'No, Irn-Bru bottles,' I'd teased.

Her pink-rimmed mouth was wide with shock. 'Suffering
Jesus, that's more than our Skoda cost. What's wrong with people,
wasting that kind of money?'

The barman had approached and Val didn't miss a beat.

'Another one of those fancy cocktails please, Samar,' she'd
said, getting his name from the badge he wore on his white jacket.
'Thanks very much. Oh, yer that handsome. Tell your mother she
did a smashing job with you.'

'I'll pass that on,' Samar had replied, bashfully. I wasn't sure
he'd come across many Vals in the first-class lounge, but he was
handling it well. The same couldn't be said for Toni, whose mortification was turning her the colour of Val's Red Russian (vodka,
fruit, ice, cherry liqueur, Samar had informed us).

My cheeks were beginning to hurt with the pain of trying to
keep my face straight when an airline rep came by to escort us to
the plane. First on, we had been welcomed with a glass of Vintage
Tattinger, before Drew, the very lovely cabin manager, had
chatted through the in-flight menu.

'Any chance they've got Lambrini and a few packets of free
Frazzles?' Val had whispered to me, giggling, when Drew had
taken our food and drink orders. 'Only I'm worried all that caviar
stuff will get stuck in ma teeth.'

And now we were sitting, or rather, lying, in a row of four
fold-down seats in the first-class section of a jumbo jet bound for

La La Land. Our thirst had been quenched by more pre-dinner champagne, we'd feasted on a meal that would have taken me the whole day to prepare and now the cabin lights were dimmed and we had the choice of watching a movie, listening to music, reading, or sampling the giddy delights from the bar. Carol had already taken pics doing all of the above, and informed us that she'd post them at intervals over the next few hours. Meanwhile, she was answering comments, tagging people and doing all sorts of other things that were way outwith the realms of knowledge I'd gleaned from occasionally dipping into Facebook or Twitter to be nosy or to check the menu of my local takeaway.

I still couldn't believe my day had turned out this way. Although, not everyone was so thrilled.

When I'd called the boys from home to let them know what I was doing, they were still at Heathrow and killing time in JD Sports before their flight to Miami. They were picking up their RV there for their tour up the east coast of the country.

'Tonight? No way! That's epic, Mum,' Mac exclaimed, and I could hear the hint of jealousy in his voice. He still remembered our first trip to LA to see Sam when he was six, and we'd been back a few times since then. Mac loved everything about it.

He'd handed the phone to his brother and Benny was equally as excited for me. 'Maybe you could come see us on the way back?'

'I'm not sure, honey. I'll see where you are and hopefully we can work something out,' I'd said, keeping it light and non-specific. By that time, I'd be missing them so much I'd be climbing the walls, but I didn't want to commit to anything in case it didn't suit Mark.

Talking of whom... 'Hang on, Dad wants to talk to you,' Benny had said. 'Bye, Mum, love you. And tell Uncle Sam we said hi.'

'Will do. Love you too, son. Miss you so much already.'

I still had a lump in my throat when Mark came on the line. 'Hey. Did I overhear all that right? You're going to LA tonight? When was that decided?' I'd recognised the tone. Confusion with a slice of irritation. He'd obviously thought this had been planned all along and I just hadn't told him.

'It's a long story. The girls ambushed me with it just after you left.'

'So it's just you? Going to LA? To Sam's place?' he'd challenged.

What was with the attitude? If I didn't know better, I'd think it was jealousy again, but it was so out of character that I was sure I must be picking it up wrong.

'Not quite. Carol and Toni are coming too, and Aunt Val has come down from Glasgow to come with us. It's turned into a Sister Sledge song.'

'Oh. Right.' Definitely some relief in there. This was just getting stranger. 'Well, look, keep in touch. I heard Benny saying something about meeting up. Let me know if that works for you. We'd like that.'

Then he was gone, leaving me with so many mixed emotions, I just shoved the whole lot to one side and carried on searching for four kaftans I'd worn in Fuenguirola when I was pregnant with Benny. I was pretty sure they were the only beach clothes that would fit me now.

Hours later, 35,000 feet above the earth, I still wasn't ready to revisit that conversation, so I left it in a box marked 'Ex-Husband Stuff' and pushed it to the back of my mind.

Instead, I pulled out my mobile and connected to WhatsApp, using the plane's Wi-Fi. I definitely had mixed feelings about the availability of Wi-Fi on flights. On the one hand, it was convenient, but on the other hand, I used to love the delicious indulgence of knowing that from beginning to end, a flight was somewhere that I could completely switch off from the rest of the world and fantasise that I was bound for LA, to a waiting movie star, for a luxurious break in his palatial home. Which, erm, was exactly what I was doing right now.

I texted Sam.

We are on the way. I can't believe you conspired against me Judas.

It was about 5 p.m. in LA right now and he was probably busy, so I didn't expect him to reply. I was surprised when the three little dots appeared to show he was typing.

Sam: I'm sorry.

Me: You're not.

Sam: Okay, I'm not. Can I buy back your love?

That made me laugh.

Me: Dinner at the Cheesecake Factory, but I'm making no promises.

Sam: I'll start saving. We'll go big.

Me:
Me:
Me:

In typical perimenopausal mood-swing fashion, something in that last comment triggered an insecurity and wrecked the moment. I ended up going for a superficial reply of...

Me: Deal. See you soon xx

I flicked my phone off and shoved it in the pouch in my seat.

'We'll go big' reverberated in my head. I was already big.

I knew it was stupid and shallow, but I hadn't seen Sam in a couple of years and, last time we met, I looked very different from the way I did now. It shouldn't matter. We were friends. My size or shape wouldn't change how he felt about me in any way. Problem was, it changed how I felt about myself. I definitely had less confidence. Definitely didn't feel easy in my own extra skin.

And yes, there was a tiny bit of me that registered that Sam was an ex-boyfriend of a million years ago, and no woman wants to bump into a former lover when she's feeling about as attractive as mud.

If I'd known I was going to do this, I'd have been down at the community centre for twice-weekly boxercise classes, I'd have got the juicer out of the hut and I'd have buried my biscuit tin in the back garden. I might also have got my eyebrows done, perhaps a bit of fake tan, sorted out my roots and attacked the forestry situation on my legs.

As it was, I was going to the city of perfection looking like I'd been marooned on a desert island for the last few years – one where the indigenous population rejected all modern civilisation except Dunkin' Donuts.

To my left, I could hear Toni fidgeting, so I reached out across the gap between our seats and stroked her hair. 'You all right, sweetheart?' I asked quietly, aware that a few people around us were dozing, including Val, who was now breathing deeply, with the occasional gentle snore.

'Yeah,' she answered, but I wasn't convinced. Something was definitely off with her.

'Want to stretch our legs?' I asked her, keen for an opportunity to chat to her. We usually only spent time together in a family group, so it was nice to have some one-on-one time.

We walked to the back of the cabin, where there was a tiny area of space outside the toilets. I didn't want her to feel I was interrogating her – plenty of time for finding stuff out in the next two weeks – so I went for casual chit-chat.

'I bet Charlotte is so jealous she's not here too. You should definitely photoshop daily pics with movie stars and send them to her,' I joked.

Toni shrugged. Again. She must have the fittest deltoids in the country. 'Doubt she'd even notice.'

Ah, was there some tension there? Had she fallen out with her sister. They were such different personalities. Right now, Charlotte was off spending her summer working as an intern for a prestigious property development company. She was driven like Carol but had that easy way with people that came straight from her dad. Everything she did, she excelled at. I could see how that would be annoying for a sibling.

'You okay there, ladies?' Drew, the lovely cabin crew manager who'd served us, was now breezing past on his way to the galley.

'We're fine, thanks,' I assured him. 'Just stretching our legs. Don't want to ruin the experience with a deep vein thrombosis.'

He was still chuckling as he disappeared behind the curtain that separated the swanky bit from behind the scenes.

Just when I was giving up on Toni engaging in any meaningful way, her curiosity got the better of her. 'Aunt Carly, what exactly is the deal with you and this Sam guy?'

The question surprised me at first. This was Sam Morton. Hollywood heart-throb.

But, of course, that was past tense. Toni wouldn't have any real idea who Sam used to be in any of his former lives. He was at the height of his fame when she was only seven or eight, before he'd made the shock decision to take himself out of the public eye and gone behind the camera. Since then, he'd had a far lower public profile but huge success, producing some of the best romcoms of the last decade. Benny was his godson, and Sam made sure he caught up with the boys whenever he was in London, but as far as I could remember, Toni had only met him a couple of times, and that was years ago.

'He's just a friend,' I answered honestly.

For the first time today, her face broke into a smile, and she nudged me. 'Come on, Aunt Carly, dish the dirt. I want to know details.'

Oh God. Truth or Lie? Truth or Lie? She was eighteen going on nineteen. That was old enough to hear what actually happened, wasn't it? And maybe sharing the story would help her trust me, and perhaps she would then share what was going on with her?

I reached over and pulled back the galley curtain just a tiny bit.

'Drew, can I have a gin and tonic please? Actually, I might need a packet of crisps too.'

How to sum up a twenty-five-year tumultuous relationship in one conversation?

I took a deep breath and contemplated where to start.

The only place that made sense was at the beginning.

9

HONG KONG, 1994
LOVER – TAYLOR SWIFT

Full disclosure: the first time we met, Sam thought I was a hooker. Which was ironic, given how things turned out.

I was twenty-five, and after a few years working in nightclubs in Glasgow, Amsterdam and Shanghai, I'd landed my dream job: managing an uber-exclusive, exquisitely trendy, illustrious nightclub in the basement of the prestigious Windsor Hotel in Hong Kong. Problem was, I'd been working and living in the chain's sister hotel in Shanghai for the previous two years, so I was well out of date with the current fashions.

In a rush to do a covert reconnaissance of the club before the staff found out who I was, I donned the only 'suitable' clubbing outfit in my suitcase – a black mini dress that barely covered my buttocks at the back, and had a zipper that ran from chest to hem at the front. I know. My only excuse is that it was the nineties and it was a throwover from when I'd lived in Amsterdam a few years before. The perfect dress for a night out in the Amsterdam nightclub world? Absolutely. But for a chic club in a five-star hotel in Hong Kong? Not so much.

The muscle-bound steward with the London accent on the

door of Asia, the hotel's basement nightspot, clearly thought the same. I can still remember every detail of my first impression:

6'2" tall. Hair, the colour of Dairy Milk, crew-cut. Brown eyes with eyelashes that you could stir tea with. Square jawline. Sun-tanned. White teeth, crowned and straight. Nose that has been broken. At least twice. Broad shoulders. Defined pecs. Washboard abs that I couldn't see, but I just knew they were there. Slim hips. This guy was an 'after' picture for a health food supplement advert.

He was clearly reluctant to let me in, but I showed him my room card and he waved me past. A few hours later, when I left the club alone, he made his judgements clear.

'No business tonight, love?'

Determined to insert a modicum of class into the situation, I gave him an aloof smile. 'Not tonight. You see, I'm very, very expensive and I don't think any of that lot could afford me.'

The following evening, when the Food and Beverage Director of the hotel called a meeting of Asia's staff and introduced me as the new manager, Sam's face was a priceless picture of mortification, but it broke the ice and sparked an undeniable attraction.

Within a couple of weeks, we were living together in his apartment in Causeway Bay. Sam had big dreams and he was working to make them happen. Already mastering Cantonese, by day he taught martial arts to kids, and was planning to open an academy as soon as he'd saved the funds to rent his own premises. By night, he made extra cash by working on the door of the club, a job that came with the extra pressure of fending off the advances of lusty customers.

We had a great time together and fell into the kind of easy rhythm that happens when you laugh a lot, have loads in common, and you're still in that first flush of love where you spend as much time as possible indoors and naked. Still, it was a surprise when, a few months later, ten minutes before midnight on New Year's Eve, the music in the club fell silent. The DJ called me to the dance floor, and my heart thudded, positive that there had been some kind of electrical shortage or a major life-threatening catastrophe. If only.

Instead, in front of a packed room of revellers, Sam Morton walked towards me, holding a microphone. 'Cooper, I love you very much.' There was a chorus of 'Aaaaahs' from the crowd and hollers of 'Go, Sam!' from the bar staff. 'Marry me,' he said.

Bugger. Fuckety Damn Bugger. My brain screamed a silent, 'Nooooooo'. I didn't want that. It was too soon. And my cheeks were burning because I bloody hated being the centre of attention. I loved him, but I already had a couple of broken engagements behind me and I wasn't ready to commit to any more than that. What was I supposed to do, though? Three hundred pairs of eyes were on us, waiting for my answer. Again, Fuckety Damn Bugger.

'Yes,' I said, because, well, I couldn't say no.

Streamers flew, poppers popped and the cheers raised the roof, and when my gorgeous, kind, smart fiancé picked me up and swung me around, I told myself we'd make it work.

For a while, we did.

But six months later, my one-year contract at the club expired and I was offered a transfer back to another Windsor hotel in the UK. Sam begged me to stay, but I was homesick and ready to see my family and friends again. Also, I was running one of the best clubs on the island. What would I do if I stayed? There was no option to extend my contact so I'd have to leave the hotel chain, and if I did that, there was no way I'd find another job of the same level.

After torturing myself with indecision and investigating every option, I decided to take the UK job for a year. That's all I was asking. If Sam really wanted to spend the rest of his life with me, then surely he could make a long-distance relationship work?

'Please don't go, Cooper. I don't want to live without you. Don't leave.'

'Then wait for me, Sam. I promise I'll come back in twelve months.' I truly meant it. The way I saw it was that if we were meant to be together, then this would work. Absence makes the heart grow fonder and all that cliché stuff.

'But don't you see, if you really loved me, you wouldn't leave?' he replied.

Wow. He didn't even try to see it from my point of view.

My indignation rose. Was that what it came down to? Emotional blackmail?

'Sam, I'm going. I have to.'

Eventually, he shook his head, shrugged.

'Then go,' he murmured, voice thick with sadness.

He got up, grabbed his jacket and left.

I slowly slipped off my engagement ring and placed it gently on his bedside table. I flew out of Hong Kong that evening, closing the door on my relationship with Sam, at least for a while.

Five years later, on my quest to revisit all the men I'd loved, I returned to Hong Kong to track down the man I'd deserted so abruptly. It took some serious detective work, but I discovered that he still visited three homeless guys who lived outside our old apartment every Friday, to take them cash and food, just as he'd done when we were together.

That's why I was sitting on the step of our former home when he drove up in a flash sports car, the first sign that he'd upgraded his life.

'What did you do, Sam, rob a bank?' I spluttered.

'Cooper! What the hell are you doing here?' Was he pleased

to see me? I wasn't sure if his expression was 100 per cent astonishment or 100 per cent delight.

'I forgot my keys. I came back five years ago and you weren't in, so I've been sitting here ever since.'

His face cracked into a huge smile as he hugged me. Delight. Definitely delight. Maybe this was it. Maybe he was the one. Maybe I'd finally found my happy ever after.

That night, the revelations about his new lifestyle continued. Incredible apartment at the Peak. Designer clothes. Not bad for a martial arts instructor, I thought.

Turns out, that wasn't quite the case. Later that evening, while Sam was out, his phone rang, and a woman left a message requesting a date with him. Then another. Then another. Only hours after my optimism peaked, it sank like a stone in Hong Kong harbour as I realised my former fiancé was making a living as a high-class escort.

By the time he came home, I was numb, just silent tears streaming down my face as I tried to understand how this had happened. 'Why, Sam?'

It took a while, but he eventually slayed me with the truth.

'After you left, I couldn't bear it,' he said. 'I didn't know what to do with myself. Everything hurt so much and I was so angry. I would go to work every night and watch all the couples, looking so happy, and I couldn't believe that it wasn't us. One night, one of the women that I trained asked me to go to a company dinner with her. It was a "partners" function and she didn't want to go on her own. I felt sorry for her, so I went. And afterwards, she insisted on paying me for my time, said it was just like a personal training session.

'The next week, she called again. Then her friends started calling and, before I knew it, I was booked out every night. Gradually I charged more and more, but the business just kept coming in. Soon after, I gave up everything else. I was making more money than I could ever have dreamt of. And it was so easy.'

His devastated expression made guilt and sorrow seep from my pores.

'So you never opened your martial arts school?'

'No,' he answered, and there was more sadness and regret in that one word than I could bear.

My silence prompted him to continue.

'At first, it was just dinner and conversation, then somewhere along the line it became... more. I didn't care. They were buying my time, I was already selling myself, so what did it matter? I was convinced I'd never fall in love again and that part turned out to be true...'

A knife twisted in my chest.

'... So now this is who I am and it works for me. No strings, no emotion, no hurt. In a few years' time, when I don't look so good, I'll take the money and run. I'll retire from this life and find something else to do. Things happen, Carly. We don't always end up how we'd imagined in life.'

Wasn't that the truth.

That could have been the end of it, but the thing with Sam was that, well, I loved him. I stayed in Hong Kong with him for a while, not as a lover, but as a friend. He wanted to try again, but getting past the 'so many people have rented my boyfriend's penis' thing was just too big for me. I couldn't do it.

A few months later, I returned to Scotland for Carol and Callum's wedding, met Mark again, and realised he'd been the one for me all along.

Back in Hong Kong, Sam's life took another incredible twist. One of his clients turned out to be a lady with serious Hollywood connections and she encouraged Sam to write about his life. It was one of those crazy occasions where the stars aligned and shot out bolts of brilliance. Sam's story, *Gigolo*, became a massive box-office hit, with him in the starring role, kicking off a meteoric Hollywood ascendance that saw him winning the types of roles that usually went to Pitt, Affleck and Damon. It seemed that the movie fans could forgive his alternative career choice because he'd delivered it up for their entertainment.

As far as my relationship with him went, there should have been nothing more to report, but a few years later, we added another chapter to our story.

Back in Scotland, married to Mark, and with two young children, I was knackered, frazzled, unfulfilled in my career and frustrated about what I perceived as my husband's serial indifference, so when my first novel was picked up by an American talent agency, I was thrilled. Mark, not so much. He didn't share my optimism that this could be great for us, and refused to take a chance on going to LA and seeking out the holy grail of a movie deal that could set us up for life.

In the end, I took my boys, a suitcase of dreams and an inflatable alligator to Tinsel Town, and my old friend, Sam, welcomed us into his mega mansion with open arms. My boys adored him, the feeling was reciprocated, and we spent weeks in a wonderful fantasy bubble, living the kind of sun-kissed, luxurious life that only happened in *Baywatch* and old episodes of *Charlie's Angels*.

I never did get the movie deal, but we had the time of our lives and it was so natural, so easy to be around Sam, that I suppose it was inevitable that the lines of our relationship would get blurred. As far as I was concerned, it was a platonic relationship. A true friendship, uncomplicated by thoughts of the sweaty bendy stuff.

And it was. For a while.

Until Sam dropped a bombshell that made me wonder if I'd chosen the wrong man.

10

LOS ANGELES, 28TH JULY, 2019
WOMAN LIKE ME – LITTLE MIX FEATURING NICKI MINAJ

'O. M. Effing. G,' Toni exclaimed, wide-eyed, over the noise of a ping in the background. 'I can't believe you were, like, legit, a movie star's girlfriend. So what happened when you took Mac and Benny over to stay with him?'

'Sorry, ladies,' Drew said, sticking his head out of the galley curtain. 'The captain has put on the seat-belt sign because there might be some turbulence ahead, so I'm afraid you need to return to your seats.'

Toni's face fell, as if someone had switched off a movie just when it got to the good bit. Baby was still in the corner. Tom Hanks was still waiting for the lift at the Empire State Building. Or maybe Richard Gere hadn't made it up the fire escape to save Julia Roberts.

The rest of Drew alighted from the galley and he followed us back to our seats. Was it my imagination or was he looking at me with a strange glimmer in his eye?

I'd just slid back under my blanket when he leant down so that he was almost touching my ear. 'I've seen *Gigolo* more times than I can count,' he whispered, with a cheeky wink.

I closed my eyes, mortified. *Gigolo.* Sam's first movie. Drew must have heard the whole thing. Actually, I doubted he'd believe it. It would be difficult to imagine that this chunky middle-aged bird ever shagged the Adonis that is Sam Morton.

'Aunt Carly, what happened next? I need details!' Toni said again, now that she'd clicked on her seat belt and snuggled down on her chair bed.

'I'll need to tell you later,' I told her, laughing. 'I don't want the whole cabin hearing about it.'

Cue yet another dramatic eye roll. I had hope for her though. This was the most interested and engaged I'd seen her for months.

'What does she need to know?' Carol asked suspiciously from my other side.

'The approximate trajectory of Saturn's moons,' I replied quickly. 'We're discussing astrophysics.'

Thankfully she was far enough away that she didn't hear Toni's giggle.

I closed my eyes for a moment, suddenly desperate to relive the rest of the story.

In my mind, I saw Sam, and he'd just bared his soul and now he was waiting for my reaction, waiting for me to tell him what he wanted to hear and...

'Is that Shirley Ballas?' Val hissed, awake again and pointing to a woman a few beds in front of us.

'Shirley who?'

Val was wide-eyed with excitement. 'Ballas! That one from *Strictly.* Oh my God, the things that woman can do. She's got years on me, but I'd need a hip replacement if I tried all that jiggly stuff. Not that I'd have the opportunity. My Don thinks the paso doble is a sex position. He went purple when I suggested we try it down the community centre.'

I stretched to see if I could get a better view, but all I could see was a very elegantly styled coiffure of dark hair.

'Shirley!' Carol, who'd heard our whole conversation, said in a sing-song voice.

We were so going to get tossed off this flight. I just hoped that if they rerouted to disembark us, we'd land somewhere the prisons had flushing toilets and progressive human rights policies.

The woman with the dark hair didn't turn round.

'Nope, not her,' Carol concluded, oozing nonchalance. 'Anyone else we're intrigued by? Want me to ask the curly-haired bloke in the corner if he's that presenter off *Top Gear*?'

Val was unimpressed with Carol's tone. 'Carol Ann Bernadette Sweeney,' she chided, using Carol's full maiden name, 'any more of that cheek and I'll be on the phone to your mother as soon as we land.'

Val and Carol's mum had known each other since we were kids, some time just after the Ice Age.

Toni leaned towards me. 'Are they always like this?'

'Since your mum was about twelve,' I confirmed. 'Any moment now, Val will threaten to ground your mother, who will then pull on some headphones and spend the next hour listening to Culture Club.'

Toni's head fell back against her chair. 'This is going to be a long two weeks.'

There was a distinct role reversal going on here.

The turbulence we'd been warned of was gentle, barely a blip that didn't stop me from slipping on my headphones and searching through the in-flight movies. I settled on *Book Club*, a comedy starring Jane Fonda, Diane Keaton, Mary Steenburgen and Candice Bergen, as four friends in their later years who are all rediscovering who they are and what they want from life. I could relate. My boys would probably be leaving home in the next few years, and where would that leave me? I'd be in my fifties by then. How did someone start over at an age when most people were beginning to contemplate plans for their retirement?

I shrugged off the introspection and brought myself back to the present. How fricking fabulous had today turned out to be? I was in first class, on a flight to LA, there was a good movie on the TV, a perfect gin and tonic on my tray and a large bag of Rolos shoved down the side of my bed in case I got peckish. I knew how to live.

I checked my watch. The boys would be landing in Miami any minute now and, God, I missed them. But I had to ease off on the apron strings, had to stop focusing 100 per cent on my boys and start to reclaim a little bit of my own life. I had to stop using them as an excuse to hide from the world.

I picked up my phone and clicked into our family WhatsApp chat.

Me to Mac & Benny: Landed yet? Not missing you at all. Nope, not a bit. But if you could both send me pics of your faces so I can gaze at them while sobbing, that would be fab.

Okay, so I didn't say it would be easy to ease off on the apron strings.

My phone buzzed immediately.

Benny to Mum: Just landed. Here's a pic. Love you x

Underneath was a snap of Channing Tatum in *Magic Mike*. My chortle probably woke up Not Shirley Ballas.

For the first time in months, I allowed myself to relax and let the bubbles of excitement rise in my chest. LA. One of my favourite cities in the world. Three of my favourite ladies in the world. One of my favourite men. And my other two favourite friends joining us soon.

It was just... The bubbles burst as something inside me brought me back down to earth. Today was like an emotional roller coaster – every time I started going up, I'd plummet right back down again. No amount of excitement could balance the fact that one of our friends wouldn't be there with us.

I took another sip of my gin and swallowed my feelings at the same time. I couldn't keep going there, couldn't keep wishing that Sarah was here, and letting my guilt over the fact that she wasn't with us cloud the way I viewed my future.

My last thought before I drifted off to sleep, was that the girls were right when they said that I had to let go of the past and start living again. I just had to make my heart believe that too.

* * *

'Ladies and gentlemen, we will shortly be beginning our descent into Los Angeles airport, where the temperature is a warm 61 degrees and the local time is 10.05 p.m. Please fasten your seat belts and return your seat to an upright position.'

No! How had that happened? I hadn't even made it to the end of the movie or the bottom of my gin and tonic, which, incidentally, someone had now removed from my tray.

I turned to face Val and, despite my fury at the missed hours of luxury, I immediately creased into giggles. When I'd fallen asleep, she'd been lying back, sleep mask on, emitting gentle, cosy murmurs. Now she was sitting bolt upright, hair perfect, wearing huge white sunglasses, screaming pink lippy and once again there was a definite aroma of Estée Lauder.

'Val! You do know it's night-time? You might not need the glasses.'

'I'm channelling my inner movie star. I'm sure Meryl Streep never goes anywhere without her shades.'

'You're right,' I told her, acting like this was completely normal. 'And the rest of you is giving out a gorgeous movie star vibe too.'

'Och, thanks, love. Someone said Tom Jones was back in business class, so I put on a bit of lippy to go see.'

I was still trying to work out if this was real life or some weird, gin-fuelled dream.

'And was it him?'

'No. It was a bloke called Shuggy from Cardiff. He said he can do a cracking version of "Sex Bomb" on the karaoke though.'

'You okay over there?' Carol asked, peering around the handbag that was sitting on Val's lap. 'You went out like a bulb.'

Above her sunglasses, Val's perfectly pencilled brows frowned at Carol's turn of phrase, but she kept her Hot Pink Pucker lips clamped shut.

'No,' I replied honestly, pushing myself up and turning my bed back into a seat again. 'I'm raging! I'm flying in first class and I should have been milking every moment and, instead, I slept half the way. What did I miss?'

Carol's ski-slope cheekbones morphed into a wicked grin. 'Supper was delicious,' she taunted. 'Fresh baked croissants...'

I groaned, my stomach rumbling its objections.

'The sweetest strawberries,' she went on.

'You can really go off a person,' I hissed to Val.

'And coffee to die for,' she said, loving every minute. 'Followed by some more champagne to wash it all down.'

I ignored her, turning to Toni instead. 'Just so you know, any disagreements between you and your mum on this holiday, I'm on your side. I'm also open to adopting you if you'd like to make it a permanent arrangement.'

'I'll definitely consider that.' Toni's laughter made the possible *Top Gear* presenter sitting in front of us turn to glare at us disapprovingly.

Val nodded her bob in his direction. 'Bet he's never done "Sex Bomb" at a karaoke,' she said in a stage whisper that could be heard in the back seats of economy.

Trying to stem my amusement, I pulled my bag out from under the seat, and took out my embarrassment of a make-up bag. It was the kind of tatty, mish-mash of ancient cosmetics that made Carol wake up screaming from nightmares. Updating it had never been a priority. For years I'd spent most weeknights sitting outside sports centres and swimming pools while the boys trained inside. I only ever wore the bare minimum for nights out with the girls. And when Mark and I went out, I just stuck to the same old stuff, because, let's face it, I could plaster on the collective cosmetic stash of *Geordie Shore*, wear nothing but a half-cup bra and some suck-it-in magic pants, and he'd still be more interested in the menu at Pizza Express.

I'd had plans to go to the bathroom, and do the whole cleanse, tone and moisturise thing, then carefully apply make-up, fix my hair, and generally alight from the aircraft looking well rested and refreshed. The reality? Now that we had minutes until we touched down on American soil, all I could do was run my fingers through my hair and slap on a bit of foundation. Hopefully, the world would be so dazzled by Val's cerise lippy that they wouldn't notice her bedraggled companion.

I needed to get better at this stuff. Now that the boys were older, I had no excuse for my shoddy grooming standards, other than being out of the habit.

There was a jolt as the wheels hit the runway, and simultaneous waves of thrills and nerves coursed up from my non-painted toes. Note to self – need urgent mani-pedi. But still, this morning? Rubbish pyjamas and self-pity on my hall floor. This evening? Hollywood.

'Hurry up, slowcoach,' Carol prompted, when we stopped at the gate. 'We're first off the plane.'

It was so obvious I wasn't used to this level of service. Back in economy, I knew I'd have at least half an hour to get my bag out of the overhead locker, and even then I'd have to take my life in my hands to cut into the disembarkation line between a bloke wielding a briefcase with sharp edges and a stroppy woman with sixteen duty-free bags and a cabin case that should never have got past the size check.

When the doors opened, I lifted Val's rainbow trolley bag down from the overhead locker, then grabbed my backpack, and followed her out, Carol and Toni now somewhere behind us, both taking photos on their phones.

As we went from the gangway to the terminal corridor, Val glanced back at them. 'I've no idea how those two ever get anything done. They're too busy taking photos to enjoy themselves. Our Josie would have confiscated their phones somewhere over the Atlantic.'

I nodded. 'She definitely would have. Then she'd have started a conga all the way back to business class.'

Val pulled a hankie out of her cardigan sleeve and blew her nose so loudly a couple of men in front of us sped up. 'She'd have loved this, you know,' Val said, and I could hear the sentimentality in her voice and see the mist form in her eyes. Josie had been her best friend for ever and they'd been inseparable until Josie's twenty-a-day cig habit left her with throat cancer. She'd died on the same day she found out, devastating everyone who'd encountered her wild, raucous ways and her huge heart.

I reached out and took Val's hand as we walked and her sad smile of thanks told me there was no need for words. The moment passed, and she shook off the sorrow as we continued to move forward. Wasn't that all we could do? Hold hands and move forward.

As Val speed walked into the ladies', moving at mighty haste in her wedges, I stood against the wall outside, waiting for Carol and Toni to catch up. Watching my sister-in-law approach was a lesson in elegance. Only Carol could make a terminal building look like a catwalk. While I was asleep on the plane, she'd obviously changed her whole outfit, because she was now wearing a beautifully cut white jacket over faded jeans and black pointed boots, her glossy hair falling in waves past her shoulders. Toni trudged behind her, looking two inches shorter despite being the same height, because she was slouching as if she wanted to make herself invisible.

Just as they reached us, Val alighted from the loos in another burst of Youth Dew and led us on a second speed walk to immigration.

'Holy Mother, this place is like Buchanan Street on the first day of the January sales,' Val gasped.

We filed into the shortest line, then chatted for the forty-five minutes it took us to reach a decidedly unenthusiastic customs officer.

Val went first, did all the fingerprint stuff and then handed over her passport.

'Purpose of the trip?' the officer asked, without even looking up.

'This will be good,' I whispered to Carol and Toni, from our vantage point behind the yellow line.

'Well, son,' she started, and I closed my eyes. We'd just spent twelve hours flying here and I was fairly sure the next sixty seconds could have us turned around and flown straight back. 'I'm here to stay with a movie star. A real one. You know that Sam Morton, the one that did all that filthy stuff in the film *Gigolo* years ago...'

The customs officer had now lifted his head and he was staring at her, open-mouthed, trying to work out if this was some kind of joke. I wanted to step forward to politely inform him that it wasn't. It was just standard operating procedure for a Glasgow granny who didn't get out much.

'... I mean, he did other movies too. He was great in that one about the fellow that saved all those rhinos.'

'Jesus, he's going to have her searched for crack,' Carol groaned.

The customs officer still hadn't said a word.

'Well, anyway,' Val continued. 'That one back there with the haircut like an altar boy from the seventies...' she gestured to me and I smiled weakly.

Oh God. Please stop.

'Well, she used to be his girlfriend – I know what you're thinking, but she's got the loveliest personality. Anyway, he's agreed to put us up for three weeks. Three weeks! My tan is going to be the same shade as my garden hut by then.'

'Toni, I'll pay you fifty quid if you faint and create a diversion,' I begged.

'No way, I'm not missing this,' she fired back. If there was one good thing in this whole sorry situation, it was that my niece had now smiled several times today. I had a feeling that a holiday with Val was going to be the best thing that ever happened to her. If they let us in the country...

Back over at the crisis point, the customs officer was clearly making a decision as to whether to let her through or call in a SWAT team.

'Ma'm, where are you from?' He already saw that she had a UK passport so he was looking for something more specific.

'Scotland, son,' she answered proudly.

'And you're here on vacation?'

Her puzzlement showed. 'Aye, son. Like I said, we're going to visit that actor who—'

The officer cracked, stamped her passport with a resounding thud, and handed it back to her. 'Enjoy your stay in the United States.'

'Oh,' Val spluttered, confused at getting caught mid-stream. 'Thanks, son. You have a good day now,' she said, all proud of herself because she'd already adopted some American lingo. 'I'll just go to that ladies' over there while you're getting sorted,' she shouted back to us. 'It's my age. I can't pass a toilet these days.'

Off she bustled, until she was just a blue canvas tote bag in the distance.

I was next. 'Sorry, about that,' I said to Chuckles behind the Perspex screen. 'I think she might have had a brandy on the plane.'

He didn't even crack a smile, but he did let us through without having us taken to a side room for body searches and further questioning, so I was eternally grateful.

By the time we reached the baggage reclaim, our cases were going in circles, I grabbed Val's, then mine, while Carol found hers and Toni's, and we followed the signs for the exit.

My stomach was back on a spin setting of excitement again.

When we got to the huge opaque glass doors that led to the public side of the arrivals hall, the four of us just happened to form into a straight line, standing next to each other, so when they slid open we strutted out, four abreast, like we were Beyonce's backing dancers. All we needed was a slow-motion shot and a fierce backing track.

The music in my head screeched to a halt when I realised I had no idea where we were going.

'Are we getting a taxi to Sam's?' I asked Carol, remembering that someone had said that he might be on location this week. When we'd last spoken on the phone a couple of weeks ago, he'd just started production on a World War Two action pic and they were shooting all the indoor action shots in Toronto. Or was it Oklahoma? He spent so much time on location that I lost track.

Carol shook her shiny tresses. 'I don't think so. Sam said he would arrange a car for us, but maybe there was a problem. We can just jump in a cab if we're stuck.'

I scanned the packed arrivals hall, picking out people with impatient grimaces, others with anxious anticipation, children who were beaming with excitement, and a couple of long-haired guys holding massive cameras, their eyes darting around the terminal. I could be wrong, but I was pretty sure they were paps, hoping to catch a celebrity on spec. It seemed like half of LA was there... Everyone except a driver holding a sign with our names on it.

'Mmmm, I don't think anyone is here for...' I stopped. There it was. A sign. But it didn't say our names.

The bloke in jeans and a black T-shirt, tinted glasses, wearing a baseball cap pulled low on his face, was holding up a placard that said, 'Hollywood Hotel for Waifs and Strays. Cheap rooms. Free biscuits.'

My gaze met his. At least I think it did, it was hard to tell with him wearing those specs. At that moment, he reached up, took them off and a slow, easy grin revealed teeth that cost the same price as my car.

'Fuck, is that Sam Morton?' said one of the long-haired, sloppy guys with the cameras to the other.

Like synchronised swimmers, they both raised their lenses,

while everyone in earshot turned to see what was going on, some of them already pulling out phones to take pictures. Sam didn't even notice.

'Ladies, I think we might have to do a runner,' I warned. The first time I'd come here with the boys, Sam was at the height of his fame and we were mobbed when he arrived to collect us. He'd scooped up two-year-old Benny and four-year-old Mac, and we'd fought our way through the crowds to the car. At the supermarket the following week, my face was plastered all over the trash tabloids, under headings like, 'Sam's secret wife brings kids home' and 'Who's the Daddy?' Mark hadn't been chuffed, but he'd understood that it was all just tabloid nonsense.

To her credit, Val sussed the situation immediately and formulated an impromptu plan. 'Leave it to me, girls. I used to deal with this kind of stuff at the Barrowlands all the time,' she announced, referencing the Glasgow concert venue that she'd worked in during the sixties and seventies. She swore she once sneaked Cliff Richard out of the back door by hiding him in a drum box.

Before we could stop her, off she went, the people in front of her parting like some biblical sea, until she reached Sam and threw her arms around him. 'Oh, Benjamin,' she yelled, 'I thought you'd got stuck at the sexual health clinic and forgotten about me. Right, come on then, let's go. My bunions are killing me and I'm dying to get these shoes off.'

The photographers decided it was a case of mistaken identity, and everyone around us immediately lost interest and lowered their phones. They also took a step backwards, and several of the men winced.

Meanwhile, Val slipped her arm through Sam's, spun him round and let him steer her towards the door, with us walking behind them, the three of us with tears of laughter streaming down our faces. Hollywood might be a cut-throat world, but it was no match for Val Murray.

Sam took it all in his stride. He and Val had first met at Carol and Callum's wedding twenty years ago, when I took him along as my fake date. Back then, he still lived in Hong Kong, but he'd travelled to Scotland with me, and Val had fallen madly in platonic love with him at first sight. By the end of the night, she was teaching him the Gay Gordons ('Just spin me round, son, and don't worry, I'll give you the name of a good chiropractor in the morning'). It was only a couple of days before Christmas, so she'd then insisted that he move into their house until after New Year. Ten days of drinking, dancing, socialising, bingo and laughing until his sides ached – he still said it was one of the best times of his life.

The moment we stepped into the warm night, a large black Mercedes people-carrier with tinted windows pulled up in front of us and Sam slid the door open. 'Leave your cases there, and we'll load them up,' he said, as the driver jumped out to help.

Val wasted no time in doing what she was told. She clambered in and immediately felt the effects of the air conditioning. 'Thank God,' she said, fanning her face with her hand. 'I've got sweat in places I don't even want to think about.'

Sam's low, throaty laugh drifted over the sound of the traffic and a few blaring horns.

Carol hugged him, then climbed in. Toni gave a shy 'hi' and followed her mum.

Then...

'Hey, you,' he said, voice oozing warmth, taking his glasses off as he wrapped his arms around me. He'd obviously maintained his extensive gym regime. It was like getting cuddled by several melons in a pair of tights. I decided to block out any contemplation about how it must feel for him to cuddle my ever-expanding wobbly bits.

I managed to get words out, despite the fact that his bulbous biceps were crushing my oesophagus. 'Hey, you,' I answered, reverting to our old form of greeting.

Eventually, he pulled back and I could look at him properly for the first time. He'd barely changed since I last saw him, when he'd stayed with us for a few days a couple of years ago. In fact, other than some grey hairs and a few lines on his gorgeous face, he'd barely changed since the night I met him on the door of that Hong Kong nightclub.

I waited for him to register that I had the appearance of someone who'd arrived here via an age-advancing, weight gaining, time-travel portal, followed by a quick blast in a wind tunnel, but his eyes never left mine.

Instead, they creased up at the sides as he smiled again. 'Where've you been, Cooper?'

'Oh, you know. Around,' I said with a shrug, loving the easy banter. It had always been that way with him.

We stood there, holding hands, grinning at each other for a couple more seconds.

'I can't believe you're here,' he said.

'To be honest, it was LA or Benidorm,' I told him. 'But you made the cut because Val wants to do one of those tours of the stars' houses.'

'I'll see if I can get Tom Hanks to wave from the window,' he joked. At least, I think he was joking. He stepped back so I could climb into the van, but then put his hand on my arm as I passed him. 'I'm glad you're here, Coop.'

I paused halfway, one foot up on the rubber step below the open door.

'Me too,' I told him. I waited for my brain to throw up some negatives, some rebukes, some limiting thoughts. None came. I couldn't decide if that made me happy or concerned.

I settled in beside Val, then we waited as Sam helped the driver load up. I loved that he didn't do the Hollywood airs and graces thing.

Zoning out of the conversation Val was having with Carol, I rewound the last couple of minutes. What had I really felt? And did it matter?

This wasn't the time for my life to get complicated with old flames. I had enough confusion going on just now. Not that I thought for a moment that Sam had those feelings for me anyway. Our time was long gone. The young, sexy, fun Carly he'd fallen in love with was long gone too. And I wasn't quite sure who she'd left behind.

11

LOS ANGELES, 28TH JULY, 2019
PICTURE THIS – BLONDIE

We drew up at the gates of Sam's home half an hour or so later. I wasn't entirely sure because I'd dozed off in the car after I'd texted my boys.

Mum to Mac and Benny: Immigration let us in! We must look respectable. How's Florida? How's the hotel? Picking up the RV tomorrow? How are you coping with the pain of missing me? Love you. Xxx

Mac to Mum: Great. They're not too smart then. Great. Great. Yes. We're numbing the pain with pizza. Love you too, Ma. xx

As the gates swept open to reveal a stunning circular driveway with a fountain in the middle, in front of a beautiful Spanish-style home, Val gasped. 'Christ on a bike, I wouldn't want to have to Hoover that place. You'd just be finished and it'd be time to start again.'

Val's housekeeping skills were legendary. She was a firm believer that most problems in life could be solved by contemplating the issue while washing your windows and putting a bit of bleach down your drains.

'It's like something off the Kardashians,' Toni exclaimed, snapping photos on her phone. I was seriously starting to worry that we'd need to get her medical help for repetitive strain injury to the thumb from constant photo snapping. Like mother, like daughter.

The Mercedes stopped at the front door, just as it opened and a tall, broad, African American man, wearing a khaki T-shirt and shorts, came out to greet us.

'Arnie!' I exclaimed, hugging him. I'd met Arnie the last time Sam came to the UK a couple of years before. A college basketball player, ex-Vietnam vet and former stuntman, he was sixty, but didn't look a day over fifty, thanks to his lifelong intensive fitness regime. They'd met on the set of Sam's last action movie, when Arnie was the body double for the head of a crack team of Navy Seals. It was Arnie's last job before retiring – not a prospect he relished – so Sam hired him as his all-round house manager and security chief. In truth, they were more friends than anything. I think Sam just enjoyed Arnie's company and liked to have someone he could trust taking care of things when he wasn't here.

'Great to see you, Cooper,' Arnie bellowed.

It was difficult to say if it was the jet lag or his gravelly Morgan Freeman voice that was making my knees tremble just a little. I suspect it was the latter.

Arnie released me from his bear hug and greeted Carol next. 'Well, look who it is, Miss Pretty,' he said, a twinkle in his eye as he flirted mercilessly.

'Keep that up and I might never leave, you old devil,' Carol flirted right back.

Carol had been to Sam's house dozens of times over the years.

When she was still modelling, she travelled to LA a few times a year, and more recently, she came here for photo shoots and freebie brand launches. Sam had given her an open invitation, so they'd become great friends. Luckily, Carol was madly in love and married to one of only a small group of men who made Sam Morton look average by comparison, so my brother had been totally cool about it. There was definitely an imbalance in our gene distribution. I'd taken chaotic, haphazard, unpredictable, and the metabolism of a sloth with concussion, while Callum got laid-back, confident, secure and finely toned. That left highly intelligent, quirky, funny, and shy for my youngest brother, Michael. I'm not sure who got the best deal, but I'm pretty sure it wasn't me.

Carol introduced Arnie to Val and Toni, before Sam ushered us all into his kitchen. I thought Val was going to have to lie down with the thrill of it. Over sixty square metres of glossy walnut herringbone floor, cream gloss cabinets and black marble work-tops, with a double island in the middle and appliances that would make Nigella Lawson swoon.

'Keep it together, Val,' I teased her. 'I know this is as close to heaven as it gets.'

She was already stroking the marble in awe. 'Sod heaven. When I die, just scatter my ashes right across this counter.'

'There's fresh coffee in the pot and Arnie has rustled up some chicken nachos,' Sam said.

'Or I can make you some eggs, or toast...?' Arnie offered, pulling mugs out of one of the cupboards.

'Nachos are good, thanks, Arnie,' I told him, my resolutions to adopt a healthy LA lifestyle being battered to death by the prospect of nachos smothered in sour cream and guacamole.

Sam pulled a couple of bottles of wine out of his floor-to-ceiling glass fridge. 'And of course...'

'Ah, now you're singing my song,' Val told him, beaming.

Wine poured, nachos out, we sat around the second island, on bar stools that positively massaged the arse, for the next couple of hours, catching up, chatting, and, in Toni's case, taking 2324 photos for her Snapchat and Insta. Val went on a roll, telling tales about all the trouble our gang of girls had got into as teenagers. She was hoarse with laughing when the conversation finally shifted to Sam and I entertaining the others with tales of Hong Kong and the laughs we'd had with the endless stream of eccentric characters who'd frequented the club there. Carol mortified Toni by talking about all the embarrassing things my brother, Toni's dad, had ever done. And Toni... well, Toni listened and laughed. Sam was wonderfully sweet with her, just as he'd always been with my boys. He'd have made a great dad.

The thought turned the dial up on a twinge of anxiety that had been lying dormant in my gut. If I'd stayed with Sam, I had no doubt we'd have married and had kids, but our lives would have turned out nothing like this. Leaving him had started a domino effect that went from part time nightclub bouncer, to a career as an escort, to a movie script about it, to fame, fortune and Hollywood. If we had stayed together, we'd probably still be living in Hong Kong, he'd have opened his martial arts academy, and we'd have lived a normal, anonymous existence. He was so comfortable in this life that he had now that I wondered if that parallel world, the one without the fame, would have been enough for him.

'Carly. Carly!' Carol said impatiently, waving her hand in front of my face and snapping me back to the present. 'You're miles away.'

I shook off the semi-trance. 'Sorry! Just, erm...' I didn't want to say, *just imagining another life with the bloke chowing down on the guacamole over there*, so I blustered a bit while lying through my teeth. 'Just a bit jet-lagged, I think. It's already...' I glanced at one of the three clocks on the kitchen wall, trying to make my excuse more plausible. One was LA time, one was New York, and one was UK. '... After 10 a.m. in the UK. I've had about five hours sleep in the last thirty-six hours.'

Sam drained his water glass and put it in the sink. His triceps were perfect too. And did I mention his abs? Just like at our first meeting, I couldn't actually see them, but I knew they were there and, right now, that was enough. 'Must be a bit of a shock to the system, being whisked off here with no warning.'

'You could call it that. I think the FBI may call it a straight-up kidnap.'

'You could be right. Come on. I'll show you to your rooms, and let you get some sleep. I haven't planned anything tomorrow, so just chill and you can see how you feel. We could go out or stay home, up to you. Carol, I thought you and Toni could take the guest house. Is that okay?'

Carol reacted with mock horror. 'That building out the back, with the roof terrace, the movie theatre, the super-king bed, the firepit and direct access to the swimming pool? Och, I suppose so.' She turned to her daughter. 'Sorry to make you slum it, darling.'

'You're so embarrassing,' Toni retorted, face flushing as she shook her head. That was more like it. At least she was actively mocking her mother instead of ignoring her. Definitely progress.

It became a group expedition as we all strolled out to the guest house, so Val could have a tour. She was practically giddy when she saw the fifty-metre, infinity-edge swimming pool, complete with high-tech lighting, a row of sumptuous cabana beds and an outdoor kitchen and bar just metres away. Pretty much made a mockery of the inflatable hot tub I'd bought from B&M back in May.

With Carol and Toni settled, next stop was Val's room, a private guest suite and bathroom on the ground floor, not too far from the kitchen, so she could nip in to gaze in awe at the double microwave whenever she felt the need.

Sam had barely heaved her case on to the luggage rack in the corner, when she had it open, and was digging out her bathing suit and swimming cap. 'Fancy an early-morning dip,' she announced. 'And if you want to get yer Speedos on and join me, you're more than welcome,' she told Sam, chuckling. It struck me that, shock and emotional trauma aside, I'd barely stopped smiling since Val arrived at my house. She was an absolute tonic. The woman should be available on the NHS.

'Okay, Miss Cooper, you're next,' Sam said, letting me go first and following me to the glass staircase that rose to the second level, before splitting and going around a gallery-style balcony to the two wings on the first floor. I noticed the 'Miss' and wondered if that was a reference to my newly almost single status. Or was I just reading too much into it?

At the top of the stairs, I stepped to the right, assuming I'd be sleeping in the same room as always, across from Sam's master suite. When Mac and Benny were younger, they used to tear out of our room first thing in the morning, to go and dive-bomb Uncle Sam across the corridor.

'Actually, I thought you could sleep along here,' he said, stopping me with a hand gesture to the left.

Was it my imagination or did he lose eye contact with me when he said that? Nope, I was definitely reading too much into everything. So I was sleeping down a different corridor, at the opposite side of the house from him. No biggie. Maybe it was because I was here on my own this time and perhaps the room he was giving me was more of a single pad. Yeah, that must be it.

'Gutted that the boys couldn't come. I miss them,' he said as we walked. And walked.

'Me too. This is the first time I've ever been away from them. If you find me curled up in a corner wailing, just show me pictures of them and say their names repeatedly until I calm down.'

His low, throaty laugh made me smile.

And we were still walking. Dear God, was this some under-hand tactic to make me exercise? The room was so far away, I was pretty sure we were now in the neighbour's house. Eventually, he opened the very last door at the end of the corridor and stood back to let me go in. It was gorgeous. Cream carpets. A beautiful old wrought-iron bed. A walnut burr bookcase in the corner. A mirrored dressing table. French doors leading out to a terrace that overlooked the pool. And another door that I was fairly sure would lead to a luxurious en suite. It was perfect. And it was also almost identical to the room I usually slept in, just a half-marathon away.

I was suddenly very aware that this was the first time we'd been on our own since I'd arrived. 'It's amazing, Sam. Thank you.'

He wrapped his arms around me and gave me a hug, then pulled back and sat on the arm of the black velvet chair in the corner. 'So how are you doing? Rough year,' he said. It was a statement, not a question.

'Rough couple of years,' I answered with a rueful shrug, as I sat down on the end of the bed, facing him.

I could see the concern on his face. 'I've been worried about you.'

'Please don't worry, I'll be fine,' I said, brushing it off. 'It's just taking me a minute to get used to my new life, but I'll get there.'

Bloody hell, I appeared to have been struck down with cliché-itus. This was Sam. Someone I'd been close to for over twenty-five years. Someone whom I'd spent endless nights with, as lovers then friends, drinking wine and chatting until dawn. Why was I acting like I'd just bumped into him while waiting for a number 42 bus? Either I was tired, self-conscious about how terrible I looked, unwilling to put a damper on the day by unloading my problems, or just depressingly unused to talking to a man who actually wanted to know the truth about how I was feeling.

Or all of the above.

If he was surprised at my superficiality, he didn't say it. Instead, he pushed himself up off the chair and kissed the top of my head. 'I'll let you get some sleep. Goodnight, Cooper.' He was almost out of the door, when he stopped. 'This will always be a place for you to come when things are tough. You know that, right?'

'I know,' I said, with a grateful smile. It was a lovely moment. Sweet. Sincere. Loving. So, of course, I charged right through it with, 'And if you need to come to a slightly dilapidated, semi-detached in Chiswick to forget your woes, the offer goes both ways.'

Fuck. I truly had the emotional depth of Val's swimming cap.

'I'll remember that,' he said, as if he was truly going to giving it deep contemplation. 'Anyway, sleep as long as you like. No plans.'

'Thanks, Sam. For everything.'

'Any time, Coop,' he murmured lovingly, then off he went, travelling the approximate length of the equator, back to the other side of the house.

Feet still on the floor, I flopped back on the bed, ready for the assault of self-doubt and recrimination that I knew was coming. What was wrong with me? Why was I being weird with him? Did I have some underlying emotions towards him that I needed to sort through? Or was I just so used to being closed off, that I'd forgotten how to be honest and authentic? Sam genuinely cared about me and I genuinely cared about him. We'd never gone for bullshit answers and superficial brush-offs. And what was I doing in my bedroom when I wasn't even bloody tired?

I let all that simmer for a moment. What did I want? What did I actually want to do right now? Other than go back downstairs and finish off the nachos.

The answer didn't take long to come. I wanted to go and get Sam. I wanted to hug him, and snuggle down, and drink more coffee and share everything that had happened. Of course, he knew the details, because we spoke most weeks on the phone, but I needed to explain to him what was really going on in my head. And I wanted to hear what was going on with him. I wanted to make him laugh, to reconnect, to hang out with my buddy, to lie on his sofa with my head on his lap and just be close to him.

Bugger it. I wasn't going to waste any more time sitting here like Nobby No Mates when, for once, I was on the same continent as Sam Morton.

Jumping up, I was about to open the door, when I stopped. Nope, not like this. I couldn't be young, sexy Carly, but I could have a stab at looking human.

I peeled off my clothes, and wandered into the bathroom, my eyes on stalks when I saw the cream marble of the shower and the rich dark woods of the wall-mounted vanity. I could have lived without the reflection I saw in the full-length, gilt-edged mirror on the opposite wall, but I just averted my eyes, deciding that if I couldn't count all my spare tyres on the fingers of one hand, it was better not to look.

In the shower, I smiled as I saw the toiletries that were already there. Coconut shower gel, shampoo and conditioner. He'd remembered my favourites. Somewhere in my fragmented heart, that gesture of thoughtfulness made a tiny crack disappear. Perhaps if I stayed here long enough, Sam Morton could super-glue the whole lot back together again.

12

SAM'S HOUSE, LA
COMPLICATED – AVRIL LAVIGNE

Re-energised by the shower and the aroma of a Bounty bar in Tahiti, I rubbed my skin hard with the super-soft towels, then took a white fluffy robe from the back of the door.

Back in the bedroom, I opened my suitcase and surveyed the chaos. In the rush to pack, I'd tossed in a mish-mash of clothes, all of which looked like Val had used them as dusters, none of which were sexy nightwear.

Sod it. The bathrobe would just have to do. It wasn't like I was going to walk in, pull the belt open and drop it to reveal my naked body in a bid to seduce my ex-lover. This was more of a 'nothing to wear, I'm comfy, and, by the way, can I take this robe home with me' kind of deal. Sam wouldn't even notice.

Feet bare, I padded out of the room, wondering if I should take a packed lunch and flare guns for the journey. Like me, Sam was a bit of an insomniac, who watched movies in bed, so I was pretty sure that despite the late hour, he would still be awake. Probably lying on the chaise in the lounge area of his bedroom. Oh yes. He had a lounge. In the bedroom. I didn't even have a laundry basket in my bedroom back home.

When I knocked on his door and there was no answer, I figured I'd guessed wrong. Bugger. Maybe this was the universe telling me to get my arse back to my room and stop wandering about in my dressing gown.

I was about to backtrack when the door opened and... Sweet Jesus. Sam. In just his jeans. Bare feet. His tanned torso naked and still in the kind of shape that was no stranger to a crunchie. And not the chocolate variety.

What sick twisted evil was the universe up to now? And why was I suddenly experiencing flutters in places that hadn't been stirred in a long, long time.

My face flushed and I just hoped the robe was thick enough to disguise the fact that I seemed to be having a reaction in the nipple area. Oh. My. God. I was actually turned on. This menopausal, knackered, sexually dormant woman, who'd spent the last few years with a husband whose interest extended to a missionary position quickie on birthdays and bank holidays, was actually feeling... it took me a moment to put a name to it. *Horny.*

'Hey. Sorry. I didn't mean to interrupt you, but I...' My throat dried up completely. I tried to clear it, setting off a very attractive coughing fit. At which point, I bent over, my bathrobe dropped open, and I flashed him. Two boobs, pointing at the floor, and a stomach that had layers.

As I desperately pulled it all back together, I closed my eyes and hoped for a quick death.

'Sorry! I was just... just...' Nope, couldn't speak again.

'Cooper, are you okay?' he asked, a smile flickering in the corner of his mouth, his eyes doing that wholly intoxicating amused twinkling thing. My hormones had another swirl for good measure.

'Yes! Of course! I... I...' Bloody hell, what had happened to my powers of speech? Just because he was standing there, in his thigh-hugging jeans, top button open, topless... 'You know, you really need to work out more,' I told him drily.

His laugh sounded like it came from somewhere deep inside his six-pack and I exhaled with relief. Ice broken. Ridiculous jokes. Situation normal. I had this.

'Let me know if you need some tips,' I said, giving him a playful punch. My hand bounced off his abs. That didn't help the hormone situation.

Ignoring his amusement, I shooed myself on into his room.

Mistake. As Carol would say, one step forward, six steps backwards.

'So I was thinking we could...'

I stopped, only registering his flinch of panic when it was too late.

My gaze scanned the room, and it took me a split second to spot that something wasn't quite right. The bedside tables. On one side, Sam's phone, a couple of books, the watch that used to belong to his dad, the pad he always left there to take notes. On the other side, a candle. A moisturiser, the kind that cost more than a flight to Alicante. Earrings. Emerald. A gold chain. On the floor below, a handbag, a pair of shoes. Red soles.

I managed a puzzled, 'Sam?' and saw the little pulse that always throbbed in his jaw when he was anxious. Shit. I made a quick decision. Act normal. Act blasé. One of us had to redeem this situation, before we drowned in a deep well of awkward. 'Honey, are you going through something you want to share?' I asked him. 'A Mrs Doubtfire phase? Only, I think you might want to get a larger size in those Louboutins.'

'They're Estelle's,' he said.

'Estelle...?' Keep it light. Casual. Just one friend chatting to another. And maybe he's forgotten that he saw your boobs thirty seconds ago.

'Estelle Conran.'

'Holy shit. Estelle Conran was here?' There was no hope of downplaying the shock. Estelle Conran, romcom queen, willowy beauty and the leading lady in the movie Sam had produced last summer. If Julia Roberts and Sandra Bullock had a love child, Estelle Conran was it.

'She lives here,' he said.

Too many questions, so I went with the most obvious, then added on a few more. 'You live together? How long have you been a thing? Is it serious? Why didn't you tell me?'

He tried to keep it light, but the pulse in his cheek was still throbbing. 'Yes, a year or so, I'm not sure and...'

I could easily have fainted, but I didn't trust the robe to hold it together and I couldn't flash him twice in one day.

'I didn't say anything because you've been going through a shitstorm of heartache and it didn't seem like the right time.'

'Oh.'

Something dropped into place in my head. That's why he'd put me in a room at the other end of the house – he didn't want me to hear him having wild, raunchy sex with Estelle Bloody Conran. My cheeks began to burn.

'I'm sorry. I should have said.'

'No, that's okay,' I countered, my voice going a little too high as I tried to act like absolutely, definitely, positively, nothing was bothering me about this announcement. 'I'm thrilled for you. I really am.' Another thought dropped. 'So where is she?'

'Shooting some retakes for the movie she's just wrapped. She should be back some time next week. I was going to tell you all about her earlier, but I couldn't get a word in.'

Or maybe a couple of words would have been handy. Along the lines of 'Don't flash your baps at me because I've got a girl-friend.' I didn't say that out loud.

Keep going. You can do this. I forced a smile. 'I hope she gets back.' *I didn't.* 'It would be amazing to meet her.' *It wouldn't.*

'Cool,' he said, and I could see his relief. Another pause. 'So what did you come to tell me? You said you'd been thinking?'

Damn. Damn. Damn. What could I say? *I was thinking we could... have a bit of a snuggle and talk for a while. I could put my head on your lap and be close to you? Because I was thinking that I just need to laugh, and to connect, and to feel something that doesn't hurt. And I was thinking maybe something more would happen. Something that I've been missing for so long.*

Actually, now I was thinking that I'd completely lost my mind. Estelle Conran.

'I was just thinking... I forgot to... eh... ask you for the Wi-Fi code.'

My last shreds of dignity and integrity just topped themselves.

'I wrote it on the pad on the side of your bed,' Sam said. 'We're like the Hilton here.'

I immediately dished out a warning to my gob. Do. Not. Say. Anything. About. Room. Service. Instead, I went romcom breezy. Bite me, Estelle Conran. 'Fantastic. Right. Well. I'll go and sort that out then. I like a browse on Twitter before I go to sleep.'

With that little nugget of glamour, I bolted out of his bedroom.

My cheeks burned with embarrassment all the way back to my room, where I sank onto the bed and covered my face with a pillow.

Never again.

I'd almost made a complete tit of myself and if I had, I could have done real damage to my friendship.

What was I thinking, going there in a flipping bathrobe? And what did Sam think I was doing. Oh shit, did he think I came to seduce him? And what would he have done? How would he have gently let down the ex-girlfriend who'd turned into a sex-chasing hot mess?

Sam was a friend. He would never be any more than that.

And those lust-fuelled feelings that had been turned back on? I was just going to have to find the off switch.

13

LA. THE NEXT MORNING
GIRL CRUSH – LITTLE BIG TOWN

'Estelle Conran! You have got to be kidding me!' Carol exclaimed.

The beautician, Crystal, nudged my ankle and I took my right foot out of the bubbling basin and replaced it with my left. 'Yeah, because I always joke about my ex-boyfriends upgrading to a genuine Hollywood star who's half my age and has a waist that's the same size as my thigh. I find that boosts my ego no end.'

Over at the next station, where she was having her nail varnish removed and replaced with a purple hue the same shade as her boob tube, Val raised an eyebrow. 'Is she the one that did that orgasm scene in the café? Our Josie once copied that at a coffee morning in the community centre. They asked us to leave.'

I turned to Carol. 'Is it just me, or is she the gift that keeps on giving?'

Carol crumbled into fits of giggles. 'No, Val, that was Meg Ryan. Estelle is the one who gave up the presidency of the USA to run off to Hawaii with the secret billionaire.'

'Aye, I remember that one. Aren't her eyes a bit close together?'

I flicked through the movie scenes in my memory, praying it

was true. Sadly, there was definitely no evidence of this genetic drawback on Estelle Conran's perfectly symmetrical face.

'I don't think so, Val,' I said sadly, as Crystal began to grate the soles of my feet with something that looked like it should be used for removing graffiti from walls.

Val nodded thoughtfully. 'Ah right. Och well. I bet you she's got no personality. The good-looking ones are always dull as dishwater.'

'Hello?' Carol chided pointedly. 'Speaking as someone who made FHM magazine's sexiest women list every year from 1995 to 2004, I can assure you that just because someone looks great doesn't mean they're dull as... as...' I could see that she was struggling to pinpoint what Val had said so she could insert the correct word. '... Dishwashers.'

So close.

Today had been Carol's idea and I was thrilled she'd taken charge. We'd slept late and when we finally emerged mid-morning, we all had tender heads and no voices, so we were less than enthusiastic about Val's plans to track down Sylvester Stallone's mansion. She'd had a thing for him since Rambo.

'Tell you what, why don't I treat us all to a day at a salon? There's one over on Robertson that I always use when I'm here and I'm sure they'll find spaces for us.'

She didn't get any arguments from us. Arnie let us know that Sam had left early for a meeting at the Peninsula Hotel with the backers of his next movie, and offered to be our driver for the day. I ignored the two gremlins of paranoia and embarrassment that were telling the rest of my brain Sam had really left because he was trying to escape after the awkwardness of last night. He was probably hiding out in the garage until the coast was clear. The minute we were out of the driveway, he'd probably commando crawl his way back into the safety of his kitchen and get online to order a panic room that shuts down if I come within fifty feet of it.

Shaking off the thought, we gratefully accepted Arnie's offer, although there was a worrying moment when we found out he drove a Hummer. It had taken three of us to give Val a heave up into the passenger seat.

Now that we were ensconced here for the afternoon, we knew it had been the right move. The salon was ultra-trendy, all mirrors and ebony workspaces, with an army of staff tackling every aspect of cosmetic improvement. We'd each been assigned our own beautician for the day, and Crystal drew the short straw, landing the biggest challenge with my long-neglected grooming standards. We scheduled in several glorious hours of pampering, with manicures, pedicures, eyebrows, lashes, tan, and for me, a hair trim and colour. I'd had those dark roots for so long I was considering hosting a farewell lunch for them. I'd never in a million years consider spending money or time on this type of thing at home, but, well, I was on holiday and it was Carol's treat. She maintained that everything was content for her posts, her blogs or her interviews. No doubt my eyebrow transformation from slug to slimline would show up in her Snapchat before the end of the day.

'Is it serious?' Carol asked, taking photos of the ombre nail art that was being applied to her toes. Her three million social media followers would love it.

'What?' I asked.

'Sam and Estelle!'

'I think so. I'm not really sure. After I flashed him, it didn't feel like the right time to have an in-depth discussion about his future.'

Carol couldn't keep her face straight. 'I'm laughing with you, not at you,' she promised, but I wasn't convinced.

'So, tell me... how do you feel about him?'

'I feel the same way I've felt for the last twenty years. He's my platonic movie star pal. He lives in LA, I live in Chiswick. He's the perfect long-distance friend and I love him like a brother. That's it.' If my manicure was accessorised by a polygraph right now, the needle would be screeching across the page.

Now it was Carol's turn to be unconvinced. Like the others, she knew all about my history with Sam, the splits, the reunions, and the torn feelings and occasional regrets.

'Carly, I love Mark, you know I do, and I've always kinda hoped that you two would get back together.'

That wasn't a surprise. I knew Carol felt that way, and Kate did too. Only Jess thought that I should definitely cut the cord and start over. Hard as it was, I knew she was right.

Down at ground level, Crystal was applying a deep red to my toenails now. I'd chosen that colour in a bid to channel my inner fierce, but so far all I was getting was my inner cynical and anxious.

Carol was still making her point. 'But you've been apart for almost a year now. Isn't it time to start seeing what else is out there?'

Maybe it was. But there was an obvious drawback to the plan of action she was suggesting. 'I know what you're saying, but...' I broke off, trying to find a new way to frame the story. How could I tell her that I wasn't sure I could ever be happy again? Not truly happy, in that carefree way I used to be. It wouldn't be fair to bring it all up again, to go back over the heartache we'd all suffered, so instead, I played to my natural personality and kept it shallow. 'Even if I felt some kind of physical attraction to Sam, it would be completely pointless. Look at him. Look at Estelle. They're perfect for each other. And much as I love him, even if – by some miracle – he was interested in me in that way, the last thing I'd want to do is to risk our friendship by getting embroiled in a complicated romantic entanglement. He means too much to me to jeopardise what we have.'

Carol pondered that for several moments, and I could see that she was considering it on a philosophical level, analysing the pros and cons, and contemplating a wise and spiritual way forward.

'You'd totally still shag him though, wouldn't you?'

I nodded. 'In a heartbeat.'

My chuckles made my feet tremble, irritating Crystal no end.

Over at the other side of the salon, I could see Toni having her hair washed at the basins. 'How are things going with Toni?' I asked, desperate to change the subject. I was almost fifty, not fifteen. My days of unrequited crushes and hormonal sex urges should be long gone.

Carol sighed, although, of course, the Botox stopped her face from showing that it was in any way perturbed by the question. 'I don't know,' Carol said, her gaze going to her daughter, all long limbs and flawless complexion. 'She still won't tell me what's going on with her. Sometimes I think we're getting past whatever it is, and then in a split second it can change and she hates the world again. I don't understand what sparks off the moods. I just don't get it.'

'You're her mother. I don't think you're supposed to get it. If it makes you feel better, I'll take the blame. She's clearly inherited my messed-up Cooper genes.'

I decided not to take offence that my sister-in-law didn't argue, just breezed right past it and went on, 'Toni's always had it tougher than Charlie. Charlie just finds everything easy. Making friends, studying, boyfriends. I think Toni's always been in her shadow, always struggled to be happy in her own skin. That's why I thought this trip would be good for her.'

'I think so too,' I agreed. 'You can never underestimate the healing powers of sun, fresh air and a sixty-something woman who is equally obsessed with Tom Jones and Sylvester Stallone.'

Hearing Carol talk about Toni was giving me pangs of longing to speak to my boys. I'd FaceTimed them this morning, but they didn't have much time to chat because they were on their way to pick up the RV. Their journey was starting today in Miami, and they were going South to the Keys to do something with alligators. They rejected my offer to put the coastguard, the local police and the nearest ER on standby. I was only half joking. After a panicked bout of internet research, I was now terrifyingly aware of the damage that could be done by a gator bite. And don't get me started on sharks and coyotes.

Crystal had just put the last coat of varnish on my toes, and inserted them into a small dryer. Sitting on a wheeled stool, she rolled up to the middle of the chair, pulled her little trolley behind her and started work on my manicure. Val was now over at the basins having her hair washed – presumably with plutonium or some other substance that could strip away nearly six decades of hairspray – and Carol had gone into a private room to have her bits waxed.

I was just about to close my eyes and zone out, when Toni was brought over to the chair next to me for her pedicure. It was like musical chairs, with beauty treatments thrown in.

Her transformation was already noticeable. Blonde highlights now framed her face, lifting her long, mousy, hair, and giving it some texture. It was in a middle parting now, and it had been styled so that it fell in loose curls that went halfway down her back.

'Wow, your hair looks gorgeous!' I told her honestly.

Normally so self-conscious, her new look was definitely making her walk just a little bit taller. She folded her long limbs into the chair next to me, and proceeded to take at least a dozen selfies, then pored over them before posting the ones she wanted to use.

It was such a strange dichotomy. Toni was so reserved, yet she felt the need to constantly post photos, painting a glamorised image of her life. Was she seeking some kind of approval? Trying to impress someone? Or was this just normal life now and I was a dinosaur who should get with the times. If so, my absolute loathing of getting my photo taken might be a slight glitch in the plan.

'Benny messaged me after I posted a pic of my hair and he said I looked like a shampoo advert,' she retorted, and I could see that she liked that. Charlie was the glamorous one, the effortless beauty who put loads of time and effort into her appearance. Toni was equally gorgeous, but in a more understated, natural way. I was glad Benny had been sweet to her. They had always been so close, such a great support system for each other. They were exactly the way Callum, Michael and I had been growing up. Although, thankfully, we didn't have social media or I might have posted something about my pissed dad or my eternally disapproving mother.

'Are you sending the pics to someone special?' I asked her, sounding like the elderly aunt who was trying to be down with the kids. In truth, I was just trying to understand her a little bit better and since she was constantly on her phone, that seemed like the best place to start.

She blinked in that way Benny did, when he was trying to get away with fudging the truth or being less than fully candid.

No, honestly, Mum... blink... I need a fiver for a collection in school... blink... and I won't spend any of it in the chippy at lunchtime... blink blink.

Toni prised her gaze away from the phone. 'Um, just my Insta timeline.' *Blink.*

I had no idea why that touched a nerve. Did she have a boyfriend she was sending them to? Or was there someone she liked? Or who liked her? Why did she suddenly look so shifty? By her age, I was on the cusp of my first engagement, so I wasn't going to judge.

I decided to probe a little deeper. 'You know, honey, if you ever have anything on your mind, or you're unhappy about anything, I'm always here for you. I'll always listen, and I'll keep it to myself. I won't even tell your mum and dad if you don't want me to.' *Blink.* I had my fingers crossed at that point. Carol would kill me if I deliberately withheld a problem from her.

'Thanks, Aunt Carly, but, honestly, I'm chilling.' I knew that meant 'happy'. Elderly aunty, down with the kids, strikes again.

'Okay, but please talk to me if you need to. Take advantage of the fact that I've pretty much screwed up or been in trouble more times than I can count.' I nudged her with my shoulder. 'Although, I think the laws have changed now about public nudity so I might not have up-to-date info on that.'

Her eyes widened, until something clicked, she realised I was kidding, and let out the most heart-warming laugh. We were making progress, I could feel it. Unwilling to push too hard though, I shut up and let her focus on her screen again.

I put my head back, closed my eyes. This was bliss. The ultimate escape. Good for the soul. Nothing could spoil it...

The buzz made me jump, and I realised that Toni had dozed off in the middle of her pedicure. This jet lag was wiping us out. My gaze went down to her screen, sitting on the armrest between our chairs.

A text.

Really bitch? Don't you fucking dare or you know what's coming.

I had to read it three or four times before I could absorb it. What the hell? Who would send something like that to my eighteen-year-old niece? Before I could wake her to ask, Crystal interrupted my fury.

'Carly, I think that's your phone that's ringing? It's coming from your purse.'

I realised that she was right and used the hand that wasn't under the UV light to tentatively retrieve it from my handbag and checked the screen. Sam. I pressed the green button to accept the call.

'Hey you, how's your day going?' There was a very faint weariness in his voice, a tightness that wasn't usually there. Perhaps his meeting hadn't gone so well.

'Yeah, good. My fingernails and my toenails are perfect, so I've just got all the bits in between to fix now. I think it's going to take a while and it'll definitely test their superpowers.'

Even his laugh sounded a little hollow. There was a slight pause and I winced. Definitely a shade of awkwardness between us now. Was this about the whole bathrobe/flashing fiasco? It was an accident and it wasn't like he hadn't seen it all before. Although, granted, it was all several inches smaller and higher back then.

'Is everything okay with you?' I asked him, hoping that whatever was bothering him wasn't serious. I knew how much he enjoyed the company of visitors from home, and I didn't want anything to spoil this time for him. Also, I might need him to dig out his old action hero wardrobe and help me find the moron who had just sent an abusive text to my niece.

On the other end of the phone, Sam sighed. 'It is. Just... you know, a lot going on.'

I wanted to point out that he'd just spent the morning having breakfast in the Peninsula. Not exactly a hard day's work.

However, I was pretty distracted, so it wasn't the time for light-hearted banter. 'I'm sure whatever it is, it'll all work out fine,' I assured him.

'Yeah, you're right. At least, I hope so.'

Another pause.

'The thing is...' He started again. Then stopped. How come I got the feeling he was furiously blinking right now?

My brain cells silently screamed at him. *In the name of the holy six pack, SPIT IT OUT!*

'The thing is...' he repeated. 'Estelle's reshoots are wrapping tomorrow, a week earlier than planned. How would you feel about meeting her tomorrow night?'

14

SAM'S HOUSE, THE NEXT DAY
FIGHTER – CHRISTINA AGUILERA

Okay, things going in my favour. The glam squad at the salon had delivered the equivalent of an Oscar-winning performance. They hadn't exactly managed to turn back time, but they'd definitely polished up the clock face. My hair was back in the pixie cut I'd worn for much of my life, with the exception of that unfortunate phase in my twenties when it went a bit wrong and I morphed into a cross between Billy Idol, Annie Lennox, and my nan after a perm and a purple rinse. The spray tan had taken me a few steps away from my natural complexion of West of Scotland Blue, and I'd been de-haired, polished, the post-flight puffy face had subsided, and the eyelash extensions and brow shape were making me look like I was wide awake for the first time since I started doing school runs in 2008.

Unfortunately, however, none of those things could even make a dent in the creeping sense of unease I'd had since yesterday when I'd spotted that text on Toni's phone.

Really bitch? Don't you fucking dare or you know what's coming.

No matter what way I played it back, there was no sugar-coating it. Unless, of course, I believed Toni's explanation.

'It's just a few of my friends taking the piss, Aunt Carly. It's a joke. I swear.' I might have accepted that if my mother-senses weren't wailing like a fire alarm and she wasn't blinking furiously as she spoke.

I pressed her to show me the conversation leading up to that point but she refused. 'That's, like, against my human rights,' she'd argued. I was fairly sure the United Nations hadn't mandated on aunties snooping on their niece's text messages, but I didn't push the point. 'And don't go saying anything to my mum, because she'll just have a berzy and blow it all out of proportion.'

'But, Toni...'

'Aunt Carly, you promised! You said you'd never tell my parents something if I didn't want you to. Well, I don't want you to tell them about this.'

Her indignation put me in an impossible position. If I told Carol, I'd break Toni's trust and she'd never come to me if she was in trouble. If I didn't tell Carol and she found out, my pal may kill me while I am sleeping. If she let me live, she'd never forgive me.

My only hope was that Carol would do a bit of snooping on her own, because she'd already sensed that something was wrong.

It was now early afternoon and we were lying out by the pool. Or rather, Carol and I were sunning ourselves, and Val was floating in the middle of the water on a giant inflatable swan. Carol had put a video clip of it on her Instagram story an hour ago and it already had over 40K 'likes'. By the end of this holiday, Val was going to be a national celebrity.

'I don't know what's got into her today,' Carol said, gesturing to Toni, who was lying in the shade on the terrace of the guest house, ignoring us all. 'I thought we were building bridges, but we're right back to square one. She's done nothing but sulk and bite my head off since last night.'

Okay, tell her. Tell her now. No don't.

My options replayed in my mind. If Toni was in trouble and we alienated her, she'd have no one to turn to. Meanwhile, she was still swearing that it was all just a stupid joke. But I should still tell Carol, shouldn't I? Aaargh, this was impossible.

Think rationally. Toni was here with us, so she wasn't going to come to any physical harm. Surely it was better to try to tease the truth out of her and then help and support her to deal with it in her own way?

Okay, that's what I was going to do. It was. Wasn't it?

'Are you still thinking about doing bendy things with our favourite movie guy, because you've been staring into space for the last ten minutes with a weird look on your face.'

I slipped straight into fake mode. 'Nope, I'm over it. I'm fairly sure if I had energetic sex with anyone, I'd need a bucket of painkillers and a physiotherapist afterwards, so I'm going to save myself the groin strain.' I almost convinced myself that I meant it. Almost. He was just so fricking lovely, and gorgeous and he made me feel... right. I sent my beating heart and tingly bits to the corner and told them to have a long think about what they were doing and stop spoiling this for the rest of me. The time for Sam and I had long gone. Past tense. And even if I was interested in him, there was clearly no way it would be reciprocated. He was in the Estelle Conran, Beverly Hills goddess league now. I was still in the league that met weekly at a slimming club and then went for the occasional splurge in Primark.

My sister-in-law, however, wouldn't get that. She pinged the string on the bottoms of her red bikini. Actually, 'bikini' was a stretch. It looked like three tops off Bisto tins, joined together with an elaborate series of string knots.

I glanced down at my Superslimmer bathing suit, guaranteed to cover the wobbly bits while cutting off circulation to the extremities. I may look a few pounds lighter, but I wasn't sure I'd ever feel my knees again.

'Oh, really?' she goaded, not even trying to hide her amused cynicism. 'You have no lusty feelings towards him at all now?'

Deflect. Deflect!

'Maybe if he put a paper bag over his head and ate a cake,' I joked, hoping that would shut her down. Sadly not.

'How are you feeling about meeting Estelle tonight then?'

I hated the very thought of it and I'd already decided she was a shallow cow with no redeeming features whatsoever. Furthermore, she'd stolen Sam. Granted, I'd left him alone for most of the last twenty years, but still, how could she? Tart. All of which was kept in the deepest corner of my brain, marked Shamefully Immature.

Instead of rising to the bait, I went for casual cheeriness. 'I think it will be great. I'm sure she'll be lovely.'

'Lovely?' Carol scoffed. 'That's only one step up from "nice".'

Nope, still wasn't rising to the bait. The truth was that I was dreading it, which was ridiculous. Sam had every right to have a young, slim, successful, globally adored girlfriend and it was none of my business. I'd been married to Mark for almost twenty years and apart from one slight blip back in the early days, Sam had accepted it and had moved on with his life. Time for me to return the favour.

Although... I checked my watch... Sam said she was arriving home around eight, so that gave me at least four hours to shower, do my hair, apply full face make-up, then repeat it at least twice when I made an arse of it. After that, I'd leave myself enough time to prise myself into whatever outfit would best cover my bumps, while giving the impression of casual elegance that suggested I'd made no effort at all.

I was just working out the timings when Robinson Crusoe

waded in from the deep and parked her swan next to her cabana. 'I'm never leaving here. Someone is going to have to phone my Don and tell him that I'm seeking political asylum.'

I put my hand to my face to help me squint against the sun. 'Political asylum? In Sam's pool?'

'Yep, I'm fleeing struggles and environmental hardship. In my native land, I have to freeze my knockers off for eight months of the year.' With that, she plumped down on her lounger and took a sip of the pina colada Arnie had made for her after lunch. If we were ever going to get Val on the plane to go home, I had a feeling we were going to have to take Arnie with us.

'You ok over there, Toni?' I hollered to my niece.

'Yes, thanks, Aunt Carly,' she raised her head from her phone, but I couldn't see her eyes for her sun specs. I wasn't going to push it for now, but she was on my radar and I was going to make sure she was ok... whether she liked it or not.

* * *

The rest of the afternoon passed in lazy luxury, and the sun was dropping slightly when I heard a warm, 'Hi, ladies,' and Sam wandered out from the house. Before I was even conscious of doing it, I'd casually grabbed my towel and covered my cellulite.

'I saw that,' Carol whispered out of the corner of her mouth.

'Shut it,' I replied, with ominous menace, before having a paradigm shift as I turned to greet our host. 'Hey, you,' I chirped, definitely not noticing that he could have stepped off the set of *Top Gun*, with that tight white T-shirt and those Rayban Aviators. Definitely not noticing. Not a bit. 'I didn't realise you were home.'

'Just got back. The meeting with the casting agents ran over.'
He kicked off his shoes.

'You look exhausted, son. Why don't you get yer kit off and get in the pool? I'll loan you my swan,' Val offered generously, over-looking the fact that the floating bird actually belonged to the newly established Republic Of Sam.

'Only if you promise not to objectify me,' Sam teased her.

Val shook her head. 'Sorry, I can't make promises.'

We were still laughing when I spotted a new arrival and my heart stopped. If I thought for one second that I had the neces-sary flexibility, I'd have put my head between my knees and hyperventilated. Estelle Conran had just left the building and was heading straight for us.

What about my preparation time? I was about to meet this goddess, and I had a puce face, wet hair, a swimsuit that gave me the contours of a melon and I was numb from the knees down. This wasn't how it was supposed to happen.

'Well, that's an entrance,' Carol murmured.

She wasn't wrong. Estelle's long baby-blonde hair flowing behind her, she catwalk-swaggered across the lawn in tiny Daisy Duke shorts, a bikini top and flip-flops, with a gold chain that wrapped around her neck and then somehow draped down between her perfect breasts and across her waist. I'd have had to remortgage my house to buy a chain that covered the same distance on me.

'Hi, baby,' she purred to Sam, who suddenly had a slight flush to his cheeks. No wonder. This woman set the pulses racing on most of the male population of the planet. I'd googled her last night, out of curiosity, not jealousy – at least, that's what I told myself. Estelle Conran, twenty-eight, size zero, earned over three million pounds last year, one of the hottest stars on the planet.

'Just remember, it's all fake,' Carol murmured.

Ah yes, the most important bit. Carol and I had thoroughly

dissected every photo of her online and although she appeared to be a natural beauty, her early photos suggested she'd had a nose job, a chin implant, breast augmentation, Botox, hair extensions, and a Brazilian butt lift. I preferred not to think about what she did to show off the last one.

Sam jumped up and kissed her, his surprise obvious. 'Babe! I thought you weren't arriving until tonight?' There was more than twenty years age difference between her and Sam, so he was old enough to be her father. A 'real hot, muscular, mega successful, wealthy, lovely, sweet, my ex-boyfriend' father.

'We wrapped early. I was missing you and thought I'd surprise you, baby,' she drawled in a *Steel Magnolias* Southern accent, before kissing him again, and holding the suction for longer this time.

Over at the glass doors, I saw Arnie pop his head out to check on developments. I caught his rueful expression and the shake of his head as he saw Estelle. I could be interpreting it wrong, but I got the distinct impression that he wasn't impressed. Excellent.

Meanwhile, were we invisible? Only, common manners would dictate that the other people present in the immediate vicinity would also be acknowledged. Or was I just being pedantic and judgemental?

My eyes flicked to Val and I saw she was right there with me, sporting the 'one raised eyebrow of disapproval' that she used to pull out of her disciplinary armour when she caught us drinking in pubs as teenagers, right before she called us by our full names and ordered us home.

'Carly Cooper, Kate Wilkes, Carol Sweeney, Jess Latham, Sarah Moore,' she'd spit through gritted teeth when she found us hiding from her in the toilets of the Dog and Kilt. 'Get up that road and don't dare stop off for a kebab on the way or I'll march you to your doors and your mothers will hear about this.'

We'd beg her not to tell them and promise it wouldn't happen again. Until the next time.

Good luck to Estelle Conran if she got on the wrong side of Val. The thought made me smile, and Estelle, who'd finally uncoupled herself from Sam, mistook it for a friendly welcome.

'Hi,' she said, walking towards me, arms outstretched. 'You must be Val.'

'Ouch,' Carol said under her breath. She really needed to stop with the running commentary.

Behind Estelle, I saw Sam close his eyes in what could only be mortification. His current babe had just mistaken me for a lady who was, although admittedly a fine figure of a woman, well over a decade older than me, with a penchant for matching accessories.

'No, I'm Carly,' I corrected her breezily, as if it were a perfectly understandable error.

Her eyes swivelled back to Sam, then back to me, then back to Sam. It was like Wimbledon without the tennis balls, but she made her point. You? With him? *Really?*

She made a recovery that was valiant, but way too late. 'Oh, I've heard so much about you. You and Sam have quite the history. Welcome to our home.'

Our home? The hackles on the back of my neck stood to attention. If she whipped off those Daisy Dukes and peed in the pool, she couldn't mark her territory any clearer. *Her* home? I'd been coming here since she was... was... actually, probably since she was still playing with her Barbies. Too late, I realised that thought didn't make me feel any better.

'Delighted to be here. Aren't we, ladies?' I said, calling in my cavalry.

Carol immediately took aim and fired a perfectly aimed torpedo of passive aggression. 'So great to meet you! I'm such a huge fan,' she enthused, sounding absolutely 100 per cent authentic. Even I was almost fooled as she moved forward for a hug, completely ignoring Estelle's top-to-toe scan of Carol's killer body. 'I absolutely loved you as Harlequin. You were fabulous.'

Estelle's sharp intake of breath almost pinged her body chain. 'That... wasn't... me. That was Margot Robbie.'

'Oh. Right. Well, she was great. Have you met her?'

Ding ding, round two. Current score, one point each.

Sam stepped in, obviously unable to bear the tension of the unfolding drama. And this was a guy who'd produced at least three movies in which the future of mankind was almost wiped out by alien invasions, terrorist plots or natural disasters.

'Babe, this is Val,' he said, steering her towards my aunt, who politely shook her hand and said it was lovely to meet her. She was never one to show her cards too soon, but I knew what she was thinking. 'And that's Toni over there.'

Over on the terrace, Toni responded by raising her head from her phone and giving a subdued wave.

'So, tell me again, how long are you here for?' Was it me, or did Estelle sound like she was one of those pageant queens who wanted to cure disease and end world poverty, right after she'd done a twirl in her swimsuit and belted out 'The Greatest Love of All' in the talent round? Maybe just me.

'Three weeks. But Val says she's claiming political asylum, so we might be here longer,' I replied, wondering if she'd get the joke and go up in my estimations.

She didn't.

Instead, she wound her arm around Sam's waist and gave him a squeeze.

'Well, we're thrilled to have you here. I'm so glad we wrapped early and I'm going to be around this week. It's going to be so great to get to know Sam's old friends.'

There was an emphasis on the 'old' and I heard a sharp intake of breath from Carol.

Ding ding, round three.

And I had a feeling this wasn't going to be over until there was a knockout.

15

SAM'S POOL, ELEVEN DAYS LATER
LOVE IS A LOSING GAME – AMY WINEHOUSE

'Ever wish you had a great big catapult?' I murmured to no one in particular. The four of us were baking to the consistency of pies in the mid-morning sun, although, as always, Val had plastered us all with factor 100, before we settled in for another hard day of doing nothing much at Sam's pool.

Carol dipped her chin and peered over her sunglasses, her gaze following mine to the same destination on the other side of the water, where Estelle was lying on a double lounger with Sam, alternating between running her fingers up and down his torso and gently stroking his thigh. 'I do,' Carol agreed. 'Although, I think a missile would just bounce off that arse. You might want to be a bit more imaginative. Tamper with her Botox or something like that.'

I savoured that thought for a moment. Estelle had been here for the last week and a half and I wanted to suggest that her next cosmetic op be one that would surgically remove her from Sam's side.

Val rolled over on to her back and yawned contentedly. 'I'm in too. I'll hide the body.'

I appreciated the support. Estelle had made it perfectly clear how she felt about us by being sugary sweet when Sam was around and ignoring us when he wasn't. I'd only had one private moment with her, and it had pretty much cemented our feelings for each other.

I'd wandered into the kitchen for a drink a couple of days before, and she was already there, making some kind of green concoction in her Nutri Bullet. I didn't want to tell her we'd been using that to make cocktails since we got there. Saved all that shaking palaver. 'I'm so glad I finally got to meet you,' she said, with such transparent disdain that I truly wondered how she managed to make a career as an actress.

'Me too,' I replied, channelling my very best Meryl Streep.

That could have been it. We could just have left it there, retreated gracefully, fully aware of where we stood with each other without a single honest word spoken. But no.

'You know, I've been meaning to say,' she began in that faux-friendly, I'm-here-for-you tone that was drenched in conde-scension.

'If you ever decide to get in shape, I could hook you up with our trainer. And I've got some great people who can work mira-cles with aging skin too. I saw some photos from, like, decades ago, when you were with Sam, and it must be so hard to feel good about yourself when you're not at your best any more.'

Ouch. My gaze met hers. She was still going for innocent sweetness, but her eyes were hard as flint and told me everything I needed to know. She was sending a message. And I was hearing it loud and clear. In my mind, her internal organs were now swishing around in that Nutri Bullet. My inner bitch, retired for almost as long as my skin care regime, dusted herself off and entered the fight.

'Thank you, Estelle, that's so kind. But you know, all that

superficial stuff means nothing to me. I think it's a bit desperate actually,' I said, feigning nonchalance. Her eyes were darkening with every word. 'I'd much rather spend my life laughing with good people and enjoying every day. That's why I've got such great friends. But you know, if you ever want to spend some time with some real women, the kind who lift each other up and have wisdom and depth, let me know. I can hook you up, sweetie.'

With that, I gave her my very best grin, then sauntered out, head held high. I could feel each dagger as it entered my back, but I relished them. I saw her. She saw me. Checkmate.

Her response had been to ignore us at all costs, while attaching herself to Sam at every possible opportunity. Our response had been to act smiley and friendly, while plotting her demise from the other side of the pool.

At the end of our row of loungers, lying on her back, Toni listened to our conversation, shaking her head. 'You lot are brutal.'

Carol shifted her gaze to her daughter. 'That's what friends are for. All for one and one for all.' She turned back to me. 'Whose slogan was that?'

'The Three Musketeers.'

'Oh. I thought it was Bananarama.'

I inserted that in the packed-out drawer in my cerebral filing cabinet entitled, 'No Way Did Carol Just Say That'.

She followed it up with a low, throaty groan. 'I can't believe we're leaving today. These two weeks have gone so quickly. I'm not ready for it to be over.'

'I'm not ready for you to go either. It's been so good,' I told her, meaning every word.

Carol Sweeney, now Cooper, had been my friend since we were six years old and we'd been through brilliant highs and awful lows. The last two weeks had definitely been a high, and having Val and Toni with us had made it even better.

For Val's sake, we'd set ourselves the target of doing one touristy thing every second day, with alternate days at the beach or pool. There had been the obligatory tour of the stars' homes, although I'm fairly sure the bloke doing the driving just pointed at random houses and lied about the occupants. Either that or Tom Cruise really did live in a Beverly Hills mansion with Eddie Murphy on one side, and Tommy Lee from Motley Crew on the other. On another day, we did the Hollywood Walk Of Fame and then Arnie drove us to a vantage point that was as close as we could get to the Hollywood sign. We spent a day at the beach in Malibu and a night on Santa Monica pier. Sam took us to the lot at Paramount Studios and gave us a tour of some iconic sets. We satisfied Carol's lust for designer shopping by wandering up and down Rodeo Drive a couple of afternoons, and Toni's more moderate shopping budget with brunch and a wander round H&M at The Grove on Sunday morning. The Rodeo Drive excursions were great for my bank balance because none of the shops sold anything over a size fourteen, so my purse stayed in my bag. We did the Getty Museum and Lake Hollywood. And we ate at the Cheesecake Factory (my choice), Nobu (Carol's pick) and Sur, as featured in the reality show, *Vanderpump Rules* (that one was Toni, and she spent the whole time snapping photos and posting them on her social media). The rest of our waking days were pretty much spent by the pool, either toasting in the sun during the day, or chatting around Sam's huge outdoor fire at night. It was like having our own private resort, one with a host who stayed very firmly in the background.

Sam had joined us on a couple of the outings, but he generally worked during the day, ate with us on a couple of the evenings, then had an early night with Estelle because they got up every morning at 5 a.m. to do a dawn fitness session with their personal trainer. On at least two of the mornings, the rest of us were just heading to bed after another night of chat around the fire, when Sam and Estelle were up and preparing their pre-workout vitamin shakes.

The whole dynamic between us and them was very... civilised. Yep, that was the word. Superficial, too. One of the things I'd been so excited about was spending time with Sam, yet I'd barely seen him and, when I did, Estelle was usually hanging off him, making sure she gave us no space. No one-on-one time for us, no relaxed conversations, no private moments. God, she was good.

I didn't blame her, not really. The guy was a catch and she was clearly just protecting her interests. Not that she had anything to worry about. I'd pretty much convinced myself that any spark I'd felt with Sam on that first day had purely been a figment of my imagination, brought on by jet lag and the shock of being here. Since then we'd been... friendly. Normal. Just exactly the way we'd been for years. And, given how he was allowing his limpet – sorry, *girlfriend* – to run her manicure through the hairs on his chest, that was exactly the way he wanted to keep it.

I should be happy for him. And I told myself that if Estelle was an absolute sweetheart, then I would be. I'd be thrilled. Maybe. But the fact that she was pretty much holding Sam hostage didn't help. And the fact that he was letting her made it even worse. His priorities were so clear, Val could see them with her huge shades on.

Carol's phone and my phone buzzed at exactly the same moment, with an incoming text to the group chat that I'd had with the girls since the beginning of time.

Kate: Holy shit, this plane has Wi-Fi!

Kate and Jess were currently midway over the Atlantic on the way here, swapping with Carol and Toni who were leaving today.

Jess: Just found a website for people who want to join the mile-high club. Glad I wore matching knickers and bra.

Kate: Eeeew, gross. Now I won't be able to pee until we land.

Me: Jess, those toilets are way too small for sex. You'll pull a muscle.

Jess: Eh, that's the point.

Kate: I'm asking the flight crew for restraints. She'll never escape them.

'They do know that they're sitting next to each other and could just have this conversation face to face?' Carol observed.

'Not as much fun though,' I said, laughing. I couldn't wait until the others got here. I was just gutted that Carol and Toni wouldn't be here at the same time.

'S'pose I'd better go pack,' Carol said with a sigh, pushing herself up and stretching in the sun, like a goddess from a shampoo commercial.

Estelle picked that exact moment to straddle Sam, blocking his view.

'Christ on a bike,' Val whistled, spotting the reaction. 'I'm off for some ice cream before that girl starts dry-humping him. It would put me right off my raspberry ripple.'

With that, she was up and gone, leaving Toni and I alone for the first time in days.

I moved along, taking the sunlounger Val had just vacated, and sat on the edge of it so I was facing my niece. I'd been waiting for a chance to get her alone for days now. 'Hey, my darling, how're you doing?' I asked her, not sure what reaction to expect. She'd been all over the place this last two weeks. Sometimes chatty and up for fun, other times moody and withdrawn.

Her sullen shrug gave me the answer to how she was feeling today. My heart sank. I was worried about her and still entirely unsure how to help, but I wasn't giving up.

'Toni, I've been thinking...'

She watched my face with those big green eyes of hers. I thought again how they were exactly the same shade as Benny's, giving me another massive pang of missing my boys. I'd spoken to them at least once a day since I'd arrived here, but I was craving their gorgeous faces.

'Is there anything you want to talk to me about? Anything I can help you with?'

Her eyes narrowed as she shook her head. 'No. Nothing. What would I need help with?' she challenged, immediately going on the defensive. I didn't rise to her combative energy.

'Okay, here's the thing, Toni. I love you and I want to protect you and have your back, the same way that your mum, and Kate and Jess and I have looked out for each other all our lives. And part of that is being aware of what's going on in each other's lives. I think there's something wrong in yours. You're not happy. And I've no idea if it's got anything to do with that text I saw...'

'It hasn't,' she spat back.

I took a breath, paused. 'Okay,' I carried on again, keeping absolutely calm. 'But you can see how I'd be worried that it might be.'

She performed her 3094th shrug of the holiday.

Fuck it, I was just going to love-bomb her and see if it helped.

'I want you to know that no matter what's going on with you, no matter if you've made a mistake, if you think it's a lost cause...

no matter what, I'll have your back and I'll love you. Because that's what we do.' I reached over and pushed her hair off her face. 'And because you're bloody brilliant, but that goes without saying,' I joked, trying to lighten the mood.

To my horror, it had the opposite effect. A single solitary tear ran down her cheek and she hastily brushed it away with the palm of her hand, then pushed herself up. 'I need to go and pack,' she said, then stopped, turned. 'Thanks, Aunt Carly. I love you too.' Yes! She was opening up... 'But there's really nothing wrong.' The shutters slammed down again. Bugger. 'I'd better go,' and then she was away, leaving me on my own, with no one except porn star Barbie and Ken across the pool.

Suddenly uncomfortable, I wandered into the kitchen, where Arnie was making lunch. It was an incongruous sight, this musclebound, handsome man, who looked like he belonged in the SAS, standing there with an apron on, chopping tomatoes.

'Can I take you home with me, Arnie? It rains, I've got no money to pay you, the house is smaller than Sam's garage and I've got a serious trash-telly habit, but it's never dull and you'll be forever adored by all of us.'

'Might just take you up on that. This life of luxury and good times is bound to get boring eventually,' he joked.

'That's my point! It's not as if Sam's great company when Movie Star Barbie is here.'

Shit. Did I say that out loud? At least I hadn't said porn star.

Leaning on the counter, I removed my foot from my mouth and popped a tomato in instead, hoping he'd just pretend he hadn't heard it.

'Not a fan, then?' he asked.

Damn. He heard it.

'Maybe I just don't get it,' I said, honestly. 'Is it a bloke thing? You're single...'

'Thanks for reminding me,' he interjected, with a chortle. 'I usually just think about that when I'm writing out the alimony checks.'

Arnie made no secret of his two ex-wives – one was a high-school sweetheart with whom he shared three children in their thirties, and the other was a Vegas dancer that he married a month after meeting her. Their happy ever after lasted until he went off to make his next movie and she hooked up with her ex.

'Sorry, but your pain is necessary to my point.'

That made him laugh again.

'You're single...' I repeated, making him stop slicing the tomatoes and use the knife to mimic stabbing himself in the heart. 'Would you be attracted to her? I know I sound bitchy and jealous...'

'Yup.' He moved on to shredding lettuce.

'But I'm not.' Okay, that was a slight lie. 'I just want him to be happy and I thought Sam would go for someone who made him laugh and who had great chat. She spent half an hour yesterday telling us about coffee enemas. I've ripped up my Starbucks loyalty card.'

Arnie's grin turned to an earnest shrug. 'We getting real, here?'

'Always.'

'He's been on his own for a long time. Ever since I've known him, it's just been short-term relationships, no commitments. Maybe he just got tired of flying solo.'

Bugger. When he put it like that...

'And, to answer your question, nope, not my type. I prefer ladies a lil' older and wiser, with some more curves on the bones,' he grinned as he said that, 'but I ain't gonna judge my bro. We're all just making this shit up as we go along.'

I now felt like a crap friend. What right did I have to come in here and judge Sam's choices? None.

'You're right, Arnie. How'd you get so wise, huh?'

'Two ex-wives and a whole lot of bruising,' he said.

'That sounds like a great title for a country song,' I quipped. 'And point taken. Whatever older, wiser, curvier lady gets you is gonna be a lucky woman.'

He was loading the vegetables into a bowl now. 'I'll be sure to tell them that. Any chance you could put it in writing?'

'A box of donuts in my room when we get back from the airport and it's done.'

His low, husky laugh was contagious. 'I'll take it.'

I headed upstairs to shower and change, and an hour later, Val and I went with Carol and Toni to the airport to greet Kate and Jess, who were coming in on the flight that Carol and Toni would take back to London.

Just going to the airport threw up another pang of missing my boys. As soon as we started driving, I pulled out my phone.

Mum to Mac and Benny: Just thinking about you two. Where are you? Whatcha up to? Would I approve?

Mac to Mum: South Carolina! Just ate grits. Tasted like something you would cook. May need to pump stomach LOL!

Mum to Mac: I preferred you when you were wee and thought I was a superhero.

Mac to Mum: Still do, Gritswoman.

The pang of missing them just escalated yet again. No one

made me laugh like my boys. Except, maybe Val, who was sitting next to me, dressed all in yellow.

'Say a word about Big Bird and I'll get violent,' she'd warned us, when she came out to the car. Even Toni laughed.

I'd glanced over at my niece, glued to her phone as always.

My worry about Toni was still niggling. I'd already decided to call my brother while they were in flight and tell him about the text. Coming from the house we grew up in, with our dramatic mother and hard-drinking dad, Callum had developed a calm, rational approach to dealing with problems, so I knew he'd keep my revelation confidential, while keeping an eye on Toni at the same time. It was the best solution I could come up with.

'I'll just go park up,' the driver – Leon, the same one who'd picked us up when we arrived – told us. 'Just text me when you're on your way out and I'll circle round to get you.'

I could so get used to this way of life.

Inside the terminal, we checked the arrivals board first. Their plane had just landed, which meant they'd probably be at least an hour by the time they got through immigration.

'Let's check the bags in first,' Carol suggested, 'then maybe we can go for a drink.'

'Sounds good to me,' I agreed, but rapidly changed my mind when I saw the gargantuan queue at the check-in desk.

'Drink first, then check in?' Val suggested, her blonde beehive acting in a periscope fashion as she scanned the area for a bar.

Target located: Planet Hollywood, just outside security, around the corner from the BA check-in desk. I ordered up three vodka tonics and a Coke for Toni, then we claimed a table in the corner. I texted our imminent arrivals to let them know where we were.

'Damn, look at that,' Carol said, eyes on the flicking numbers on the departure board. 'Delayed for two hours. Noooooo. Why don't I have a private jet? I'm gonna ask your brother to buy me one for Christmas.'

'I'll see if I can find one on eBay,' I told her, in the same tone I'd have used if she'd asked for fleecy slippers and a dressing gown. 'Anyway, I know the delay is a pain, but at least you'll get a few minutes with Kate and Jess.'

'Yep, every cloud has a silver spoon,' Carol whistled, completely unaware why Val, sitting next to her, was now shaking her head woefully. 'What? What did I say?'

Thankfully, the drinks arrived, taking the heat off.

'You know, I can't thank you enough for making me do this,' I said to both Val and Carol. 'I don't think I realised how much I needed to be dug out of the rut I was in. This has really given me a chance to breathe and pull myself together a bit.'

Val reached over and squeezed my hand. 'You're welcome, pet.'

'I mean, obviously I'm still a hot mess and I've got no idea how my future looks,' I admitted ruefully, laughing because it was absolutely true. 'But I love you all and you've reminded me how much I need my friends and my family.'

'Don't have me filling up, because this eyeliner is fresh on an hour ago,' Val pleaded, her voice emotional.

'I don't want to go home!'

Toni's outburst was so violent and sudden, so out of left field, that it took me a moment to register it.

Carol was a picture of confusion as she looked quizzically at her daughter. 'I know, sweetheart, but...'

Toni had already turned to me, pleading, 'No, I mean it. I don't want to go. Aunt Carly, please let me stay with you and Aunt Val. I'll be no bother. It's just that... that... Don't make me go home.'

Carol reeled like she'd been slapped.

'But, honey, why? Look, Toni, if there's something wrong...'

My heart was thudding. I should have told Carol about the text. I was a rubbish pal.

'Aunt Carly, please. Let me stay?' she begged. 'I'm not back at college until next month, so it's not as if I'll be doing anything anyway.'

'Well...' I turned to Carol, trying to judge her thoughts by her expression alone, a tough job as she hadn't had the ability to frown for a decade. Was she okay with Toni staying? Or not? And was anything I said going to be completely wrong and make her feel I was undermining her parenting? The bar was busy and I was fairly sure that no one else in the room was having a conversation as excruciating as this one.

'I mean, it's okay by me. If it's okay with you. But if it isn't, that's cool. I mean, whatever works for you,' I stuttered, losing the ability to form intelligent, cohesive sentences.

'But the flight...' Carol began, processing the info.

'If it's too late to change it, I'll pay for a new flight out of my own money,' Toni pleaded, sounding increasingly desperate.

My heart was breaking for her and something in her voice sparked a reaction in Carol too.

'You don't need to do that,' she turned to me, 'but, Carly, are you sure?'

'Of course! Yes! I'm sure it'll be okay with Sam too.'

Toni threw her arms around me and then stretched over to hug her mum, clearly assuming that she'd got her wish and oozing relief.

'Anyone waiting for a couple of very attractive pals?' Jess's voice.

We'd been so caught up in the moment, we hadn't even realised that Kate and Jess had found us.

I'm not sure the men in suits at the next table appreciated our squeals.

Greetings over, Carol got up. 'Here, one of you take my seat, I'm just going. Toni's going to stay here with you, though. I'll sort it out when I check in.'

'Yay!' Kate cheered, completely oblivious to the drama, but just happy to have Toni here with us for longer. Some said it took a village to raise a child. In our case, it took a group of pals who loved all of our offspring like they were our own.

'I know it's only a week until we come back, but we'll miss you,' I told Carol, hugging her again. 'Give my brother my love.'

'I will. Won't miss you lot at all though. You know what they say...'

We were all on the edge of our bar stools...

'Absence makes the heartstrings wander.'

Jess turned to me, reacting with her usual deadpan observational skills. 'Thank God she can make a living on her looks.'

Carol was too busy hugging Kate to hear Jess's playful dig. Not that she would have cared anyway.

After another round of kisses (mine) and tears (Val) and uncomfortable goodbyes (Toni), Carol grabbed her Chanel suitcase and matching trolley bag and waved goodbye, then glided off towards the check-in desk. I watched her go, until she disappeared out of sight, in awe of her ability to walk in four-inch heels as if they were flip-flops.

'I'll just text the driver and tell him we're ready,' I announced.

'Oooooh, get her. Texting her driver. The week before she came here, she spent four days in her pyjamas. How quickly they change,' Jess teased, lifting Carol's glass and finishing off her drink.

True to his promise, Leon was waiting outside, engine

running. Toni and I loaded up Jess and Kate's cases, then we all filed in to the back of the van: Val first, then, Jess, Kate, then...'

'Stop! Wait!'

It took me a minute, but... 'Carol?' I spun round, and there she was, looking uncharacteristically flustered.

'These shoes are not meant for running,' she gasped, her breathing heavy as she leaned on her case for support.

'What's wrong? Is your flight delayed again?'

She was still trying to get her breath back. 'Nope.' Breath. 'Got to the check-in desk.' Breath. 'Gutted to leave.' Breath. 'Thought what am I doing?' Breath. ''Cause you know I hate to miss anything.' Breath. 'So thought, fuck it, I'm not letting you lot have a holiday without me. I texted Sam and he said it's cool with him.'

I was hugging her before she got the last word out.

'Yaaayyyyyyy!' came the chorus from the van. Even Toni looked thrilled.

I had a sudden image of Estelle's face when she realised that there would now be six of us instead of four. She'd be straight on the phone to one of her three therapists and the force of the frown might even snap her Botox. Shame.

'I need you to do something though,' Carol told me, when she climbed in to join the others.

'Anything!'

'Can you call your brother and tell him our two-week holiday is now three? He can't divorce you.'

'Absolutely. I'll take the blame. I'll say I need you here to keep me out of trouble'.

There was an element of truth in there. With Toni here, we weren't going to do anything too wild, reckless or crazy.

At least, that's what I thought.

I couldn't have been more wrong.

16

SAM'S KITCHEN, THAT EVENING

WHAT'S LOVE GOT TO DO WITH IT? – TINA TURNER

I doubted that the soundproofing in Sam's house had ever been tested by six women who were shrieking with laughter, tears streaming down their faces. On the way back from the airport, we'd stopped at a supermarket and bought a mountain of food and drink to replenish Sam's stocks. We didn't want him to think we were taking advantage of his generosity. Not that he would, of course, but it made us feel better about the oestrogen invasion of his home.

When we'd arrived at the house, Sam and Estelle had already left for an event, so we'd had a quick change then settled round one of the kitchen islands with snacks and vino. Five hours later, we were still there, Chinese food had been added to the equation and Arnie had restocked the kitchen wine fridge for us.

Thankfully, I'd just finished the story of my bathrobe/flashing debacle (leaving out the bit where I went there with thoughts of fondling his body parts), when we heard the clipping of heels, announcing that Sam and Estelle had arrived home.

'Sam Morton!' Kate greeted him, sliding off her stool, arms

wide. She was slightly tipsy, but still registered his tux. 'You don't scrub up too badly for an old guy.'

Behind him, I saw Estelle's perfect lips purse together. She just did not get our deprecating humour at all. I was fairly sure she was counting down the hours until we left and was indeed now totally dismayed to see that we'd added two more to our numbers.

Kate wasn't wrong about Sam, though. His hair was swept back, his suit was sharp and he was utterly, intoxicatingly handsome. Much as I hated to admit it, he and Estelle, in her deep navy Balenciaga gown (she'd dropped the designer into the conversation over breakfast, when she'd been describing her outfit for the night) and tumbling mane of caramel hair, looked perfect together. Definitely Movie Star Barbie and Ken now. Urgh.

They'd been to an awards ceremony, where Estelle was being honoured for her humanitarian work. Not that I was making harsh judgements, but I had an inkling that her publicity team may have been involved in influencing that acclaim, because as far as we'd seen, her cup of human kindness wasn't exactly overflowing.

'You don't look too bad yourself, Kate,' Sam said warmly, immersing her in a hug.

Jess was next. 'Nah, he's totally let himself go,' she said, feigning disgust as she nudged Kate out of the way and took her place.

My inner health and safety officer was suddenly concerned that Estelle was bristling so much she may split that Balenciaga frock, shooting sequins across the room. She could have someone's eye out.

We introduced Estelle to the newcomers. Of course, we'd already given them a full rundown of her snide disdain for us, but they covered it up well with wide smiles and handshakes. Jess wasn't into hugging strangers unless she'd found them by swiping right on Tinder.

'Is your room okay?' Sam asked Jess. Since Carol and Toni were still in the guest house, Arnie had put the girls in the suite next to mine – a twin room, decorated in classic California whites and pale woods, with a huge bathroom and walk-in closet.

'Nope, there's only one steam room in it and the safe isn't big enough for all my diamonds,' Jess quipped, making him laugh.

Estelle had clearly had enough of all the cosy joviality and stepped forward into centre stage. 'I'm just off to bed. Early call in the morning and Scorsese is so demanding. Coming, darling?' Was it me or did she ramp up the sultry stuff when she threw out that question?

Sam. Rabbit. Headlights.

His gaze caught mine and I tried to send him a telepathic instruction. *Don't go, Sam. Say no. Hang out with us. You know you'd prefer it to a night of passion with a global celebrity who's been on the cover of* Vogue, Vanity Fair *and* Sports Illustrated. *Okay, maybe not, but there's some Kung Pao chicken left and we're happy to share.*

'Eh, sure,' he said, but it was to Estelle, not me. His telepathic receivers were clearly being blocked by Estelle's sequins.

Was it my imagination or did she respond with a smug grin of victory? My imagination. Or maybe the wine.

'You guys enjoy the rest of the night and just help yourselves to anything you need. It's good to have you here.' I was so busy thinking how lovely he was, that I was startled when I realised he was now talking to me. 'We're scouting locations tomorrow, so I'll be away early in the morning and I'm not sure when I'll be back.'

'Oh. Okay. It'll be tough, but I suppose we'll find something to do around here,' I joked, making him smile again. He was almost out of the room, when I blurted, 'Sam!'

He stopped so suddenly that Estelle nearly dislocated a shoulder trying to hang on to his hand. Shit, it was the bloody wine again. Goddammit. It was determined to challenge Estelle dominance and ask him to stay and hang out with us. It was the equivalent of hoping the popular kid at school picked your gang to hang out with. Pathetic. Sad. And now everyone was staring at me.

'Erm... Thank you. We really appreciate you letting us stay here.'

His eyes were locked on mine again. 'Sure. You know I love to see you all. Goodnight, Cooper.'

This time, I managed keep my gob shut and let him go.

'Oh no,' Kate said, in the low wary voice she usually reserved for the arrival of serial killers in crime shows. 'There's something going on with you two. It's gone all awkward and weird.'

'It's not!' I said, completely aware that I was being both very awkward and very weird. 'I just wanted to spend a bit more time with him, that's all.'

'That's all?' Jess asked, lifting her eyes from her phone.

'Definitely.' I couldn't meet Kate's eyes again, so I was delighted when Jess pivoted to a completely new subject. 'Okay. Do you think this is the real Channing Tatum?' she asked, holding up her phone so we could see a pic on her Tinder app. 'Only if it is, I might need to pop out for a couple of hours.'

I really hoped she was kidding, but Val took charge, swiping the phone out of Jess's hands and popping it down the front of her bra. 'I'm not having you sexticating...'

Ironically, Carol was the first to suss out what Val meant. 'Sexting, Val. It's called 'sexting'.'

'Well, whatever it's called, I'm not having you doing it any more, Jess Latham.' As always, the full names came out when she was chiding us.

'Eeeeeew, I'm never going to be able to not see Channing Tatum in your boobs. I'll never have sex again,' Jess moaned.

'Good. Because you're going to catch something if you carry on like this and I saw a programme about those genital warts and they can make you walk funny.'

'Excuse me, forgot my purse.' Estelle had picked that exact moment to walk back in. She picked her Lagerfeld clutch off the worktop and backed out of the room, horrified.

Toni put her head on the island, shoulders shaking, while the rest of us bit our tongues.

'That was probably more information than she needed to hear,' Val said. 'Anyway, I'm off to bed. I've found the BBC on that telly and I want to catch up with *EastEnders*. Love you all, lassies.'

She blew us a kiss and marched off, handbag under one arm, wine in the other.

'I think I'll turn in too,' Carol said, stretching. 'Toni, come with me and we'll call your dad and Charlotte. I'm going to lie through my veneers and say you begged me to stay here so he doesn't call in the lawyers.'

Another grin from Toni. Since we'd got back from the airport, she'd reverted to her happier mood from a couple of days before. I wondered if this week's sulks and strops were because she was dreading going home? I wasn't entirely sure, but I had another seven days to try to suss it – and her – out.

'Shit, Val's away with my phone,' Jess groaned, before taking off in pursuit, leaving just Kate and me.

'LA has been good for you,' she said, grinning. 'Loving the hair and the tan. You've managed to put on outdoor clothes and everything.'

'I know. I'm like a new woman,' I agreed, laughing as we began clearing away the dishes and food boxes. 'I've even brushed my hair five days in a row. It's progress.'

'Have you spoken to Mark?'

'Every day.' That was surprisingly true. Mac and Benny would put the phone on loud speaker for at least part of our daily calls, and Mark would chip in too. It had been strangely easy. Almost friendly. 'The boys are having a great time and he sounds happy too. I hope so. I'm still finding it strange that I'm not there, though. And not just because I miss them. Don't judge me for this, but...' I paused. 'I want them to have a fantastic holiday, I promise, but it still stings that they're having a great time without me. I mean, who's organising what they do every day? Who's nagging them to get their clothes in the washing machine? Who's telling them to get off their phones and moaning at them for watching fourteen episodes of *The Walking Dead* in a row? Those are my jobs. Who's doing all that?' I suddenly felt emotional and wanted to call them to hear their voices.

Kate switched on the tap and began rinsing plates. 'You have to let them do their thing,' she said gently. 'I understand though. I'd find it hard to think of Bruce and the kids having a brilliant time without me. It's that whole "needing to be needed thing", isn't it?'

I thought about that as I took her rinsed plates off the drainer one by one and put them in the dishwasher. It was time to loosen off the cords. I knew that. But I still wasn't ready to fill the gaps that would be left there.

'What about Sam?'

I'd moved on to the cutlery now. 'What about him?' I tried to channel innocence, but she didn't buy it.

'Oh, I don't know,' she chirped. 'Maybe just the fact that he was one of the biggest loves of your life, and now you're here, in his home, and he's the same lovely guy as he always was and you'd need to be dead from the neck down not to have any kind of response to that.'

'Sssshhhhh,' I hissed. 'I'm pretty sure Estelle has this place bugged. One wrong word and she'll storm in here and stab me with her Louboutins.'

I was only half-joking. In her last movie, she'd played a devious international assassin with a quirky taste in killing methods. There was a fairly good chance she'd picked up some tips.

'Val would protect you. I'm fairly sure she has some kind of impenetrable force field in that handbag of hers. She never goes anywhere without it. But come on, spill. Do you think there could be anything between you again?'

'Kate, have you seen his girlfriend? I look like her elderly aunt, the one who works in a pie shop and likes comfortable shoes. Estelle Conran is half the planet's wet dream.'

Everything rinsed, she flipped off the tap. 'Yeah, but she's not you,' she said simply.

'Thank God, because she'd need to use a body double for nude scenes.'

I closed the dishwasher and leaned back against the cool marble of the island, letting Kate's words sink in.

'The thing is,' I said, 'I'm not even me any more.'

Wow. How had we gone from riotous fun to deep and profound so quickly?

Her expression changed to a sad smile. 'You will be. You just need time.'

I wasn't sure that all the time in the world would help, but I wasn't going to argue. Instead, I picked my wine glass back up, took another sip and then went for full disclosure, using her words from earlier.

'I'm not dead from the neck down though,' I conceded. 'I've thought about him. About us, and everything that happened. It would be impossible not to. But there's no going back. Our chance passed a long time ago.'

Kate dropped the last of the rubbish in the bin. 'Any regrets about that?'

Regrets? Her question took me back to the last time I had the chance to choose a life with Sam. It was the next chapter in the story that I'd been telling Toni on the flight on the way here. The History of Sam Morton and Carly Cooper, year 2008 AD – the one where Sam drops a bombshell that leads to a crossroads and a decision that would shape the rest of my life.

And I would never know if I made the right choice.

17

LOS ANGELES, JUNE, 2008
WHITE FLAG – DIDO

I'd come to LA on a mission to sell my first book, *Nipple Alert*, to a movie studio, so that it could be a global success, dollars would fall from the sky, and I could spend the rest of my life wearing leopard print and having lunch once a week with Jackie Collins at the Chateau Marmont. I had brought the boys with me, but Mark had stayed at home, not even pretending to be happy that I'd come to Hollywood to chase my dreams.

However, there was already a whole lot of acting going on in the family. At almost three, Benny was pretending to be Buzz Lightyear, jumping off any high surface shouting 'To Infinity and Beyond'. We already had a standing reservation at Accident and Emergency. At four and three quarters, Mac was showing a real talent for impersonations. Unfortunately, it was always of the bad guys in movies, and I was already having nightmares in which I'd see his face on FBI Most Wanted posters.

Bottom of the performance scale were Mark and I, who were acting really badly as a married couple. It was amazing how quickly the happy ever after had been derailed by the stresses and strains of everyday life. When we'd said our 'I do's' at that brilliantly rushed ceremony in New York, I'd been absolutely certain that I was marrying my soulmate, the guy I'd love until the end of time, one who had promised to do everything he could to make all our dreams come true.

I was sure nothing could break us and I still felt the same, but that didn't mean we wouldn't get a few dents along the way.

Straight after the wedding, Mark got a transfer to the London office of his legal powerhouse, a competitive yuppie-fest that demanded sixteen-hour days and unflinching commitment. I could almost live with that. We'd moved into the house next door to Kate, and my pals had pretty much taken up residence in my kitchen, so I wasn't bored or lonely. However, I was broody. I bought my first ovulation kit and we became that cliché couple, having sex on demand, to a biological schedule, then seething afterwards because Mark would fall asleep when I was still lying with my legs up a wall to give his swimmers the best chance of success.

Still, we didn't give up. Kate had her third child, Carol had her twins. Sarah's were approaching their teens and Jess was thinking about having another to keep her toddler, Josh, company. And oh, the irony. I'd spent years of my life trying to avoid getting pregnant, and now my ovaries seemed to have downed tools and organised a walkout.

Three years later, it was all worth it. Mac had come along, then Benny, and the happy ever after was back on the horizon. However, I was the only one sailing towards it. Mark was too busy working to even get in the dinghy. The long days didn't change, and the weekends were spent sleeping or preparing for the week ahead. Oh, the predictability of it all. I was the frustrated suburban housewife who felt her husband took her for granted and didn't pull his weight. Once upon a time, I was a driven, ambitious, life-loving, twenty-something with an admittedly chaotic but thrilling love life. In just a few years, I'd become the one thing that I absolutely, definitely, positively didn't think I'd ever be: normal.

My only hope of opening our lives back up to thrills and excitement was the possibility of making my writing career a success, so when Hollywood came knocking, I answered the door. The soulmate who'd promised all that richer-or-poorer stuff tried to slam it shut.

It had started with a phone call from Ike Tucker, a big-shot talent agent who specialised in book to movie deals. My publisher had sent him my novel and he wanted me to come to LA to work with him on pitching it around the studios. Was I interested? I'd started packing before I got off the phone. This was it! My big chance! My dream!

I was rudely awakened when Mark had refused to come with me, because, well, the truth was, he was a realist. In in his fact-based world, the chances of me landing a movie deal were so miniscule that he was absolutely certain it wouldn't happen. In Mark's mind, that meant there was no point in even trying, and definitely no point in spending money we didn't have and disrupting our lives for the sake of an unattainable dream. We should just accept our lives for what they were. Embrace normality. Settle for what we already had.

But I couldn't. I was restless and I was miserable, and I definitely wasn't ready to concede defeat to a husband who wouldn't know excitement if he tripped over it on his way to another long day at the legal coalface. I was a dreamer who was stuck in a rut, with two admittedly gorgeous toddlers, but how many days could I pass singing Barney songs, baking cakes and speaking in words of one syllable, then writing my *Family Values* columns and my next book while they were asleep, and hoping my husband would make it home before midnight?

I wanted more. A big shiny future was being dangled in front of me and I couldn't resist it. Besides, it was the summer holidays and Mac would be starting school in August, so this was going to be the last chance to go on an extended adventure. This wasn't some crazy whim, it was a genuine opportunity and if I didn't take it, I'd always be wondering, what if?

So, despite Mark's furious objections, I'd waltzed through the brand new Terminal 5 building at Heathrow, with one kid dressed as Buzz Lightyear and the other one as Woody (I didn't have the emotional strength to argue), and jetted off to La La Land to stay in one of Uncle Sam's guest suites.

It was like a parallel universe in LA. At home I was a cook, a cleaner, a babysitter, a financial planner, bill payer, holiday organiser, car fixer, stressed-out working mum of two toddlers. I hadn't had a proper conversation or decent sex for as long as I could remember. Here? For the first time in years, I could exhale. The sun was shining, and all I had to do every day – with the exception of a few meetings my agent had set up with movie producers – was hang out at the beach and pool, play with my boys, and when they were in bed, I could chill with one of my best mates in his incredible home, watch movies, eat our favourite foods and chat about his day at the giddy heights of movie stardom. It had been a long, long time since I'd felt that happy or that relaxed.

For a while, I almost convinced myself that it was real, until the sting from the persistent phone calls from my pissed-off husband burst my bubble.

A month after I'd arrived, the movie deal hadn't come in, Buzz and Dr Doom (Mac had gone over to the dark side by then and decided he'd rather be a baddie) were starting to speak with an LA twang, and Mark was getting more and more insistent that we come home.

'Mum, Mum, Mum, Mum, MUM!' Mac said excitedly. That

was his thing. He'd been born in a perpetual state of excitement and enthusiasm, so he repeated everything he said, in ascending volume, until someone answered him, by which time he'd usually forgotten what he wanted to say.

'Yes, my darling?'

His tone would suggest I was miles away, but I was actually lying between them on the sofa, watching old episodes of *Scooby Doo*.

'Tomorrow, can we, can we, can we...' I stroked his hair as I waited, unable to guess. It could be anything from 'get pizza' to 'see if Spiderman can come for a play date'. 'Can we phone Dad and tell him to come play with you and me and Uncle Sam? I miss him.'

'Me too,' added my little Benny Bear, from somewhere deep in my armpit. I was aware that Benny's declaration may not be particularly heartfelt, given that he spent all day agreeing with everything his brother said.

Mac when he wakes up: 'Mum, Mum, Mum, MUM, I'm hungry!'

Benny: 'Me too.'

Mac at the park: 'Can you push me on the swing? I want to go so high I can see the Death Star!'

Benny: 'Me too.'

Mac in the evening: 'Mummy, I love you more than chips. With tomato ketchup.'

Benny: 'Me too.' (Pauses, looks around.) 'Where are the chips?'

I'd almost forgotten Mac was waiting for an answer. 'Of course we can call him. I'm not sure he'll be able to come play though, because Daddy has to work.'

'Not fair,' Mac pouted. He got no arguments from me.

Even after two more mysteries had been solved by Scooby and

the pesky kids, I was almost reluctant to let the boys go to sleep because I was avoiding Sam, for two reasons. First, despite my happily married state, I'd been having obscene thoughts about doing things to Sam that would use muscles I'd forgotten I had. And secondly, well, there was the trifling matter that a few nights before, he'd told me he was falling in love with me again.

We'd been at Mammoth Mountain, a ski resort a few hours north of LA. The boys were in bed in the fancy two-bedroom suite, and Sam and I were drinking coffee at the dining table, a real wood fire crackling in the background.

There'd been a tension between us for days, the heavy weight of a conversation that we'd been putting off because we were both too scared to have it. Sam got there first, taking my hand. 'I'm falling in love with you again,' he'd said softly.

I'd lost the ability to breathe.

How many life-changing moments were we destined to have? Sam had asked me to marry him years before. I'd said yes, but then left and broke his heart. I'd gone back to find him years later, and that time my heart was shattered by his new career choice. He'd begged me to reconsider, but I couldn't. I left him again, married Mark.

Now here we were again. He'd told me he loved me. Asked me to think about trying again. And despite the fact that I wanted him so badly it hurt, I somehow managed to stay on the right side of monogamy. My boys had been asleep in the next room, and I couldn't betray their father for the sake of an incredible, wanton, wild, fan-fricking-tastic night of passion. No matter how much I wanted to.

Instead, I told him I had to think about it, had to work out my feelings for Mark.

A few nights later, back in Sam's house in LA, I was, very

maturely, still avoiding the issue, torn between two men I loved. But which one did I love more?

Before I had a chance to do anything I'd regret, to cross a line with Sam or to break a vow to my husband, Mark took it out of my hands the next day by arriving unexpectedly. My boys were fairly sure their magic powers had made it happen. It was either that, or the Gods Of Marital Panic, so I let them believe their version.

'I can't believe you're here,' I told him, overcome that he'd travelled all this way for us. There was a whole cauldron of other feelings too. Relief, mostly. A bit of shame. And I ignored the tiny tug of regret that any illicit thoughts or feelings for Sam had just been squashed by Mark's size elevens. No more wondering what if. No more torturing myself over how I felt.

For the next two weeks, we had the kind of family holiday that makes you wake up happy in the morning and then go to sleep hours later, still smiling. Sam had gone off on location, so the fog of confusion cleared. Mark was the boys' dad. We were a family. I had no right to break up their lives. More than that, I still loved him. No matter what, when I thought about how the rest of my life would look, Mark was by my side. We'd been brilliant together once, and I knew we could be that way again. Mark promised to meet me halfway. He wasn't going to work as much. He was going to be more involved with us. We were going to recapture the kind of happiness that I'd experienced with no one else but him.

When the fortnight came to an end, Mark's vacation was over and he had to go back to work. I was staying in LA a while longer to fulfil my meetings with the movie companies.

After he'd gone, I knew it was time to be honest with everyone, including myself.

One night a couple of weeks later, I found Sam sitting outside on the terrace by the fire and went to him.

I didn't even have to speak.

'You're going back to Mark, aren't you?' he said.

'I am.' I could feel a piece chip right off my heart. I couldn't be with Sam, but I couldn't lose him from my life either. 'Are we over, Sam? Is this it?' I asked, terrified of the answer.

He took a sip of his beer and stared into the flames for a moment. 'Carly, we've been through worse than this and survived it. I love you, no matter what. And if that's as friends, then I'll take it.' Man, he was killing me. 'Besides,' he went on, a sad smile, 'I'm Benny's godfather. I can't deprive him of my godfatherly brilliance.'

The chip in my heart got bigger. If it was a movie, the end credits would roll over the footage of me and the boys landing back in London, then rushing through the terminal, the doors opening and ta da! There's Mark, arms wide, and we rush to him and he wraps us in a loving embrace and we all live happily ever after.

Only, as we'd already found out, life wasn't like the movies.

18

LOS ANGELES, 13TH AUGUST, 2019

GOD IS A WOMAN – ARIANA GRANDE

'You did what? Jesus, I think my womb just clenched,' I gasped, gripping the phone and praying I'd misheard.

Mac repeated it, just in case I hadn't been traumatised enough the first time. 'We went bungee jumping off a cliff. It was epic, Mum. Although, Benny couldn't speak for an hour after it. I think his brain was rattled.'

'Your mother is fricking rattled! Tell me that your father isn't injured.'

'Of course not. Why?'

'Because I want him to get home in one piece so I can kill him.'

Mac's throaty laugh made my womb stand down from fear level one. God, I missed them. 'Dad!' I heard him shouting. 'Mum says she's thrilled we went bungee jumping and we've to make sure we have loads more adventures like that on this holiday.'

'Mac Barwick,' I spat, doing the full name thing of the pissed-off Scottish mother. 'You are going to be grounded until you're thirty.'

I heard the rustle of him removing the phone from his ear.

'And, Dad,' he shouted into the distance again, 'she's saying we should try skydiving next.'

'Make it forty,' I threatened, trying to keep the amusement out of my voice. 'Now let me speak to your brother so I can let him know I'm writing you both out of my Will if there are any more death-defying stunts.'

Another rustle, and I heard Mac stage-whisper, 'Don't tell her about the swimming with sharks.'

'Hi, Mum,' Benny greeted me with his usual quiet cheeriness.

'Benny Barwick, I love you...'

'I can hear a "but" coming,' he said wisely.

'But I'm relying on you to be the sensible and mature one there.'

'How does that work? I'm the youngest. I should be the nightmare.'

He had a point. 'Yep, but we both know that your brother is an adrenalin junkie, and going by what Mac just told me, your father is clearly on drugs.'

His chuckles were the equivalent of fluffy unicorns for the soul.

'Now try to come back in one piece because I kinda like you guys the way I made you. Okay?'

More chuckles. 'Copy that.' He must have been watching *Chicago Fire* again. 'Anyway, Mac's shouting that we need to go. Something about getting shot out of a cannon. We'll call you if we survive. Love you, Mum!'

And he was gone, leaving me sitting at the kitchen island in a puddle of maternal stress. I tried to shrug it off, telling myself they'd be fine. They would. I'd see them again in just over a week, and in the meantime, I had plenty of people here to keep my mind off missing them.

It was the morning after Kate and Jess had arrived, and I'd got up early to drink coffee and write my weekly column for *Family Values* – the kind of magazine that was only read by people who had three nannies, who hothoused their little darlings in cello and Mandarin before they were five, and had a conniption if their child went within ten feet of any food that wasn't organic. By some miracle, I'd managed to sustain the weekly load of tossed-up bollocks for over a decade. My general formula for writing it was to conjure up the most irritating parental habit or trend I could think of, then write 800 words extolling the virtues of it.

Thanks to Carol and my experiences on this trip, today's was easy – an essay on why you should always fly first class (but leave the nanny and the kids in economy). I was 100 per cent sure that at least half the people who read my weekly witterings agreed with me, and the other half would quite happily see me choke on my vanilla soymilk skinny cappuccino with a macadamia twist. I'd once written a whole column on why that should be the coffee of choice for the busy mum who lunched. It was that or yet another piece on the merits of subjecting your baby to classical music and high-brow literature in the womb.

I'd just shivered, reminded myself that I only did it for the money, and pressed send when Kate wandered in with Jess and Val, all dressed in trainers and some combination of Lycra or loungewear.

'Where have you lot been?' I asked, curious.

'Five-mile jog,' Val fired back, flicking on the kettle.

That was a shock. The last time I saw Val jogging was vivid in my memory. 13 July 1985, the day of the Live Aid concert, and she was running to get to the off license before it closed, because an impromptu party had kicked off in her house and the adults had run out of beer, Martini and Babycham. She was also trying to cheer up my Uncle Don, because he'd just found out that she'd phoned in and donated their entire summer holiday fund to Bob Geldof.

'Wow, seriously?' I asked, thinking LA was changing us all.

Kate crumbled first. 'No, of course not. We were using the telescope in the back garden to try to spy on the next house along the canyon. Apparently, Matthew McConaughey lives there and he does naked yoga in the mornings.'

Jess took her shades off and yawned. Her mass of red, Deborah Messing hair was tied up in a messy bun and her ivory skin was even paler than usual.

'You look knackered, Jess. Jet lag kick in?'

'Erm, yeah. Something like that.'

Kate shot her a knowing look. 'Jess Latham, you'll never go to heaven.'

I took a sip of my coffee, trying to act cool. Jess was the kind of person who shared things in her own time and if she thought she was being interrogated she'd clam up and tell us nothing. It was understandable. She'd absolutely been through the wars in her love life. After the affair with the married MP splashed her across the newspapers and made her a household-name tart (her words, not mine), she really thought she'd turned things round when she married Mike, the journalist who had exposed her affair. Within a few months, she was pregnant and I'd never seen her so contented, so absolutely blissfully happy and it stayed that way until the moment she found out that Mike was shagging around behind her back.

Distraught, heartbroken, and with a young baby to support, she'd surprised us all by marrying Keith, a lovely builder, and going off to live in France. About ten years ago, Keith dropped dead on a building site. Heart attack at forty-two. It took Jess a long time to even look at another man, but when she did, the occasional one-night stand had been the most she could manage.

'I've been in love three times,' she used to say. 'That's more than enough for any woman. Except Cooper.' I didn't take offence.

The occasional one-night stand had turned into something much more frequent in recent years thanks to dating apps, but Jess was rightly unapologetic. The way she wanted to live her life was her choice, and none of us judged her for it. As long as she was happy, took safety precautions, used condoms and carried pepper spray, we were all for it.

'Something to share, Jess?' I probed gently. 'Or will I wait until you've gone to the loo and Val tells me everything?'

'Every detail,' Val agreed, nodding.

'Okay, okay! God, you lot need to learn about boundaries and personal space.'

I chose not to point out that she was the worst of us when it came to interfering in each other's lives. 'I went out last night to meet someone I'd hooked up with online.'

I almost spluttered my coffee across Sam's marble island.

'When? We didn't go to bed until 3 a.m.'

'Eh, yeah. It was about three thirty. I got back at six,' she admitted, shame-faced, before attempting to use bravado to wiggle out of it. 'I've had about an hour's sleep, I'm close to the edge, and jurors now consider sleep deprivation as a solid base of defence in murder trials, so it's probably wise if you lot stop meddling in my business.'

That made me laugh. 'You do you, boo. I'm fully supportive of your decisions regarding your own lady garden.'

'Aye, but does she have to have so many gardeners?' Val quipped.

Thankfully, Carol and Toni chose that moment to appear, both of them in pyjama shorts and vest tops, make-up free, with their hair pulled up in high ponytails.

I pulled a move out of Toni's playbook, sighed and rolled my eyes. 'If I rolled out of bed like that, I'd spend the first hour of the day walking up and down the street so all my neighbours could see me.'

Carol came over and hugged me from behind. 'Ah, but you're beautiful on the inside,' she teased. 'Under this gorgeous exterior, I'm completely shallow and a bit of a cow.'

Kate rattled up four mugs on to the worktop – Val already had tea and Toni wasn't a fan of hot drinks in the morning – and poured coffee from the pot that was on a machine that looked like it could power a space shuttle.

'What's our plan for today then?' I asked. 'Anyone got anything they want to do?'

I could have been staring into an eclipse, and I'd still have spotted all the shifty glances that passed between them.

Suspicion made my voice drop a couple of notes. 'What's going on? What am I missing?'

'Okay, hear us out,' Kate pleaded.

If they were making Kate do the talking it must be bad. They knew that she was the one most likely to win me over because I couldn't refuse her anything. She knew too much.

'Carol has been invited to cover the launch of a new laptop for one of her clients. It's a big swanky do and would be great for her to be there,' Kate began, her tone and body language not necessarily matching such a positive announcement.

'O-kayyyyy,' I said, slightly suspicious.

Carol took up the reins. 'It's a big earner, and I'd be crazy not to do it. Especially since it's over here.'

Even better! So what was the problem?

'And they've said that they'll pay my travel and I can bring guests. They'll pay for them too.'

I was already trying to work out what I had in my case that I could wear to a fancy launch. Another trip to the Grove might be on the cards, unless Estelle had a designer frock that was really stretchy.

'That sounds amazing!' I enthused, to more shifty glances. Even Val was staring into her tea.

'When she says "over here", she doesn't exactly mean Los Angeles,' Jess explained and, oh God, she was physically squirming. Jess hadn't squirmed since she'd had a chlamydia false alarm that gave her psychosomatic symptoms.

'So where is it?

As I raised my coffee, Kate's eyes met mine, and I saw the apprehension in the furrow of her brow.

'New York,' she said quietly.

I knew my cup was burning my lips, but I couldn't move it. It took me several seconds of stunned silence before my trembling hands could slowly, carefully return it to the table.

'No,' I said, quietly, definitely, shocked that they would even suggest it. I wasn't going back to New York. No way. I couldn't do it. They knew how I felt about it, so why would they do this to me? How could they think it was something I'd even consider? Were they crazy?

'Hear us out, Carly, please,' Kate begged, and my suspicions rose even further until I was in full-scale conspiracy mode. Was there even a launch? Had this been planned all along? Was this some kind of fucked-up ploy that they'd all been in on?

She mistook my furious silence for the green light to go on.

'It's time. We should do this.' A pause. '*You* need to do this.'

'No. No, I don't. Did you lot plan this all along?'

I could see Carol was genuinely surprised by this, so I scored that accusation off my list, while she argued the point.

'No! I swear. But, okay, I did call and offer to do the job this morning because I realised it made sense.'

'How does it make sense?' My voice rose just as Arnie walked

in the door, read the room, then promptly turned and walked out
again.

'Because you'll never get past this if you don't face it,' Jess said
impatiently. She'd never been great at sympathy or emotional
turmoil and I could see by her irritation that I'd already passed
her tolerance point. 'And because we've already told Hannah and
Ryan that we're coming.'

The explosion in my chest was so violent that I almost
buckled with the pain. How could they? These were the people I
loved more than anyone and they were backing me into a corner
of pain. Hannah and Ryan. Sarah's children, kids we'd loved since
they were little and who were now grown adults with their own
lives. Lives that were being lived without a mother, because Sarah
was dead, and so was her husband, Nick, both killed by all the
decisions that had led to her being in the wrong place at the
wrong time. My decisions.

'And Hannah was okay with us coming?' I asked. Last year,
we'd thought about making the trip to New York – the first time
we'd have been there since Sarah's funeral the year before – but
Hannah had said she was too busy at work. I didn't believe her.
She didn't want us there. And I knew why. She didn't want to see
me. She'd never actually vocalised it, but I knew, because I'd feel
the same. It was easy to keep up polite conversation in our calls
and texts, but actually seeing someone, being with them, was a
whole different level of pretence and I knew that Hannah didn't
feel ready for it. I didn't blame her. The truth was I had been
relieved because I couldn't bring myself to face her either.

'Yes! She wants us to come. All of us!' Jess assured me. I didn't
believe her.

'Come with us,' Kate begged. 'It's only for a couple of days and
then we'll be back here and I know you'll feel so much better.'

I slowly stood up, shook my head. 'No.'

None of them said a word as I walked right past them and out of the door.

I've no idea how long I'd been staring at the ceiling when there was a knock at my bedroom door. I had a hunch it would be Val. She would have been my first choice of negotiator in any situation that called for serious mediation.

'Can I come in?'

Sam's voice. Unexpected, but probably the only one I could face right now.

'Sure,' I croaked, my throat tight with unshed tears.

The door opened and he crossed the room, almost silently, in a college T-shirt and shorts.

'Hey, you,' he said, his tone making it obvious that he knew exactly what was going on. He sat beside me on the bed, his back against the headboard, and I pushed myself up so that our heads were level. 'How are you doing?'

'Had better days,' I said, still struggling to get the words out. I tried changing the subject, 'I thought you were going out on location today?'

He shrugged. 'It was postponed. A problem with the weather.'

It was seventy-five degrees outside, the same as almost every other day in this city, so I doubted that was true. Had he cancelled because he knew the girls were going to spring this on me this morning? Was he part of the conspiracy? Or was I actually losing my mind?

Silence. He'd always been good at that. Of all the men I'd loved, Sam was the best listener, the best talker, the one who knew what you needed without asking. It was what had made him – for that crazy few years back in the nineties – one of the most in-demand escorts in South East Asia.

After a few more minutes, I managed to form my words. 'They want me to go back to where Sarah died.'

'I know,' he said softly.

'I can't,' I blurted.

He took my hand, and moved it over onto his lap, where he held it between his, as if transferring some kind of energy between us.

He didn't argue. 'Okay.'

'You think I should go.' It was a statement, not a question.

'I think that sometimes you need to face pain, otherwise it never leaves you. It will consume you and then you find yourself, years later, regretting the choices you made.'

For a moment I wondered if we were still talking about me, or if this was something he'd learned for himself. Either way, I knew he was right.

'I'm scared.' There, I'd said it. That was the truth of it.

'Of what?' he asked.

'Of the guilt. That I'll hate myself even more than I do now.'

He rubbed the back of my hand with his thumb. 'That could happen, and I could tell you all the reasons you're wrong, but you won't believe me. It's almost two years now, Carly, and you haven't been able to work this out, so maybe, for once, you just need to let go and trust the people who love you.'

Another silence, but his words flooded my brain, drowning out the white noise, ebbing and flowing until finally they were still and made perfect sense.

'I hate that you're usually right about this stuff. It's your least attractive quality,' I said grudgingly. He knew me well enough to hear what I was saying. I was going to go.

'I thought that was my feet,' he argued.

'Yeah, those too.'

His face came towards me and for a weird second I thought he was going to kiss me on the lips, but his mouth just made a quick, sweet contact with my forehead, before he climbed off the bed.

He was almost at the door, when I realised the conversation wasn't done. 'Sam, can I ask you something?'

'Always.'

'Does Estelle make you happy?'

I was hoping he'd hesitate, but he didn't. 'She does.'

'I'm glad you've found happiness.' I realised I meant it now. My chat with Arnie had shifted something inside me. 'You deserve it.'

The gorgeous Sam Morton looked at me with a sad, sympathetic smile. 'I think maybe it's time you started looking for it too.'

19

NEW YORK, 13TH AUG 2019
TRUE COLOURS – CYNDI LAUPER

Back at home, I drove a twelve-year-old Mini that didn't lock and had a window that fell down if I drove at over 40 mph. Mark might earn a good living, but in London it definitely didn't stretch to anything close to my current standard of travel – I'd now flown in first class and on a private flight in the space of a couple of weeks.

The plane that the IT company had chartered to fly their bloggers and influencers from the West coast to New York for the two-day trip was like a party in the air. Free food. Free alcohol. Lots of people taking pictures of themselves enjoying both. There was also quite a bit of fraternising and people spending unduly long periods in the bathrooms. I didn't investigate.

I had no idea how Carol had managed to wangle seats for us too, but if I had to make this journey, at least it was on a busy flight that gave me little time to wallow. Although, it did feel strange without Val and Toni after two weeks of being with them round the clock. Val had opted out, claiming that another flight would play havoc with her varicose veins and Toni chose to stay and keep her company. I suspect she was looking forward to the space she was going to get without her mum and me around and Sam had offered to take her along to some of his studio meetings. Carol had made Sam swear he wouldn't let her borrow his car or his credit card. Sam had agreed but I wasn't sure he could withstand the pressure of a teenager who was desperate to hit the shops. I was pretty sure his American Express card was in serious jeopardy.

Kate and Jess slept most of the way, their body clocks completely destroyed by two flights in two days. Carol networked like a demon, accepting all requests for joint selfies and posing up a storm. I still found it incredible to watch her in the wild, and see her treated like the legend that she was by the younger stars of the industry. The minute she was on show, my chaotic, hilarious sister-in-law became a polished, switched-on professional – Carol Sweeney, the former top model, still a household name and now a social media influencer and commentator who'd refused countless requests to feature her family in their own reality show. Callum had squashed that possibility. Said he spent enough of his life making sure he got good angles.

I passed the five hours in the air alternating between trying to calm my inner panic, and trying to take my mind off it by making notes for my next two weeks' columns on my phone. Inspired by my surroundings, one was a commentary on mummy bloggers and the other was a recommendation piece on ten travel essentials for the exhausted mum. For research purposes, I might need to sniff a couple of Joe Malone diffusers in duty-free on the way home to London next week.

Talking of which... I picked up my phone and saw that I had Wi-Fi, and typed out a text on our family group chat.

Mum to Mac and Benny: Where are you now? Your mamma is missing you (I may have mentioned that before) xx

I expected a wait, so I was pleasantly surprised to see the three little dots begin to pulsate.

Benny to Mum: Nearly at Washington DC. Dad said we've to have an educational day tomorrow. Going to Smithsonian. Yassss! Mac says he wants us to drop him off and he'll hitchhike to somewhere more fun (😊 😊 😊).

The smiley face was contagious. Benny was interested in the world around him, but Mac? Unless it was a basketball or a potential girlfriend, he wasn't interested. The thought of him being forced to spend a day of his holiday in a museum would horrify him.

The next text told me I was right.

Mac to Mum: Ma, they're making me learn stuff. Call a lawyer.

I fired off a reply.

Mum to Mac and Benny: Oh son, hang in there. You'll get through this. #prayforMac

Mac: You're not funny.

Benny: You are.

For the first time today, my shoulders lowered from somewhere around my ears. The last couple of years had been the worst of my life, but these two had made every day bearable and I couldn't love them more.

I wondered if Mark ever read our conversations. He was probably way too busy behind the wheel of the RV. Over the last couple of weeks, they'd driven from Miami up the east coast, through Florida, Georgia, South Carolina, North Carolina, Virginia, and now they were in Washington DC. I wasn't sure if they were going any further north, but Mark and I had talked about doing that tour for years. And yes, it did still make my teeth grind just a little that Superdad had only kicked in now that I wasn't around. Better late than never.

Mum to Mac and Benny: Guess where I am?

Mac: Michael Jordan's house.

Mum: Why would you even think that?

Mac: Wishful thinking.

Mum: I'm just going to tell you cos you'll never guess – on a private plane!

Typing that made it sound exciting, but I wasn't going to share my anxiety with them. I grew up in a home where the atmosphere had been dictated by my parents' moods and tensions and I'd vowed never to repeat that, so no matter whether I was up, down or falling to pieces, I slapped on a smile and made sure the boys had a consistent, happy home.

Benny: No way!

Mum: Way!

There was a pause while I waited for more. And waited. And waited. It was a couple of minutes before the reply came.

Benny: Dad is asking if you are with Uncle Sam?

Ah. I should have thought about that. It hadn't even occurred to me that Mark would assume I was with Sam, perhaps jetting off somewhere exotic. This whole jealousy thing was so unlike him that I still didn't see it coming.

Mum: No. With Carol, Jess and Kate, just about to land in New York. Please let Dad know. And call me any time. Miss you guys so much!

Mac: Do you miss me enough to come save me from this museum?

Mum: Not that much. Love you tho xxxxx

Mac and Benny: Love you too, Mum

I waited to see if anything else was going to come, but when the screen stayed blank, I slipped the phone into the seat pocket in front of me, waiting for the pangs of longing for my boys to subside. I was actually going to be on the same coast as them, although I would be about 250 miles further north. This was the longest I'd ever been away from them and it was sixteen days too many. Was this how it was going to be from now on? Separate holidays? And what about birthdays? Christmas?

I used to look forward and imagine our house of the future being like a John Lewis ad at Christmas. Or maybe Aldi. Mark and I would be dressed in matching festive jumpers, I'd be a size ten, because I'd finally mastered a diet, and the house would be decorated to grotto standard. 'Have Yourself A Merry Little Christmas' would be playing in the background, cinnamon candles burning, and we'd be beside ourselves with excitement when Mac, Benny, their wives and children burst in the door, for a week of wonderful food, games and long walks in the country-side. For the purposes of this dream, I overlooked the reality that I'd rather snuggle under a blanket with a cup of tea and a box of Matchmakers to watch *Love Actually* for the hundredth time than pull on outerwear and walk anywhere.

In all my fantasies of the future, never once had I been sitting on my own, with a microwave turkey dinner because it was the boys' turn to visit Mark that year. Or Mark and a new partner. Or Mark and his new partner and their triplets, who'd all wear matching elf hats and become a viral sensation. Or...

I stopped myself. Closed my eyes. I knew what was happening. My anxiety over New York was taking hold, and my imagination was pushing my brain to a place of doom that would crush me. I fought to get a grip on it. It would be fine. We'd work out a compromise. And if we didn't, I could always sit outside Mark's new house in my festive jumper, clutching a turkey sandwich and watching my sons have a great Christmas with their dad and their new step family.

Eyes still closed, I tried to control my breathing and slow it down. When I'd decided to leave Mark, I hadn't thought any of those things through. I'd just been in pain, and hurt, and desperate to be alone, so I'd gone into steamroller mode, making decisions, clearing the decks. Had I been too hasty? Should I have given it more time?

I picked up my phone again and typed some notes for another column.

Ten reasons to wait before calling time on a marriage.

Number one. Separate holidays.

Number two. You'll never be a John Lewis advert...

I was pretty sure I'd manage another eight before this trip was done.

* * *

It was after 7 p.m. when we touched down at LaGuardia. Outside the terminal, in the humid, sticky early-evening heat, we jumped in a cab and gave them the address to which I'd sent cards, gifts, and on one occasion, my children, for the last decade. My pulse quickened again just hearing it being said out loud.

In the back of the yellow cab, Kate slipped her hand into mine. 'You've got this,' she whispered.

I wasn't so sure. Every bone in my body wanted to have the car turn round and head right back to the airport.

Hannah and Ryan were six and five when I met them; gorgeous little things that were thankfully too small to realise why Mummy and Daddy didn't live together any more. Sarah's first husband, her children's father, had been an abusive sociopath who'd controlled her to the point that she wasn't allowed to leave the house without him. We had no idea. In our naïve and scattered youth, we'd all gone our own ways and when she'd stopped returning our calls, we'd let it slide. Big mistake. We got a chance to change that a few years later, when we met again. By that time, their father was out of their lives and it stayed that way.

Since then, Hannah and Ryan been family, like cousins to the rest of that generation in our self-built framily, but ones that lived so far away we hadn't been close by to hold their hands and help them through the loss of their mum.

For once, I wanted traffic to slow us down. Maybe a puncture. Anything to delay the inevitable.

We pulled up outside the destination on a beautiful tree-lined street in Greenwich Village in record time. The Gods really were messing with me today.

My heart was thudding, my palms were sweating, and with

every bit of me, I was dreading the reunion I'd been putting off since the last time I left this city, dressed in black and devastated.

I loved Hannah and Ryan with all my heart. Last time I saw them, after Sarah and Nick's funeral here in New York, they were still numb, catatonic with grief. Late that night, we'd stood on the Brooklyn Bridge and scattered their ashes into the East River and then we'd held each other, all of us together in our grief. But now, time had passed and they'd had chance to think, to work through timelines and apportion blame. Despite what the girls and Sam said, I knew it was all on me.

We buzzed the intercom on the brownstone and waited. Nothing. We buzzed again. It seemed like minutes, but it may only have been seconds, until a light behind the doorway came on.

The door opened and for a moment I couldn't comprehend what I was seeing. It was Sarah, standing there in the doorway, the light behind her like a halo, illuminating her long dark hair.

But it wasn't her. The hair was longer. The frame taller. The face younger. Hannah. At twenty-six, she was a mirror image of her mum at that age.

Carol, Jess and Kate stood back, as I walked towards Sarah's daughter, my arms automatically opening.

'I'm sorry,' I whispered, waiting for her reaction. No matter what she did, I would accept it.

Because whatever way the truth was sliced, diced or moulded, I was the reason that her mum wasn't answering the door here tonight.

20

GLASGOW, 1999
ETERNAL FLAME – THE BANGLES

'I still can't believe this is happening today,' Sarah had beamed, already looking so much younger than the person I'd bumped into in the frozen food aisle at Tesco just a couple of days before. We'd spent the last forty-eight hours joining the dots between our last meeting almost a decade ago and now. After hours of laughing, crying, regret and resolve, I'd persuaded her to come with me on my search for the second love of my life. Or was it the third? Nick Russo. The guy I'd met in Benidorm when I was seventeen and on my first and last holiday with my pals. He'd walked into a bar and I'd fallen in love with him on sight. I'd said goodbye to my virginity, and then, thirteen blissful nights later, I'd said goodbye to Nick. He'd made me promise we'd meet again one day.

Twelve years later, I'd travelled to his hometown of St Andrews hoping this was the day.

'Are you excited about finding him?' she'd asked, as we got dressed in the hotel that morning.

This was the first stop on my mission to track down all my ex-boyfriends, and I'd already blown my Mastercard on a swanky suite in the Old Course hotel, just because Sarah's face had lit up when we passed it on the way into town. If it didn't work out with Nick, there were five others to find after this one, so I was going to have to get either some self-control or yet another credit card.

After a bit of detective work, we'd discovered he was the owner of one of the most popular bar-restaurants in the town. He was thrilled to see us, and we'd had a long boozy dinner, before Sarah had bailed out and left Nick and I to have a romantic moonlit walk on the beach. Years of anticipation, months of planning, hours of preparation and I was finally back with him again and I felt... happy. Not blown away. Not blissed out. Not ecstatic to be close to him. Somewhere along my travels, we'd lost our romantic attraction.

The next morning, I took off to search for number two on the list – Joe Cain in Amsterdam. That could have been the end of Nick's chapter in my life, if it weren't for the fact that Sarah stayed behind for a few days and found her old self, her confidence and a husband. I wasn't the right girl for Nick, but that's because his perfect woman was my sweet, gorgeous friend. By the time my quest was over, they were engaged, and they married in a beautiful old church in St Andrews on a sunny day in the first May of the new century. Nick adopted Hannah and Ryan, by then seven and six, and claimed them as his own. The perfect family.

Three months later, they travelled with us to New York for my wedding to Mark and Sarah fell madly in love for the second time in a year, this time with the bustling, heady atmosphere of the Big Apple.

'I never want to leave here,' she'd announced, on the last day of the trip.

'Then don't,' I'd told her, pumped up on the roaring success of my mission. I'd taken a chance, I'd gone after what I wanted, and I'd reconnected with Mark, the boy I'd met at fourteen and dated on and off my whole life. The right one was there all along. I just had to take a risk to find him. 'You could stay here if you want to,' I went on, enthusiasm building. 'Why wouldn't you? Nick could open a bar here, you could teach, and the kids could have a great life.' The picture I painted was so vivid, my friend had bought the print.

Back in Scotland, Nick had franchised out his bar in St Andrews, then, over the next few years, he set about creating a chain of identical outlets across the UK and the east coast of America. He was able to get a US visa because he was investing in a business and bringing capital into the country. They went to court to get official permission to take Hannah and Ryan to live in the US and their biological father didn't fight it. He'd already moved on to his next family and had little interest in the one that had left him. The feeling was mutual.

New York was everything they hoped and they adored it unconditionally.

They created a life that was exactly as I'd drawn it. Nick's bar in New York, a cool, cosmopolitan speakeasy in SoHo, was a great success and Sarah landed a fabulous teaching role at the international school. We visited at least once a year, sometimes twice, determined to raise our children as one big extended family. Nick and Sarah Russo were set to live happily ever after.

Until they weren't.

In 2017, on a warm Sunday afternoon, my mobile phone rang.

'Girls, it's Sarah! She's on FaceTime,' I yelled to Kate, Carol and Jess, who immediately grabbed their drinks and came to join me at the table in my garden, leaving the rest of our broods to carry on cooking, chatting and, in the case of the kids, fighting a volleyball tournament to the death, using a large net curtain slung over my washing line.

'Happy birthday, Cooper!' she bellowed as soon as I answered the call.

'Thank you! God, I'm old. Ancient. We all are.'

'Except me,' Carol chirped. 'I'm frozen in time.'

'Only because you've had too much Botox,' Jess shot her down. Harsh but true.

'I wish you were here,' I wailed. 'It's been waaaay too long.'

'It has. Tell that husband of yours to get his act together. He's wrecking our social lives.' Sarah adored my husband, but she definitely disapproved of his workaholic habits. We'd planned to visit her twice that year already, and had to cancel both times because Mark couldn't get away from work. I hadn't seen her in person since they'd been over at Christmas and we missed them beyond words. 'Speaking of which, where is he?' she asked.

'Working,' I admitted, with a rueful grimace.

Sarah gasped. 'On a Sunday? When his wife's having a birthday party.'

'Don't get us started,' Kate cut in. 'We already plan to remind our darling Mark what his priorities should be. Although Jess seems to think she requires electric probes for his dangly bits to get the message across effectively.'

'Ouch,' Sarah squirmed. 'Although, if the end justifies the means...'

I went for a quick change of subject. 'Anyway, where's your other half?'

'He's still in bed. It's 8 a.m. here. We're having a lazy morning and then we're going to meet the kids for lunch.' She still called them kids, although Hannah was twenty-four and working in a real estate company and Ryan was twenty-three and in his final year at college.

'Did you decide what you're going to do for Nick's birthday yet?'

Mr Russo's big day was the week after mine. Over the years, we'd had many joint celebrations, and if it wasn't for Mark's errant priorities, we'd be over there right now, preparing for another one. This one was special – Nick was a few years older than us, so he was about to turn fifty.

'Uh, I've got nothing,' Sarah groaned. 'I want it to be something special, something he'll always remember.'

'What about...' I paused to build up the moment. 'Flying lessons! Nick would love that.'

'You think?' she asked, sounding doubtful.

'Absolutely!' I assured her. 'He mentioned having a hankering to learn the last time he was over here,' I enthused. 'That's it! It's the perfect present! And they do those dual lessons, so you could go with him.'

Sarah spluttered. 'I'd rather be subjected to Mark's electric probes.'

'Sarah Moore Russo, where is your sense of adventure?'

'I let it go for a lie-down about five years ago and I haven't seen it since,' she joked. 'You know I hate all that adrenalin-rush stuff. Besides, I'm flipping terrified of heights.'

That should have been it. I should have let it go. But at that moment I was so carried away with my own brilliant idea, so chuffed that I'd solved her problem, so determined to push her into something I thought she'd love, even if she wasn't sure herself, that I wouldn't let it go.

'Book it! It'll be amazing and I promise you'll thank me. He'll be completely blown away and, you never know, you might catch the bug. If so, we demand to be flown anywhere for free until we croak,' I joked, loving her giggle on the other end.

At some point that week, on my stupid advice, Sarah booked a joint flying lesson for her and Nick, and another ten for him to do alone.

The following Sunday, they showed up at the local, provincial airport that was the base for the flying school.

A terrified, apprehensive Sarah, and a delighted Nick, climbed into a Cessna, with an instructor of twenty years.

One that had been out playing poker and drinking Jim Beam with his mates until 3 a.m. that morning.

Forty-seven minutes later, the pilot made a mayday call.

Thirty seconds later, the plane came down, crashed into an electricity pylon and then finally came to rest when it landed on a nearby lake.

The investigation would conclude that there was a mechanical issue which almost certainly caused the crash, but the situation was exacerbated by the reduced faculties of the pilot, due to lack of sleep.

It ruled accident, and fell short of naming who was at fault.

It didn't have to because we all knew it was me.

The truth was, if it weren't for my crazy ideas, Sarah Moore would never have met Nick Russo.

If I hadn't got married in New York, Sarah wouldn't have visited that city that year.

If it weren't for my encouragement to live in the moment and go after what she wanted, she might never have packed up her whole life and moved to New York.

If I hadn't given her that idea for an adrenalin rush and badgered her into booking the flying lessons for Nick, she'd never have organised that flight.

And if they'd never taken that flight, they wouldn't have died when it crashed to the ground, claiming the lives of everyone on board.

If it weren't for me and my stupid, ill-thought out schemes and exploits, Sarah and Nick would still be alive, and Hannah and Ryan would still have their parents. I might not have caused the engine to fail, or poured bourbon down the pilot's throat, but if I hadn't coaxed Sarah into going there, she'd never have been in that situation.

So what right did I have to live my life like nothing had happened? What right did I have to sleep easy at night, to love and to seek love back, when Sarah had lost it all?

How could I possibly be happy, when my recklessness had taken away two people we loved, and left nothing behind but guilt, sorrow and holes in our lives where Nick and Sarah Russo used to be?

21

NEW YORK, AUGUST, 2019

Sarah and Nick were everywhere in their home. They were in the black-framed photographs that lined the hallway, showing unposed images of family moments throughout the years. They were in the duck egg blue of the wall panels – Sarah's favourite colour. And they were in the plaid of the carpet runner that climbed the stairs, St Andrews tartan, a nod to the town Nick grew up in.

Sarah was there, right there, in the face of her daughter. It took my breath away to see how much Hannah resembled her mum now. The long dark hair, pulled back in a low, messy pony-tail, escaped tendrils framing her face. The smile, too. Wide, open, but hinting at a shyness that lingered just under the surface.

At the door, we hugged like we were hanging on in a storm, until Carol interrupted the moment. 'Right, you two, I love you both, but if you don't let me past, I may pee in the hallway and I'm trying to stop doing that when I go to other people's homes.'

My tears turned to gratitude for the perfect distraction. 'My sister-in-law, ladies and gentlemen,' I said solemnly, standing back for her to sweep past.

'Come in, come in,' Hannah beckoned. 'Leave your bags there and we can sort them out later.'

We followed her into the kitchen. Like Kate, Sarah's homes had always had a table in the middle of the room, operation central for her family and friends, and we all automatically took the chairs that we'd sat in on the many times we'd visited this house before. I couldn't bring myself to look at the empty one at the end of the long plank of glossy ebony.

'Coffee or wine?' Hannah asked.

Kate and Jess were in sync with, 'Wine.'

'Coffee,' I said, at the same time. I didn't want to say that my choice was influenced by worry that a drink or two would make it impossible to maintain the gargantuan effort it was taking to hold it together.

Hannah flicked a button on the integrated barista machine on the wall of the gloss cream units behind her. The kitchen had been Nick's domain. RUSSO, his restaurant in St Andrews, the one we'd tracked him down to all those years before, had turned out to be just the first in a chain of six: two in Scotland, one in Manhattan, two in upstate New York and his newest one, opened just before his death, in New Jersey.

When he died, Hannah had stepped up from her management role in HR to take over the company, a transition made easier because she'd worked part-time in the restaurants since she was a teenager, so she was familiar with every aspect of the operation. If only Sarah could see how brilliant her daughter had been since her parent died...

I stopped myself. *Hold it together.*

Hannah chatted as she poured the wine. 'Ryan said to say hi and sorry he couldn't be here.'

Ryan was younger than Hannah by a year and a half, so they'd always been close. A sporty kid, Sarah had been thrilled when Ryan had landed a four-year soccer scholarship at a college in Columbia, South Carolina. He'd graduated just a few weeks after the accident and I knew from Hannah's emails that he'd found it difficult to adjust to his whole life changing in such a short space of time.

'How's he doing?' Kate asked, taking the first full glass.

Hannah hesitated. 'It was rough at first...' She didn't need to elaborate. 'But he's getting there. You know he spent the last couple of years drifting in and out of jobs, just trying to find his place, but now that he's gone back to South Carolina he's so much better.' The previous January, Ryan had been offered the role of assistant soccer coach at the college he'd attended for four years.

Hannah's relief was palpable as she went on, 'He's so happy to be back there and I think it's helped beyond words that he's somewhere he feels comfortable and that he belongs. They're like family and they're taking care of him.'

Every one of us at the table understood that concept.

There was a click of sky-scraper heels as Carol charged back into the room, hair scraped back from her face, already changed into a body-hugging red minidress that clung to her every curve. 'Okay, my Uber is outside.' I'd completely forgotten that the initial purpose of this trip was for her to attend some flash launch. 'I'm off. I'll be back as soon as they've milked me to a dry husk for the sake of corporate profits.' And she called me dramatic.

Jess went for the cynical approach. 'You mean as soon as they've plied you with food and champagne, and paid you massive sums of money to have your photograph taken next to some ridiculously expensive, price-inflated piece of technology that was probably built for twenty quid in a factory with the bare minimum of health and safety standards?'

Carol stopped, and I was pretty sure I almost saw a frown line. It was either a trick of the light or a definite indication that she needed to top up her Botox. 'Yep,' she said, as if it was obvious. 'That's exactly what I said.' She blew us a kiss and then her heels clicked right out the door.

For the next couple of hours, mostly thanks to Jess and Kate keeping everything light and chatty, the conversation flowed. We talked about everything except the people that connected us. It was superficial. Breezy. Like the conversation you would have with a casual friend. Not the difficult, antagonistic conversation that needed to be had between people who were grieving and those who were responsible for that pain. Sure, Hannah was making an effort to be polite tonight, but she couldn't look me in the eye. This was all surface stuff and I knew she was only behaving this way because Sarah had brought her up well.

She kept up the façade of normality until we'd exhausted all areas of small talk, and a painful silence descended. To my surprise, it was Hannah who broke it first.

'Mum would love that you're all here,' she said, leaning over to refill Kate and Jess's glasses. 'I'm glad that you called me, Aunt Kate. I really am.'

Kate reached for her hand. 'Me too. I can't tell you how much we've missed you.'

Hannah bustled to her feet, perhaps unable to bear the emotion of the moment.

'Another coffee, Aunt Carly?' It was the first time she'd actually made eye contact with me.

I shook my head and Kate glanced at me, checking up on how I was doing.

Hold it together.

'Anyone fancy a walk?' I blurted, suddenly feeling a desperate need to get some air into my lungs before my chest exploded.

Jess didn't even try to hide her initial reaction of horror. I knew she'd much rather take a cosy kitchen with wine and snacks than outdoor exercise on a warm Manhattan night. 'You want me to walk? For no purpose? There isn't a shopping mall or a bar at the end of it?'

'No purpose at all,' I confirmed. 'Just a walk.'

'I think that's a great idea,' Kate jumped in, sussing that the walls were closing in on me and I just needed some space.

'Me too,' Hannah agreed, her relief visible.

The clock on the wall showed eleven o'clock when we passed it on the way out. The temperature had dropped outside, but it was still warm and humid. Without making a plan, we turned right and began to walk, no destination in mind. The pavements were narrow, so Jess and Hannah naturally fell into step in front, with Kate and I behind them.

'How are you holding up, honey?' she asked me, in hushed tones that couldn't be heard by the two in front.

'My heart is breaking for her and I can't stand the thought that me being here must be so painful for her.' I could have said so much more. That my heart was racing. That the guilt was crushing me. That I'd do anything at all to take back what I'd done.

Kate's pace slowed so the gap was a little bigger, making sure our conversation was only between us. 'You need to talk to her. It's the only thing that is going to help.'

'I know.' I did. I just wanted to wait for the right moment. But was there ever a right moment to bring up something as important at this?

We turned left off 6th Avenue on to Canal Street, the cafés and food outlets still open and busy. I'd walked the streets of New

York many times in my life, absorbing the energy of the city, but tonight, nothing could get past the feelings of sadness. New York would always be Sarah's city. Without her, it didn't feel the same.

We were still wandering with no real purpose, turning corners, crossing roads, when I caught sight of a building so familiar it took my breath away. The blond stone steps of the New York City Marriage Bureau were just in front of us.

Kate registered my sharp intake of breath, and knew exactly what had caused it.

'Anyone want to sit for a while?' she asked.

'Yes!' Jess blurted, before realising where we were and laughing. 'Oh my God, that was one of the best days ever.'

Hannah looked confused as she sank down on to the steps next to us. The four of us were in a row, huddled together so we could hear each other clearly.

'Carly and your Uncle Mark got married here. Only it nearly didn't happen because we all got waylaid in a bar round the corner and we were having much too much fun to interrupt it for the actual ceremony bit.'

Hannah pulled her knees up and wrapped her arms around them. 'The bar is a McDonald's now.'

Something inside me deflated at that announcement. Sometimes progress sucked.

Chin on her knees now, Hannah went on, 'My mum pointed it out to me years ago. She told me that story so many times. It sounded like quite a day.'

'It was perfect.' I wasn't entirely sure if I'd said that out loud. 'The perfect day with the perfect people. I wouldn't change a thing.' I definitely vocalised that because I could hear my voice crack as I ended the sentence.

Hold it together.

I've no idea why that suddenly seemed like the right place to have the conversation I'd been avoiding for so long. Perhaps it was the feeling that this was somewhere I'd felt so loved, so protected. Mark and I had been so completely and spectacularly in love. My girlfriends had been by my side. And life had yet to kick the crap out of my naïve optimism that nothing could touch us, that we were an unbreakable gang who would live the best lives.

'Hannah, I'm so sorry,' I said, repeating my words from earlier, but this time, having the strength to go further. 'I know you and Ryan must blame me for your mum and Nick's deaths and I understand. I really do. I blame me too. I know it's a cliché, but I'd do anything to be able to go back and do it all differently and I'd give anything to have them here with us. I don't know what I can say to you, because words can't bring them back, but I didn't want you to think I've just moved on with my life. I can't. And the reason that I'm not asking you to forgive me is because I know you never could. I'll never forgive myself either.'

Her eyes, her mother's eyes, were cloudy as she turned to me, and I saw her brow crease. 'I don't understand.'

My heart sank. I was making an arse of this. Making it worse. I needed to explain myself better. I was still trying to find the words, when she continued.

'Aunt Carly, why would you think you were responsible?'

There was screaming, the uncontrollable, excruciating sound of pain, but it was all inside my skull. She didn't know. She had no idea. But...

'I pushed your mum into buying the flying lessons for Nick. She wasn't sure and I coaxed her into it. And if I hadn't...'

'No,' she interrupted me. 'Aunt Carly, that's not how it happened at all.'

My throat was tight as I answered. 'What do you mean?'

I watched as her body slumped, as if she was finally taking a stone out of a dyke and letting the grief consume her. She sobbed, a heart-breaking, guttural sound that made me fly to her side, so that I could wrap my arms around her. Her whole body shook as she wept in my arms, and my heart broke for this young woman who'd been through so much.

Eventually, as her tears slowed, there was sadness in every word as she began to explain. 'I know my mum spoke to you about the flying lessons, but she decided not to do it.'

Now I was the one who didn't understand.

'Then Nick borrowed her laptop and he saw the website there, realised what she was planning. He was so into it, and gutted when I told him that she'd changed her mind. Me. It was me. And I was the one who played a game between them. Nick told me not to let her know he'd found out, but to persuade her to do it because he thought it would be a blast. So I did. I coaxed her into booking it, even though she was so scared, and I thought I was so smart, because Nick was delighted. Then...' Another sob. 'Then they died. I understand how you've been feeling, Aunt Carly, because it's exactly how I've felt from the moment I found out they were gone.'

As her tears fell in rivers, Jess and Kate reached out to her too, desperately trying to use physical touch to sooth her.

A couple with a small dog walked past us, just giving a glance to the four women on the steps, one of them holding another, tears blinding all of them.

'That's why I couldn't face you all since the funeral. I know how much you loved her and the thought of seeing you just killed me because, to me, you're all part of her. It just hurt too much. I'm so sorry. I know I should have been braver. Just one more regret on the pile. I wish I could go back, I wish I could change every-thing,' she was choking out the words now.

My arms were still around her as I held her tightly, stroking her hair. 'No, no, no, you don't have to apologise to us. Hannah, it wasn't your fault. It really wasn't. It was just fate. Just the way things turned out.' Even as I was saying it, the blanket of angst and despair and regret and rage that had clouded every day since Sarah died began to lift, replaced with nothing but concern for this special woman.

It took a few moments, but Hannah eventually pulled back, used the bottom of her T-shirt to wipe her face, managed something close to a smile. 'You weren't saying that a minute ago when you were blaming yourself,' she said, with the kind of understated, acute perception that her mother delivered into every messed-up situation I found myself in.

'I know, but I've got double standards and I reserve the right to use them whenever it suits me.'

Like a lifetime of moments I'd spent with Sarah, Carol, Kate and Jess, we somehow pivoted from tears of devastation to the comfort of laughter.

'That's very true,' Kate confirmed, as an explosion of feelings hijacked my mind. Sorrow for Hannah, who'd borne the weight of this unfounded guilt. Incredible relief as a chunk snapped off my own mountain of guilt. Sadness that we'd waited so long to have this conversation and an overwhelming regret that we had been so wrapped up in our own self-loathing that we hadn't found a way to comfort each other over the last two years.

'Now you know all this, you don't hate me? You're not disgusted?' Hannah went on.

'Hannah, please... we love you. You did nothing wrong. And I know if your mum was sitting here right now, she'd be mad as hell at you for blaming yourself. You need to let it go, my love. You need to forgive yourself because no one, including your mum and Nick, would ever blame you for this. Let those feelings go.'

'I don't know if I can,' she said, her expression earnest, full of sorrow.

'Well, you have to,' I said, squeezing her again. 'You now have four aunts who know exactly what's going on and we're not standing for it. Actually, three, but we'll fill Carol in later.'

Hannah managed a sad smile. 'I always loved your friendship, you know. My mum used to say that, after us, it was the biggest blessing in her life.'

'Ours too,' Kate said. 'That's why we're here. And we've got you, Hannah, we really have. None of this is on you, I promise.'

A hesitation, then Hannah dried her eyes again. 'Okay. Thank you. So much. I can't tell you how much this means to me.' We could all see that she meant every word.

Another few moments passed in a soothing silence as we all rebalanced on the shifting landscape of the truth. I hadn't caused the accident. All this time, beating myself up, had been so point-less and there was such a release in that. But...

'Are we good?' Jess asked, sniffing, then kicking in with a bit of levity. 'Any other problems? Any more irrational regrets or feel-ings that we want to discuss?'

I shrugged awkwardly, making both Kate and Jess groan.

'What?' Jess asked, exasperated.

'It's just that...' I paused, then decided to get it all off my chest. My guilt may have decreased, but it hadn't been wiped out completely. 'I can't help wondering what would have happened if my crazy scheme hadn't brought them together in the first place. That was the first step and it was down to me. If I hadn't been so reckless and fickle, Sarah could have met someone else, had a completely different life.'

Hannah thought about that for a moment, before pushing herself up from the stone step. 'I think we should go home. You need to see something,' she told me. 'You all do.'

22

NEW YORK, HALF AN HOUR LATER

RISE UP – ANDRA DAY

In the centre of the screen, Sarah was sitting in an overstuffed cream armchair, her dark hair loose around her shoulders, just a bit of mascara and lip gloss on her beautiful face. The pale blue of her shirt brought out the indigo of her eyes, and her straight-leg jeans were the old battered favourites that she'd had since we were teenagers. She'd found it hilarious that the tears and frayed patches, earned over years of wear, had caught up with today's fashions to make her trendy. Her legs were pulled up beneath her, and her feet were bare. It could be a scene from a Ralph Lauren campaign, the casual elegance of a woman who was absolutely comfortable in her own skin.

Hannah's face filled the viewer now, her eyes investigating something on the top of the camera, checking a setting or perhaps adjusting a lens. At maybe nineteen or twenty, the confidence that maturity had given her wasn't quite there yet and she chewed her bottom lip as she worked.

'Okay, Mum, I think that's it,' she said, backing up, satisfied that she'd mastered the video. With the same easy grace as her mother, she took the other armchair in the frame, identical to her mum's, separated by a small, beautifully carved, dark wood side table. I recognised it. Not long after Sarah and Nick and the kids had moved here, I was visiting her for a few days and we'd spotted it in a mid-town flea market. Sarah had fallen in love with it, but she was never one to indulge herself. I'd circled back the following day and bought it for her birthday. When I gave it to her, she'd cried. They'd moved a few times since then, but the table always went with them, and now it was in the corner of her bedroom, between the armchairs they were sitting in.

Hannah pulled her legs up underneath her, mirroring Sarah, subconsciously chewing the end of her pen as she checked the notepad on her knee, then spoke to Sarah. 'Remember, don't refer to me in the first person – speak like you're talking to strangers who don't know you. Don't worry about any mistakes though, Mum, I'll edit them out.'

'I think you might have to edit a whole lot of this out,' Sarah said, flashing that shy grin that was so quintessentially her. 'I reserve the right to approve the final edit. You know, like Beyoncé.' That made them both giggle, their laughs so similar it was like listening to the same sound in stereo.

Hannah turned to face the camera, cleared her throat, projected her voice in a very succinct and professional way. 'Hannah Russo. Psychology. Interview with Sarah Russo on 14 July 2015. Topic: The Science of Soulmates. Sarah...' Hannah began, and her mum's expression flinched with surprise and a little amusement. Not 'mum' any more then. 'We've had many discussions on the subject of soulmates. As you know, many in the science world believe that the concept of soulmates is a romantic notion with no basis in fact. Yet, you are a firm believer in soulmates and their validity in our lives. Today I'd like to talk to you about why you hold those beliefs.'

Hannah cleared her throat again and any parent who'd ever

watched their child at a sports event, or a recital, or a concert would recognise Sarah's expression of encouragement and pride.

'So tell me,' Hannah went on, eyes flicking to her notes again. 'What does the term "soulmate" mean to you?'

Sarah took a moment to consider her answer. That was her way. She was thoughtful, pensive – qualities that were there when we were kids, but that really came into play when she qualified as a teacher and knew that everything she said reached the ears of people who could be inspired or informed by her words.

'I think that the answer is right there,' she said softly. 'To me, a soulmate is someone you are destined to be with, someone who is connected to you at the very deepest level, with an unbreakable bond that endures a lifetime.'

Hannah nodded while her mum spoke, her eyes flickering occasionally to her notepad, queuing up the next question. 'Do you feel you have a soulmate?'

Sarah's smile widened. 'I do.'

'Can you tell me when you discovered that, how it came about?'

Again, Sarah paused, reflected. 'I discovered that the night I met my husband. It's a funny story...' Sarah leaned forward, speaking in hushed tones. 'Do you want me to actually share the story of how we met? Give all the details?'

Hannah leaned forward, matched Sarah's tone. 'Erm, yes please. If you just tell me everything, I can edit out the bits that aren't relevant later.'

'Okay.'

They both sat back, cleared their throats, smoothed down their shirts and adopted the professional posture they'd had before.

'I met my husband back in 1999. Actually, that's not quite true. I met him for the first time when I was seventeen years old, on holiday in Benidorm. I had a holiday romance with his friend, and he had a holiday romance with mine. I guess in a way it was the perfect start to an unusual story, that, to me, shows how sometimes fate leads you to where you're meant to be and to who you're meant to be with.'

There was a brief pause as she gathered her thoughts. 'I'd just come out of an incredibly toxic relationship. I won't go into the details...' For all of Hannah and Ryan's lives she'd protected them from the truth about who and what their father really was: an abusive, controlling bully who treated Sarah like a possession. 'I'll just say that I finally found the courage and opportunity to leave him. At that point, I pretty much thought my life was all mapped out for me. I'd gone back to college to train to be a teacher, I had two young children, and I had no time or energy for relationships. More than that, I wasn't interested in meeting someone. I'd seen the worst of what relationships could bring and I was so happy to have escaped, that I promised myself I'd never jeopardise my freedom again.'

Hannah was still listening, her head moving slowly up and down, reinforcing the validity of her mother's points.

'It was a shock, then, when serendipity led to a meeting with an old friend I'd lost contact with. You see, there had been a group of us that had been inseparable for years, until my husband had effectively cut everyone I loved out of my life. One of the great joys was to rediscover those friendships again.'

Hannah still said nothing, letting her mother's story unfold.

'My friend was going to meet an ex-boyfriend, the holiday romance from many years before, that she wanted to reconnect with, and she persuaded me to go with her. My children were spending time with their father, and I had nothing planned so I went along with it, just delighted to laugh again. It had been a long time...'

A breath, then she shook off the sadness.

'So I went. My friend...' She broke off, leaned forward, and went to informal, hushed tones again. 'It was your Aunt Carly, you know that, don't you?'

'Mum, how many times have I heard this story?' Hannah drawled. 'Of course I know.'

'Okay,' Sarah whispered, then sat back and reverted to her camera tone. 'When we met my friend's ex, it became clear that there was no longer any chemistry there, no romantic interest from either of them, but I had a very different experience. As soon as I saw Nick, it was like a bridge came down and joined us. It was like I knew him. I could see who he was. It was unexpected, especially as I'd met him very briefly many years before and barely remembered him, yet this time... it was like finding a piece of me that I didn't know I'd lost. The wonderful thing was, he felt the same. I've heard people talk of love at first sight, and I believe that exists.' A low chuckle escaped her. 'The friend I mentioned earlier swears she's experienced that many times.' That thought obviously amused her and I felt my heart swell a little because she was referring to me with such amusement and tenderness in her voice.

I watched, spellbound, as she went on, 'But I think this was more than that. It was a recognition. A feeling of having found your person. A deep connection that felt like coming home, of being exactly where you belonged, a love that was so strong it could endure anything.' She broke off. 'Is that too cheesy?'

Hannah rolled her eyes. 'You're always too cheesy, Mum. It's who you are.'

Their giggles were infectious.

'Right, I'm going to come in with a question.' Eyes down to the pad again, then back to her mum. 'So what you're saying, Sarah, is that you and Nick recognised each other as soulmates?'

Sarah nodded. 'Yes. Because this felt like it was more than just a meeting in this lifetime. I don't know whether I believe in reincarnation, but I choose to believe that Nick and I knew each other in another lifetime. Our souls are intertwined. And when our story ends in this life, we'll be together in the next one too.'

'And Aunt Ca—' Hannah stopped. 'And your friend, the one who led you to your husband, did she find her soulmate too?'

Sarah thought about that for several seconds. 'Yes, I think she did. But, here's the thing. I think "soulmates" are more than just romantic partners. I truly believe my children and my four closest friends are my soulmates too. In this life, that friend led me to where I was supposed to be. I've had the most incredible marriage, and there are no words to express how blissful my life has turned out to be. No matter what happens over the coming years, I'll always be grateful because I found the people I belong with.'

'And if there is a next life?' Hannah asked, her academic interest in the topic now replaced by something more emotional, as if this were just a mother and a daughter, having one of those beautiful moments that they would always remember and treasure.

'Then I'll find my children and those friends in that one too.'

'Okay, Mum, thanks. That's perfect. I'm gonna ace this course.' A giggle, then a pause. 'I've got a question, though. Not for the tape, just for me,' Hannah said, although obviously the tape was still running. 'If you could change anything about your life, what would it be?'

Sarah didn't even pause before answering. 'Not a thing. I know that's a cliché, but I truly mean it. You and Ryan are everything. Nick is the other half of me. And my girls, your aunts, are my sisters. I'd have felt lucky to even have one of those blessings in my life, but to have so many...' she tailed off, and I could see a tear running down her cheek. 'Because of you all, I know what love is. I know how to give it and I know that I'm loved. And really, that's all that we want in life. Love. Compassion. Forgiveness. Acceptance. Laughter. To have people who care if you're happy, who will celebrate with you, and who'll stand beside you in your worst moments. I have that. So no, I'd change nothing. No matter what happens, I've lived my best life.'

The camera clicked, then the screen faded to black. For several moments, no one spoke, all of us struck dumb with grief, with love, and with absolute gratitude that we'd been Sarah Moore Russo's people.

The sound of the doorbell was a snap back to the present. Hannah got up to answer it, while Jess, Kate and I stayed with our thoughts.

'She lived her best life,' I repeated, intertwined triffids of sadness and happiness strangling my words.

Next to me, Kate nodded slowly, playing with the bangles on my wrist as she spoke. 'And if she hadn't met Nick that wouldn't have happened. You need to let it go, Carly. All of it. Every bit of guilt and grief.'

Before I could answer, the door opened.

'What did I miss?' a tipsy Carol chirped, then sensing the atmosphere, 'Oh fuck, who died?'

Somewhere in my head, I could hear Sarah howling with laughter at that. She always loved a bit of gallows humour.

The clock on the wall chimed 2 a.m., but suddenly I wasn't tired.

'Sod it, come on,' I said, jumping up, grabbing the bottle of wine from the table. In the first act of old, spontaneous Carly Cooper that I'd manage to muster up in a long time, I got bossy. 'We're going out again.'

'I've just got in,' Carol objected. 'And my feet are killing me.'

'Put your trainers on,' I ordered, summoning an Uber on my phone.

And that's how, twenty minutes later, five women, one of them in a very flash evening dress and trainers, stood on the Brooklyn Bridge, the place we'd scattered Sarah and Nick's ashes, sharing a bottle of wine.

'To Sarah,' Kate said, taking a swig, then giving the bottle to Jess.

'To friends. And to forever love,' Jess said, with uncharacteristic emotion, before taking a drink and passing it along.

Carol held the bottle up to the stars. 'To us and to Sarah and Nick, who'll always be together.'

My turn next. I took the bottle in one hand, and slipped my other one into Hannah's hand as I turned to face her. 'To letting go of guilt and sadness. Because the most special woman in the world would want us to. Both of us.'

I took a sip and then passed the bottle on to Hannah.

'To my mum and Nick,' she said, holding the bottle high. 'And to my aunts, who are four of the greatest gifts my mum ever gave me. And to living your best life.'

'To living your best life,' we echoed.

In my mind, I heard Sarah's voice again, and she was telling me to get started.

23

NEW YORK, THE NEXT MORNING
STRONGER – KELLY CLARKSON

The sun was streaming in the window of the bedroom when the beep of an incoming text and a feeling of suffocation woke me.

'Carol! Carol!' I croaked, nudging her in the ribs. 'You're cutting off my windpipe. I think I'm close to death.'

There was a rush of oxygen as she lifted the arm that was slung over my neck, murmuring, 'Sorry. Thought you were Callum. You smell the same. Is that weird?'

Was it weird that I smelled the same as my forty-eight-year-old brother? 'Yep.'

She pushed herself up and pulled off her sleeping mask, to reveal a scrubbed-clean, flawless face.

'What is wrong with you?' I asked her, appalled. 'Why can't you come home drunk, stay up talking until 4 a.m., then wake up the next morning with last night's make-up on, looking completely crap like us normal people?'

She just pulled her mask back over her eyes and ignored me.

'Whassup?' Kate groaned from the next bed, squinting against the sunlight.

We were in Sarah's guest room – my favourite bedroom in the

house. White bleached floors, and walls that were a riotous stipple of her favourite shades of blue, it had two double beds, with a huge chaise that doubled as a single bed over at the window. Sarah had designed it that way so that the five of us could sleep in the same room when we visited. Said she didn't want to waste a moment that we could be together, so she'd leave her own bedroom and come and sleep here with us so we could talk until we drifted off. Those were some of the very best times of my life.

I waited to be felled by the pain that thoughts like that brought me, but to my surprise I felt my cheeks lift into a smile. A sad smile, but still a smile. Carol's arm of crushing death aside, I felt lighter. Like I'd had a weight on my chest and now I could breathe properly again for the first time in months. Years. Last night had changed everything and I felt... It took me a moment to name it: free.

I pushed myself up on my elbow and spotted the vacant area of Kate's bed. 'Where's Jess?'

Kate scanned the room, like she expected Jess to be hiding behind a plant. 'Dunno. Must be downstairs.'

'I went down for a glass of water an hour ago and she wasn't there,' Carol murmured, making me panic and reach for my phone. If she'd gone out, she would have texted. Yep, there it was.

Two texts waiting. I opened the one that had arrived at 9.17 a.m. from Jess.

Gone out for a run. Won't be long.

Dear God. One friend who looks like a goddess, and another one who voluntarily does exercise after only five hours sleep.

'She's gone out for a run. Forget what I said about you lot last night. I need new pals, ones who handle hangovers with carbohydrates. Why is she jogging alone, without telling us she was going? There are way too many serial killers out there.'

'And you need to stop watching the crime channel,' Kate countered.

Beep! I jumped as my phone rudely chided me that I hadn't yet opened the other text. I pressed on it, my cheeks automatically going to a grin when I saw it was on the family group chat.

Mac: Mum, guess where we are?

Me: Jail?

Mac: Nope.

Me: Court?

Mac: Nope.

Me: Michael Jordan's house?

Mac: You're not taking this seriously.

Beside me, Carol groaned again. 'What is that noise? Carly, open a window and throw a shoe at whoever is making that bloody racket. Use one of my Louboutins. I'll take the loss.'

'What?' I lifted my gaze from my phone and immediately heard what she was referring to. Outside, someone was sounding their horn like their life depended on it. I fired off another text to Mac.

Mum to Mac: I am interested! But if it's anything dangerous, I don't want to know.

I pressed send, then climbed out of bed and padded over to the window, glancing down when Mac replied.

Mac: Definitely dangerous.

'I swear I'm going to murder Mark when I get a hold of him,' I muttered to no one, as I reached over to pull the curtains back. 'He's being a complete... Aaaaaaaaaargh!!!!!'

My scream brought Carol and Kate rushing to the window.

'Serial killer?' Carol gasped as she moved. She'd never been great at reading reactions.

It was a scream of pure joy, not fear, as on the street below was a huge white RV, and on top of it, waving at us, were Mac and Benny.

I threw my head back, exploding with laughter, then opened the window.

'You two get down from there right now or I'll tell your mother and I've heard she's a total dragon,' I warned them, laughing. The neighbours must be wondering what the hell was going on. We were definitely lowering the tone of the neighbourhood.

'She is,' Mac shouted back. 'But we put up with her because she feeds us.'

'I've absolutely no idea how you managed to raise such cool kids,' Kate teased.

I was already on the way out of the room, rushing down the stairs, reaching the front door just as Hannah was pulling it open.

'I think you've got visitors,' she said, chuckling. Her face had a brightness that wasn't there last night either. We'd both found some kind of solace and peace.

The boys stormed in, and were accosted by hugs from everyone in the house, Kate and Carol squealing with delight as they cuddled their nephews. Back at the doorway, I watched as

Mark jumped out of the RV and walked towards me. For a moment, it felt like some kind of time warp. I'd only seen him two weeks ago, but he looked different. Or perhaps I was just seeing him differently, through eyes that weren't watching the world through a veil of guilt and sadness.

His jeans were his favourites, Levi's that I'd bought him years ago because I thought they made him look like George Michael in the 'Faith' video. His white T-shirt showed off his tanned arms, his hair was a little longer, flopping over his forehead, the way that it used to do when we were young and crazy in love. The whole picture, the mood, my happiness, the sheer joy at seeing my boys, somehow it all combined to make me throw my arms around him.

'What are you doing here?' I quickly realised that, especially given our recent tensions, that question could be misinterpreted, so I swiftly corrected myself. 'I mean, I'm so glad you're here! It's amazing!'

'Oh, we were just in the neighbourhood and thought we'd pop by.' Did I mention he smelled good too? 'Is it okay?' he asked, suddenly uncertain. 'If it's not a good time, or if you still have things to work out, I'll grab the boys and take off. I just knew it would be tough for you to come here so I thought seeing the kids might make you feel better.'

Oh, my God, this man. He drove me crazy, but there was no arguing with the fact that he'd been in my life forever, and much as some of it had been awful, he'd always been on my side. Well, mostly. Unless the tussle was between me and his work, in which case he bought popcorn and waited for me to keep swinging until I passed out from frustration.

'What did I miss?' came a voice from behind him, as Jess wandered up the path. 'Is it "phone in an ex-husband" day?' Only I'd rather not play that game.'

Jess's antagonistic relationship with her ex-husband Mike was the stuff of legend. It was about as vicious as it got and had been that way since she caught him cheating on her.

'Yeah, it's a new service. I'm on an app,' Mark joked with her. They'd always had similar senses of humour, so, ever since we were teenagers in the same gang at school, they'd had a high sarcasm brother/sister vibe.

I intervened before she could come back with something inappropriately cutting. 'Mark brought the boys to visit,' I explained, ushering her in.

Mark followed us into the kitchen, where Kate and Carol were helping Hannah, who was already grilling bacon and pouring a white gloop into a waffle maker. My boys would never want to leave.

Mark joined them, pulling out the seat next to Mac, while I sat across from him next to Benny.

'I may hug you many times in the next few minutes,' I told my youngest son. 'So brace yourself and take one for the team. And don't think you're safe over there,' I gestured to Mac. 'There are plenty more hours in the day.'

'Save me,' he said to his dad, out of the corner of his mouth. 'I'll pay you money.'

My mind took a snapshot of the image. Mark, Mac, Benny and me, around a table, all tanned, healthy, laughing at our bad jokes. We'd used to have so many moments like this. When had they stopped? When had we let it go?

I shook it off. This wasn't a time for reflection. If hearing Sarah's words last night had taught me anything it was that I had to live in the moment. Seize the day. And this one came with my boys, my friends and waffles.

'Okay, so tell me everything,' I begged, squeezing Benny, who launched into a blow-by-blow account of every day of the trip so far. The adventure, the excitement, the laughter, the fights – all of which were between him and his brother, and all of them, he claimed, were Mac's fault. Mac took it on the chin and didn't argue. Or perhaps he was just too busy focusing on his food.

They'd finished their brunch by the time we got up to the present moment. 'And then yesterday, when we were in Washington DC and you said you were coming to New York, Dad worked out that it would only take us four hours to drive here, so we decided to surprise you.'

It had taken over thirty years of knowing him, but Mark had finally shocked me. This was the kind of thing that I'd do, and he'd spend hours with a flow chart explaining why it was such a bad idea and pointing out the potential pitfalls. He didn't do spontaneous. He didn't do random acts of madness. Maybe the bungee jump had given him concussion and this temporary episode of crazy fun was the result.

The concussed one had a question. 'What time is your flight back to LA?'

Shit. The flight. They were just here, and I was going to have to leave them.

Carol checked her phone. 'In... three hours. Actually, we should probably start getting organised.'

My heart sank. I wasn't ready. It was too rushed.

'What are your plans for today?' I asked the boys, trying to keep it light and hide the fact that I was contemplating handcuffing myself to Benny's wrist.

'We thought we'd go to Central Park for the rest of the day, then maybe catch a comedy show or a movie tonight. Then we thought we'd maybe do the Natural History Museum tomorrow...'

'Shoot me,' Mac begged. 'Or at least drop me at a basketball court and come get me when the geek is done with the boring stuff.'

I was fairly sure the geek made a rude gesture to his brother, but my mind was on other things.

'Mum, I wish you weren't going back today because you could have come with us and...'

'I'll stay!' I blurted. 'Just for another day. I soooooo need some boy time.'

'Seriously? Yasssss!' Benny cheered.

Lots of other actions happened at precisely that moment. Carol, Kate and Jess's heads whipped round in my direction, Hannah grinned and nudged Mac with her shoulder. 'Told you I was keeping you here,' she giggled, looking thrilled at this development. So like Sarah. She took everything in her stride with a huge smile too.

Meanwhile, I looked searchingly at my soon-to-be-ex-husband.

'I mean, if that's okay with you?'

What if he said no? What if he was horrified? Thought I was crashing his party? Muscling in on his time with our sons?

Yet, the way he was staring at me...

Mark Barwick, my soon-to-be-ex-husband, smiled.

'That's definitely okay with me.'

And suddenly I was smiling right back.

24

LATE MORNING, SAME DAY
UPSIDE DOWN – DIANA ROSS

'You sure you know what you're doing?' Kate had asked me before they left for the airport. We were in the bedroom, packing, all the logistics already worked out. Kate, Jess and Carol would fly back today on the return leg of the launch-party charter flight, and then the boys would drop me at the airport tomorrow and I'd fly back to LA alone. My menfolk would then head back south for the last few days of their trip. It was the perfect solution.

'Absolutely! I just want to spend the day with Mac and Benny,' I'd said, flippantly.

'And Mark?' she'd asked pointedly, throwing an inflatable Statue Of Liberty that she'd bought for Val into the case.

'Well, sure. Mark too. I can't exactly ask him to sit in the van while the boys and I are out exploring Manhattan.'

I was sure I saw a flash of scepticism and heard a muttering about protesting too much.

As we waved them off in their Uber, Hannah dropped a front door key into my hand. 'I need to go to work, but take this and please come and go as you like. You know where everything is.'

'Thanks. We will completely take advantage of your lovely

hospitality,' I joked, then gave in to an urge to throw my arms around her. 'You know, I'm so proud of you, Hannah Russo. You're pretty kickass, you know that?'

'Yeah, I blame my aunts. They made me like this. You wouldn't want to mess with them.'

With a cheeky wink, she was off, and I was sure it wasn't my imagination that she was walking a little bit taller today. I was just sad that I'd been such a coward and unable to face her before. We'd wasted so much time, both of us wrapped up in our guilt.

Once again, I shrugged off the melancholy. Sarah was still gone, and there would never be a day in my life that I wouldn't miss her, but there was an incredible release in not feeling responsible, so today, I was going to smile and I was going to live, and I was going to enjoy every moment because that was exactly what Sarah and Nick would have wanted.

We decided to leave the RV parked at the house, and walk up to Central Park, stopping for ice cream on the way. The boys had been here a few times before, so the crowds were no surprise to them and they got a buzz from the excitement of the city.

Mark and I walked behind them, our shoulders touching, his hand just naturally slipping into mine when we were navigating obstacles. Somehow, the busy streets and sunshine and the happiness of all being together made it easy to chat for the first time since we separated. As we strolled, I told him all about the trip so far, about LA, about Sam, about Estelle.

'Yeah, the boys told me about that. What's she like?'

'Oh God, not you too!' I drawled. 'Why is the entire male species obsessed with her?'

He playfully dropped his arm around my shoulders. 'I've only been obsessed by one woman,' he said playfully, tickling me, to the horror of a couple of camera-clad tourists who had to walk round us. 'She's a bit of a handful though.'

'Is that a fat joke because I didn't pack my magic pants?' I shot back, making him buckle with laughter.

Oh God, this felt good. And normal. And... and... did I mention good?

A couple of streets back from the park, we popped into a cycle-hire shop and picked up bikes. It was the best way to cover the square miles of greenery, but my thighs were trembling at the prospect.

'Right, you lot, I want you to know that if this kills me, I love you very much and there's a hundred quid hidden behind the toilet rolls in the bathroom cupboard for emergencies. I knew you'd never find it there.'

It was a standing joke that that they could wipe out galaxies on the Xbox, code a program on a computer, but taking a cardboard roll off a toilet roll holder and replacing it with a new one was absolutely beyond their capabilities.

We cycled for an hour or so, stopping off whenever we wanted to check something out, before arriving at the basketball courts at the Great Meadow. Mac had his ball out of his backpack and was on the court before Benny even took his cycle helmet off. Mark and I found a shady spot under a nearby tree. I took a blanket out of my backpack and spread it on the ground, then reapplied some factor 50.

Mark pulled off his baseball cap and stretched out against the tree.

'You look good, Cooper,' he said, and I tried not to notice that the cycling had pumped up the muscles on his thighs even more than usual. Bloody hell, what was happening to me? I hadn't given his thighs a second glance in years. I wasn't sure when we stopped noticing each other. Probably around the last time he told me I looked good. I think I was in my thirties at the time.

'It's the tan. Underneath this I'm still a haggard specimen of a woman.'

'Why do you do that?' His gaze bore right into my soul and I felt myself flinch. He hadn't looked at me like that for a long time.

'What?'

'The self-deprecating stuff.'

Oh, too many things to unpack there. I went for the most obvious. 'It's the Gods Of Menopause. They make you feel shit about yourself and then apparently they kick in some good stuff at the end of it that makes it all worthwhile. I haven't got to that bit yet. When I dig out the G-string bikini and shave my legs, you'll know I'm there.'

He rolled over, his head dangerously close to my lap. I had a ridiculous urge to run my fingers through his hair, but gave myself a metaphorical slap. This wasn't the right time, the right place, or the right marriage. 'I was worried about you when I heard you were here. I know there are too many memories. Things seemed good with Hannah though.'

'They are. Do you want to hear about it, or do you want to have a sleep while the boys are busy?' I knew he'd choose sleep. Listening to me talk about emotional stuff was on his list of least favourite things, in between athlete's foot and the congestion charge.

'I want to hear about it.'

Well, bugger me and call me interesting. Who was this guy? Actually, I already knew the answer. This was Mark Barwick 1999. Maybe even Mark Barwick 2008. But he bore no resemblance at all to Mark Barwick 2010 – 2017 – that guy would have stopped twice on the way here to call the office, and right now he'd either be sleeping or taking notes for a Skype meeting he was planning for later. He certainly wouldn't be asking his wife about the emotional ups and downs of her week.

Yet, Mark Barwick 1999 and 2019 was interested, so Carly Cooper 2019 told him all about it. The bigger shock was that he listened. Asked questions. Engaged.

When I began to tell him about our toasts at the bridge, he even leaned over and wiped away tears that came out of nowhere and dripped down my cheek, then he took my hands in his and held them softly.

'It's not sad tears,' I told him, thinking how good his touch felt.

'I know that,' he replied. 'In all our lives together, you've cried more when you're happy.'

He was right. When I was sad, I was more likely to hold it in, to swallow back the pain. For a lot of years with Mark, there were buckets of happy tears. When we met again, when we married, when we bought our house, when we had our boys. We'd had a lifetime together and much of it had been incredible. Over the last few years, I think I'd forgotten that.

I carried on, managing not to crumble when I told him about Hannah's final words.

To Living Our Best Lives.

'Fuck,' was his final verdict, and I could see that had hit him somewhere deep in the chest.

'Really? You're a lawyer who makes cohesive arguments for a living and that's all you've got?' I asked, amused.

'Sorry. It's just that...' He stopped.

'Go on,' I prompted, but he shook his head.

'No. This isn't the right time or place.'

'Don't start with that, Mark. Say what you feel. I'm done with robot Mark. I want to see the real guy again.'

'Okay, fine,' he said. 'I just think... what a waste it's all been.'

'What's been a waste?'

'Hating yourself. Blaming yourself. Stopping yourself from being happy.'

Had I done that? The first two, yes, but the last one?

'Carly, I know that I've been a pretty shit husband for the last few years...'

I didn't argue.

'But the truth is that I could have been perfect and I honestly think we'd still have split. You've been so unhappy, so consumed by misery, that even if we did have a shot at making us work, I don't think you could have taken it.'

'So it's my fault?' I snapped, irritation rising. Was he gaslighting me here?

'No!' he countered urgently. 'Shit, I'm making such an arse of this. Carly, there's no excuse for how crap I've been, and I take all the responsibility for that. I swear. That's what I wanted to talk to you about when we got home. Since I moved out, I've... Christ, I'm a cliché. I've realised what I was missing. I've realised where I went wrong. I lost myself somewhere and I lost sight of what mattered. Then I lost you. God, I'd do it all so differently if I could go back. The whole balance of my life was fucked, and I was so consumed by making my career work that I didn't have the sense to see my mistakes at home, or to change them. That's why, I've realised that...' He stopped, as if he was weighing up whether or not he should say something. 'I want to fix it. That's what I was going to tell you when we got back home. I knew I'd fucked up before I came here and being with the boys has just reinforced that. It's been so good to be with them and I know I'm running out of time to be that dad that I want to be to them, the one who is there in the mornings, and who hangs out with them after school. The one who is part of their lives every day. This has been two of the best weeks of my life and I feel like they've given me another chance. I just hope you can too. I want to try again, Carly. With you. Us.'

Silence. Crickets. Nothing. The shock had paralysed me. For years, I'd been desperate for him to say those things and to really mean them, not just spout off empty promises. Now, I could feel that he'd had some kind of real change, that he was absolutely serious about being the husband and dad I'd begged him to be.

'Carly, you're not speaking. Babe? Are you okay?'

I was definitely not okay. And I definitely, for once in my life, could not speak because I absolutely didn't know what to say. He wanted to try again? That sentence ricocheted around my skull. Try again.

Two weeks ago, if someone had told me this would happen, I'd have thought they were insane. We could barely spend time in the same room.

But now?

He wanted to try again.

I couldn't stop hearing it.

'Hey, what you two looking so serious about?' Mac plumped down on the grass, his hair soaked with sweat, his T-shirt off, his cheeks red with healthy exertion. His interruption killed our conversation. I decided to up his monthly allowance.

'Oh, you know, usual stuff… how we're not letting either of you go to Magaluf or Zante until you're in your forties.'

His low, throaty laugh made a couple of teenage girls lying on the grass a few metres away turn to look with curious smiles. A thought struck me. When I was that age, I was already writing Mark's name on my jotters at school and lurking at the sports pitches to watch him play football. I was already convinced that – unless George Michael did a detour to the council estate I lived on, spotted me hanging out at the bus stop, and whisked me off to a life of fame and fortune – I was going to marry Mark. It took me a while to get there, but I did. And for a long time it was wonderful. Was I wasting over thirty years of my life by throwing away the last chapter, the one where we had finally got past all the pressures of bringing up children, building careers, trying to pay mortgages and juggle a hundred other things? We were, hopefully, coming into a new, easier time in our lives. Were we supposed to be together so that we could enjoy the payoff of a more contented, carefree future?

'I'm hungry.' It was Benny who interrupted the heavy stuff this time. He'd be getting his allowance raised too.

'You've been hungry since you were six. I think it's a boy thing,' I told him, ruffling his hair and watching him squirm at the public display of affection. 'If you go more than half an hour without eating, your body goes into panic mode and screams for Wotsits.'

'I think you might be on to something there,' he replied with mock sincerity.

'Okay,' I surrendered, grateful for the distraction and desperate for an excuse to delay answering the question that was still written all over Mark's face. 'Let's go and eat before you faint. I couldn't afford the hospital bills here.'

If anyone was watching us, they'd think we were such a bonded, happy family. Maybe we could be again.

We ate in one of our favourite New York restaurants, an Italian pizzeria across from the east side of the park, with our bikes chained up outside. Afterwards, we cycled some more, played baseball in the park's North Meadow, ate ice cream for the second time and lay around on the grass, talking, laughing, being a family. I couldn't remember a more perfect day.

By the time we got back to Sarah's home... would I always call it that? I think I would. Anyway, by the time we got back, all we had the energy to do was crash out on the sofa and watch an old

Fast & Furious movie. It wasn't the one with Charlize Theron, so I didn't feel the pressure of hair comparisons.

Hannah joined us when she got back late from work. I wondered if she wanted to talk more, but she flopped next to Benny on the couch, opened a bucket of popcorn and told us that her favourite thing in the world was to chill and watch Vin Diesel and the late great Paul Walker. She immediately went to the top of the boys' 'favourite cousin' list.

It didn't even occur to me to change the sleeping arrangements we'd always had in this house. At least, not until we all trudged upstairs, exhausted but as happy as I could remember. Benny crashed out instantly the moment he sat on the bed, flopping onto the pillow, sound asleep in seconds. I've always been so jealous of his ability to do that.

Mac was in the bathroom, as Mark pulled off his T-shirt. He'd already changed into the fleecy shorts he wore in bed.

He glanced at Benny, making sure he was asleep, before picking up the conversation from earlier. 'Listen, what we were talking about in the park... will you think about it? I really hope you'll give it a chance. I want to make you happy.'

'I will. I just need some time...'

'I get it. I'll wait,' he said, grinning at me with the kind of tender love that used to make me melt to mush.

The moment was broken, though, when his eyes suddenly went from bed to bed, as if he was only just registering that this might be an awkward moment. Every time we'd stayed here, Mac and Benny would top and tail in one double bed ('Muuuuuuuum, he's got his foot in my face again') and Mark and I would take the other.

Mark gestured to our usual bed. 'Are you going to...?'

Another feeling from the past made an appearance, when I felt a physical yearning for his arms to wrap around me, to cuddle in and spoon until morning. But...

'No,' I answered, and I knew he would sense my regret. 'I don't want to give mixed signals to the boys. Not yet...'

He got it. I knew he would.

I kissed a sleeping Benny on the head, hugged Mac when he came out of the bathroom, and said goodnight to Mark, before climbing under the lightweight blanket on the chaise under the window.

This was Sarah's bed when the girls were all here, and I knew it was crazy, but I felt her here, sensed her breathing.

Sarah had always been the one with smart, rational advice in every situation.

I just wish she could tell me what I should do now.

25

NEW YORK, THE NEXT MORNING
BABY CAN I HOLD YOU – TRACY CHAPMAN

'Okay, so what are the rules for the rest of the week?' I asked my sons over brunch. We'd slept late, all of us too tired to spring into action, and too content to care that we weren't up and about.

'Nothing that can break bones or put our internal organs in a different place,' Benny recited, word for word, the order I'd given earlier.

'Correct. I'm putting you in charge, Benny.'

Benny punched his brother's arm in triumph, evoking protests from Mac.

'Ow! Why does he get to be in charge?'

'Because you're much more likely to throw yourself out of a plane.'

He couldn't argue.

Mark drained his fresh orange juice. 'Right, you two, go and grab your stuff and sling it in the van.'

Benny snapped his fingers at his brother. 'Come on, get to it. Let's move it, pronto,' he barked, before grinning mischievously at his dad and me. 'I think I've gone power crazy, but I kinda like it.'

Mac sighed and shook his head. 'You are such a tit,' he told his brother.

'Hey!' I interjected, outraged.

Mac immediately looked sheepish. I was about to follow through with the bollocking, when I remembered that I wouldn't see them for a week, and didn't have the heart to scold him. Instead...

'I said he's in charge!' I said firmly. 'So that's *Sergeant* Tit to you.'

The two of them crumbled, while Mark put his head in his hands. 'You can't help yourself, can you?' He was feigning exasperation, but I could see the laughter in his eyes.

When the boys were gone, Mark raised his gaze expectantly and I knew immediately what was coming so I cut him off as gently as possible.

'Don't ask.'

'What? I wasn't going to say a thing,' he protested with mock innocence. Patience had never been his strong point.

'I need more than twenty-four hours,' I chided him, then slipped my hand near his and rubbed his palm. It was a familiar touch, a gesture that I'd made thousands of times before, yet today it felt almost illicit. 'It's a lot, Mark. Give me some time. Let's talk when we get home.' I didn't tell him that I'd lain awake most of the night thinking about it, wrestling with so many different feelings and questions that were impossible to answer. The one that came up again and again, was 'did I still love Mark enough to make it work with him?' I wasn't sure of the answer. And goddammit, in the few moments when I did doze off, I had vivid dreams in which Sam was standing to one side, just watching, waiting, and I'd...

'Carly? Are you ok?' Shit, I must have drifted.

'Sorry! Fine. Just tired,' I blustered. And confused. Really, really confused. Why couldn't I get Sam out of my mind?

'Are you sure you don't want to come with us? Spend the rest of the week?'

I'd thought about that too, but...

'No. The girls put so much effort into doing this and I'm so grateful. I think it's the loveliest thing anyone has ever done for me.' That wasn't meant to be a dig, but he flinched and I realised how it sounded. I wasn't going to apologise or backtrack though, because it was true. We were never going to sort things out if we couldn't be honest. 'Besides, if I don't go back, Val will come and get me and she's already marched me out of far too many places in my life.'

That made him laugh. In his youth, he too had been marched out of the occasional pub by Val. When it came to our crowd, she'd been an equal-opportunities discipline enforcer.

'Sam will be glad you're back,' he said, with a very subtle but unmistakable edge in his tone. 'I bet he's loving having you all there.'

Something tightened in my chest. Must have been the way I was lying last night. That, or the fact that there was a definite bite to his comment. What was with the jealousy these days? It was bizarre.

'Yeah, he is. Val is objectifying him on a daily basis, so that keeps him going,' I giggled. 'Estelle isn't impressed. Fairly sure she's already called Homeland Security and asked to have us deported. Of all the women on the planet, why did Sam have to pick Estelle Conran?'

Mac gave a dramatic shake of the head as he came back into the room. 'I still can't believe Uncle Sam is dating Estelle Conran. Take me back with you, Mum. I beg you,' he joked, pleading dramatically. At least, I think he was joking.

'Sorry, son, I'd be doing you a disservice if I took you, on account of the fact that she's pretty rude, pretty obnoxious, and your Aunt Val may well have drowned her with an inflatable swan by the time we get back. Don't ask.'

'My life sucks,' he groaned. 'But tell Uncle Sam we said congratulations and let him know I'm available for adoption.'

It was a joke that had been made many times before, but this time I saw Mark's jaw clench as he tried to supress his rising hackles.

I moved the topic along. 'Will do, son. Right, are we good to go?'

To Mac's joy, they'd abandoned plans to visit the Natural History Museum, and decided to head south after they'd dropped me at the airport. They were going to try to get back down to Florida by the following evening. Something about racing at Daytona. I decided it was better that I didn't know the details.

Everything packed, the guys said their goodbyes to Hannah, then headed out to the van. I took her hands and we stood there just like that for a moment, as if we were holding on to the connection, savouring every moment until we had to let go.

'I'm so glad we came,' I told her, lump sliding right into position in my throat. 'I'm not being glib when I tell you that this has changed my life. I'm so grateful.'

'I second all of that,' she said, walking that fine line between laughing and crying. We didn't need to bring it all up again. We knew that this had been a turning point for both of us.

'Remember, we're family. We're always there for you, so please, please lean on us. Tell Ryan that too. We like it. We're at that age where it makes us feel useful.'

'My mum always thought it was hilarious how you dealt with emotional situations by making jokes.'

'Did she tell you about...'

I didn't even need to finish the sentence. 'The time you got asked to leave a funeral? Yeah.'

I sent a silent reprimand up to Sarah.

'Not my finest hour.' I admitted.

There was a honk on a horn outside.

'Natives are getting restless. Goodbye, my darling.' I threw my arms around her and hugged her tight. I was so sad to leave her, but at the same time there was a peace, a deep feeling that she was going to be okay.

I paused in the hall, touched one of the pictures in the black frames on the wall. Sarah, me, Carol, Jess and Kate, on my wedding day, the five of us hanging on to each other, helpless with laughter, as we reached the marriage hall with only minutes to spare. I sent her a silent message. I knew she could hear.

Goodbye, beautiful. We'll see you at a kitchen table again soon.

I gently closed the door behind me.

'Are you okay?' Mark asked when I climbed into the passenger seat of the RV.

'I am.' He started up the engine. 'We've decided we're going to come over to visit Hannah every year. Sarah would like that.'

I wondered if he was going to say something about the cost of that, but he didn't.

'I think you should,' he said, surprising me. I was beginning to think I had no idea who this new Mark Barwick was at all... but I liked him.

Mark switched on the music and the intoxicating brilliance of Michael Hutchence oozed from the speakers. INXS had been one of our favourite bands back in the days when we listened to albums over a bottle of wine and a plastic tray of chips.

I waited for the usual complaint to come from the boys in the back – something about ancient music and could we please put on some Drake – but nothing came. Surprised, I turned round to see Benny with his earphones in, eyes closed, and Mac deep in concentration on his phone. I almost left it. I was so close to just turning back round and singing along to 'Need You Tonight'. But there was something in the angle of Mac's brows, the firm set of his lips, the pulse in the side of his jaw that made the nerve endings under my skin begin to crawl with dread and fear.

'Everything okay, honey?'

No response. He was still scrolling through something on... it looked like Snapchat. Or maybe it was a group chat on Whats-App. It was hard to tell when it was upside down and I didn't have my specs on.

'Mac!' I said, louder this time, startling him. 'Is everything okay?'

There was a split second where I could see he was deliberating whether or not to tell me. Thankfully, he came down on the right side of it.

'Mum, you should probably see this, but please don't lose it and go mad.'

Now I was getting seriously scared.

'I'm only showing you because I know you'll help her.'

Oh fuck, he really had got someone pregnant. And he needed me to help! I was almost fifty and I was going to have to start again with nappies and prams and bring up my son's child because the girl already had her career planned out and wasn't ready to be a mother.

'Help who?'

'Toni.'

Toni? What did Toni have to do with Mac's child's baby mamma? I didn't get it. Maybe there were two Tonis?

'Our Toni?' I clarified, and now it was his turn to be confused.

'Yeah, our Toni. Who else would it be?'

'Honest to God, this is excruciating,' Mark interjected,

keeping his eyes on the road. 'Mac, your mother has gone into full-scale panic mode inside her head, so she's jumping to 237 wrong conclusions in the time it takes you to answer every question. Best thing to do is just tell her really quickly what's going on so that she'll calm down to just moderately traumatised.'

Staring at him, I pursed my lips in irritation, even though every word he'd just said was absolutely correct.

'I think Toni's in trouble, Mum.'

My gut started to twist. I'd known for days, maybe weeks that something was wrong, but I hadn't been able to get to the bottom of it.

'What's happened? It doesn't matter what it is, Mac, tell me the truth and tell me everything. You know I'll do what I can.'

He stretched forward in his seat, turned his phone round to show me the screen.

'It's a group chat with a load of the guys who do the fantasy football stuff. Toni was dating one of them – Paul Dorico's big brother, Taylor. Paul's cool, but Taylor is a dick.'

'What age is this guy?' I knew nothing about him but I already hated him. If he was harming Toni and Mac disliked him, that was all I needed to set off my inner tiger aunt.

'Nineteen. Maybe twenty. I think he was the year above Toni in school.'

'Okay. So what's happened?' I was already beginning to get a pretty good idea, but I needed to find out if I was right. And for once, I really didn't want to be.

'She dumped him because... well, because he was a dick. And because he's off his face on MDMA every weekend and becomes an even bigger idiot.'

'Glad to hear it.' It was all I could manage to say over the noise of the screaming in my head.

'But the thing is...' I could tell Mac was hating every moment of this. It wasn't in his nature to spill secrets, but I was so grateful that he had the maturity to realise that Toni needed support from an adult for whatever was going on. '... He has some photos. Toni sent them to him months ago, right at the start, when she thought he was a good guy.'

'How do you know this?' My feeling of dread was growing by the second. It didn't take a genius to suss that the photos wouldn't be of cute puppies.

'Because he told one of my mates. I asked her, but she said it was rubbish and I believed her 'cause he bullshits all the time. Only, I guess it wasn't because... Look.'

He held his phone closer, and I could see a picture of a female, topless, hands covering her breasts as she leaned into the camera, as if trying to tease the person the photo was meant for. The face had been cut off, but her brown hair fell loose over her shoulders. It wouldn't have been enough for a stranger to make an ID, but it was enough for us, because there, on her shoulder, was a tiny mole, the same one I'd seen every time my niece lay on a sunlounger next to me for the last fortnight. It was Toni.

'He says he's got more, but I think he's just putting this one up because she dumped him.' An image flashed up behind my eyes. A text.

Really, bitch? Don't you fucking dare or you know what's coming.

Don't you fucking dare what? Dump him?

You know what's coming? The photos?

'Mac, when did Toni start seeing this guy?'

He shrugged, thinking. 'Maybe about six months ago?'

It all made sense. Carol had first mentioned Toni's mood shift just before Mother's Day, and Toni had definitely been upset and edgy at Kate's barbecue. Had all this been brewing then? Had she already sent the photos and realised it was a mistake? Was her every waking moment consumed by fear over what he'd do? She checked her phone constantly, but I'd just put that down to teenage habit. It now made absolute sense that her unpredictability and outbursts must have been a result of relief or fear over what she saw there.

Oh God, poor Toni. She must have been in hell and so scared.

As I continued to process it all, my swirling gut morphed in to pure, visceral rage that made my head explode. How dare he? How fucking dare he do this to her?

'Thanks for telling me, son. I promise I'll handle it and we'll sort it. We've got her. Don't worry.'

The uncharacteristic anxiety on his face began to soften. I turned back to the front, my breaths coming hard as I tried to get my head around it.

'You okay?' Mark asked, one hand on the steering wheel, the other taking mine. 'I can contact someone at the office to look into the legal side of this. See what can be done, what the options are.'

Mark specialised in corporate law, so I knew this wasn't his field.

'Yeah, that would be great. But please, can you ask on a hypothetical basis? Don't say it's Toni or discuss her identity with anyone.'

'No problem. Leave it with me. I'll do everything I can.'

Wow. I'd forgotten what it was like to have a true partner, someone who stood beside you to help fight your battles and protect the people you love. I'd also forgotten what a decent guy Mark really was.

The flight I'd booked back to LA left from Newark, and when we pulled into the drop-off zone my stomach was lurching. I didn't want to leave my boys. To my surprise, I didn't want to leave Mark either. But I knew I needed time to think about his proposition, had to decide whether I wanted to give our relationship one more try.

We all jumped out of the RV and Benny got my case from the back. I squeezed him tight, then did the same to Mac. 'Remember what I said about your internal organs and take care of yourselves and your dad. I love you so much.'

'Ma, we'll see you in about four days,' Benny said, trying to console me. 'And you'll probably FaceTime us at least 500 times before then. You won't get a chance to miss us.'

'Yeah, you might have a point. But give me another hug anyway so I can make sure I qualify for Needy Mother of The Year.'

'You won that a long time ago,' Mac joked. At least, I think he was joking.

The boys jumped back into the van and left me with Mark. He put his arms around me, then his lips touched mine and for a few seconds I was lost in him.

'Come back to me, Carly. Please.'

'Let me think things through.' My head was still spinning, and it wasn't fair on him or our family to make a snap decision now. For once in my life, I was going to take my time. Be measured. Make sure I was thinking with my head as well as my heart. And besides, I couldn't focus on this while my stomach was churning over all this stuff with Toni.

'Take as long as you need, but remember I love you.'

'I love you too.' I meant it. I just wasn't sure if it was enough. I waved until they were out of sight and then took a deep breath. Somehow, I had to decide exactly what I wanted.

Meanwhile, I had absolutely no idea how I was going to handle it, what I was going to say or do, but I had almost six hours on a flight to LAX to work out how to help my niece.

26

LOS ANGELES, 8.12 P.M
WHEN WE WERE YOUNG – ADELE

It was like night and day, touching down at LAX from a domestic flight instead of an international one. No immigration queues, no fumbling for passports, no worrying if some devious criminal had somehow managed to stash three kilos of crack in your Ted Baker trolley bag... Again, that last one might just be me.

For the five hours and fifty-three minutes of the flight from New York, I'd allowed myself to be a seething mess of mixed emotions. The pain of losing Sarah was more acute than ever, but there was also a true sense of gratitude and relief that my misconceptions and guilt had been laid to rest. Confusion and uncertainty over my feelings for Mark and our future had my stomach churning. But I was overwhelmed by how good it had felt to be a family again.

All of these mixed emotions sat right next to apocalyptic anger at that spineless prick who was targeting Toni. However, as I marched through the arrivals terminal, geared up for my last four days in LA, I wrapped that rage in a box and sat on it until it was shut. Anger was no use to me. Toni needed calm reason and support, and a solid, effective plan to deal with this and that's what I was going to deliver. Until I spoke to her though, I just wasn't quite sure how that plan would look.

I'd texted my flight details to Kate and she'd offered to ask Arnie to come and get me, but I'd told her not to bother. I didn't want to trouble him when it was just as easy to jump in a cab. I scanned the signs above me, and followed the one for the exit, head down, feet moving fast as I charged through the sliding doors into the daylight and...

'Cooper!'

It was loud, male, out of breath.

I stopped, turned around, really hoping it was nothing to do with three kilos of crack in my trolley bag.

'Sam? What are you doing here?'

Under the baseball cap and the dark glasses, I could see his face was flushed. 'Oh, I don't know... I went out for a jog and took a wrong turn,' he said, the heavy dose of sarcasm making it clear it was a ridiculous question.

The absurdity of it cut right through my fury and made me laugh for the first time since I stepped out of the RV at Newark airport. Sam Morton. Hollywood icon. Sweating his bits off in the middle of LAX and not a paparazzo in sight. I loved it.

'I came to collect you, but you came out of arrivals like your arse was on fire and I was waiting at the other end,' he explained, his breathing starting to regulate. 'I called you, but...'

'Sorry. I was a bit distracted. Stuff on my mind.'

He didn't ask. I didn't offer.

There was a weird pause until he snapped back into action. 'Uh, okay. Cool. Any chance we could go get the car and get out of here?'

'Absolutely. Just as long as you promise not to give up the movie career for a job driving taxis. You'd be pretty crap at it.'

He took my trolley case from me, and started walking in the

direction of the nearest parking structure. 'I'll bear that in mind. Thanks for the tip.'

We were in his open-top Jeep and on the freeway by the time I noticed something felt weird.

I gasped dramatically. 'Sam, I've just realised something… this is only the third time we've been alone together since the day I got here.' For the purposes of maintaining my dignity and composure, I refused to allow myself to revisit the dressing-gown moment of mortification or the meltdown over the girls' announcing we were going to New York. Instead, I reverted to type and went for really bad wit. 'Does Estelle know you're out? Oh my God, Sam, she's probably alerted the authorities that you're missing. She'll be sending an army of drones into the sky right now to track you down.' I went into full-scale drama-queen mode, scanning the skies like Gerry Butler in that drone/lake/save the President scene in *London Has Fallen*.

'You're really not funny, do you know that?' The corners of his mouth turned up though, betraying his words.

'I've been told,' I said, giggling. 'By the way, the boys asked me to tell you that they were missing you and Mac wants to come and live with you because he's got a massive crush on Estelle. She might want to take out a restraining order.'

'I'll let her know. And yeah, I was thinking we hadn't had any time together and tomorrow I'm away on a set visit that I can't put off – that's why I came to get you. All part of the service.'

There were a few seconds of silence as my mind went low and ambushed me with thoughts of a very different kind of service Sam had once provided. God, he was hot. And kind. And funny. Did I mention hot? More than that, he had been one of the most important loves of my life. I just wasn't sure that my heart was still putting that in the past tense. Thankfully, he couldn't read my mind, and if he could, he was intent on changing the subject.

He broke the pause with, 'So... can I ask you something? And bearing in mind we've got a twenty-five-year history and have always been straight with each other.'

'You mean, apart from the time I promised to come back to Hong Kong and didn't? Or the time you forgot to mention you were the number one tax write-off for every bored, wealthy woman on the island?'

His chuckle was carried over the noise of the traffic around us. 'Yeah, apart from those times.'

'Excellent. Okay, I'm all ears,' I told him, enjoying the escape from reality that the easy banter was delivering. Whether we'd been friends, lovers or somewhere in between, that had always been there with us and I loved him for it.

'On a scale of one to ten, how much are you hating Estelle?'

'Twelve,' I shot back immediately, then groaned. 'Look, I'm sorry, Sam, but why would you ask me that? You know I'm going to be honest with you and then you'll hate me until the end of time.'

'I don't hate you,' he sighed, staring straight ahead.

'I wanted to love her, and you know I'm a girls' girl. It would have been amazing if we'd hit it off and we could have spent every morning together doing the downward dog and comparing thigh gaps...'

He still had his eyes on the road in front, saying nothing.

'... Okay, I haven't got a thigh gap, but you know what I mean. She's just so... territorial. And I understand. If you were mine, I'd be territorial too.'

Bollocks! Why had I just said that? I'd had that thought last week, but it was one that was supposed to live inside my head and never see the light of day, especially not in front of Sam. Shit. Damn. Bugger.

'Hypothetically speaking,' I added weakly. 'And get your eyes back on the road, because if we die in this car, the media reports will only mention the celebrity and I'll get forgotten. My ego couldn't take it.' My brain was sending cease and desist orders to my gob, but it wasn't listening. 'Anyway,' I kept rambling right on, 'I guess all that's important is that you love her. My opinion doesn't really matter. I just want you to be happy.'

'I do. Maybe she'll grow on you when you get to know her better.'

That was obviously his way of telling me that she was going to be around for a while.

There was a pause, so I filled it with a bit more internal dialogue, berating myself for being so frank and stupid. I should just have said she was lovely and been done with it, because... Anxiety set off a chain of irrational thoughts that escalated straight to full-scale catastrophe. *If Estelle and I clashed, she might give him an ultimatum. He might be forced to choose between us. He'd pick her. I'd lose my lifelong friend. I'd be devastated. Crushed. And... I loved him too much to lose him.*

My heart was drowning out the roar of the wind now. Before he could say anything, I blurted out, 'Sam, please forget I said anything. I'm tired. Emotional. It's been a heavy couple of days.'

For a moment, I thought I'd pissed him off beyond repair, but he reached over and took my hand. 'Kate told me what happened with Hannah and about the video you watched and about going to the bridge. I'm glad you got some kind of resolution. You've had me worried for a while.'

That wasn't news. Since Sarah died, he'd been the soothing voice and the wide shoulder on the other end of the phone more times than I could count.

My hand tightened a little more around his. 'I'm sorry, Sam. I was a mess and I was so grateful for your friendship. I always will be,' I told him. Deep and meaningful declarations weren't usually our thing, but it suddenly seemed important to let him know how much he meant to me. 'To be honest, I haven't really had the chance to process everything that happened in New York. I think I need some time just to adjust to a different story from the one I've been telling myself all this time.' I didn't add that maybe I was referring to more than just my guilt over Sarah and Nick. Maybe I'd been telling myself an inaccurate story about my marriage too.

He nodded. 'I get it. You could always stay in your LA holiday home for a bit longer. It's perfect for emotional trauma and navel-gazing.'

'Thank you,' I said, laughing. 'But you know... all that luxury and having things done for me would wear thin after a while.'

'You're right. It's all kinds of hell,' he jested, before going on. 'Mark and the boys stopping by was pretty cool.' There was a slight question in there somewhere, but I ignored it.

'I can't tell you how good it was to see the boys. They're just all kinds of freaking awesome, they really are. Remind me I said that next time I'm moaning about them.'

He returned his hand to the wheel as he changed lanes, so he could veer right on the 10 as it transitioned on to the PCH. On the left, I could see the Ferris wheel and the roller coaster on the Santa Monica pier. When the boys were small, and I'd brought them here on my failed attempt to crack the movie industry, we used to go to Mother's Beach in Marina Del Rey most days, and on the way back to Sam's house in the evenings, they'd beg me to stop here so they could play on the pier for a while. I usually gave in, their joy like a transfusion for the soul. Even now, it was one of my favourite memories, one I'd bring out when my faith in life was running low.

I shook off the melancholy. Five more minutes and we'd be home... Hang on, not my home. Sam's house. Sleep deprivation and all this turmoil must be muddling my brain.

I was so distracted by the memories that I almost lost track of what we were talking about. The boys. How great it was that they'd come to visit me in New York.

Sam took my hand again. 'And good to see Mark too?'

'Yes. I don't know. Yes, it was, I think. But it was just... a lot.'

'How are those decisiveness classes coming along?' he teased, but there was a tightness I didn't recognise in his voice.

'He wants to call off the divorce and get back together.'

I heard a sigh, but I didn't pick him up on it. It was understandable. There was history there. When Mark and I had been at breaking point years ago and Sam had asked me to stay with him, to start a new life with him and the kids in LA, I'd almost done it. Almost. But in the end, I'd gone back to Mark because he was the boys' dad and because I loved him. He was my always. And maybe he still was.

'What did you say to that?' Sam asked. 'Is that what you want?'

'I don't know. I told him I needed some time. It's... complicated.'

'It's always complication with you, Cooper.'

'I know. It's a curse,' I joked, trying to lighten things up a little as we turned off the PCH and began the climb to the Palisades. 'I think that after Sarah died, I just didn't feel that I had the right to be happy. Don't get me wrong, Mark and I had problems, but I detonated my marriage, my life... everything. I was so wrapped up in grief that I could barely breathe. If that hadn't happened... I don't know.' I paused. 'What do you think?'

'I think it's up to you.'

I let his hand go so I could punch his arm. 'Sam Morton, that is such a cop-out. Why are you so shy about giving an opinion all of a sudden? You usually have loads of them.'

He indicated to turn into his street. 'Because I don't want to be an asshole.'

'You won't be. I'm asking your opinion. Just like you asked mine earlier.'

'Look how great that turned out,' he quipped, oozing sarcasm again.

Sam's gates opened as we approached them, and he swung the Jeep around and stopped outside the front door. I thought he was going to stay put, to finish the conversation, but instead, he jumped out and reached into the back seat for my case.

I was already out of the car when he got to my side, and for the first time since the conversation began, we were face to face.

'I want to know what you think,' I told him. 'It's important to me.'

'Why?'

'Because it just is. What's your problem?'

Aaaargh, why did he bring out the worst in me? I knew I sounded like a stroppy cow, but it felt like the atmosphere had shifted, like I needed to challenge him in some way that I couldn't explain.

In return, he seemed irritated and for a moment I thought he was going to dodge the question again.

'Okay, fine,' he snapped back. I brought out the worst in him too. 'I'll tell you my problem. Last time Mark asked you to go back to him, you went. And how did that work out for you?'

27

LONDON, JULY 2010

CLOWN – EMILE SANDE

'What day is it today, baby boy?' I asked my seven-year-old, Mac, as I woke him up with a torrent of tickles that made him shriek.

'Christmas!' he squealed.

I stopped, feigning irritated despair. 'Christmas? It's July! You always have to steal the joy, don't you?'

That made him giggle even more. It was one of our standing jokes. If he went for Christmas, everything else was an anticlimax.

Before I could chide him further for making fun of his mother, I felt a weight crush down on my back. Five-year-old Benny had escaped his bed and climbed on me, his arms crushing my oesophagus, but I didn't care. This was my favourite part of the day, the first moments of the morning with my boys. Mac was always up to mischief that would make me laugh, and Benny always had a smile that would melt my heart.

I moved the party downstairs, Benny still on my back, Mac rolling himself down each step like a stuntman, then stopping at the half landing to check for mutant zombies that could be lurking around any corner. Just another normal morning in Chiswick. I really had to stop him watching *Power Rangers*.

They both climbed onto chairs at the kitchen table, then poured their cereal and milk, while I sliced up bananas and spread it on their toast. Breakfast was usually some combination of fruit, cereal, yoghurt and toast, mostly because if I gave them free choice, Benny would have prawn cocktail crisps and Mac would have a family-size pack of Milky Ways and a Mint Magnum.

'You still haven't guessed what day it is today,' I said, slightly miffed that Mark hadn't already prepped them.

Benny's spoon stopped halfway to his mouth. 'Is Ronald McDonald coming for a play date?'

Sometimes, I wasn't sure if we were living in the same world, but I appreciated his imagination, so I let it pass. 'No, he's at chicken nugget school today. Any other guesses?'

The back door opened, and Mark came in from his morning jog. I was kind of hoping that he'd give it a miss today, but he'd got up at six and headed out as normal – 5 a.m. on weekdays, 6 a.m. at the weekend. He grabbed the towel he always left at the door for his return. It was the kind of detail he was good on – anything to do with his daily routine, his job, our long-term future. He was a man who was already paying more into his pension than anyone I knew. I was just hoping I made it to retirement age with a job.

'Hey, babe,' he said, kissing the top of my head, and then, 'Morning, boys.'

Benny and Mac gave him their very best grins as he kissed them both, then stole a piece of Mac's banana to riotous objections.

I waited for some comment about the significance of today. And waited. And then waited some more. Nope, nothing. And

Benny and Mac both had the attention spans of custard, so they'd completely forgotten that I'd asked them anything.

Was this all part of some elaborate prank? You know, that one where everyone acts like they've forgotten an important occasion, until the poor victim is on the brink of madness, then they all jump out and shout 'Surprise'?

Mark went off for a shower and I poured another coffee, my bubble of excitement definitely popped. I sat with the boys and dissected the merits of Hong Kong Phooey versus Top Cat. It was the kind of highbrow current affairs debate that expanded my mind.

'Can we go to the park today, Mum? Can we, can we, can we?'

I wondered if Mac would ever get out of the whole repetition thing, because it was definitely going to cause raised eyebrows in the corporate boardrooms of life when he was older. Although, he was already convinced that he was going to be a racing driver or a pizza delivery guy, so I might be worrying unnecessarily.

I'd made no plans because I was sure Mark would have today covered. He would. Definitely.

'We'll see, sweetheart. I'm not sure what we'll be doing yet.'

'Can we go and see Charlie and Toni?' Benny asked, spraying banana. His cousins were four years older than him, and they treated him like a living doll – feeding him, giving him drinks, playing with him for hours. He didn't even mind that they'd dressed him in a furry yellow jumper and called him Winnie the Pooh all last weekend.

There was a thud from the hall and one from my heart straight afterwards. Bugger! I'd been standing by the letter box every morning this week to make sure that I was first to check the mail. I was about to commando-crawl out to the hall to retrieve the package, when Mark walked back in holding it. He was also dressed for the office. On a Saturday. I'm not sure which of those bothered me most.

'Letter for you,' he said, holding out the A4-size manila envelope. There was a question in his tone, but I brushed it off.

'Oh. That's the... eh... lingerie catalogue I ordered,' I told him, proud of coming up with a way to kill the conversation stone dead. Other men loved the whole sexy underwear vibe, but it had never been Mark's thing. He'd made a token effort with a few sexy camis for Valentine's days, but they were a couple of sizes too large (yep, that somewhat spoiled the moment) and still in the back of my drawer. They'd come in handy if I ever required a wind sock to check the weather conditions. 'Are you going into the office?' I said, unable to hide my amused intrigue. This definitely must be a joke. It had to be. There was no way he'd forgotten.

'Yeah, we're debriefing after the pitch for the Regen Corp case yesterday. All the partners want a full rundown on the meeting.'

'Oh.' My stomach flipped. The biggest pitch of Mark's career. The one that, if it came in, would also deliver the partnership he'd aspired to and worked towards since he qualified. And the one that would almost certainly consign my dreams to the big wheelie bin of life.

He pulled on his suit jacket. 'You two be good for Mum, okay? I love you,' he kissed them both and I melted a little inside. He was a good man, Mark Barwick. He loved me, loved his boys. Even if he was a complete workaholic and messing with his wife by setting up some twisted surprise on me today. 'Right, I'm off. I should be back around lunchtime though, so maybe we can do something later?'

Ah, there it was. Dangling a carrot, making sure I kept the rest of the day free. I liked his style.

'Yeah, sure. I'm just going to take the boys to the park, maybe see the girls, so I'll be around. Just give me a call.'

It was my turn for a kiss. 'See you later. Love you,' he murmured, then off he went.

As soon as I heard the door close, I ripped open the brown envelope.

Contract.
> *Carly Cooper.*
> *Associate Writer.*
> *Project: Family Comes First*

Oh Jesus, it was here. It was actually here. I already knew the terms of the agreement, because the assistant to the assistant to the assistant (it was Hollywood, that's how it worked) to the producers had been emailing back and forth for weeks.

I picked up my mobile and texted Kate.

Contract is here. It's official. If I make it big, it was lovely knowing you, but I'll be at the spa with Reese Witherspoon. xxxx

No answer. Bugger, she must still be in bed. Kate and her husband, Bruce, enjoyed an interlude of passion every Saturday morning. I tried not to be jealous. After all, Mark liked an interlude of passion at least once a month and a bonus one if there was a bank holiday.

Sigh.

The boys finished their breakfast and went off to play, while I sat down and read every word of the contract. Twice.

Still no reply from Kate.

I had to stop myself from drumming my fingers on the table. Where were all the people in my life? This was one of my biggest moments, on one of my biggest days, and I was sitting alone at my kitchen table feeling extremely sorry for myself.

Ping! Text. Hurrah! Someone had remembered!

I picked it up – not Kate.

Sam: Did it arrive?

I checked the clock, 9.30 a.m., so that was 1.30 a.m. in LA.

Me: It did. Why are you still up?

Sam: I'm a movie star. I'm supposed to be up all night with cocaine and a harem.

Me: So you're sitting alone like a saddo drinking beer?

Sam: Sure am.

That made me laugh, because I knew it was true. When I'd done the trail of hope to Hollywood a couple of years before, it had amused me no end that nights out and dinner parties were usually over by ten, because most of the successful people in the industry got up in the middle of the night to work out, meditate, or whatever else they did to connect with their inner superstar.

I was about to make further fun of him, but he jumped the queue by texting first.

Sam: Have you told Mark yet?

Me: …

…

…

...

I typed and deleted at least four excuses, or fudges of the truth, then went with...

No.

I knew that, right now, Sam would be sighing, and trying to come up with the right thing to say. Problem was, there wasn't a right thing in this situation and I only had myself to blame. After my failed trip to LA a couple of years before, I'd been offered some scriptwriting work, but it had frittered out. I'd been devastated, but what could I do? Mark was right. Jobs in Tinsel Town were too precarious, too sporadic, and it didn't work when we lived in the UK and were raising a family.

I accepted it. Came to terms with it. The End.

The big dream was over.

That is, until a month ago, when my LA agent had got in touch with an offer to join the writing team on a new comedy drama *Family Comes First*.

My first call had been to Sam. 'Did you do this? I mean, if you did, I'm eternally grateful and I'll give you the internal organ of your choice should you ever need it...'

'It's nothing to do with me,' he'd said, very definitely.

'Sam...?'

'Cooper, I swear. If I was behind it, I'd tell you, because you'd find out anyway. You did this on your own.' I could hear in his voice how happy he was for me.

I just hoped my husband felt the same.

I planned to tell him that night. And the next. And the next. But I never quite got the words out. I did, of course, tell the girls though.

'Are you going to wait until you're unpacking your case in LA before you actually let Mark know about this?' Kate had asked. She always could read my mind.

That old career-limiting chestnut. Writing in LA was the dream. Married life in Chiswick was the reality. Without a husband who was on board with the dream, I didn't see a way I could do both.

Problem was, I hadn't quite refused the LA job. And by that, I mean I'd made positive noises all along and they were sure I was ready to jump on the plane. In my head, I had a fantasy life where Mark thought it was a great idea, told me we'd work it out somehow, and then supported me as I took my little guys to LA and beautifully juggled writing and motherhood. My dashing husband would then fly over whenever possible and we'd have missed each other so much, he'd ravish me at every opportunity.

Like I said... fantasy.

But there was one tiny nugget of hope. If he didn't make partner, then perhaps I could persuade him to take a chance on this. Sure, it was a gamble. Shows got cancelled all the time. Projects got shelved before they even got started. Mark, who needed security, concrete plans, bloody pensions, struggled with the very thought of those kinds of risks. But if the partnership didn't materialise, if his morale was low, if he started to question his commitment to the rat race, maybe – just maybe – I could persuade him to take a chance on this. On me.

The ping of another text interrupted my thoughts.

You'll work it out. Goodnight, Cooper...

A wave of sadness. I knew Sam was cutting short the conversation because he didn't want to interfere in my marriage. He'd tried that once before. He'd wanted to love me, to build a life over there, but I'd chosen Mark. At the time, my husband had made big promises: he'd work less, he'd be more present, he'd support my career, he'd do more with the boys, we'd make time for each other. It had lasted for a while, then life had taken over and we'd slipped back to the same old ways.

Did I resent it? Quietly. In a pathetically passive way. I made deals with myself. When the boys were older, I'd focus on my dreams again. By that time, Mark would have found a better work/life balance and we'd reignite our romantic spark and have endless laughs and great sex until it was time for the Zimmer frames.

But maybe we could have all that now? Except the Zimmers, obviously.

'Mum, you didn't tell me what day it was today?' Mac had wandered back into the room, clutching a light sabre.

Before I could answer, my phone buzzed again.

Another text from Sam.

And, Cooper... happy birthday.

I had never missed someone more.

Before I could reply, our early-warning system advised us of an imminent arrival.

'Daddy's home!' Benny squealed, as the front door opened again.

It was Mark. But not just any Mark. This was excited, alive, thrilled, enthusiastic, grinning, gorgeous Mark.

'We got it!' He picked me up, swung me around. 'The Regen contract. We got it! We didn't think we'd hear until next week, but they called while I was in the office.'

The boys were picking up on his energy and squealing with delight, so he put me down and scooped them up.

'This is it, boys! Daddy's got a brilliant new job! How will we celebrate?'

'Can we get a swimming pool?' Mac blurted, excitedly.

'Beans!' Benny shouted. 'Let's get beans!'

If my heart hadn't plummeted to my walnut floor, I'd have been dancing with them.

'Yes! A swimming pool and beans. At the same time.' The boys were still cheering when Mark put them down and let them conga off back to their toys.

All his attention came back to me as he kissed me, his hands on my face, the way he used to do once upon a time when we were young and besotted and he couldn't get enough of me.

'I know I've been so wrapped up in this, and I'm sorry.'

'That's okay,' I said, smiling. It wasn't, but I couldn't bring myself to dent his joy – even if mine had just left the building.

'Babe, this is going to set us up for life. Better salary, great pension...'

Argh, that fucking pension!

'Security for the boys.' There it was. The kicker. Mark's job would give us the kind of stability that mine never would.

'And, Cooper,' he said, his voice low now, oozing happiness and love, 'I bought you this.' He pulled a little velvet box from his jacket pocket and held it out to me.

Still wordless, heart still thudding, desperately trying to balance love and despair, I took it, opened it.

'It's an eternity ring,' he whispered, as he took the beautiful band of diamonds from the velvet cushion and slipped it on my finger. 'Happy birthday, my love.'

He hadn't forgotten.

Through tear-filled eyes, I stared at the ring sitting snugly on my finger. Eternity.

'Oh, and I think we might have visitors,' he grinned, pulling away, reaching over to open the back door.

Kate. Carol. Jess. Sarah. Husbands. Kids. Our whole extended framily.

'Surprise!' they cheered.

Somewhere in the midst of the hugs and kisses and celebrations, I slipped the brown envelope into the bin.

28

BACK IN LA, 2019

FIGHT SONG – RACHEL PLATTEN

'Cooper – you came back!' Kate exclaimed cheekily, setting off a rousing cheer from the others, all of them sitting on stools at Sam's outdoor bar, except Val, who, despite the late hour, was lying in the pool on her shiny new Statue of Liberty inflatable lilo, balancing a cocktail in one hand and a book in the other. There was a snapshot I'd keep in my mind until the end of time. She was obviously taking her political asylum in the Republic of Sam very seriously.

I gave a mock bow of thanks, shrugging off the melancholy Sam had caused with his comment.

'I'll tell you my problem. Last time Mark asked you to go back to him, you went. And how did that work out for you?'

We both knew the answer to the question. All the promises Mark had made about spending more time with us, about supporting my career, about nurturing our marriage had all drifted away on a raft of work, commitments and pressures. There were payoffs, of course. We lived in a nice home, the boys loved their lives, and I carved out a career that I could work around taking care of my family. Somewhere along the line, I decided that was enough and I made it work. Until I couldn't. Sarah's death had changed everything. The grief and pain wiped out the energy I need to carry on the façade that I had a happy marriage and a fulfilled life. I'd loved Mark Barwick for most of my life, but that wasn't enough to stop us from falling apart.

Maybe the last few days had changed that. Maybe I could believe what he said about learning lessons, changing, priorities. Maybe it was time to make myself happy again.

I jumped as Sam's voice cut through my thoughts. I hadn't realised that he'd come out behind me. 'Ladies, I'm hitting the road. My flight to Toronto leaves in a couple of hours.'

What? He hadn't mentioned that. He'd said he was going out on set tomorrow, not tonight. Had he just booked it? Was he making it up because he wanted to get away from me after our blowout? We were only going to be there for four more days and he was going off in a sulk?

Well, screw Sam Morton. What did he know? He was the one who was living with a female who spent half an hour a day getting her arse vibrated so it was pert. What right did he have to lecture me on life choices and personal fulfilment? If he was going out of town, then at least I could spend the rest of the holiday free of his sanctimonious judgement. I ignored the fact that my heart was screaming a rebuttal to that thought.

I watched as he hugged everyone, then nodded in my direction as he passed me.

'See you later, Cooper.'

Then he was gone.

'Holy crap, what happened there?' Jess gasped. She was on the end stool, sitting next to Arnie, who was now up and following Sam into the house.

'Don't ask,' I said curtly, way too pissed off and heartsore to go there. Right now, I had a different priority, and she was noticeably missing from this gathering. 'Where's Toni?' I asked, keeping my voice light and casual.

'In bed,' Carol replied, with a sigh. 'The poor thing has come down with some kind of bug. She's been sick as a donkey since we got back.'

I didn't want to admit that I knew all about that bastard bug.

'I'll just go and say hello.'

The sliding glass doors to the bright and airy guest house were wide open, but the door to the bedroom was closed. I knocked. No reply.

'Toni? It's me.'

Nothing.

'Can I come in?'

Nothing.

Anxiety was now making my skin prickle. There were two options. Give her space, or…

I opened the door gently in case she was sleeping, a fair guess given that the curtains were closed. But no. She was sitting up, staring straight ahead, and even in the dim light, I could see her hair was limp, her skin was pale, the circles under her eyes were dark and desperate.

'Oh, honey,' I whispered, closing the door behind me.

She didn't object, didn't cry, didn't say a word when I crossed the room, sat on the edge of the bed and wrapped my arms around her.

'Toni, this can't go on. We need to talk.'

'I'm fine. I'm just not feeling well,' she sniffed.

No. No more. We were done with this. She was hurting and it was time for it to end, even if that meant some uncomfortable truths.

I let her go and went over to the curtains and pulled them

open. At least I tried to. They didn't budge. I tried again, almost dislocating my shoulders in the process.

'Aunt Carly, there's a switch for that,' she said, and I turned back to see her flick a chrome knob beside the headboard. The curtains slid open.

'Eh, I knew that,' I blustered, trying to make her smile. It didn't work.

Back over at the bed, I sat down, took her hand.

'Sweetheart, the next five minutes are going to sting, but there's no other way. I know about Taylor Fuckwidget...' I couldn't remember his surname and that seemed apt. 'I know about the photographs, and the post he put up. And I know that text I saw came from him.'

She visibly shrank as she wailed, 'Noooooo.'

'Toni, honey...'

'I'm so... so... sorry,' she sobbed, crumbling in front of my eyes.

'Toni, why are you sorry? This isn't on you.'

That softened the sobs, as she looked up at me with those beautiful big eyes and I thought about Toni at eight, at ten, at fourteen, that happy, carefree little kid who had always been shy but who bubbled with happiness and laughter.

It was taking every bit of me to hold down the rage at what had happened to her, because that wasn't what she needed right now.

'What do you mean?'

'Hang on,' I told her, before going into the bathroom and coming back with toilet roll and baby wipes. I gave her the toilet roll first. 'I couldn't see any tissues, but you need to blow your nose. I can't concentrate when there's snot.'

That caused a glimmer of a smile – it was a start.

I took out a baby wipe, sat back on the bed, and gently wiped her face of tears.

'Okay, the version I have of this story. Tell me if I've got any of it wrong.'

There was still fear in her face as I began to speak.

'You were seeing this boy, and he told you he liked you...'

'He said... he said he loved me,' she whispered.

I sighed. 'Bastard.'

There was a flash of surprise. We always made a point of being respectable grown-ups who didn't swear in front of the kids. That had just gone right out of the electric-curtained window.

'Anyway, he asked you to send him pictures, and you knew you probably shouldn't, because we've told you all a million times not to do that...' I wasn't letting her off the hook completely. 'But you liked him...'

'I thought I loved him.'

'So you did send him the photos.'

A nod.

'And then what happened?'

A pause, until finally, 'He wanted to have sex.' Her voice was husky from crying. 'And when I said I wanted to wait a while; he didn't like it. I kinda saw... I don't know how to explain it. I got scared. I saw who he was, so I told him I didn't want to go out with him any more. He said if I dumped him, he'd show people the photographs.'

'When was this, Toni?' I needed to get it all straight in my head.

'I started seeing him at the beginning of the year.'

'Och, sweetheart.' I pushed her hair back off her tear stained face. 'Why didn't you come and tell me when it got messy?'

She shrugged. 'I couldn't tell anyone. I didn't want to say what I'd done.'

'I might have to come back and talk about that later,' I told her, trying to make her smile. It almost worked. 'Tell me what's happening now.'

She sighed and her eyes filled again. 'He posted one of the photos on a chat, but you can't see my face. He sent a screenshot of it to me to prove he'd done it. He says if I really do finish with him, though, he'll post the other photos online. That's what that text you saw was about.'

Really, bitch? Don't you fucking dare or you know what's coming.

It all made sense now. Dump him and he'd post more photos of her.

'There is another one too. A worse one. Where my hands aren't covering me. I'm sorry,' she sobbed again. 'I really am. I don't know what to do.'

'Toni,' I said, gentle but firm. 'Enough. Please stop crying.' I took both her hands again as she swallowed back another sob. 'Okay, here's what we're going to do. You know how your mum and I...'

'Oh God, please don't tell my mum!'

I just kept right on talking. 'Your mum and I, and Aunt Kate and Jess, and Aunt Sarah when she was here... We've all been friends our whole lives. And I can't tell you how many mistakes we've made, and how much trouble we've got into and how many times we've bailed each other out. We're experts at messing stuff up and fixing it. Well, except Aunt Kate. She's pretty angelic. Anyway, I need you to trust me. We – both of us – are going to tell your mum. And then, if it's okay with you, we'll tell the others because they love you and I don't want you to be worrying that they'll find out some other way. They'll have your back too, and we'll come up with a plan to stop this happening to you. I promise, Toni – we've got you, my darling. We'll take care of you.'

'But...' she began to argue, then realised that she was out of options. This was the only life raft on the boat.

'Is that okay?' I asked.

After a few hesitant seconds, she nodded.

I called Carol in, and we sat her down, and between us, we managed to get the whole story out again. She was devastated, upset, regretful, sorry, furious... all the emotions that were completely natural for a mother in this situation. Most of all, though, she reacted in exactly the way I knew she would – she held Toni, told her she loved her and that we'd work it out.

A couple of hours later, sitting around a table with Val, Jess and Kate, it had all come out.

'Jesus suffering, Toni, you should have told us,' Val chided gently. 'Didn't we all get into bad situations at your age. The problem is, all these bloody cameras and this bloody internet. I'd ban the lot of it, I really would. Except the Tom Jones videos.'

'Val's right. We all made mistakes at your age,' Jess agreed, then in her usual no-filter, blunt manner, went on. 'Your Aunt Carly probably made the most though. Didn't you once go to a club in Amsterdam where everyone was naked?'

I shot her daggers. 'I think we're moving slightly off topic here. Anyway, are we all agreed on the plan?'

Naturally, Toni looked terrified, but she was bolstered by the positivity coming from the rest of us.

'Right then. Go ahead and call him,' I urged her, as encouraging as I could be.

We'd already worked out that it would be early morning in the UK so hopefully he'd answer.

She put her phone on the table so that she was the only one

he'd be able to see on screen and pressed the FaceTime button with a shaking hand.

'You've got this,' I promised, holding her free hand under the table. 'Remember, just pass him to me when you're ready.'

She nodded, staring at the ringing phone. We'd decided that I would be the adult intervention in this situation, because Carol didn't trust herself not to completely lose it. Also, just in case there was any comeback, it was far better to have an anonymous person dealing with this, rather than a YouTube influencer with three million followers who could propel it right into the public eye. That wouldn't help anyone, least of all, Toni. Val had volunteered, but she would almost definitely make death threats so we'd put the kibosh on that. Kate was too nice, Jess would have him arrested. So in the end, it came down to me and Carol settled for furtively recording the whole thing from the side, out of shot, so he wouldn't realise she was doing it.

Still ringing.

'Yo,' he said, as the screen cleared, and a Justin Bieber lookalike appeared. 'Wellllllllll, look who it is.'

Keep calm, I told myself. Toni knew what to say.

Toni managed to keep her voice steady. 'I got your screenshot of the photo you shared.'

'Didn't think I'd do it?' he leered.

I've never felt the urge to punch someone more.

'Didn't show yer face though. Not that kinda guy. It was just a bit of a laugh.' His smirk elevated my blood pressure straight into the hypertension bracket.

'It wasn't funny.'

'C'mon, Toni, chill out.'

'I want you to delete them. You promised.'

'Changed my mind.' He shrugged, like it was nothing. Like he was high on power, Getting off on hurting our girl.

'Taylor, please...' She was doing so well, but I could hear the anxiety starting to build and she was squeezing my hand so hard my fingertips were turning blue.

'I'm going to hang on to them. You know, in case I ever need... a favour.' The way he said it made it entirely clear what the favour was.

I cracked. My eyes flicked to Toni's, I nodded, she slid the phone around so that he had full view of me on the screen. We'd practised this. I was going to be cool. Be calm. I was going to maturely point out the error of his ways, and I was going to persuade him that deleting them was the right thing to do.

'Taylor, I'm Toni's aunt. And I just wanted to have a chat about this situation.'

So far, so good. Cool. Calm. However, the shock in his face and the sneer of his lip sent me down a slightly different path. I think it was the same one as Liam Neeson in *Taken*.

'Listen up, you little fucker, if you dare, just *dare*, to do one more thing to hurt my niece, I will hunt you down and I will remove your balls, layer by layer, with my cheese grater. It will be slow, it will be painful and you'll never have sex again. Or cheese. Do we understand each other? Excellent. Now delete the photos or I'm coming for you and you really, really don't want that, you insidious piece of crap.'

I hung up to a stunned silence, five women staring at me open-mouthed.

Jess eventually shrugged. 'Well, that got the point across. Not exactly the adult, mature approach we'd discussed.'

Adrenalin was still causing havoc with my heartbeat. 'I used the word "insidious". That's totally mature.'

Silence.

'Any other thoughts?' I asked, slowly coming down from white hot rage.

Carol slipped her phone into the pocket of her robe. 'I... erm... think you were clear and well understood,' she nodded, as if I'd just read the weather forecast.

In my peripheral vision, I saw Toni nodding, and I was scared to look. If she was rocking back and forward, distraught, I'd never forgive myself.

But no.

Her face had cracked into the first real, natural smile we'd seen for months.

'Aunt Carly... thank you.' Her shoulders had lifted, her eyes were brighter and, to my relief, I could see that she absolutely meant it. 'But remind me never to piss you off.'

29

LOS ANGELES – FOUR DAYS LATER
HOLD MY HAND – BRANDY CLARK

'She's like a different girl,' Carol said, gesturing to Toni, who was attempting to surf across the pool on the swan in a race against Val on her inflatable Statue of Liberty.

We were just hours away from our flight home and we were at Sam's poolside, taking advantage of our last few hours of California sun. We were also trying to sweat out the last of our overindulgence from the night before. Sam was still in Toronto on the World War Two set – apparently there was some issue with the director – and Estelle had gone to a residential boot camp in Montecito (a departure that had evoked not a single complaint from us), so Arnie had taken us all to a celebrity restaurant called Craig's, in the hope of finally satisfying Val's mission to track down Sylvester Stallone. He wasn't there, but on the way to the toilet, she did introduce herself to a lovely bloke who said he was going to be in the next series of *Grey's Anatomy*. He didn't mention what his role was, so there was every chance he was corpse number three at a natural disaster, but he had a Patrick Dempsey jawline so we didn't care. Val brought him back to the table and pointed out that Jess was single.

Actually, I wasn't sure that was strictly the case. Every night since we'd got back from New York, I'd heard Jess creeping past my room on the way out in the middle of the night. And every morning, she'd creep back in then come down for breakfast looking like someone had attached her to a whirligig and spun her round for several minutes. Apparently, the Tinder action in LA was relentless, and she was making the most of it.

Maybe that's why she was now lying next to us, looking like someone had rained on her casual sex parade.

Carol, meanwhile, was still beating herself up on the other side of me. 'I can't believe I didn't realise what was happening. I feel like the worst mother ever.'

'Don't be ridiculous. Have you seen what I feed my kids? I'm definitely the worst mother ever.'

That at least made her smile. She was right about Toni though. The last four days had been an absolute joy and she was just like a normal eighteen-year-old again, one without the weight of the world on her shoulders. We had no way of knowing if Taylor had deleted the photos from his phone, but he'd taken them off the Whatsapp chat and he hadn't published any more. I think what was making a huge difference with Toni, though, was that she now felt supported. Seeing the bond she'd developed with Val was wonderful too. The girls, like my boys, were missing someone in the grandmother role, due to the fact that my mother was resoundingly disinterested, and Val, well, no girl could ever replace her Dee, but she had plenty of love and hairspray for a whole squad of nieces.

Kate stretched out like a cat purring in the sun. 'Sam's going to have to replace all these loungers because they're pretty much moulded into the shape of our bums,' she said, laughing.

It was true. We'd barely been off them since we came back from New York. We'd spent lazy days at the pool, and cosy nights by the fire or – with the exception of last night – in Sam's movie theatre watching films that weren't even out in the cinema yet. Turns out he was on an awards panel and was sent copies of all the new releases. Val said she was bringing her Don here and they were just going to camp out in the movie room for a month.

Jess put her Sex On The Beach down on the table next to her lounger. 'Have you heard from him?' she asked me.

'Who?'

'Brad Pitt,' she answered drily.

'Nope, I think he's trying to get back with Jennifer Aniston.'

Jess threw a flip-flop at me.

I sat up and pulled my psychedelic kaftan over my shoulders. The girls called me Joseph and started singing 'Any Dream Will Do' every time I wore it. 'I refuse to answer questions about Sam Morton on the grounds that I'm a complete emotional screw-up, who always seems to say and do completely the wrong thing. And also, I'm still fairly sure Estelle is monitoring these conversations and one wrong word could get her so fired up her lip filler could explode.'

'*I close my eyes...*' That was Val, in the pool, singing her heart out.

How was I going to get through the rest of my life without seeing every one of these women every single day? In the last three weeks, despite all the emotional traumas, I'd never laughed more or ever felt so loved in my life and it was all thanks to these women. My soulmates. And in my heart, Sarah was included in that too.

I shoved my feet into my furry sliders, an impulse buy from Venice Beach. I think the fumes from all the hippies smoking pot had made me high. 'I'm going to go and finish packing. What time are we leaving for the airport?' Just saying that made my stomach lurch. I missed Sam. I missed Mark. I really, *really* missed my boys. So on the one hand I was desperate to get home, but on the other hand I was dreading leaving. I still hadn't come to a decision about Mark, either. It was just all too complicated.

Jess checked her watch. 'In about an hour.' The time check made her get up too. 'I think I'll just go and see if Arnie has sorted out our lift to the airport.'

'Hopefully Sam will be back by then,' Kate said. 'I'd hate to leave without saying goodbye.'

I tried not to let my feelings show on my face. Sam. I hadn't heard from him since he dropped me off after bringing me home from the airport, and I hadn't contacted him either – mainly because I didn't want to disturb him, but also because, okay, I was annoyed. I felt judged, but I didn't want to think about that right now because I was too freaked out by the thought of leaving without seeing him.

Taking my iced tea, I schlepped on up to my room to get myself organised. I jumped in the shower, then dried off and pulled on a pair of cropped jeans and a grey Clippers basketball T-shirt, then towel-dried my hair and left it to dry. When I came here, I was hoping to channel pixie cuteness. Now I was channelling Boris Johnson after taking a wrong turn and wandering through a car wash.

'Hey, you.'

The surprise made me yelp. 'You really need to stop that sneaking up on people stuff,' I chided.

Sam leaned against the doorway, in jeans and a white T-shirt, surveying the scene of chaos in front of him. I may have slightly overdone the shopping for the kids. I had no idea how I was going to get four boxes of trainers, eight T-shirts and three pairs of goggles into my case. 'Good to see you're organised as ever.'

'Good to see you're critical as ever,' I shot back.

Shit. A bit too harsh.

He flinched, his eyebrows raising quizzically. 'Something wrong, Cooper?'

My brain started throwing out orders to the rest of me. Say no. SAY NO. Just thank him for his wonderful hospitality, tell him how much his friendship means to you and then walk away quietly leaving no chaos in your wake.

'No. Everything's fine.'

Ah, crap. This man had lived with me. He knew that when I said 'fine', I actually meant *irritated, pissed off and if you hang on five minutes, I'll come up with everything you've ever done to annoy me.*

'Glad to hear it.'

And I'd lived with him. I knew that he wouldn't push me to tell him the problem because he thought that my reluctance to be open and truthful was incredibly immature. He might have a point, but that didn't matter. My brain was still shouting out orders like a shop steward who was worried about workers getting out of line. Keep it civil. Stay friendly. You're only here for another forty-five minutes.

'I didn't make a mistake going back to Mark last time!' I blurted furiously. My brain clapped a hand to my forehead and slunk away to have a lie-down in a dark room. 'I know that's what you think, but you're wrong and it really pisses me off that you're judging me. I know it hasn't worked out now, but we had another ten years of a good marriage after I went back to him. And what matters most is that the boys have had great lives, and haven't had to deal with parents on different continents, going back and forward always missing one of them.' My voice was getting higher by the second. There was a real possibility cracks would begin to appear in the French doors to the balcony. 'And I know my career might not exactly have hit the giddy high spots of... of... some high-flying Hollywood producer or his Emmy-winning, yoga-bendy girlfriend, but I'm okay with that. So, if you don't mind, keep your opinions to yourself and stop making me feel like you're some wise oracle of knowledge and I've disappointed you.'

For a moment, I thought he was just going to turn and walk away. Confrontation wasn't his thing. He was way too zen. I'd only seen him lose his temper once and that was twenty-five years ago, in Hong Kong, when I told him I was leaving.

'Really? Is that where we're going with this?' Oh, bollocks. He was seething. The little muscle at the side of his jaw was bulging like a plum. It always did that right before he wiped out the bad guys with a rocket launcher in his action-movie days. 'Disappointed? Of course I'm fucking disappointed! You've wasted half your life on a guy who didn't love you enough, didn't go out of his way to make you happy.'

'Mark does love me!' I shot back. 'We don't all have bloody...' I gestured to the ceiling – no idea why. '... Chandeliers! And people to run around after us. And more money than we know what to do with. My life might have been lacking some things that I'd have liked, Sam, but at least there were people in it, at least I'm not fifty years old and shagging someone half my age who couldn't make you laugh if she was... was... wearing a fucking clown suit and riding a unicycle!'

Aaargh, what was I saying? A clown suit? My brain was now rocking back and forward, weeping.

'Things you'd have liked?' he yelled back. Okay, maybe he hadn't heard the bit about the unicycle. 'Carly, from the minute I met you I knew you wanted to have this big crazy life. Look at all the things you did! You were the most driven, most adventurous person I'd ever met. You had all these huge dreams and you could have done anything—'

'I did do something! I raised a family.'

'At the expense of your dreams! I know Mark loved you, but it was all on his terms. What about your terms? Why didn't your dreams matter?'

'Because… because… life just doesn't work like that!'

It was lame, but it was the best I could do.

It was twenty-five years since we last had a fight like this, but we were making up for it now.

His eyes were blazing. 'It should have. You should have been with someone who made you count.'

It was out of my mouth before I even registered that I was going to say it.

'You mean like you?'

He reeled back as if he'd been slapped, then stopped. Stared.

'Yeah,' he said, all volume gone. When he spoke again, it was softer, quieter, but I could still hear the anger. 'You should have stayed with me.'

I brought it down a few notches too, but inside I was still blazing. 'But who knows if things would have been different if I'd stayed here with you? There would still have been kids to raise, jobs to do, and someone always has to make sacrifices for that. We all have big dreams, Sam, but sometimes real life happens, and someone needs to do the school runs and take out the bins.'

He stepped backwards out of the door, turned, then stopped, turned back.

'Have it your way, Cooper. Believe whatever you want to. And by the way,' his voice was even lower now, 'no matter what you think about Estelle, she's not going to rip out my heart and destroy it. If she said goodbye, it wouldn't hurt. I'll take that any day over the kind of pain you left me with last time you walked away.'

I don't know how long we stared at each other, speechless, before we heard the sound of a throat being cleared.

'Erm, sorry to interrupt,' Kate said. 'But Leon is here to take us to the airport. He says traffic is heavy, so we need to go now. Sorry.'

'That's okay. We're done here,' Sam said.

This time he was the one who walked away.

30

THAT NIGHT AND THE NEXT MORNING, LOS ANGELES AND LONDON

PROUD – HEATHER SMALL

'Jess, I beg you – instead of watching me drinking the gin, could you just hit me over the head with the bottle, so I can go straight to the blackout stage?'

Jess shook her head. 'Nope, you deserve to suffer. That was brutal.'

'Could you guys hear everything?' I groaned.

'Carly, the whole of Pacific Palisades heard you. I'm pretty sure Matthew McConaughey had to call a halt to his naked yoga because you were disturbing his peace.'

I let my head drop onto the table and I didn't even care that it was sticky or that everyone else in the airport bar was probably wondering if I'd fainted.

As it turned out, the traffic hadn't been too bad after all, so we'd got here three gins ago. Maybe four. I'm sure Val bought doubles.

'I just lost it. I don't know what's wrong with me,' I mumbled into the wood.

'I blame the menopause,' Val announced, making several people around us choke on their drinks. 'When I was going through the change, I was forever just blurting out whatever was on my mind. Although, my Don says I'm still doing it, so this must be the longest menopause in history. I also took a liking to rhubarb, but we never got to the bottom of that. Anyway, love, he'll forgive you,' she went on, patting the bottom of her bob to make sure it was still a perfect dome. 'Sometimes a good barney is what you need to reset a relationship. Gets rid of all that sexual tension.'

Carol nodded sagely. 'Val's right. It's just water under the tunnel. He'll get over it.'

'I thought age was supposed to bring wisdom,' Toni drawled, earning a loud cackle and an elbow in the ribs from her great-aunt.

Hearing Toni so upbeat and funny was the only thing that could have got my head off that table right at that moment, although there was a definite sticky residue and I really wished I'd cleaned the table before my dramatic gesture. Anyway, the return of her sparkle and her dry sense of humour was a joy to see, so it was worth it.

My phone buzzed.

Benny: Mum, we're at the airport. Boarding soon. Mac says he's hand-cuffing himself to a chair because he doesn't want to come home.

Mum: Tell him to go marry someone with an American passport imme-diately. But only if I can come live with them too.

Mac: I'll go off grid. You'll never find me.

Me: I got you chipped when you were a baby. I'll find you. PS: the vet that did it got struck off.

Mark: Is this the nonsense you lot always talk on here?

Benny: Yep. Welcome to paradise.

Wow. Mark Barwick had just joined one of our chats. Another first. Maybe he really was changing. Maybe…

I shut the thought down. I couldn't go there right now, not when Sam's bollocking was still reverberating in my brain.

'Let's do a video for Dad and Charlie,' Carol suggested to Toni.

She held up her iPhone so they were both in the picture. 'Right, you two, we're on our way. Time to get rid of the twenty-one pizza boxes that are probably now stuffed under the sofa…' She wasn't kidding. It was a standing joke that my brother could eat his body weight in chips and still retain the body of an Adonis, while I gained two pounds just taking the Chinese take-away menu out of the drawer. 'Love you both and we can't wait to see you!'

With that, she and Toni both blew kisses and giggled as they ended the clip.

My phone buzzed again.

'Suffering mother, it's like a shop for those sex aid things in here with all this buzzing,' Val exclaimed, making Kate and Jess howl with laughter.

Mark: Carly, shouldn't you be boarding by now too?

'Oh my God, that man and his need to organise things!' I exclaimed.

'What's up?' Kate asked, while Val and Jess listened in. Carol and Toni were too busy filming another content piece for Carol's Instagram. Something to do with travel masks, which they were now holding to their faces. We were so getting thrown out of here.

'Mark and the boys are just boarding and he's asking why we aren't boarding now too. I mean, how does he even know our flight times?'

'He asked me for an itinerary,' Jess said. 'You know he likes his details.'

It was like one of those scenes you see in sitcoms, where everyone realises something at exactly the same time. Or rather, Kate, Jess and I all realised something at the same time. Carol and Toni were still doing social media videos and Val was trying to listen to the people at the next table talking about a suspicious rash.

'Shit!' Jess vocalised it first. 'We should be boarding! We've completely lost track of time. Six of us here and not a sensible one among us,' she bellowed, jumping up, grabbing her coat, her bags, her friends. She practically pulled Carol out of her seat by her collar.

'Hang on, hang on! I need to post this video,' she wailed.

'No time!' Jess argued. 'I'm not missing a bloody flight because you're getting paid a grand to talk about aloe vera. Let's go!'

That got her moving, still tapping away on her phone as she grabbed her stuff and ran alongside us. Thankfully, her ability to multitask was far greater than her ability to articulate any well-known phrase or saying.

We ran – and I mean sprinted – all the way to the gate – with Val shouting 'out of the way, it's a medical emergency' to everyone in front of us. We reached the gate with red faces, exploding lungs and only seconds to spare. A decidedly unimpressed ground-crew member ushered us on and helped us find space for our cabin bags, our jackets and the giant bags of M&Ms that Val had bought for Don in the duty-free. No first-class for us this time. We were in two rows of three back in economy, because when Carol and Toni had skipped their flights, they'd just booked seats next to ours for the homeward journey. Carol was clearly horrified, but she didn't have time to moan. Our bums had barely hit the seats when the safety announcement came on and the airplane began to pull back from the gate.

The holiday was over. Done. It had been three of the best weeks of my life and I would treasure it always, for the laughs, for the friendships, for the closeness it had given me to Toni and Val, but especially for the peace I'd found over Sarah's death. I closed my eyes, hoping that wherever she was, she could hear what I was thinking: *We miss you, pal. We always will. And we'll look out for Hannah and Ryan, I promise.*

'Ladies and gentlemen, I regret to inform you that unfortunately Wi-Fi service is not available on this flight...'

That made me smile. I was pretty sure Wi-Fi wasn't required to get through to my friend on the other side.

Kate was sitting next to me.

'I had a great time, Kate,' I said quietly, taking her hand. 'I can't tell you how much I love you for this. I mean, I loved you anyway, but even more now.'

'I love you too, Coop,' was the last thing I heard before three weeks of emotional overload, a potential reunion with my husband, a huge fight with one of the other loves of my life, too many laughs to count and at least three large gin and tonics took effect, and I fell into a deep, exhausted sleep.

Twelve hours and ten minutes later, I woke up as the wheels were touching the tarmac at Heathrow.

'Did I do it again? Did I miss the whole flight?'

I didn't require an answer, given that it was daylight outside and I could see the terminal building approach as we taxied towards it.

We hadn't even come to a standstill when mobile phones all over the plane began to ping as people began to switch them on.

'This is ridiculous, so it is,' Val said. 'I mean, what's so important that folk can't be out of contact for a few hours without everyone needing to speak to them. No wonder people get stressed. In my day...'

'Oh crap. Crap. Crap. Crap. Oh crap.' All of which came from Carol, sitting directly in front of me.

I was about to lean forward, when my phone sprang into life in my hand.

Mac: Mum! OMFG!

I made a mental note to have a word about his language. Yes, abbreviations counted.

Benny: Mum! Have you seen Aunt Carol's Insta???????? You're going to kill her.

Mark: Call me. I think you're going to need someone from work.

Someone from work? He was a lawyer. Why would I need someone from his work?

'Oh crap. Crap. Crap. Crap. Oh crap.' Still Carol.

That horrible ice-cold fear feeling – the one that comes when you know something really bad has happened but you're not sure what it is – began in my gut and spread instantly through every vein.

I leaned forward, putting my face into the gap between Carol and Toni's seats.

'Carol?'

My sister-in-law turned to see my face peeking through, and I could see she was ashen.

The fear feeling got even worse. 'What's happened?'

Her mouth moved a couple of times, but nothing was coming out. For a second, I wondered if she'd had a stroke.

It was Toni who managed to get her words out first. 'You know Mum was posting the face mask video when we were running for the plane?'

I tried to nod, but my head was wedged solid.

Toni went on anyway. 'She posted the wrong one.'

I didn't understand. 'It wasn't aloe vera?'

Toni shook her head. 'No. She posted the one of you talking to Taylor Fuckwidget on FaceTime.'

31

CARLY'S KITCHEN, SHORTLY AFTERWARDS
TAKE A BOW – RIHANNA

The first thing I saw when I got in the door was Mark's stone-cold expression of rage and fury. I'd been feeling nauseous since I saw the video, and now, seeing his reaction, I definitely wanted to throw up.

'Seriously? Christ, Carly, what were you thinking? How many times have we warned the kids never, ever to put anything on film that they wouldn't want the world to see?'

'But I didn't think...'

'That's the problem – you didn't think!'

This was exactly how I always imagined it would be to get a bollocking from my dad... if my dad hadn't been a nightmare of a drunk who generally didn't give a toss what we did as long as it didn't interfere with his relationship with Jack Daniel's. The point was, though, I suddenly felt like I was six years old and getting scolded. Not what I needed right at that moment. I wanted to turn round and go right back to the airport and get on a flight to anywhere, preferably somewhere that someone would wrap me up and tell me it was all going to be ok and... argh, why was Sam the first person that came into my head?

Mac and Benny were sitting at the kitchen table, both of them heads down while their dad gave a full-scale reprimand on social media misuse. To. Their. Mother. I wouldn't blame them if they put themselves up for adoption after this.

I could have tried to defend myself, tried to mitigate the damage, but there wasn't much I could say to minimise threatening to slice off a guy's balls with a cheese grater, especially now that 1.2 million people and counting had watched the video. 1.2 million. That's what happens when a social media influencer with three million followers posts something outrageous and shocking, and then switches off her phone because she's on a twelve-hour flight with no Wi-Fi.

Carol had, of course, deleted the video, but it was too late. It had been shared, retweeted and picked up everywhere, including the websites of all the major tabloids.

The fallout had already been beyond anything I could imagine. I'd had an email from *Family Values* magazine, cancelling my column. Seems they've got some kind of bias against people who threaten others with slow, excruciating torture. Plus, the British Cheese board are one of their sponsors and they weren't too chuffed either. Something about positive cheese messages and optics. The fact that a few of the taglines were calling me the cheesy ball slicer didn't help.

There was also an email from my agent, saying that the morning telly guy who'd hired me to ghost-write his autobiography no longer required my services. This is a guy who had blown over a million quid on cocaine and got caught in an S&M four-way with three high-class hookers who revealed his safe word was 'courgette'. Yet, it would seem I was now at least one step lower on the desirable poll than him.

To be honest, though, the only people whose opinions I really cared about were the two boys sitting at the table staring at their feet, and Toni. Had I made it so much worse for her? Had I just pushed my shy, sweet girl into a spotlight that would burn her? At the airport, she'd been too shocked to speak, too stunned to react, so I had no idea what she was thinking. Carol just kept repeating a tearful mantra of 'Oh fuck, sorry. Oh fuck, sorry,' until Callum had whisked them away, shouting over his shoulder that he'd call me later. I couldn't work out if he was mad, sad, or just wanted to get his wife and daughter home to try to work out how to deal with this mess. Val had gone with them, as she was staying with them for a couple of nights to spend time with Callum and Charlie, before flying home to Glasgow later in the week.

The thing was, Carol had messed up by posting the video, but if I hadn't gone full psycho vigilante on the call, then it wouldn't have gone viral and had over four thousand comments raging from, 'This is a disgrace' to 'Put this chick in charge of shutting down Brexit. She'd slice off Boris's balls.'

I pointed this out at least fifty times in the cab Kate and I had shared home. She'd listened to me berating myself for forty minutes, so she was probably now having a lie-down next door with a cold compress over her head.

How had I fucked this up so badly?

How many times had I warned the boys about the dangers of the internet?

How was I going to fix the wooden floor in my kitchen after Mark had worn a hole in it with all his pacing up and down?

And how was I going to get out of this mess?

A thump at the door provided me with a ray of hope. Please let it be Carol and Toni. Or Kate. Or anyone else that mattered and who would tell me this was going to be okay. Or at least Derren Brown, so he could wipe this from our memories.

When Mark went to answer it, I sagged on the kitchen chair. 'Boys, I'm so sorry. I know I've really embarrassed you and I'm mortified that this might affect you too. Please disown me. If you want to live with your dad until it dies down, I'll understand. I'd hate it, but if being around me is a problem...'

'Carly.' That was Mark, and I didn't even need to look to know that whoever was at the door, it wasn't good news. He had the same tone as when he told me the repairs were going to cost a grand after I left the bathroom tap running and flooded the house. 'These officers would like to speak to you.'

Officers. I could hear Val in my head, whistling a low, horrified 'Suffering mother'.

'Mrs Barwick...'

I didn't want to point out that I'd never officially taken Mark's name, so I was still a Cooper. Didn't seem like the right time.

'We've received a complaint against you for threatening behaviour. We've also come into possession of some video evidence that backs up that allegation, so we'd like you to come down to the station with us to discuss the matter further.'

Again, suffering mother. This was unbelievable. Jail? And again, the worst part was the look on my boys' faces – total shock and fear.

'Boys, don't worry, please,' I begged them. 'It'll be okay. I promise. It'll be fine. I'll sort it out.' None of which was based on anything but hope and a desperation to make them feel better. I was hardly going to tell them there was every possibility that the next time they saw me I'd be sitting behind a plexi-glass screen, wearing orange, with tattoos on my knuckles.

'I'll call and get someone down to help you,' Mark said. Turns out his prediction that I might need a lawyer wasn't as crazy as I'd thought.

In fairness to the police officers, they were very polite, and they didn't put me in handcuffs, so at least the neighbours weren't scandalised by the sight of me being huckled off to jail. Although,

I was pretty sure Kate would have thrown herself in front of them and sacrificed herself in order to help me escape.

But no. Twenty minutes later, I was down at the local nick and having my rights read to me. Once upon a time, in my wild crazy nightclub years, that wouldn't have been a total shock, but how had this happened to a middle aged mother, who never broke the law and even paid her parking tickets on time?

'It's within your rights to have a lawyer present when we question you. Do you understand that and wish to wait for legal representation?'

'No, thank you.' I just wanted to get this over with and get back home, presuming I wasn't about to be detained at Her Majesty's Pleasure.

The room they took me to was like every interrogation room I'd ever seen on the TV. Brick walls. Large one-way mirror. Desk. Two chairs on either side. Big bloody lock on the door.

They kicked things off by explaining that the criminal complaint had been made by Taylor Fuckwidget's father – they didn't actually call him that, but I couldn't hear them over the wailing in my head, so I missed what they said – in response to a video that had been posted online. Apparently it contravened at least three acts of a law to prevent online abuse. There were only a couple of things going in my favour. The first was that I didn't actually use the guy's name. And the second was that, because of the angle Carol had shot it at, it was almost impossible to get a clear look at his face. What was clear though, was me, on camera, threatening a twenty-year-old man with mutilation by cheese grater.

I explained everything from start to finish, in the most honest way that I could. And yes, I'd seen *Line of Duty*, so I threw in a couple of 'whereupon I's and 'the alleged victim's. I'm not sure it helped my case.

I was there for about an hour when a suggested resolution was reached. If I accepted an official caution, all further action would be dropped.

I thought about it. It was a tempting solution. No further action. No court. No threat of worse. It would all be over. Except...

The first thing that came into my mind was that an official caution might have to be declared when applying for a new visa to visit the USA. I only knew this because George who worked in the butchers on the high street had told me he got knocked back for an ESTA visa because he once got done for vandalism after spray-painting 'Vegans Kill Carrots' on the underpass next to the fruit market. If I couldn't get a visa, then I couldn't go to the USA, and if I couldn't go to the USA, then I couldn't go and see Hannah and I couldn't go... Bugger, I couldn't go and apologise to Sam when he blocked me on all means of communication for being a complete bitch. If he didn't come to the UK, then I'd never see him again. Never hug him. Never hear him laugh. Watch him smile. Never hold his hand. Touch his face.

'No,' I blurted.

'What?' the older cop fired back.

'I don't want a caution. I can't. It's not you, it's me.' I might have been getting my TV shows mixed up. I'm not sure Martin Compston ever said that in *Line of Duty*. 'What are my options?'

'Mrs Barwick, this isn't like a menu, where you get to choose from a selection of punishments.'

'I know, I'm sorry. I really am. But what else can I get?'

They clearly thought I'd lost my mind.

'Look, you don't seem like some criminal mastermind,' the nicer cop said, 'and, to be honest, if some... *person* did that to my daughter I may have had a similar reaction. But the point is, we need to be seen to be doing something here. My advice would be to wait for a lawyer and take it from there.'

That's when they led me to a holding area, plonked me in a room, and banged the door.

So hello, well of despair. I was wondering when I'd get back to you.

I was lying on a cold slab of concrete, in a breeze-block cell, with just a thin piece of plastic-covered foam on top, and I couldn't help but contemplate the fact that at that very moment, I seemed to have found myself unemployed, skint, single, publicly shamed, facing national humiliation, my mother had denied knowing me (I actually didn't know that for sure, but if I was a betting woman I'd put my gas bill money on it), my kids may never forgive me...

'Stand up and move back from the door. You have a visitor.'

And my lawyer was at the door.

Christopher Atwell, the partner in Mark's law firm who dealt with criminal cases, was standing outside, all three-piece suit and professional.

'Nice to see you, Carly,' he said, as if I'd just met him over a turkey vol-au-vent at the company Christmas dance.

'You too,' I murmured, wondering if this was some psychological ploy to play mind games with the cops.

'Come on, let's get you home.'

'Really? I can go? I don't understand.'

'All charges have been dropped. It was pointed out to the complainant that his son had breached Section 33 of the Criminal Justice and Courts Act 2015, prohibiting the distribution of photographs such as the ones in question. After discussions with all concerned, the authorities have decided it's not in the public interest to pursue this matter. There was also a bit of a backlash. A couple of newspapers started petitions. Free the Chiswick Cheese Slicer.'

I have never wanted to die a swifter death than I did at that moment.

After a few signatures on bits of paper, I came out blinking into the sunshine.

Freedom, as the bloke with the blue face would say.

'Home?' Christopher asked.

'Home,' I agreed. I didn't add that somewhere in this absolute clusterfeck of a morning, I'd already made my mind up that it would only be a flying visit.

32

CARLY'S HOUSE, TWENTY MINUTES LATER
I HAVE NOTHING – WHITNEY HOUSTON

When I opened the door of my house, there was complete silence, and my first thought was that everyone had abandoned me. My boys had taken me up on my suggestion, they'd gone to Mark's house, and he was already petitioning the courts for sole custody. Perhaps I'd be allowed weekly visits as long as I was supervised and searched on the way in for cheese graters. It had been at least an hour since my last major catastrophisation so I was due one.

It was only when I got near the closed kitchen door that I heard the sound of a voice. Then another. Then another. Then...

'Cooper!' Kate's startled reaction when I opened the door.

It was like the Last Supper. Only in Chiswick. With better shoes.

The whole framily was there: Kate, Jess, Carol, Val, Toni and Charlie sitting at the kitchen table, none of the first four showing any signs of jet lag. Mark, Bruce and Callum were standing over at the sink with my boys. The thought struck me that Mark looked like he'd never left. Like he belonged there.

'Mum!' that was Benny and it came with the biggest grin and the tightest hug.

I squeezed him until my arms hurt, milking the moment in case the police had second thoughts and stormed back in for me.

'Ha, it's Al Capone.' Mac. Of course. As soon as I released his brother, he stepped into his place.

I tried to read the boys' reactions and the atmosphere in the rest of the room, but I was so tired and drained I wasn't sure I was getting it. This couldn't be right. No-one seemed pissed off at me. Even Mark had stopped scowling. But what mattered most was...

'Toni, I'm so sorry. I really am.' I was so anxious, that my voice had risen a couple of octaves. 'You know I'd never do anything to embarrass you. At least, not deliberately.'

'She's never had any control over the accidental stuff though. She used to have me pure mortified with her antics,' Val interjected. It wasn't helpful.

'I hope you can forgive me, Toni,' I went on, feeling utter despair that all the progress we'd made to rebuild her self-esteem and get her back to a happy place had been undone.

There was a silence as I waited to hear my fate. I could mess up my own life. In fact, I'd done it on several occasions. But I just couldn't do that to anyone else. They didn't deserve it. Especially not the kids.

'They want you and Mum to go on *Loose Women*,' Toni blurted.

'They're going to name and shame us?' I gasped, already picturing the look of scorn on Holly Willoughby's face.

'No! They think you're both fab! They loved the video. Actually, they wanted me to go on too, but I passed. I said I'd talk to *Heat* though. I think it's important that I speak up for people this happens to.'

'What? I don't understand. I didn't embarrass you?' She didn't look mortified or sad at all. She looked... determined. Strong. Empowered.

'Yeah, you did.'

Ouch. I'd been hoping for a reprieve on that one. Now we were getting to the truth of it.

'But my face isn't shown anywhere and even if the photo goes viral – which it probably will – it's just my body with nothing actually showing. Taylor wouldn't dare post the other photo now that the police are involved. Part of me hates that everyone is talking about me, but I didn't do this, so I'm not going to let it define me.'

Well, snap, girlfriend. These kids were so much more mature than we ever were. Or are now, actually.

Carol put down her mug. I suspect it had something other than coffee in it. Actually, maybe that's what was happening here. They were all under the influence of something. 'The post got so much publicity that we've been inundated with calls from the media.'

'I know – Free The Chiswick Cheese Slicer.' I admitted, cheeks flushing with mortification.

'Yep, that's it,' she laughed. 'The public is on our side. People are sick of guys like Taylor Fuckwidget using stuff like this against innocent women and girls. Cooper, if anyone should be apologising, it's me. And I have. To Toni. At least a dozen times. I was the one who messed up by posting it. I'm sorry to you, too. You were just protecting my daughter and I've landed you in a police station.'

'It's okay, I'm not getting charged,' I told her quickly, desperate to set her mind at ease.

'I know. Christopher Atwell called Mark and told him.'

'Oh. I kinda wanted to break that news,' I said, a little deflated. My gaze automatically went to Mark. After all his outrage, I was looking forward to letting him know he had nothing to worry about. He wouldn't have to spend the next period of his life bringing the kids to visit their mum in prison. Always a bonus.

'Sorry if he stole your lightning,' Carol said, immediately sussing what I was thinking. Actually, now I was thinking about thunder, but this wasn't the time to be pedantic.

'All right, sis?' Callum said, budging in beside me on the kitchen bench and giving me a hug.

'I am now. Are you still talking to me?'

'Absolutely. I wouldn't have expected less than what you did. You were looking out for my girl. Even if it did cause a national scandal. Do me a favour, though. I love you, but don't go on holiday with my wife again. My heart can't take it.'

He kissed my cheek, then got up and wandered back over to where the menfolk were gathered.

The relief was indescribable. So that only left Mark to reason with later. He'd been furious this morning, and I wasn't sure if he'd calmed down or if he was just putting on a show because I was no longer on a wanted list. Right now, I just wanted to soak in the strange turn this had all taken and enjoy the moment, celebrate the fact that my family hadn't disowned me.

'So, Toni, tell me all about this interview with *Heat*.'

33

LATER THAT NIGHT

THINK – ARETHA FRANKLIN

'That was some day,' Mark said, as he picked up another empty beer bottle and put it in the half-full black plastic bag he was carrying in his other hand.

It was almost midnight and the last of the stragglers had just left. Kate and Bruce had gone back next door, Jess had gone home to wait for her ex to drop off Josh. Callum and Carol and the girls had headed off to plan their media activity, taking Val with them. The last words I heard her say as she went down the path were, 'If you go on *This Morning*, I'm coming. I love that Phil Schofield, especially since he stopped dyeing his hair.' And finally, Mac and Benny had gone next door to the living room to launch an invasion on the PS4. They seemed to have completely brushed off everything that happened this morning and emerged unscathed from their mother's criminal antics.

I took my glass of wine and opened the back door, then sat on the step. 'I'm just enjoying the breeze,' I told Mark, then added over-dramatically, 'when you almost lose your freedom, you start to appreciate these things.'

His sense of humour seemed to have returned because he

laughed, then put the bag down, grabbed his beer and joined me on the step.

'I'm sorry about this morning,' he said, gently nudging my shoulder with his. 'I totally overreacted. I guess my ability to roll with the punches has got lost along the way somewhere.'

'You could be right,' I said, softly. 'I warned you though.'

'What do you mean?'

'Twenty years ago. When we met again at Callum and Carol's wedding. I think I was sitting in a tree, crying in my bridesmaid dress after I'd done something mortifying and you asked me if my life was always a drama or a disaster. I told you it was, and you said you'd get used to it. I don't think you ever did.'

He smiled at the memory, but it was tinged with something else. Maybe sadness or regret. 'I guess I was more of a prude than I realised.'

'Not a prude,' I argued. 'Just someone who prefers to play life safe. I get that. I really do.'

He sighed. 'How come I feel like I can hear a "but" coming?'

'But it's not me,' I said, delivering it. 'I love you, Mark...'

'Ah shit, another "but" is on the way,' he groaned.

'But we're not the right fit any more. I think I've realised now that when we were young, the whole opposites-attract thing worked for us. I loved your stability. I loved the safety I felt when I was with you. I'd grown up in such a hot mess of a house, with a pissed dad and a mum that didn't much care, so you gave me the same feeling as I've always had when I'm with the girls: like I belong. Like they've got my back. They care.'

Where was all this coming from? It was like I'd cracked open my soul, all this emotion and insight was just pouring out and I couldn't make it stop, even though it was making my heart hurt.

'Back then, you loved that I was wild and unpredictable. It

intrigued you. Amused you. But the thing is, that doesn't work for a lifetime. One of us had to change and it was me. I became smaller. Stopped chasing my dreams. Settled for normality. I fitted around your way of living, instead of holding on to mine. Please don't think I'm blaming you for that. It was all me. I let it happen.'

'I can see that,' he said mournfully, 'and I'm sorry.'

'Don't be. Like I said, it was my choice, and the truth is, I'd do it again for our boys to turn out exactly the way they are. This is the life I chose because I wanted them to grow up with all the safety and stability I never had.'

'Another "but"?' he asked.

'But it's not right for me now.'

He winced when I said that, but I kept going.

'I think losing Sarah was the turning point. I was too broken to keep the act up. And it's a cliché, but it made me realise that life is short. That's why I wanted to separate. I couldn't keep living a life that wasn't right.'

'Carly, please... I told you in New York, I know I've made mistakes too. I went too much the other way, cared too much about doing things right, not stepping out of line, building financial security...'

'Is this where you try to woo me with your pension?' I asked, teasing him. To his credit, he laughed with the joke and I wished, for a moment, that I could make this work, that we could start from scratch with open minds and optimism, but I knew we couldn't. 'I know you think you want to take risks and make life an adventure, but I also know that's not you, Mark. This morning proved that.' It wasn't a rebuke or a criticism, just a statement of fact. 'Something bizarre and unpredictable happened and you freaked out, went straight to furious. And I immediately shrank back. The truth is, I was sorry for embarrassing you and Toni and the boys – although Mac told me today that I'm badass and he made it sound like a good thing...'

That made him smile.

'But I wasn't sorry for what I did. That prick deserved it and I'd do it again. I should have stood my ground when you were going off on one, I should have defended myself, held my head high, but I didn't. I changed who I am for you and I can't keep doing that. And you can't change who you are for me. I'm sorry.'

He didn't say anything for a long time, just sat there, staring ahead, processing it all. It was more proof of what I'd just said. I wanted a man who would fight for me. Inside, down really deep, I was still the same person I was at eighteen. I was the girl who went off looking for adventure, who fell in love hard, who wanted someone who would declare his love and sweep her off her feet. Okay, so now the only guy with the muscle to pick me up and sweep me anywhere would be The Rock, but the sentiment remained. For twenty years, I'd kept that girl down. It was time she got to come out and live her life again.

'I should argue, but I can't,' he said honestly. 'I know you're right. I just hate it.'

'Yeah, I've always hated it when you're right too. I tended to deal with it by calling you names under my breath and using your razor to shave my legs. Sorry about that too.'

Another sad smile as he shook his head and another silence while we both processed what we were saying. We were done. Our marriage was definitely over. Perhaps, in time, we'd see that something much better had been left behind.

'Friends?' I asked him, praying that he'd accept this. For the boys' sakes, but for ours too.

After a moment, he put his arm around me. 'Friends.'

I should probably have drawn a line under that and bowed out while the going was good, but that was the thing: I didn't want to, and hadn't I just promised myself that I was going to live on my own terms from now on?

'There's something else,' I said, before I could change my mind. 'You might not like it, but eventually you'll see that it's for the best.'

'Oh God, I don't know if I'm ready for this,' he groaned.

'The thing is, it involves the boys, so you need to be.'

I spent the next half-hour telling him everything, and to his credit, he listened, didn't comment, argue or judge.

'What do you think?' I asked him when I was done.

'I think I really hate it,' he said eventually and I could see the pain and despondence in every crease of his face. 'But I think you've got to do what you've got to do and I've got to get used to it. Go do your thing, Carly.'

'Really?' I hadn't expected that. I'd been braced for arguments, for him to push back and fight for what he wanted. He didn't. And relieved as I was, there was a little piece of me that knew that lack of passion was exactly why it was time to say goodbye to our marriage. I wanted more.

'Really. Fuck, I hate being the mature one,' he said with a low, rueful chuckle.

'I hate that you're so mature too.' It was true, but I said it gently, bumping his shoulder with mine. There was a pause, as we both shifted to the new landscape, adjusted to what we'd just agreed.

'Thank you, Mark,' I said eventually. 'I need you to know something though. If I could go back, I'd make all the same choices. I've loved you beyond words and I'm so thankful that we've spent the last twenty years together.'

We were both blinking back tears now. 'Likewise, Cooper. It's been some ride.'

I reached over and hugged him for a long time. 'I love you,

Mark Barwick. Always will.'

His voice was husky as he replied, 'You too, my love. You too.'

We sat like that for a while, calm, reflective, my head on his shoulder, until he broke the silence. 'We should tell the boys soon. I don't want them to get any mixed messages.'

'You're right. Let's do it now. Let's go ask them if they'd be ok with it.'

He inhaled sharply. 'Now? I was thinking maybe tomorrow. You know, limit the life changing events to one a day.' That made me laugh.

'Here's the thing you never understood, Mark,' I teased him. 'Sometimes in life, you've just got to close your eyes and jump in. And it's time for me to make a fuck-off big splash.'

34

THE NEXT MORNING
GOOD AS HELL – LIZZO

'You sure about this, guys?' I asked them, as I was bent double at the kitchen table, pulling on my ankle boots. 'You know, I understand if you want to stay with your dad, and he meant it when he said that was okay with him too.' I didn't want to say that I was happy beyond words that they'd stuck with me, but I felt it in every single piece of my heart. Mark and I had explained everything to them last night, and then told them my plan for today. If they'd objected, I would have scrapped everything, so I'd held my breath as they went from surprise, to contemplation, and then – when they saw that their dad was cool with it – to something between excitement (Mac) and calm, happy acceptance (Benny). When Mark left, it was with hugs, love, a little regret, but the absolute certainty that we were doing the right thing and we were all going to be fine.

Now, I'd only asked my boys if they were sure because I wanted to check their feelings hadn't changed overnight.

'Hell no,' Mac exclaimed, taking the last bite of his toast. 'I'm not missing this for anything.'

'Me either,' Benny said. 'Even if it's a disaster. It might be like one of those horror movies that you can't stop watching even though the serial killer has a machete.'

'Thanks for that. I'll bear it in mind. Nothing can be as bad as a serial killer with a machete,' I said, chuckling despite the nerves that were flipping my stomach from side to side. 'Okay, I'll go watch for the taxi. I'll shout you when it gets here.'

In the lounge, I stared out the window thinking how absolutely apt this was.

When I was eighteen years old, I'd packed up and gone off to Amsterdam with no money, no job, just the hope that I'd land on my feet.

When I was thirty, I quit my job and my flat, and went off to find all the men I'd ever loved, with the hope that one of them would be the right guy.

And now? I clearly hadn't learned a thing because I was almost fifty, and here I was going off to apologise to a man I loved, with just the vague hope that he wouldn't slam the door in my face.

This was crazy. Ridiculous. Completely irresponsible.

Yet, despite the terror, I couldn't stop grinning because I hadn't felt this alive in a long, long, time.

I spotted the approaching car. 'There's the taxi. Right, boys, let's go, and even if you think it's a really bad idea, just humour me, okay?'

We bundled everything into the car, three bodies, two back-packs and a trolley case, and told the driver we were off to Heathrow. Only twenty-four hours since I landed there, I was going back. I was going to apologise to Sam. I was going to tell him how I felt and...

My phone started ringing in my bag and it took me a moment to find it, to fish it out, and to see Kate's name flashing up.

'Hey, lovely!'

'Carly! Where are you?'

'Just passed your house on my way to Heathrow. I was going to call you when I got there.'

'No way!' There was a change in the tone, as if she'd put me on to speaker. 'Cooper, why are you going to Heathrow?'

'Okay, don't freak out...' I decided that I had at least twenty minutes until we got to the airport, and the boys were both occupied on their phones, so I may as well jump right in and tell her. 'But here's the thing, Kate. I messed up. I really did. I was a complete cow to Sam, and I know now that it's because I was confused, and I didn't want to leave, and I was jealous...'

'Jealous?'

'Yes! Jealous that Estelle got to be with Sam even though she has the personality of a cabbage.'

Mac shook his head, laughing and I chided myself for the low blow. Even though I meant it. How I felt about Estelle didn't matter. What actually did matter was...

'I love him, Kate. I do. Not just as a friend. I love him in all the ways. So last night, I told Mark I couldn't go back to him... It's okay, the boys are with me and they know. We worked it all out and it's going to be fine.' I knew I was rambling, but I was just running on nervous energy and so excited to be telling her. 'Anyway. I'm going to LA and I'm going to tell Sam I'm in love with him and I know it'll be a disaster because I'm a chunky, middle-aged woman with her own lips and a forehead that moves, and he only dates goddesses now, but I need to tell him anyway. Because I do. I love him. I think I always have, but it was never the right time for us. It's still not the right time, because he's happy with Estelle, and he probably hates me because I was a cow to him...'

'STOP!' she screamed. I almost dropped the phone. 'Carly, come back. Right now. This minute. We need to talk and it's important. There's some things you need to know.'

'But, Kate, I can't. Didn't you hear me? I'm going to...'

'Carly, call it off. You can't do it. I need to talk to you first. Come back here right now.'

I was starting to get scared. 'Tell me!'

'Sam's married!' she blurted.

The shock almost made me drop the phone. Mac and Benny's heads whipped round, eyes wide, jaws dropped. He'd married Estelle. Fuck. I'd blown it. I was too late. Everything went numb, except for the searing pain in my chest, but I couldn't buckle in front of my boys.

Instead, I gulped for enough air to speak, then tapped the driver urgently on the shoulder. 'Excuse me, can you turn round please. Take us back to where you collected us.'

I could see in the rear-view mirror that he wasn't pleased that a fare to Heathrow had turned into a ten-minute drive round the block, but to his credit he didn't complain.

'You okay, Mum?' Benny asked, taking my hand.

'I am.' I wasn't, but I couldn't crumble in front of them. They needed to know this was going to be ok. 'Sometimes things just don't work out the way you expect, my love. Life is just like that.' I was trying so desperately to hold it together.

Mac went for the practical angle. 'You've still got us. And trash telly. How about we chill out on the sofas for the rest of the day and we'll give you the remote control.'

Don't cry. Don't cry. 'I've never felt more honoured. I get the remote for the whole day?'

'Until midnight,' he confirmed solemnly.

I put an arm around each of them and kissed their heads. They didn't even squirm once. 'Well, if I'd known all I had to do to get the remote was come up with some crazy heartbreak, I'd have done it ages ago.'

The car stopped as we pulled up outside my house. I paid,

then paused at the end of my path.

'Boys, I'm just going to pop next door to see Aunt Kate. You go on in and I'll be home in a few minutes.'

'Sure you're okay, Mum?' That was Benny again, his concern almost pushing me over the edge, taking my cool, pragmatic act with it.

'I am,' I assured him, lying through my teeth.

I walked the few steps to Kate's house, in a daze, one foot in front of the other, trying to get there before I fell apart. Her front door opened at exactly the same time as I opened her gate.

'Hey you.'

Sam Morton. In Kate's doorway.

I blinked, deciding it must be jet lag or the fumes from the taxi's exhaust.

Nope, still there.

'Sam? What the... what the... what are you doing there?'

'I was in the neighbourhood...' he said, and I could hear the laughter in his words. 'And I heard that the Chiswick Cheese Slicer lived around this way...'

There it was. Mark had almost combusted when he saw the video, yet I knew Sam would think it was hilarious and love the fact that I was standing up to a creep.

'So I thought I'd come see if she needed to be bailed out of jail.'

Ah. Kate had told him about that then.

Kate! That threw up her words from just a few minutes ago.

'But Kate said you're married.'

Kate's living-room window flew open. I hadn't even noticed that she must have been watching us all along. 'Sorry about that,' she said, wincing. 'It was the only thing I could think of to make you stop and come back and it just flew out of my gob. You know I'm no good in a drama.'

'That might be the worst thing you've ever done to me,' I told her, but I could feel the corners of my mouth turning up. I took a few steps forward, towards Sam. 'So, just to clarify, you haven't married Estelle?'

'Nope. You see, I'm a bit in love with someone else. And I don't think she's a cow. Or chunky. Or middle-aged. And I like that her lips are normal and her forehead moves.'

'I WAS ON SPEAKER WHEN I SAID ALL THAT?' I bellowed to Kate. The window opened again, and her head popped out.

'Yeah, ehm, sorry. I actually think that's probably the worst thing I've ever done to you.'

I didn't have time to agree, because Sam was speaking again.

'And I love everything about her. Every single thing. I always have. I just couldn't tell her because I didn't think she felt the same and my heart couldn't take another break.'

'Yasssss!' It was only a whisper, but enough to make me turn, to see that Benny and Mac were a couple of metres behind me, at the end of the path, and they were both punching the air. They'd always adored Sam, and they'd taken the news really well last night, especially when, to his credit, Mark had explained that he thought Sam was right for me. Seems like we all did.

I took another few steps towards him. 'If she promises that she's madly in love with you and that she'll never break your heart again, will you give her a chance to prove it?'

'Depends.'

'On?' I asked, heart thudding.

'Whether she'll stay for good this time?'

In a few more strides, I reached him, and kissed his gorgeous, perfect lips. I only stopped when I realised I hadn't answered his question.

'For good this time, Sam. For always.'

EPILOGUE

The champagne was on ice and the dulcet tones of Tom Jones were oozing from the sound system. Over at the floor-to-ceiling glass wine fridge, Val and her husband, Don, were dancing arm in arm to 'Delilah'. Sam had flown them both over to Los Angeles, first class of course, as a wedding present. A wedding present to me. In ten hours, we'd be getting married outside, in the beautiful grassy garden behind the pool. Matthew McConaughey was welcome to watch if he put some clothes on.

Mac and Benny were thrilled about the wedding, and so happy to be in LA. They'd already picked their rooms for when we were here, although we'd agreed to stay in London for two more years and just come here during school holidays.

Sam had moved production of his next movie to Pinewood Studios, so he would be with us for most of the first year at least, until the movie wrapped. We weren't sure exactly how it would look, but Sam and I agreed that the boys came first. Mark and his new girlfriend, a lawyer from his office, felt the same, so I was pretty sure that, between us all, we'd figure it out.

There was a cheer as Kate and Bruce joined Val and Don in

their kitchen dance, quickly followed by a groan from Kate's daughter, Tallulah. All the kids were congregated round the island. Kate's three, my two, Charlie and Toni, Jess's son, Josh, and Hannah and Ryan. The next generation of the framily. I knew that they'd always have each others' backs because it was how they'd all been brought up. If Sarah could somehow see this, could see them all laughing together, she'd know that Hannah and Ryan were going to be fine. We had it covered.

We had Toni covered too. She was almost unrecognisable from the young woman she was six months ago. She held her head high and spoke with confidence, something that she'd got used to since the video came out. She'd left her fashion course at college, admitting it was never a good fit for her, and she was taking a year out to decide what she really wanted to do with her life. I had a feeling it would be something progressive, something that truly mattered to her. She was now as big on social media as her mother, but as well as influencing ethical trends, she'd become a spokesperson for several anti-bullying, cyber safety and teenage mental health groups. It was like she'd finally found her own skin and it fitted her perfectly. I couldn't be more proud.

Callum and Carol were sitting at the other island, with my youngest brother Michael and his family. They'd all travelled here for the wedding and I couldn't be more grateful to have them here, especially as my mother couldn't make it. She was on her own honeymoon after marrying a golf pro she met in Marbella in an intimate beach ceremony last week. They hadn't invited any guests because they said they only needed each other. They were obviously totally compatible.

Turns out another couple had found they were pretty well matched. On the bar stool next to me, Jess was leaning on Arnie, his arms draped around her shoulders, her engagement ring sparkling on her finger. Apparently, it had been lust at first sight and that had quickly become so much more. All those nights she'd been sneaking out while we were in LA, hadn't been for Tinder dates. She'd been sneaking out to Arnie's flat above Sam's garage. His third marriage was definitely going to be the lucky one.

I was sure my second one was going to be special too, even if a tabloid had run a story speculating that I was Sam's new-age, spiritual advisor, a complete fruitcake who ate nothing but bread (thus the hips) and who was a throwback to the hippy generation. I think they must have spotted me in the multicoloured kaftan. Either that or Estelle had leaked the lie out of spite. Although, rumour was that she'd now shacked up with one of the guys from the next *Fast & Furious* movie. Mac and Benny had never wanted to meet her more. Traitors.

'I love you, Cooper,' Sam murmured, kissing my neck.

I pulled back so I could see his face. 'Yeah, about that...'

Sam groaned. 'Oh God, what now?'

'I'm thinking... maybe Carly Morton has a ring to it?'

His throaty laugh did incredible things to my insides. 'You do whatever you want to, my love. I'll take you any way you come.'

Sam Morton. Not the former Hollywood heartthrob. Not the successful producer. Not even the one who used to do some dodgy stuff in South East Asia.

Just my future husband. The one I loved no matter what, and who didn't want to change a single thing about me either. And that's how I knew we were going to be together until the final credits rolled.

ACKNOWLEDGMENT

As always, this book wouldn't exist if it wasn't for the spectacular team at Boldwood Books: Amanda, Nia, Ellie, Megan, Jade, Rose and everyone else in the Boldwood squad. I adore working with every single one of you. Special thanks to my editor and friend Caroline Ridding, who is the kind of brilliant talent and inspiring support that every writer dreams of having. I'm so grateful for your guidance, encouragement, positivity and your cool head in a crisis. And there have been many!

Thanks too, to all the fabulous book bloggers, journalists, and reviewers who have supported me over the last two decades. I can't tell you how much I've appreciated every word you wrote.

As I said at the beginning of this story, my readers have made my twenty years in this business possible and I'm so thankful to every one of you. I truly hope you'll stick around to see how the next twenty years pans out.

My books wouldn't exist without my very own 'framily', my awesome band of girl friends who've been there for every good time, bad time, caramel wafer and drama. There have been many of those too. Thanks ladies. I owe you even more cocktails.

Gratitude and love to my own family, the Sunday night Zoom gang, who haven't disowned me yet despite the fact that I'm frequently really embarrassing.

And to my girl, Gemma, and my boys, Callan & Brad – who have given me endless laughs, love and cups of tea while I make up imaginary friends on the keyboard. I heart you all. Beyond words.

Finally, John Low... Twenty seven years and counting. And I'd do it all again. Everything. Always.

Love,

Shari xx

MORE FROM SHARI LOW

We hope you enjoyed reading *What Now?*. If you did, please leave a review.

If you'd like to gift a copy, this book is also available as an ebook, digital audio download and audiobook CD.

Sign up to Shari Low's mailing list for news, competitions and updates on future books.

http://bit.ly/ShariLowNewsletter

What If? the first instalment in Carly Cooper's story is available now.

ABOUT THE AUTHOR

Shari Low is the #1 bestselling author of over 20 novels, including *My One Month Marriage* and *One Day In Winter,* and a collection of parenthood memories called *Because Mummy Said So.* She lives near Glasgow.

Visit Shari's website: www.sharilow.com

Follow Shari on social media:

 facebook.com/sharilowbooks

twitter.com/sharilow

instagram.com/sharilowbooks

bookbub.com/authors/shari-low

ABOUT BOLDWOOD BOOKS

Boldwood Books is a fiction publishing company seeking out the best stories from around the world.

Find out more at www.boldwoodbooks.com

Sign up to the Book and Tonic newsletter for news, offers and competitions from Boldwood Books!

http://www.bit.ly/bookandtonic

We'd love to hear from you, follow us on social media:

 facebook.com/BookandTonic

 twitter.com/BoldwoodBooks

 instagram.com/BookandTonic

Printed in Great Britain
by Amazon